Almost Perfect

A NOVEL

E.F. Dodd

*For my girlfriends. Without your love, support
and encouragement, none of this would be possible.*

Books by E. F. Dodd

(NOT) LOOKING FOR LOVE SERIES
Risky Restoration
Earning It
Almost Perfect

THE STANDARD OF LOVE SERIES

A Higher Standard

Changing Leaves and Catching Feelings

Chapter 1

September 20th

*D*ave stared down at the pile of receipts, invoices, and other assorted scraps of paper with notes scrawled illegibly in the margins which Ryker—the new manager in name only—had left heaped together in a tangled mishmash of information. He squinted in the dim light and struggled to shut out the riffs of Jackson's guitar as he ran through soundcheck on the stage a few yards from the bar. Since Jackson was doing him a favor by playing a Wednesday night on short notice, Dave wasn't going to ask him to dial it down. He blinked, rubbed his eyes, and refocused on the torn page in front of him. It was either the listing of condiments his boss wanted to include on that week's inventory refill, or a partial grocery list. It could go either way.

Feedback squealed through the speakers and pierced Dave's already tattered concentration. The manager's office door burst open, and Ryker glared at him from the doorway, his bushy eyebrows resembling irritated caterpillars. He jabbed a stubby finger at the stage, where Jackson fiddled with his amp. "Jesus Christ, Richardson, get your head out of your ass, your nose out of that file, and do your goddamn job!"

Calling the collection of haphazard information in front of him a "file" was a stretch. And while technically it wasn't Dave's job to translate Ryker's pile of crap into something that resembled a restock list, liquor inventory, and the following week's server schedule, if he didn't, chances were good that come next Saturday night Tonic would be running low on both booze and staff. Man was he glad he didn't have to be back here until the following Wednesday. He needed this week off like he needed air. Air that wasn't stale with the scent of old cigarettes and spilled beer.

Dave straightened the stack as best he could and tucked it into a clipboard beneath the bar. He snapped off a sarcastic salute. "Sure thing, boss."

Ryker's only acknowledgment was to grunt and slam the door hard enough to rattle the hinges. "Dick," Dave mumbled under his breath and headed to the stage where Jackson gave him an apologetic grin.

"Sorry, man, I'm not sure what's up with . . ."

Dave waved a hand in the air, brushing off the apology. "Not your fault. The system here needs a complete overhaul, but some people refuse to see it that way and insist on using shit that's been here since the seventies."

Kneeling down, he checked certain cables, monkeyed with a few of the looser connections and adjusted the spacing of the stand-alone mics—thankful nothing sparked or shocked him. With a grin, he looked up at Jackson as he wrapped electrical tape around an old cord. "Anyway, you're the one doing me the favor by playing tonight. If you hadn't agreed to fill in at the last minute, we would've been screwed. I don't know what I would've done if you hadn't come back to town this week for your reunion."

"No worries, man," Jackson said, shrugging broad shoulders and adjusting the strap of his guitar. "Happy to help out. It's not like anything is really going on until Friday anyway, so I'm a bar manager's two favorite things—cheap and available."

Although they'd grown up together, their paths had forked after college with Jackson leaving Rochester for the sunnier skies and milder temperatures of North Carolina. Dave's was more of a U-turn that brought him circling back home within the last few years.

Dave snorted. "As 'head bartender,' I wouldn't know what the bar manager prefers."

Jackson frowned. "Yeah, Ryker getting that job over you is bullshit, man. If I were you, I'd be thinking about making a move." He glanced toward the door, just like he had been since getting to Tonic an hour ago.

Dave ignored the comment about Ryker, although he wholeheartedly agreed with it. The guy was more useless than a bag of dicks and half as smart. He was a living, breathing example of nepotism at its finest, since the only reason he had this job was his dad owned Tonic. But rather than discuss either the slap to his pride, or the general sense of detachment he'd felt in the months since being passed over for the asshole, Dave rocked back on his heels and regarded his best friend. He noted the anxious set of his jaw and antsy way he twisted the tuning pegs of his guitar. "What's going on with you?" he asked.

Jackson jerked his eyes from the door. "What do you mean?"

Dave cocked his head and studied Jackson for a long moment as he fidgeted while trying to look normal. Was he . . . *blushing*? The combination of the darkened bar and Jackson's beard made it difficult to tell, but Dave thought he was. Rising to his feet, Dave gave Jackson a good-natured shove. "You've been staring at that door like the lottery guy is going to walk in and hand you millions. What gives?"

The color in Jackson's face deepened to a ruddier hue. He rubbed his neck with one hand and stroked his fingers over the frets of his guitar with the other. The one thing he wasn't doing was meeting Dave's eyes. Realization hit Dave full force, and he grinned widely. "You invited a girl."

Jackson finally looked at him, his expression somewhat sheepish. "Yeah, I did."

Another shove. "Well, shit, man, why didn't you tell me? I'll dust off our finest table for her."

Jackson laughed and rubbed the back of his neck again, glancing once more toward the door. "Let's not get carried away. She might not show."

Dave gave an incredulous snort. "Please. When was the last time a girl said 'no' when you asked her to come see you play?" He rubbed his chin. "When was the last time you *asked* a girl to come see you play?"

"I didn't tell her I was playing," Jackson said. "Just that I'd be here at Tonic to see a"—he cleared his throat and looked away again—"decent band."

Dave's mouth fell open. "What?" If he had even an ounce of Jackson's talent, he'd tell every single girl he met. Even the ineptest nerd whose voice cracked at the mere thought of a girl had a chance with the ladies if he could play guitar. And if he could play guitar and sing? Game over.

Jackson turned away and kneeled down to adjust an already perfectly set amp. Dave refused to let him off the hook and walked around behind it. "Dude, what's the deal?"

With an anguished grunt, Jackson pushed himself back to standing and raked a hand over his hair. "Fuck, man, this girl . . ." He shook his head, a smile hinting at the corners of his mouth. The slight twitch of his lips was camouflaged by his beard before he scrubbed at his chin.

"I don't know. I only met her a couple hours ago, but . . ." The smile broke free, wide and goofy.

"Jesus, who is this girl?" Dave grinned and waggled his brows. "And does she have a sister?"

"Not sure." Jackson's grin went from dopey to mischievous. "But she's got two cute friends."

"Cute?" Dave asked with a derisive curl of his lip. "'Cute' isn't really my thing."

"Okay, so, not cute. Pretty, attractive, whatever. One blonde, one brunette. If she shows, so will they." Jackson clapped Dave on the shoulder. "Who knows, brother. Maybe you'll have your own miraculous ten minutes."

I'd rather have five quiet minutes to deal with the liquor order, Dave thought, but pasted on a grin for Jackson's sake. "Maybe so, man. Maybe so."

An hour later, Dave saw Rodney leading a group to the table he'd set aside for Jackson's mystery woman. A tall redhead in a blue dress led the way, followed by a brunette who had "resting bitch face" down to an art form, and then a blonde.

A blonde in a white dress that poured over her curves like spilled milk. Even in heels she was diminutive, especially when compared to the redhead who looked positively Amazonian next to her. Long, honey blond curls ribboned down the center of her back to right above her trim waist. The brunette said something to her, and she laughed. Logically, Dave knew there was no way he could hear it from across the nearly full bar. That one woman's laugh couldn't compete with the din of the crowd. And yet . . . he imagined the sound of it tripping down the vertebrae of his spine. He cleared his suddenly dry throat, grabbed a tray, and headed for their table.

V watched the bartender saunter back to the bar after taking their order. She couldn't help but notice how his faded Jimmy Buffett T-shirt stretched across the strong set of his shoulders. Not in a gross Miami metrosexual way, but in a way that made V want to feel the softness of the worn cotton beneath her fingertips.

"He's cute," Kez said from her left, jolting V from her ogle-fest.

"Hmm?" she asked, trying to sound disinterested.

The smirk on Kez's face told V she'd failed spectacularly. One red brow rose in an arch so slowly it resembled time lapse photography. The corner of Kez's mouth tugged upward to match when she replied, "The bartender. He's cute."

V flushed, grateful for the mood lighting of the bar and praying it was dark enough to keep Kez from seeing it. "Really? I, uh, hadn't noticed. Well, I mean, yeah, maybe just a little." *Smooth, really smooth,* V thought, then averted her eyes from Kez's too knowing gaze, willing her friend to drop it and praying Rae, the third member of their trio, hadn't heard her lame deflection.

She was saved by Rae elbowing Kez in the side and pointing to the stage. After a yelp, Kez looked to where Rae pointed and her whole demeanor changed when she saw the bearded, tattooed giant they'd met earlier in the hotel bar standing on stage. He held a guitar and grinned at Kez like she was Christmas morning. Kez looked like she wasn't sure if she should rush the stage or vomit.

Given that the three of them had traveled to Rochester that week-end on Kez's half-cocked plan to crash her ex's reunion and get a glimpse of his new fiancée . . . her somewhat conflicted response to Jackson, the guy on stage, was understandable. Because Kez insisted closure was the purpose of this trip. Confirmation she was done with her ex was the goal. Only now it seemed things had changed. Things like the panicked half-turned on half-nauseated face Kez was making in response to the hot guitarist.

V felt a passing warmth at her back, then heard "Here you go, ladies," right before a glass of prosecco appeared in front of her. When she looked toward the voice, her eyes collided with the bartender's. For the span of two heartbeats, someone picked up the needle playing the record of the night. The air around V paused and the noise of the other patrons faded into a quiet hum. Dark whorls of chocolate spun through with flecks of honey drew her in until she thought she might drown in their warm, welcoming depths.

Then Kez moved next to her, bumping her elbow in the process, and the world restarted. Everything around V came whooshing back into focus and she blinked once, twice, and then a third time to try to dispel whatever had settled over her in that brief moment.

The bartender was still there, just behind her left shoulder with a smile spreading slowly across his face to crinkle the corners of the eyes she'd just been lost in. "I'm Dave. If you need anything, just ask."

The words were innocuous enough, nothing out of the ordinary, and certainly appropriate to say to a table of patrons. And yet . . . they seemed like . . . more. More of what, V had no idea. But something in the way he'd said it, in the silky way those words coasted over her, made them less of a passing comment and more of a promise. Before she could even process what in God's name was going on inside her head, Dave was gone—bounding up to the stage to introduce Jackson.

V gave herself a mental shake and took a long swallow of her drink, letting the bubbles dance over her tongue. *What was wrong with her?* Instantly, she knew the answer to that question. Two years without a satisfying sexual experience was enough to make any woman want to rub up against a hot bartender like a cat in heat. She heard her mother's voice in her head. *Vivian,* ladies *do not publicly lust after a man.*

V crossed her legs and tried to concentrate on the music rather than the throb of awareness pulsing low and urgent within her, but it was no use. Her eyes kept wandering back to the bar. Back to Dave.

He leaned against the wall, a study in casual masculinity—broad shoulders emphasized by equally enticing arms crossed over a toned chest. They could've used him as the musculature model in her college physiology class. Not bulky or brawny, but lean and tapered. Like a surfer. V could easily picture him coming out of the ocean, shoving damp hair out of his eyes as he—

"You know I won't judge you if you drag him off to the backroom," Rae said.

V startled so badly she almost dropped her forgotten glass of bubbly. "Wh-what?"

This time the brow that arched at her was brown, not red, when Rae glanced over. "C'mon, Doc," she said. "Everyone in this bar can tell you want to bone the bartender." Her shrug was a slight lift of one shoulder, allowing her long brown hair to tumble forward. "I'm simply giving you permission to do it."

"I . . . I do not!" V said, even as the telltale heat rose in her cheeks.

"Want to, or need permission?" Rae asked, a twinkle in her green eyes.

"I don't . . . I'm not . . . we aren't. . ." V spluttered to find words. She took a drink, then a deep breath and looked at Rae. "We aren't having this discussion."

"Doc," Rae said, shaking her head. "There's no need for any more discussion. You just eye-fucked that guy within an inch of his life. No one here is going to blame you if decided to *actually* bang him." She sat back in her chair, swirling the ice in her drink. "Sex with a bartender is like a rite of passage. It's basically required to happen before you can claim your rightful place as a member of the female tribe."

"Do you know how insane you sound right now?"

"No more insane than you've had to be after dating the latest loser your mom picked out for you," Rae said with a shudder. "How a man can claim to be versed enough in the human anatomy to sell medical equipment, and still not know how to find the clitoris is beyond me. Of course, anatomy classes are probably taught by some old fossil who wouldn't know a clitoris if it came up and—"

"Can you please stop saying 'clitoris'?" V whisper shouted, glancing around them. Kez had gone to the bar for another drink, so the two of them were alone. Although given Rae's volume, Kez—and everyone else at the bar—could probably still hear her.

Rae was unfazed. "All I'm saying is that you and your clitoris could use a little fun after suffering through college, med school, residency, and whatever else it is you had to go through to become the badass you are today. The reward for that should be more than Such and Such Somebody the Third who your mom thinks is going to be a great son-in-law but in reality is—and don't bother to deny it—a two pump chump on a good night." She angled her drink at Dave, who remained—V hoped—far enough away not to hear anything Rae said. "As a proud connoisseur of bartenders throughout our great nation and others, I'm willing to bet Dave there could not only find your poor neglected center of sexual pleasure, but he would worship it until you lost the power of speech. I'm telling you, Doc, you owe it to yourself to let him render you mute."

V glanced at Dave just as he happened to look over at their table. He winked at her, and she quickly looked away, making Rae laugh.

V shot her a look. "That's not the point of this trip, Rae. We're here to support Kez through . . . whatever it is she hopes to accomplish. My meeting someone is not on the agenda. And anyway, we're only here for a few days."

Her friend's grin widened. "Meeting a guy wasn't on her agenda either, but it's safe to say that ship has sailed. And anyway, can you name a better way to spend a long weekend than with a guy who looks like that?"

"You know that's not . . ." V frowned. It wasn't that she had a problem with casual sex, or those who had it. Rae's sexual conquests were a reliable source of entertainment and had been since Kez introduced them to one another a few years ago. And while she admired Rae's control over her own sexual destiny, V just didn't see the same appeal in it.

Sex for the sake of sex wasn't what she wanted. Sex required a relationship. With someone suitable. Someone with whom she had things in common. Someone she could introduce to her family. Someone with the right qualities. Qualities that did not include how well he filled out a T-shirt, or his knowledge of erogenous zones. Although, based on her last boyfriend, she was starting to think that knowledge should rank higher on the scale of importance.

Rae slid her chair closer to V's. "Look, I know a casual tryst is more my style than yours. I'm familiar with your 'minimum' requirements before getting down to business with a guy. Although, the litany of your requirements could hardly be called minimum."

V tried to protest, but Rae kept going. "All I'm saying is you could, perhaps, just this once, put aside your list of the nation's most boring, blue-blooded bachelors and choose your male companion based on how good his ass looks in those jeans instead of your Excel spreadsheet outlining your compatibility scores."

There was no way for V not to look in Dave's direction after Rae's descriptor. The man did look unbelievably good in those jeans.

"Take it as far as you're comfortable going," Rae said, then stretched her face into an exaggerated leer and twirled an imaginary villainous mustache. "Or, if you're feeling truly adventurous, as far as I would."

V couldn't help but laugh. "I can't imagine the places your mind goes, Rae." She held up a hand when Rae opened her mouth. "Nor do I want to." Biting her bottom lip, she snuck another look at the cute bartender, considering Rae's advice. Which was, on its own, wholly terrifying.

Rae wasn't wrong in her characterization of V's dating life. She'd learned from an early age what qualities or standards were important to consider in choosing a man. *Learned* wasn't the right term, since her mother had essentially ingrained said qualities into her brain as soon as she realized V no longer considered boys "yucky."

"It's important," her mother had said, "to find someone who's going to match you in life, Vivian. Someone from the right background, with the right family and the right goals in life. Someone who will help you lead the life you want and have the future you deserve. Don't waste your time with dalliances that lead nowhere, or boys that aren't worth it."

V snuck another glance over to where Dave worked behind the bar with a casual grace to his movements. The tingle of awareness rippled through her again, and she suppressed a shiver. Would it be so bad to experience a snippet of what Rae was encouraging? Put aside what she wanted in the long-term and have a little fun while they were in town?

Sensing V's wavering, Rae nudged her shoulder. "C'mon, Doc," she wheedled. "Give the chastity belt a break for the weekend and take a walk on the wild side."

V frowned. "It's not like I'm some sort of nun, Rae. I just have certain . . . requirements of the men I date."

"Please," Rae scoffed. "Your lab coat is your habit and your stethoscope your rosary." At V's wince, Rae backpedaled. "Okay, okay, so it's not *that* bad. But, c'mon, V! You have to admit your dating life has been blander than a communion wafer. It's like you specifically choose guys who are duller than dirt." She narrowed her eyes. "And before you deny that, please remember, I'm pretty much a human lie detector."

When V laughed, Rae shook her head. "I'm serious. How else would I know my client is lying when I ask if the leaked pictures of them licking whipped cream off their twenty-one-year-old nanny are fake or real?"

"How is that even a question that comes up?"

Rae shrugged nonchalantly. "The world of PR is often twisted and kinky, which is why I'm so good at my job." She waggled her eyebrows at V. "But don't try and change the subject. I'm not telling you to date him. I'm telling you to shelve your dating requirements for a day or two and take the guy for a test drive, feel the wind in your hair and his hands in your pants."

At V's renewed frown, Rae amended her idea. "Okay, fine, his hand chastely touching just above your knee, whatever. I'm telling you, Doc, that man," she nodded in the direction of Dave, "radiates BDE."

"BDE?"

"Big. Dick. Energy," Rae explained. "And you, my friend, need to plug in and recharge your battery."

"Who's the blonde?"

Dave's head snapped up from the old-fashioned he was making. "What?"

Shay, the head server, frowned and her lip piercing shimmied in protest. "The blonde in the white dress you've been staring at for the last hour. Who is she?"

Automatically, Dave's eyes flickered back to V and lingered there.

"Someone important, then," Shay said, her frown morphing into an excited grin. "Tell me more."

Dave pulled his eyes from V's profile and back to the drink he was making. "I don't know her."

"But you want to," Shay said, bumping his hip with hers. "Which means you know *something* about her. You know I'll get it out of you eventually, so go ahead and spill it."

Ice rattled in the shaker as Dave shook it harder than was strictly necessary. "She's here with a girl Jackson met."

"And?"

Dave huffed out a sigh. "And what, Shay?"

"And why are you staring at her like she's on the dessert menu?"

"You mean other than the fact she's fucking gorgeous?"

Shay glanced back at the table where V sat with her friends. "Can't fault you there. To be honest, I wouldn't kick any of the three of them out of bed for eating crackers."

Dave snorted. "You're such a poet."

Her tattooed shoulder rose and fell in a careless shrug. "What can I say? I'm a woman of many talents." She leaned a hip against the bar back. "But tell me more about Blondie over there and why she's caught your eye."

Dave opened his mouth, but Shay shook her head. "And don't give me any more bullshit about her being gorgeous. Gorgeous women come in here on the regular and try to get with you, only to leave disappointed. So, it's more than her looking like a modern-day Grace Kelly with a better rack."

"Shay," Dave said, her name a warning.

"Ah, touchy touchy," she said, grinning and rubbing her hands together. "Now I know there's something more here."

Dave rolled his shoulders uncomfortably. He didn't know how to put into words the jolt he'd felt when he made eye contact with the blonde, or how it had pushed the air from his lungs. Shay would make some joke about Cupid's arrow or something, and then he'd feel like an idiot. And it wasn't like he'd done anything more than take her drink order.

Prosecco, although he was willing to bet she preferred champagne. Veuve seemed a little more her style, although he had no clue why he thought that. It didn't matter, though, because since Ryker's arrival, their booze list ran more to swill than sauvignon. Which meant prosecco was as highbrow as things got now. Thoughts of his boss made him frown and slam the freezer bin.

"Ah, c'mon, D," Shay said, mistaking his irritation with Ryker for ire at her. "I was just messing with you. You want to keep this mystery lady a mystery, that's fine with me."

Dave put the old-fashioned on Shay's tray, along with two different IPAs and a draft domestic. "Take these to table eight, nosy."

"Sir, yes sir!" Shay dipped a saucy bow, while managing to balance the full tray, and sashayed out from behind the bar.

"Excuse me." The soft, Southern voice had Dave's body turning before he even knew he was moving.

Her white dress glowed under the light from the Edison bulbs strung above them. Small hands rested lightly on the scarred wooden bar. For some reason, he'd thought she'd have longer, tapered nails. The kind he associated with women who looked as expensive as she did. But hers, although manicured, were short and square with pale pink polish. There was a small crescent-shaped scar above the knuckles of her right hand.

She noticed him looking and smiled. "Hazards of the job."

"I'm sorry?"

Her right hand flexed on the bar, and she pointed at the scar. "Small children can get rather squirrelly when they don't feel like cooperating."

"You're a teacher?"

Her smile was quick, as was the shake of her head. "No, I'm afraid I don't have the requisite patience for that." Blue eyes met his, and he felt that same jolt of energy pierce his chest. "I'm a doctor."

"Wow," he said, for lack of anything better.

Her laugh was soft, like her voice. "Sometimes I feel the same way."

Dave shook his head. "Sorry, that was stupid."

"I'll let you in on a little secret, Dave," she said, leaning a little over the bar. It brought the scent of some sort of flower to his nose, delicate yet spicy.

He leaned toward her but stayed silent.

"It's never a stupid idea to say 'wow' when a woman tells you what she does for a living. Because most of the time, it's like that old line about Ginger Rogers and Fred Astaire."

"Can't say I know that one," Dave admitted.

She smiled at him. "They had the same job—both of them were dancers, partners actually in all those old movies from the 1930s. People would go on and on about how great Fred Astaire was. Until one day a cartoonist said, 'Sure he was great, but don't forget that Ginger Rogers did everything he did . . . backward and in high heels.' The same could be said for women in most professions these days. We're doing the same jobs men are, except in the face of more challenging circumstances."

"Backward and in high heels."

"Exactly." She nodded. "So, there's nothing wrong with you being a little in awe of it." Her smile turned impish. "In my opinion, it's the proper response."

Dave laughed. "I'll remember that."

"I hope so." She extended a hand to him. "I'm Vivian, by the way, but most people call me V."

"V?" he asked, taking her hand. It was smooth and soft, cool to the touch.

She lifted a shoulder with a knowing smile, as though she were used to the question. "The redhead with a preference for tequila is Kesler. We met in elementary school. 'Kesler' and 'Vivian' were a bit formal for kids, so we came up with something a little more casual."

"I see," he said. "Well, it's nice to meet you, V." Without thinking, he brushed the pad of his thumb over the scar above her knuckle. Her fingers tightened on his.

"Likewise," she said. Seconds passed and Dave didn't want to let go of V's hand, didn't want to lose the feel of her. She didn't seem to mind, as she made no move to pull away. Fleetingly, he wondered what would happen if he tugged her closer. If he drew her across the bar and into his arms. What would she feel like against him? What would those pretty pink lips taste like under his?

Startled by the direction of his thoughts, he cleared his throat. The noise seemed to bring her out of whatever she'd been thinking, and she dropped his hand. He missed the contact.

"Um, yeah, so . . . Was there something I could get you?"

V smoothed a hand over the ends of her curls. "Yes, right. Prosecco. That is, I came over to ask for another glass of prosecco. Not from you, or anything." Her cheeks pinked up and Dave enjoyed the sight of it. "What I mean to say is that I'll pay for it, of course."

The blush deepened and she closed her eyes. "Sorry, my brain seems to have misfired at some point after my wonderful Astaire/Rogers repartee. Can we just rewind the last minute or so and start again?"

He grinned and turned away from her, only to turn immediately back to face her. "Good evening, miss. What can I get you?"

Her answering laugh was tinged with gratitude. "I'd love a glass of prosecco, please." She slid her credit card across the bar to him.

"Coming right up."

Chapter 2

*S*ince when was a well-washed concert T-shirt sexy? V wondered to herself while watching Dave parcel out drinks to a nearby table just before last call. *Had it always been, and she'd never noticed before? Or was it this T-shirt in particular? Were all Jimmy Buffett T-shirts so well-tailored?* The cotton hugged Dave's shoulders like it had been stitched just for them, all snug and perfectly draped. Not too tight, not too loose, but juuust right.

"Seems like you're at least contemplating taking my advice," Rae said, bringing V out of her disturbingly adult version of Goldilocks. She set down her half-empty glass of prosecco. No need for any more of that stuff to fuel further thoughts of the hot bartender. Not that she needed something other than the mere sight of him to fuel anything.

"I'm . . . considering it."

Her admission made Rae grin and pump a fist in the air. "Yes! I knew there was a secret sex kitten hidden in there somewhere. There's no way a woman with your shoe collection wouldn't have one somewhere longing for her day in the sun."

"You're so weird."

"Is it wrong for me to be fully invested in helping you select something tall, blond and built from the bar menu?" Rae's red lips dipped down into a playful pout. "C'mon, Doc, let me be your wing woman tonight! The opportunity so rarely presents itself, I can't believe you'd deny me the joy of experiencing it just once."

"What are you even talking about? We go out together all the time."

"Yeah, and instead of guys like him"—Rae surreptitiously tilted her glass toward where Dave was talking to a spiky-haired server with a lip ring—"you end up spending all evening talking to some asshat in a sport coat."

"What is your aversion to sport coats?"

"Nothing, in the right context. Like at a steeplechase or cocktail party. But at a sports bar? Talk about pretentious. And yet they seem to drag you in like some sort of tweed tractor beam. But tonight, you've finally presented an option with which I *want* to help. A man who doesn't look stuffy, boring or, as previously discussed, wouldn't know how to find your cli—"

"Do not"—V clamped her hand around Rae's wrist—"say that word again. You've made your point, okay?"

"Ladies," Dave said from behind them. She froze, immediately wondering how long he'd been standing there. Rae grinned and V wanted to strangle her. She turned to find Dave smiling down at where she gripped Rae's arm.

"Everything all right here?" Dave asked. "Need anything?"

Rae chimed in before V could. "Actually," she drawled, and V felt her stomach clench in anticipation of whatever outlandish request Rae was about to make.

"I wonder if you could settle a little debate we were having," Rae continued, and the cramp in V's belly worsened.

"Happy to help any way I can," Dave said, resting a hand on the back of V's chair.

"Well, you see, Doc and I were just talking about . . ."

Please, for the love of God, don't let her say clitoris, V prayed silently.

"Men's fashion," Rae finished.

Dave laughed and V relaxed a fraction. "I don't know that I'll be much help in that department," Dave said. He gestured at his T-shirt. "You're looking at about as fashionable as I get these days."

"Ah," Rae said, green eyes twinkling. "So, no sport coats, then?"

"Uh, sport coat?" Dave questioned, a line appearing between his brows.

"You know," Rae said, "A blazer. A suit jacket without the suit."

Dave laughed again. "Sorry, no blazers, I'm afraid. I do own a few suits, though. For funerals, weddings, and stuff like that."

"Good to know," Rae said, and V glared at her.

Rae ignored her. "One other question, if you have a moment."

Dave surveyed the bar, then looked back at Rae. "Sure."

"What are the odds of a fashionable guy like yourself being single?"

V's cheeks went hot, and she tried to kick Rae under the table. Rae, being well-versed in V's chosen methods of retaliation, had wisely shifted her legs to the other side of the chair. V's heel whiffed unsatisfyingly through the air without impact.

Dave's chuckle made V lift her gaze to his, and she felt the snap when their gazes collided and held. Without looking away, Dave said, "I'm very, *very* single."

"Also good to know," Rae said, but this time V didn't shoot her a glare. Shifting any of her attention away from Dave was a physical impossibility.

He flipped his hand on the back of her chair to crouch next to her, his fingertips grazing her shoulder with the adjustment. His forearm was next to her upper arm, not touching, but close enough for the warmth of it to tease her bare skin. "What about you . . . Doc?"

The nickname Kez and Rae gifted her never stuck out to her before. Had never seemed worthy of notice, other than to acknowledge they were speaking to her. But when Dave said it, that single syllable became much more interesting and made V want to hear it said in that rumbly voice of his in other, more private settings. Her throat went dry, and she reached for a sip of her now flat prosecco. "Me?" she asked, proud of forming a word, albeit one in any kindergartner's vocabulary. His proximity was doing strange things to her brain.

He nodded slowly, eyes never leaving hers. "Yeah, you."

She could smell his cologne, or aftershave, or hell, maybe *he* just smelled like a woodsy paradise. If he looked this good, why wouldn't he smell the same? If it didn't come from a bottle, he was sitting on an untapped pheromonal gold mine. V resisted taking a deep breath, because one more solid hit of that scent was going to permanently short-circuit her frontal lobes.

When she shifted in her seat, her calf brushed his jean-clad knee and V didn't miss the dilation of his pupils. "I am without a dance partner for the weekend."

Dave smiled. "No one moving you backward in high heels?"

"Not at the moment."

"Well, then"—he shifted his grip on her chair, bringing his arm in brief contact with hers—"consider this my audition." The touch could've been accidental. It was nothing more than a whisper of sensation and should not have felt as illicit as it did. But oh *did* it.

V swallowed and clarified what was really up for discussion. *If she actually went through with it.* "You understand this show will have a limited run, don't you? The curtain falls on Sunday."

Dave was undeterred. "What if I earn rave reviews?"

V smiled. "I like your confidence, but your leading lady and her entourage are only here through Sunday."

"No chance of taking the show on the road?" His eyes were playful, but intense as he gazed up at her.

She tucked a curl behind her ear, their arms brushing again. "At this time, that's not under consideration."

"What I'm hearing"—Dave's grin was equal parts choir boy smile and bad boy smirk—"is there's at least a chance."

"Okay, I'm not sure what is going on here," Rae said, "but whatever it is, I am one hundred percent on board."

Surprisingly, V was too. For once, she considered Rae might be right. There wasn't really anything wrong with indulging in a little fun with a cute guy. Even if the guy were a significant departure from her norm of buttoned-up men in button-downs. Which meant they probably had nothing in common and all that would come out of this would be a funny story to mention every now and again. That one time she let her hair down and lived a little. Reached a toe over the line into territory Rae knew all too well.

Not that she was going to stray too far over. Just a toe, maybe the ball of her foot, but nothing more. She was *not* going to lose control here. The rest of her was going to stay firmly planted in the land of common sense. Where doctors dated bankers, lawyers, or other doctors. And didn't get all tingly when a bartender smiled at them. Tingly, flushed, and warm in places that had been cold a long time.

Before she could overthink or convince herself otherwise, V took her phone from her clutch and unlocked it. Passing it to Dave, she said, "We'll need your contact information for callbacks."

"Of course," he said, typing a number into her contacts. Instead of handing V back her phone, though, he hit send and waited for two rings before hanging up. At her questioning brow, he said, "I need to make sure I have contact info too. How else can I send over my headshots?"

"And by headshots, you mean what exactly?" Rae interjected.

"Don't answer that," V cautioned. "Don't even think about responding to her."

"Spoilsport," Rae said with a frown.

"Pervert," V retorted, her lips matching the downward slant of Rae's.

Dave laughed and stood up. "I look forward to our collaboration Doctor . . .?"

"Walters," V answered. "So do I Mister . . ."

Again with the sizzling grin. "Richardson."

Dave Richardson. V's insides did a little flip-flop she'd neither experienced nor seen described in any textbook or discussed in any year of her residency. Had to be the result of flat prosecco, because she certainly wasn't having a physical reaction to learning this man's full name. That would be ridiculous.

"Hey." Kez reappeared at the table, face flushed and eyes bright. "Sorry, I was . . ." She glanced at the stage where Jackson was packing up his guitar.

"I just bet you were," Rae said, and Kez scratched the side of her nose with a middle finger.

Looking at where Dave stood just behind V, she asked, "What did I miss?"

"Just a little dance number," Dave said, shooting V a wink she felt all the way to her toes. Toes she realized were inching farther and farther into uncharted territory.

September 21st

Dave stared at the contact entry in his phone until the numbers blurred into one another. He blinked, bringing them back into focus. Ten digits formed the number below V's name. The circle above it was empty, because he wasn't a total creep who'd take a secret picture of her to keep on his phone. He pushed away the thought of having one there, because that was nuts.

A picture in a phone contact was reserved for something lasting, not a fling. And V had made it clear their relationship, if you could even call it that since its half-life was shorter than that of the guacamole in his fridge, had an end date that would coincide with her flight out on Sunday. Given that it was already five o'clock on Thursday afternoon and he hadn't heard anything from her, he'd started to wonder if she even *wanted* to see him again. If he'd been wrong about the banter and the chemistry and that certain undeniable—to him at least—spark of attraction between them.

Which explained why he'd been staring at his phone, specifically her contact information in his phone, for the last fifteen minutes. There was no rule that he couldn't call her. Nothing that prevented him from sending a quick text. But each time his finger hovered over the number, he hesitated. He didn't want to spook her. She'd been adamant about the parameters of what she wanted, which made him think she'd reach out if she wanted to see him. After all, she'd asked for his number, not given him hers. He'd been the one to call himself from her phone. So . . . he should let her contact him. Right?

Dave groaned and tossed his phone to the coffee table. Where it proceeded to ring and scare the crap out of him. Hastily, he scrambled to pick it up, fingers fumbling to lift it from the smooth surface of the table.

In his mad grab for it, he knocked the remote to the floor and brought the TV blazing to life with the countdown to Thursday Night Football.

Finally, his dexterity returned, and he picked up the phone. Jackson's number reflected back at him, and he swiped to answer.

"Hey man," he said, ducking under the table to retrieve the remote.

"Hey," Jackson responded.

"Fuck," Dave swore as his head connected with the underside of the table.

"What's going on?" Jackson asked.

Rubbing the back of his head, Dave muttered, "Nothing, just dropped the remote." He muted the TV and sat back on the couch. "What's up?"

"Probably the same thing as at your place. Thinking about a girl."

Dave snorted. "What makes you say that?"

"You mean other than the way I saw you looking at Kez's friend V?"

Dave made a noncommittal noise somewhere between a grunt and a harrumph.

"Yeah, like I said. Same thing here."

"I don't know, man," Dave said. "You and Kez seemed awful cozy last night."

"You mean while she was telling me about her plan to crash her ex-boyfriend's high school reunion to get a peek at his new fiancée?"

"Uh . . . what?"

It was Jackson's turn to grunt-harumph. "You heard me."

"Well . . . shit, dude. That's . . . I don't even know what to call that."

"I can think of several words to use, none of which make me feel any better about the situation."

Suddenly, V's desire to keep things between them to a fun and flirty weekend didn't seem so bad in comparison to the world of shit Jackson was getting ready to dive into.

"So, I guess that means you're not going t—"

Jackson didn't let him finish. "Not going to let her waste any more energy on some fuckwit that was stupid enough to let her go? Pretty much."

Not the answer Dave had expected. "Are you sure, man? Whatever she's got going on seems a little . . ." *Batshit crazy?* No way was he voicing that to Jackson, though. He settled for, "I don't know, intense?"

"Maybe so," Jackson agreed. "But there's something there with her, man. I can feel it. I have no fucking clue what it is yet, but I can't deny it's there."

Remembering how he'd felt when he laid eyes on V, Dave had a decent idea what Jackson was talking about. He was silent for a beat. "But you haven't talked to her since last night?"

"No," Jackson admitted. "I can't decide if it's too soon to reach out to her. She's already skittish enough about things. I don't want her to balk into a complete one-eighty. I mean, I just saw her twelve hours ago. I feel like I need to give her room to breathe, or she'll shut me out completely."

"Probably a good call," Dave agreed.

"What about you?"

"What about me?"

"Don't be a dipshit," Jackson said. "What's your plan with V?"

"To not fuck things up with her before they've even started by being too clingy?"

"Solid plan," Jackson said. "And that leaves things exactly where?"

With me spinning ridiculous scenarios while committing her number to memory. Again, no way was he sharing that.

"With me on my couch staring at the TV while waiting to hear from her."

"Sounds familiar." There was a pause, then Jackson added, "Only more pathetic when you say it, though."

"Hey, you're the one who called me. Which makes you the pathetic one. I was content to stew in solace."

"Sure you were." Jackson laughed. "Feel like stewing in the company of friends? Maybe over beers and a slice?"

Dave looked around his apartment and decided solitude was overrated. "Sounds good. Geno's?"

"Meet you there in fifteen."

"Look what the cat dragged in," Shay said, pulling a chair up to their table at the back of Geno's Pizzeria.

"Don't you get enough of this guy at work?" Jackson asked her.

Shay grinned. "More than enough. But, he is the one who makes the schedule, so it's wise to schmooze when I can." She cocked her head, the silver ring in her lip winking under the florescent lights. "Although, I have to say I'm surprised to see you two here."

"Why's that?" Dave asked, taking another slice.

Shay rolled her eyes. "Because if I'd hooked up with a lady that looked as good as either of the ones the two of you idiots managed to chat up last night, I damn sure wouldn't be sitting in the back of Geno's the next day." She wiggled her brows at Dave. "Although, you left alone last night." A quick head jerk in Jackson's direction. "This big, bearded bastard's the one who left with all three ladies. I don't know, boss man," she said with a theatrically mournful expression. "Maybe you're losing your touch. Or maybe, you don't have what it takes to romance a beautiful blonde. I mean, why would she waste her time with you when I'm sure she's got the pick of the litter wherever she goes."

Dave knew Shay was only giving him the standard ration of shit she always did and meant nothing by it. Which made the sting of her words that much more of a surprise. He'd never put much stock in how others viewed his career choices. Not when his parents pressed him about still working at Tonic, or when his former coworkers told him he was crazy for leaving. But the idea V might question it, or him for making it, didn't sit well with Dave. Nothing about their conversation from the night before gave him the impression she was anything other than genuinely interested, though.

He shook off his discomfort as garden variety paranoia. They'd been having fun last night. A little playful teasing about the idea of a no-strings hookup while she was in town. She barely knew him, so there was no reason for her to be thinking beyond a few days of fun. For that matter, why was he?

"I've got everything she could want, or need," Dave said with more bravado than confidence.

Shay snorted. "If that's the case, then what the fuck are you two doing here instead of hanging out with them?"

Jackson wiped his mouth. "I've got to side with Shay on this one, man." He grinned at her. "As much as it pains me."

Shay stuck her tongue out at Jackson.

Dave nodded. "Agreed both as to the side and the pain." Rising from his seat, he said to Shay, "Be on the lookout for flying pigs on your way home."

She threw a balled-up napkin at him. "For that, I'm taking your pizza."

Dave caught the napkin in midair. "It's the least we could do. How would I function without you there to knock my ass off my shoulders when I need it?"

Shay laughed and reached for a slice. "Helping you poor, pitiful Ryan Gosling lookalikes is my singular goal in life. You've got it so tough, after all."

Chapter 3

Buzz buzz.

V looked up from her final notes on an article review to glance across the coffee table at Kez.

Kez picked up her phone and checked the screen. "Not mine," she said and went back to her laptop.

Rae was out on the balcony taking a crisis call or something, so it had to be V's phone. If only she could find it.

Buzz buzz. She shuffled the papers in her lap and lifted a separate stack off the cushion next to her. Not there. Shifting that stack to the table, she tugged her messenger bag over closer and peered into its depths.

Buzz buzz. The phone illuminated at the bottom of the bag, and she reached down to pull it out. Her stomach fluttered when she saw the screen.

Dave Text Message

V cleared the message to stop the buzzing, but didn't open it. Exchanging numbers last night had been fun and in the moment.

They'd been flirting and he'd been smiling, and she'd been . . . well, she hadn't been her normal reserved self, that was for sure. She'd given into Rae's peer pressure about living a little, broadening her horizons and experiencing . . . well, experiencing *Dave*. All of that had seemed acceptable last night, with the music and the lighting and *the smiling*.

But there on the sofa in her hotel suite, away from the heady atmosphere of Tonic and the easy flow of things with Dave the night before, she was second-guessing herself. If she were honest about it, she'd been second-guessing things since getting up for her Thursday morning staffing call.

Thankfully, that morning, Kez saw her ex for the first time in years and created an excellent distraction from V waffling on whether she should've given Dave her number at all. Waffling that turned to irritation when she didn't hear from him all day. It was one thing for her to have second thoughts, but totally unacceptable that he would.

Only he wasn't, apparently. Instead, he was right there in her phone behind the words "Dave Text Message." For the briefest of seconds, V debated ignoring the text. But that was impossible. Not just because she wasn't going to ghost someone, but because she wanted to know what he said. Because in between vacillating over whether she should've given him her number, she remembered the *zing* she'd experienced when his fingers brushed her shoulder, and the teasing glint in his eyes as he'd claimed to be auditioning. The chemistry between them was palpable and, even if it were a purely physical reaction, she couldn't lie to herself about its existence any easier than she could deny wanting to feel it again.

Decision made, V swiped right to open the text.

Dave: *I figured someone had to break the ice.*

V's lips tilted up, and she glanced over at Kez, but she was hunkered down over her laptop, typing away and not paying any attention to anything outside her screen.

V: *Isn't there some bartender joke about using a polar bear to do that?*
Dave: *I wonder about my brethren sometimes.*
V: *So, you've never stooped to using cheesy pickup lines at work, then?*

Bubbles appeared for a long time, then.

Dave: *I'm trying to figure out how to say something without coming off as a complete douche.*
V: *Ah, the ancient conundrum of the first text thread. "How not to seem douchey."*
Dave: *Exactly. What I'm mulling over is an honest statement, but it also comes off . . . cocky?*
V: *The not-so-distant cousin of douchey. A relative sometimes welcomed, but who often overstays his welcome.*
Dave: *That's the one.*
V: *Well, how about this? I promise to deduct only half as many points from whatever it is you want to say as I normally would. Given your preamble, I feel like you deserve the benefit of the doubt.*
Dave: *Okay, that seems fair. Here goes. I've never used a cheesy pickup line, because I've never had to.*

V swallowed a laugh, checking once again to confirm Kez remained engrossed in whatever she was working on. She tapped a nail to her teeth as she formulated a response. Dave was quicker.

Dave: *No bubbles? Dammit, I KNEW that was going to come off as douchey. I'm really not trying to be douchey, cocky, or any of their other less desirable relations. I'm just being . . . honest. Pickup lines aren't something I've had to use, because I've found genuine conversation works just fine for me.*

His answer struck V as personal. Like Dave was offering her an unvarnished version of himself. She felt inexplicably protective over this exchange between the two of them and was suddenly hyperaware of Kez sitting across from her on the couch. Not that Kez had a clue as to who V was texting or the subject of those texts, but still . . . she couldn't dispel the distinct desire for privacy before responding.

She checked the time on her phone. Six thirty. "Hey, Kez?"

Kez looked up, her face in the lawyer permafrown she wore when working. She blinked and the line between her eyes disappeared along with the firm set of her mouth. "Sorry," she said. "This freaking guy . . ." She gestured vaguely at her computer screen, then shook her head. "What's up?"

"I'm thinking about calling it a day on this." V waved a hand at the piles of research around her. "Should we see if Rae can take a break in running her empire and join us for a dinner order?"

Kez glanced through the double doors where Rae was pacing the balcony, her hands moving almost as much as her lips as she barked out orders to someone on the other end of the line. With a feline stretch, Kez unfolded her long limbs from where they were tucked under her and stood, digging her knuckles into the small of her back so hard they popped. "I'll go interrupt her world domination to get an idea of what she wants to do."

V nodded. "Sounds good. Seems like a good night for pizza and PJs to me."

Kez grinned at her. "I'll second that."

Scooping up the various papers strewn across the couch, V plopped her phone on top and saw new texts from Dave. Her heart gave an excited thumpity thump thump and she made herself walk normally to the bedroom instead of heading off in a dead run to check them. In the semiprivacy of the shared bathroom, she re-opened their text thread.

Dave: *Huh, maybe I was wrong about the genuine conversation thing, because this one seems to be going poorly. Pickup line it is then. But you have only yourself to blame for not responding to my last text. So . . . here goes.*
Dave: *I'm going to complain to Spotify about you not being in this week's hottest singles.*
Dave: *God, was that as lame to read as it sounded in my head?*
V: *Sorry! I was talking to Kez. I can confirm that the whole "genuine conversation" thing managed to cancel out the douchey quality of your earlier statement, thereby eliminating the need for any deduction of points. I'm sorry to say, though, that the Spotify pickup line . . .*
Dave: *Yeah, I know. It's pretty bad. Please believe I did my best to pick the lowest level offender.*

V giggled and secretly admitted to herself the Spotify line wasn't half bad.

V: *Like I said, at a minimum you deserve the benefit of the doubt, so I'll take you at your word.*
Dave: *Okay, now that the ice is officially broken . . . what are you doing tonight?*
V: *You do realize what time it is, don't you?*

Dave*: Why does this feel like some sort of trap?*
V*: Because despite the fact you were about to ask me to do something with you tonight, when it's already after six o'clock, you seem at least somewhat intelligent.*

Bubbles, bubbles, bubbles.

Dave*: Is this something like the three-date rule for sex?*

V laughed out loud. Cheeky. Very, very cheeky.

V*: Wow, going there already?*
Dave*: I think there's a gross pickup line in there somewhere.*
V*: You'd be the one who'd know.*
Dave*: Touché. Seriously, though, I feel like I've unknowingly violated some girl rule.*
V*: Technically, there is no pending violation, because you didn't ask me to do anything. Had you asked, then yes, you would've broken the rule of having enough respect for a lady to ask her early enough in the day to make plans. Otherwise, if you ask and she says yes, then it seems as though she were just whiling away the day waiting on your call.*
Dave*: So . . . you weren't lounging around with hearts in your eyes thinking of me and watching the phone?*
V*: Why? Were you?*

The phone rang in V's hand, and she jumped. *Dave* was the caller ID. Why was he calling her? They were texting. They hadn't moved into phone call territory yet. She looked at her panicked reflection in the mirror and bit her lip.

"Hello?"

"Yeah," Dave said in that deep timbre she remembered from the night before. It rumbled into her ear, and she watched heat bloom on her cheeks in her reflection.

"What?"

"Yeah," he said again. "You asked if I were lounging around staring at my phone and thinking about you today. The answer is yeah, I was."

"Oh," she said, smiling at herself in the mirror. "That's . . . good?"

His laugh was a rough tumble of sound that shot straight down her spine. "You sound as though you're not so sure of that."

V cleared her throat and turned away from the mirror. "No, I . . . I'm sure th—"

"V?" Kez stuck her head in the bathroom. Seeing V on the phone, she mouthed "sorry" and started to back out.

"It's okay," V said to Kez, but it was Dave who answered.

"I'm glad to hear you say that," he said.

Flustered, V said, "I wasn't talking to . . . hang on a second, okay?" Tucking the phone against her shirt, she looked at Kez. "Sorry, what?"

Kez looked at her like she was being a giant weirdo. Which, to be fair, she was. "Rae is on board with PJs and pizza. Food should be here in about twenty minutes. Does that work for you?"

"Yeah, that's great," V said, keeping her phone pressed to her chest. "I'll be out once I wrap up this call."

When the door clicked shut behind Kez, V lifted the phone to her ear. "Sorry about that."

"No problem," Dave said, all relaxed confidence and smooth baritone.

"Right," V said. "So, listen, Kez and Rae ar—"

"It wasn't a line," Dave interrupted.

"What?"

"When I said I'd been thinking about you all day. That wasn't a line, V. It's the truth."

Why was that so sexy?

"Okay, that's . . . good to know."

He laughed again and again the sound of it tickled its way into her ear and lodged in some deep recess of her brain. "Just for clarity, that time you *were* talking to me?"

V laughed. "Yes, I'm now speaking to you." Deciding to match his honesty with her inquisitive side, she asked, "If it is true, though, why did you wait all day to text me?"

There was a weighted pause, then Dave said, "Because I wasn't sure about the parameters of . . . whatever we're doing here." She could almost hear him grinning into the phone when he continued. "And it seems like I guessed right about you being a big fan of rules and boundaries. Boundaries I wasn't sure if I'd break by reaching out first. Then, thanks to a friend, I realized I should stop being a chickenshit and pick up the damn phone. So . . . here we are."

Here they were, indeed. This guy was . . . unexpected in all the right ways.

"Here we are . . . not going out tonight," she teased.

"No? Not even with my admitting to being a chickenshit?"

She couldn't hold back a giggle. "Like you said, I'm a woman comfortable with rules and boundaries."

"Got an extra handbook I can review?"

"Fresh out, I'm afraid. Looks like you'll have to learn on the fly."

"I'm pretty quick on my feet," he assured her. "Maybe we could discuss this in person over dinner tomorrow night?"

"Maybe we could," V said. "But things are a little up in the air here, so I'll need to get back to you on that."

"Okay," Dave said. V detected a note of disappointment in his voice, but he rallied. "Then I'll call you tomorrow. In the morning."

"And you thought you needed a handbook," V said, laughing.

He laughed and said, "Have a good night, Doc." Before she could respond, he added, "I should probably make sure it's okay if I call you that, or if you prefer V."

"No," V said, then shook her head, even though he couldn't see her. "I mean, yes."

His chuckle made her groan inwardly. Why could she not play it cool for an entire conversation with this man?

"What I mean is," she said, trying again, "it's fine if you call me Doc, or V."

"All right," he said, and she heard the smile in his voice. "Good night, Doc."

September 22nd

"It's six in the freaking morning," Jackson grumbled when he answered Dave's call the next day.

"Are flowers too much?" Dave asked, scrolling through a local florist's website.

"Everything other than death or a lost limb is too much at six in the freaking morning," Jackson said and yawned into the phone. "If the flowers aren't for a funeral arrangement, then you could've waited until after eight to call me."

"No one died. I just need advice on whether flowers are too much."

"Jesus, I need coffee for whatever this is going to be," Jackson said. "I know I'll regret asking this, but too much for what?"

"For a first date," Dave said. *Roses? No, too cliché. Lilacs? Too . . . grandmotherly.* Panic set in as Dave clicked past bouquet after bouquet.

Jackson grunted into the phone. "I take it your call with the good doctor went well yesterday."

Daisies? No, not sophisticated enough. Dave suppressed a groan.

"Did you seriously call me to ask one question and then sit there?"

Jackson's voice startled him from his flower fugue. He'd almost forgotten he'd called him. "Huh? No, sorry," Dave said, tuning back in to the conversation. "Yeah, it was good. We texted, then talked. So, yeah, it was good."

"So, the two of you are going out tonight, then."

"I hope so."

"You hope so?" Jackson asked, and Dave heard the clink of what he assumed was a coffee mug followed by a grinding sound. "I thought you said things went well."

"They did. Great, actually."

"Then why don't you know whether you're going out with her tonight?"

"Because she said things were complicated with them right now, whatever that means, and I need to check in with her this morning to make sure she's free." Dave clicked on something called a peony and waited for the larger image to load. "I'm guessing that complication has something to do with what you mentioned yesterday."

Jackson made a noise of acknowledgment. "Yeah, I'd say that's a decent guess."

Too focused on his own impending flower crisis to drill down on whatever Jackson had going on with Kez, he said, "Flowers. Too much, not enough? What do you think?"

Jackson slurped what was most likely the aforementioned coffee. "What time did you get up this morning?"

Dave shrugged, then remembered Jackson couldn't see him. "I don't know, why?"

"Because you sound like someone who chugged four energy drinks with an espresso chaser, man. You need to relax and stop overthinking this. More importantly, you need to confirm you have a date before buying flowers. One step at a time."

Dave blew out a breath. "You're right. I just . . . really clicked with this girl, you know?"

"I have an inkling of what you mean," Jackson said drily. "Which is why you need to get your shit together and stop spinning out about flowers. First, make sure you know where you're going to take Dr. Walters if she agrees to go out with you. Doesn't make sense to show up with a bouquet, but no destination."

"I'm not a total moron," Dave said, slightly offended.

"Despite all evidence to the contrary," Jackson muttered.

"I'm thinking the Canal House over in Pittsford," Dave said.

"Very nice," Jackson said. "Color me impressed."

"Yeah, I think she'll like it." Dave refused to let the relief he felt at Jackson agreeing with his suggestion show in his voice. He'd agonized over it between the hours of three and four that morning like a crazy person.

He glanced back at his laptop to see a flower that resembled what would happen if a rose and a cabbage had a baby with the rose winning the color contest.

"What do you think of peonies?"

"I don't think of them," Jackson said with a laugh.

"Why did I call you?"

"I've been asking myself that since I answered the phone."

Dave snorted. "Fine, thanks for not helping me."

"Here's a bit of advice before you hang up." Jackson paused dramatically. "Wait until at least nine before calling the doctor, okay? At least if you *want* her to go out with you tonight."

The line went silent in his ear, signaling Jackson's departure from the conversation. Dave tossed his phone onto the table next to his laptop. Only two hours, fifty-one minutes to go.

Chapter 4

"I understand, Mrs. Franklin, but we've been over this before in several prior visits. Sarah Ann's condition isn't something that can be cured through overprescription of medications."

The base of V's skull started to throb with the telltale beginnings of a raging headache. A headache that followed Sarah Ann Franklin's appointments with alarming frequency. Not because of the patient. Sarah Ann was a lovely eight-year-old who suffered from anxiety . . . which was made worse by her mother choosing to ignore it, or when she deigned to acknowledge it ask why all this couldn't be "fixed" with "a pill, or something."

The grooves next to Mrs. Franklin's lips were more pronounced on the screen of V's laptop than they were in real life. They deepened as she frowned at V.

"Really, Doctor Walters, it's not like I'm asking you to give her Xanax or Valium or anything. I just want to make sure we're exploring all treatment options here."

Except for treatment options like the therapist V mentioned to her on several different occasions. V resisted the need to rub the back of her head. She couldn't afford to show this woman any weakness.

"I understand your concerns, Mrs. Franklin, and can assure you we are all focused on doing everything we can for Sarah Ann."

Her cell vibrated on the table with an incoming call, but she didn't glance at it. She'd learned that the hard way with this particular mother, who'd bitched up a storm the *one* time V dared check her phone during an appointment. Regardless of the fact she was only checking to see if her nurse were calling with the latest round of test results. It had been "insulting" and "belittling" and Mrs. Franklin felt as though her and Sarah Ann's time "wasn't being valued."

This woman was a giant pain in her ass. If she hadn't felt so sorry for Sarah Ann being saddled with this witch as a mother, she would've found a way to refer them out completely.

"Well, I suppose that's all we can ask. Even though, I think this latest information I mentioned would be helpful to Sarah Ann."

The "latest information" came from some parenting magazine with zero medical support. V consciously dialed down her response. "I appreciate you bringing that to my attention, Mrs. Franklin and we will definitely look into it. But for now, we need to keep Sarah Ann on her current medications to give them time to take effect."

With a few more put-upon huffs from Mrs. Franklin, V was able to end the telehealth appointment. She sat back with a sigh and dug her thumb into the tightening muscles at the base of her skull, trying her best to ward off the knots that would inevitably result in a headache.

Her phone buzzed once, and she picked it up with her free hand.
Dave Voice Mail

The smile that started was unstoppable and before she knew it, she was grinning as she lifted the phone to her ear.

"Hey, Doc," Dave said, "it's Dave. Although, you probably guessed that from your caller ID, so I'm not sure why I mentioned it."

Was he nervous? The idea of the suavely confident bartender being nervous to leave a voice mail caused a little flutter in her belly.

"Anyway," the voice mail went on, "I'm calling as instructed yesterday evening to see if you're free for dinner tonight. Just give me a call and let me know, okay? I'm really looking forward to it."

V checked the time on her computer. She had roughly fifteen minutes until her next telehealth appointment. She pressed the return call icon under the voice mail.

One and a half rings later, she heard, "Doc, hey."

Again, she noticed the sound of her nickname on his lips. Noticed and very much enjoyed it.

"Hey," she said. "Sorry I couldn't take your call. I was with a patient."

"With a . . . patient? Uh, are you . . . did you go back home already?"

She would be a lying liar who lied if she tried to deny the ping of pride she felt at the disappointment in his voice.

V laughed. "No, it was a telehealth appointment."

"Oh." She grinned at the relief she heard in that one syllable. "So, you're still in town?"

"Still in town," she confirmed. "And, thanks to your friend, available for dinner."

"Thanks to my friend?"

"Yep, Jackson has been drafted into . . . well, it's a long story, but suffice it to say if he's with Kez tonight, that means I'm free."

"That's great," he said, his enthusiasm making her grin wider. "I was thinking I'd swing by to get you for dinner around seven, if that works."

"That should be fine," V said. "I'll meet you in the lobby."

"Perfect," Dave said. "See you tonight."

V disconnected and clasped the phone to her chest, her wide smile stretching her cheeks. This weekend was working out much better than she'd thought it would. Due in no small part to Dave. She tried to remember the last time she'd been this excited for a first date. And couldn't. It was ironic that her past first dates seemed much more like auditions than anything with Dave did. Which made sense because those dates were designed to find something long-term and this was just for fun. That thought dimmed her smile.

She chided herself for being silly, because the thought of leaving him behind shouldn't impact her smile *at all*. Dave was nothing more than a nice little distraction, and she'd do well to remember that instead of acting like a giddy schoolgirl with a crush. That thought chased her smile away completely.

Her phone buzzed against her chest, and she jumped.

Dave: *Really looking forward to seeing you again, Doc. Also . . . I like calling you that for some reason I can't explain.*

V's hand came to her lips, where her smile had reappeared in full force.

"Need a paper bag?"

V startled and turned to see Rae lounging in the doorway of the shared bathroom. "What?"

Rae fluffed out a small paper bag, likely the same one she'd gotten from her earlier run to the package store that afternoon. "A paper bag," she repeated. "You've been in here for over an hour, even though you've been ready longer than that, and you look like you could either vomit, hyperventilate, or both." She shook the bag. "An accessory for each of those occasions."

"I don't think I have time for any of those," V said, dropping the gloss she'd applied for the third time into her clutch. "Dave should be here any minute." That knowledge made the butterflies in her stomach take flight and lodge in her throat.

She must have looked a little green, because Rae said, "A to-go bag then." She folded the bag into thirds and passed it to V. "Tuck it in there just in case."

"You're nuts." V laughed.

"Says the woman who's about to puke because she's got a date with a hot bartender. Between the two of us, Doc, it's obvious who's a little off in their perspective here."

Brown eyes and a dimpled smile flashed into her thoughts, and V bit her bottom lip. This had seemed like such a good idea earlier. To take Rae's advice and go out with a guy who didn't fit into the cookie cutter shape of "V's Boyfriend," because he didn't check the necessary boxes. Only now, two days and several flirty texts later, she wondered if he didn't fit because she had the wrong criteria for the part.

She'd never considered the possibility before, largely because she'd been too absorbed on other things, namely: a) graduate summa cum from a great college, b) score admission to at least three med schools on the list she'd been cultivating since middle school, c) get chosen for a residency at a prestigious hospital on the list she'd started in junior high, and d) the final, ultimate goal of being a doctor.

The single-minded focus she'd devoted to making all these things occur meant V had little interest in, or time to devote to, figuring out what she was looking for in a guy. It had been easier to just let her mother imprint her with what to look for. Just like it had been easier to say yes to the guys her mother had suggested, because that way, V was never more invested in them than she was in her path to achieving the goals she made for herself. Only now that she had, now that the last, most important item had been checked off her life to-do list, she was left feeling as though maybe she should've devoted one single ounce of the energy she'd poured into school and achieving her career goals into figuring out what *she* wanted in a man instead of relying on her mother to figure it out for her.

She gave herself a mental shake. "I'm not about to puke," V said. "I'm just a little nervous, that's all. Which I think is perfectly understandable. Given we don't know this guy." That was why her stomach was flip-flopping like a fish out of water and certainly not because she couldn't stop wondering whether his lips felt as full as they looked.

"Uh-huh," Rae said, sounding thoroughly unconvinced. "You're more than welcome to join me and Chris if that will make you more comfortable."

"I saw enough of the two of you over lunch, thanks," V said. "I don't think more of . . . *that* is going to make anyone more comfortable." She'd made the mistake of joining Rae at the hotel bar for lunch. They'd left with full bellies and the bartender's phone number stored in Rae's phone.

"Don't be so uptight, Doc."

"I hardly think I'm being uptight by not wanting to see you engage in any further cherry stem contests."

"*Pfft*," Rae dismissed V's comment. "It was never a contest. I won hands down. Although, I have to admit," she added thoughtfully, "I was impressed with his dexterity and speed. I mean, five knotted cherry stems in under ten minutes is definitely worthy of further examination."

"As lovely as that invitation sounds, I think I'll pass."

"Suit yourself," Rae said with a small shrug.

With one last look in the mirror, V left the bathroom. Rae's hand on her arm stopped her in the doorway. "Seriously, Doc," she said. "You need me, I'm there. Even if my cherry is mid-knot."

"That's disgustingly sweet of you," V said. Her phone chimed with an incoming message.

Dat Ass *peach emoji*: *Hey, I'm downstairs. I know we said we'd meet in the lobby, but I'm happy to come up, if you want. No pressure, just making the offer.*

"Regan Murphy!" V wiggled her phone in Rae's face. "Did you change his contact info in my phone?"

Rae cackled. "Some of my best work, if I do say so myself."

"You're unbelievable," V said, but couldn't completely squash her laughter as she edited the contact to read "Dave—Tonic."

Rae squeezed her shoulder. "Have fun, Doc. Don't overthink it, just enjoy yourself."

Tingle, tingle, tingle. V's nerve endings fired in relentless waves of awareness when she stepped into the lobby and spotted Dave. Dark wash jeans molded to strong thighs and the butt that Rae couldn't resist commenting on. Tonight, he wore a dark green dress shirt with sleeves rolled up to showcase tanned forearms. He turned around, running a hand through that sexy tousle of blond hair, and spotted her. His hand stopped where it was, pulling his hair back from his face and making V's heart stutter, skip, and then resume beating at a much quicker rate.

In his other arm, he cradled a bouquet of peonies in bright shades of pink, purple, and fuchsia.

Belatedly, V realized she'd stopped in her tracks at the sight of him. Battling a blush, she forced her legs to resume movement. Each step made the erratic thump of her heart louder in her ears, so by the time they stood in front of each other it resembled the low thud of a base drum.

"Hi," he said right as she said, "Hey."

Even more awkward was his coming in for a hug at the same time she held out a hand, so her nails ended up poking him right in the gut. He emitted a little "Oof" sound, and her other hand flew to her mouth.

"Oh, gosh, I'm so sorry!" The hand at his abdomen flattened against it and she clumsily patted his stomach. *Good Lord, woman, get ahold of yourself.*

Hastily, she dropped her hand from his abs, cheeks now fully engulfed in embarrassed flames. "Sorry for . . ." V waved a hand at his midsection, her voice trailing off because she wasn't sure how to finish the thought. Sorry for what? Groping him? Fondling at least four of the six-pack he was carrying under that shirt? Wanting to keep her hand there?

Dave caught her hand, his broad calloused palm wrapping around hers. "No worries." He cocked his head to the side. "Let me have a look at you, Doc."

He stepped back and used his grip on her hand to spin her in a slow pirouette. Like they were alone, and he had all the time in the world to study her, instead of standing in a busy hotel lobby surrounded by people. His thumb brushed the underside of her wrist in the last quarter of the spin, like steel grazing flint and shedding sparks all the way up to her elbow.

One full turn and their eyes met. "Even prettier than Wednesday night, and I didn't think anything could top that dress." His voice was a low rumble that hit deep in her belly and spread outward.

V cleared her throat. "Thank you."

He held out the flowers, then paused. "I didn't consider the lack of a vase situation."

She took the bundle of blooms from him with a smile. "We'll figure something out. These are beautiful."

"They made me think of you," he said, a shy smile on his handsome face. He squeezed her palm. "Hungry?"

Oh boy was she. Wait, what? No! Get. It. Together, she thought sternly, with a mental headshake to dispel *that* line of thinking. Had it really been so long since she'd experienced physical attraction to a guy that one touch and a good line reduced her to a quivering mass of hormones? Given her body's red-hot response to the feel of his hand on hers, the answer was blatantly obvious. Yes, it had been that long. Too long. So long, in fact, V wanted to climb this man like a tree and stay there until Sunday.

"Doc?"

V blinked up at Dave. "Yes?"

He grinned. "I asked if you were hungry."

"Oh, yes," she said, nodding too rapidly. "Starving, actually." *Had Rae actually taken over her brain?*

"Well, we can't have that," Dave said, and tucked her free hand in the crook of his elbow to lead her to the front doors.

"Thank you so much, Lisa," V said to their waitress. "Dinner was lovely."

"It was my pleasure," the young woman assured her as she handed Dave the peonies now ensconced in a vase that had somehow become a complimentary gift from the restaurant. "I hope we'll see the two of you again soon."

"I think you can count on that." V looped her arm through his, which sent a strong burst of masculine satisfaction coursing through Dave. It was a signal that, at least for tonight, she was his.

"Did you have enough to eat?" he asked as they waited on the Uber.

"Are you kidding me?" V asked. "I couldn't eat another bite. That place was amazing."

"And you got a gift to take home," Dave said, moving the vase in his arms.

"Yes, sorry about that," she said with a small smile. "I really didn't mean for them to send us home with that. I just didn't want the flowers to wilt over dinner."

It was exactly what she'd told their waitress, but the way she'd done it had been so charmingly respectful that the woman had fallen all over herself to assist. Dave was starting to see that one of the most important rules in V's little handbook was the golden one. She went out of her way, it seemed, to be kind to others.

When she'd noticed a gaggle of young women seated together, one with a sash and a crown, she'd signaled their waitress.

"Lisa, could you send a bottle of champagne to that table?" She indicated the table of women. "Seems like they're celebrating something special." Before Dave could do anything, she'd slipped her card into Lisa's outstretched hand and bought the bachelorette a bottle of bubbly.

It was that same innate sense of kindness, Dave supposed, that made V agree to accompany Kez on her bizarre reunion weekend.

Over dessert, he'd finally gotten the full story of what brought them to Rochester.

"Wait, wait, wait," he'd said as his spoon crunched through the caramelized sugar on his crème brûlée. "She and Miller broke up how long ago?"

V arched a brow at him as she sliced into her cheesecake. "It doesn't matter how long ago they broke up. What matters is that he'll always be the asshole who broke her heart."

"Which means the three of you had to come here to crash his reunion?" There seemed to be several steps and a whole lot of logic missing from the plan.

V had simply shrugged and said, "It's what Kez needed to move on." She closed her mouth around a bite and hummed, and Dave made note of that sound and his desire to hear it later. And to be the reason she made it.

In a single dinner, he'd been presented with examples of her loyalty, kindness, and the fact that she genuinely seemed to love her work with troubled kids. Everything about her brightened when she talked about her job. He was simultaneously happy for and envious of her. Having a job you not only enjoyed, but honestly loved was something he only wished he could relate to. Not that he had anyone to blame but himself for his current predicament, but it didn't make it any more pleasant to go to work each day.

Their car pulled up, and he opened the door for her. Once she and the peonies were situated, he joined her in the back seat. "We'll drop these at the hotel and then head to our next stop."

"Next stop?" V asked with a laugh. "What else is on the menu for tonight?"

"Let's just say I want to see how well you move backward in high heels," Dave replied.

Chapter 5

The answer to that question, it turned out, was exceptionally well. Dave should've guessed that was the case when V had almost vibrated out of the car with excitement at the mention of a dance club. It was another piece of the oh so interesting puzzle that was Doctor Vivian Walters. He'd never imagined the doctor so prone to an innocent blush would be the one at the center of the dance floor with moves his whole body noticed.

But that's what he found when he returned from the bar, drinks in hand, only to discover the table they'd appropriated was empty except for Rae's date Chris. Because, of course, V texted Rae the minute Dave mentioned the dance club to see if she and Chris wanted to join them. He'd seen the all-caps of Rae's excited acceptance from across the back seat of the car. Chris appeared not to share her enthusiasm.

He set a beer in front of the guy and asked, "What happened to the girls?"

Chris smiled and picked up the beer. "Take one guess," he said, angling the neck of the bottle toward the dance floor.

Dave lifted his own beer and looked in the direction Chris pointed. Their table was slightly elevated, which offered Dave a bird's-eye view. The bottle stopped halfway to his lips, and he stared open-mouthed at the dance floor.

On it, V and Rae were at the center of a ring of admirers, male and female. Those girls could flat out *move*. The music seemed to flow through them. They came together, then whirled apart, but always in sync with the other. V did some type of spin move and dropped down, rolling her hips as she writhed her way back up. Dave abandoned his beer and maneuvered his way to the edge of the crowd, eyes on V the whole time.

The band started a new song with a heavy beat and a sensuous rhythm. V easily picked it up. Hands in her hair, her hips swayed side to side, swiveling in a seductive lure designed to drive Dave insane. Tight jeans clung to her curves and her shirt gave tantalizing peeks of her cleavage. An outfit that was alluring over dinner had his fists clenching with the need to touch her as she danced. When she turned and gave him her back, Dave's eyes locked onto her ass.

V knew Dave was watching, and it sent a victorious spike of energy coursing through her. She let the rhythm of the throbbing bass of the next song guide her body.

Her hips shimmied and twisted. She piled her hair on top of her head and then let it fall as she dropped to the ground. Flipping it back as she wriggled her hips on the way up, she peeked over her shoulder and saw Dave in the shadows just off the floor, watching. Even from a distance, she could feel the weight of his gaze.

"Girl," Rae's voice sounded in V's ear over the music. "I hope you know that man is making plans for you right now. Very naked plans."

V said nothing and basked in the thrill of his eyes on her, tracking her like a lion watching a gazelle. Only she welcomed his predatory stare. The way it raked over her skin in an almost tangible way, outlining the curves of her body.

Risking another glance back at him, she took in the clench of his jaw and the way his hands fisted at his sides. Like he was holding an invisible rope to keep from coming to her. A slow smile spread across her lips and his twitched in response.

Turning once more, V pulled out some of her best moves, lifting her arms and rolling her hips. And then he was behind her, strong arms snaking around her waist and pulling her flush against him. Running his hands down her arms, he guided her hands to clasp his neck. His fingers slid back down her arms and along her rib cage.

When she shuddered, V felt his laugh against her back. Again, he gripped her hips, pulling her tighter against him. She heard his low groan in her ear and felt the ridge of him pressing into her backside. When he started to move with the beat, she had no choice but to follow.

Dave nipped her earlobe and V's body simmered with sparks. His laugh at her ear was dark and full of dirty promises. She matched each of his moves in a hotly sensual display. His hands left her hips and roved over her body. She arched into his touch, not caring who was watching or what the two of them looked like. Her breath quickened as her nipples peaked beneath her shirt, and she couldn't bring herself to feel embarrassed or self-conscious. All she felt was Dave. He was everywhere as he worked his hands over her, drawing near but never quite touching anything truly risqué. Her body blazed to life, sizzling with need for this man.

"Doc." The word was a guttural sound seemingly torn from Dave's throat. "I'm about four seconds from throwing you over my shoulder and taking you to bed. If that's not something you want, I need you to tell me that. Now."

V didn't think, didn't analyze, didn't consider anything but the throbbing center of need that threatened to swallow her whole if she didn't have this man naked and on top of her within the next fifteen minutes. Wanting him consumed her with a ferocity that was terrifying.

When she didn't answer right away, Dave spun her around to face him. "Talk to me, Doc," he said, voice tight and strained. "Tell me what you want here."

"I . . ." V couldn't find words to say how badly she wanted him.

He stepped closer to her, shepherding her off the dance floor and into a little alcove. His hands cupped her jaw and he leaned in close to be heard above the music. "I need words here, Doc. Words that tell me whether I'm alone in this, or if you're with me."

V had no words, but she did have action. Fisting his shirt in her hand, she dragged him closer and pushed up on her toes to seal her mouth to his. She felt his initial surprise give way to hunger, and he lifted her against him. He kissed her like she was air he needed to breathe, or as though his very survival depended on that kiss. It was harsh and raw and real, and she loved every possessive second of it. Her fingers tightened in his shirtfront, and he growled into her mouth, backing her into the wall. Dave gripped her thigh and hooked her leg over his hip. He pressed into her, the hard length of him leaving no question about how badly he wanted her.

Breaking the kiss, he touched his forehead to hers, his breath coming in jagged pants. "I need actual words, Doc."

V managed a shaky exhale. "Yes."

"Yes, what?" Dave pressed.

She met his eyes, dark pools roiling with desire. Raising a hand to his cheek, she said, "Yes, to all of it."

Dave's nostrils flared and he straightened, locking his hand around hers and weaving his way back to their table. Rae and Chris were seated next to the beer he'd ordered and never tasted. Dave tossed a few bills onto the table to tip the waitress.

"Leaving so soon?" Rae's catlike eyes twinkled up at them.

Dave responded with a jerky nod and Rae laughed. She put a hand to the back of Chris's neck. "Let's go, handsome. No need to hang around here all night. I've got better plans for you."

"Are you sure you're okay with them staying at your place?" V asked softly as she glanced at Rae and Chris in the very back of the Uber.

At that point, Dave would have agreed to host a sleepover for Attila the Hun if it meant getting V into bed. He nodded. "Yeah, it's fine. Probably better for her to stay with us than go back to some random guy's house."

V laughed, and Dave didn't think he'd ever get tired of hearing that sound. "I'm pretty sure we've known each other only a few hours longer than they have."

"All the more reason for the two of you to stick together, then," Dave said, letting his fingers trail up and down her arm. "Not that you have anything to worry about with me," he hurried to add. "I just meant . . ."

V's hand dropped to the inside of his thigh and his pulse went tachycardiac. "I know what you meant, Dave, and I appreciate it."

He forced his brain out of his groin and back to where it belonged. At this rate, things were going to be over before they even started. He needed to get a grip, so he didn't immediately maul her once they were alone. But Jesus fucking Christ, he'd almost lost his damn mind in the club watching her dance. And when she kissed him . . . *Fuck.*

The ride to his apartment was like a scene from an action movie, when the hero and villain have fought their way across an apartment lobby with nunchaku and ice picks and are within moments of the climactic end . . . only to land in an elevator with a grandmother and her shopping cart. During the forced break in the action, they stare daggers at each other over her head while the muzak plays, each of them equally anxious to get back to the battle at hand. This Uber ride was the elevator and the other people in the car the grandma. His palms itched with the need to touch V, and he longed to haul her into his lap and kiss her until she couldn't remember her own name. The teasing circles she traced along the seam of his jeans in dangerous proximity to his crotch weren't making things any easier.

"Keep doing that, Doc," he growled into her ear, "and I'm not going to be able to stop myself."

V's fingers paused in their circuit over his thigh, and she blinked up at him. "Isn't not stopping the point of tonight?" Her voice was soft and her lips close to his ear so only he could hear her. His eyes almost crossed when her hand moved north, and her pinky dragged against the bulge in his jeans.

Doc played dirty, it seemed. Yet another side of this woman he liked. Except now . . . now she'd opened the door to a world he doubted she was well-versed in, teasing pinky and sultry pout notwithstanding. He decided to test his theory.

"I'm all for that, beautiful." Dave whispered the words against the shell of her ear, earning a little shiver. She tucked her bottom lip between her teeth and glanced away, even as she leaned closer, and that pinky gave another teasing stroke.

He let his hand slide back down her arm, only this time instead of stopping at her bicep his thumb brushed down the side of her breast. On the upsweep, he dragged his thumbnail over her nipple and back again. She emitted a little squeak and her hand instantly moved away from his groin.

Following her lead, Dave drew his hand back to rest on her shoulder. But he couldn't resist teasing her a little. "For clarity's sake, is this a pause, or a full stop?"

Blue eyes narrowed on him. "What do you think?"

Dave shook his head, needing her to understand his next words with absolute certainty. "Doesn't matter what I think, Doc. When it comes to pausing, waiting, hesitating, considering, or stopping any portion of tonight, only one person's opinion matters—yours. Because I can tell you, I've been at full steam ahead since I met you."

V smiled. "And if I said I just wanted to eat ice cream and watch reruns of *Private Practice?*"

"I've got mint chocolate chip and plain vanilla with chocolate syrup and Addison Montgomery is a goddess, so that's no hardship for me." He grinned back at her. "Assuming, that is, you were planning to include me in the evening of dairy delights and medical dramas."

"Who are you?" V asked with a laugh.

"I'm just a boy standing in frmwhsh . . ."

The rest of his words were stifled by her hand over his mouth. "No, uh uh, nope, no way. That's too much. Taye Diggs and Kate Walsh at their finest are one thing, but there's no way you enjoy watching rom-coms from the nineties. I refuse to buy into that line of baloney."

Dave kissed her palm where it pressed to his lips, which made her smile and drop her hand away. "Okay," he said, "how about this? I'm the lucky sonofabitch looking forward to spending the night with you in whatever form that takes. Simple enough?"

V looked at him for a moment, blue eyes roving over his face until finally she said, "I think I can work with that."

Chapter 6

Dave's apartment was neat and clean. At least V thought it was when she, Rae, and Chris received the quickest tour in the history of time. It consisted mainly of Dave pointing and naming rooms, "Living room, kitchen, guest room down the hall. Help yourself to anything in the fridge."

That constituted the entirety of the tour and the limited five minutes she and Dave spent with Rae and Chris before heading to Dave's bedroom. It was rushed, but not forced. More of a comical display of how badly he wanted to be alone with her. While it was true she didn't know him well, or technically at all, she believed him when he told her they could take things at her pace tonight. That hers was the final word on whatever happened. The truth of it, the bare honesty of his words, lodged in her mind. It didn't make scientific sense, this innate belief that she could trust him, but she didn't question it.

His bedroom door snicked closed behind him and he leaned against it, watching her take in his space. Now that they weren't setting a land speed record through the place, she could take her time looking around. Get a sense of the man from his surroundings.

The first thing her eyes went to, though, was the bed. The *large* bed in the center of the opposite wall. It was neatly made, which did squiggly things to her clean freak insides. The comforter was a deep green, and the man had pillows with shams. *Coordinating* shams in a green and tan checked pattern.

A book sat on the nightstand to the left, along with a framed photograph. V moved closer to get a better look. The book was *Daisy Jones and the Six* and the picture was of Dave in between a woman and a man who looked roughly his age. All three of them were grinning with their arms looped around each other. Behind them was a firepit and a mountain range rose in the distance.

"That's me with my brother and sister from a trip to the White Mountains a few years back."

"Camping?"

Dave laughed. "My sister won't camp. If there isn't a hotel, she isn't interested."

"Sounds like my kind of girl," V said, shooting him a grin over her shoulder.

"No interest in roughing it, Doc?" Dave asked, pushing off the door. She turned back to the photo. "None whatsoever."

Dave came to a stop behind her, close enough for her to feel his heat, but not yet touching her. "Are tonight's accommodations up to your standards?"

Her pulse fluttered at his proximity. "Yes," she said to the picture of his siblings, "although the main living area passed in a bit of a blur, so I'll reserve judgment on that for now."

His answering laugh ruffled her hair. "I'll let management know of your complaint." He took another step forward. One hand touched her hip while the other swept her hair to the side and exposed her neck and shoulder.

Dave's lips landed on her shoulder in a soft kiss. When V tilted her head, he kissed his way up the slope of her neck to the corner of her jaw. His mouth brushed the shell of her ear. "How we doin', Doc?"

She shivered and leaned back to urge him to continue. "I'm . . ." The word came out too breathy, a sigh rather than a word. V cleared her throat. "I'm good."

The hand on her hip tightened, pulling her backside flush with his groin. It became obvious how Dave was doing in the moment. He kissed the throb of her pulse beneath her jaw. "Glad to hear it," he said, teeth scraping her jawline. "But let's see if we can't move that up from just 'good.'"

He turned V to face him, his hand curving against her jaw. She still had on her heels, but even with them the top of her head only reached his chin. The broad expanse of his chest met her gaze when she turned around and above it the hollow of his throat beckoned to her. V wanted to put her lips there, to taste that slip of tanned skin at his open collar. The desire was unexpectedly primal. A much baser instinct than she was used to experiencing.

She didn't dwell on that thought, because Dave angled her face up, his fingertips teasing the hair at the base of her skull. His eyes were so dark it was hard to see where pupil stopped and iris began. His gaze dropped to her lips, and he lowered his head, dusting his lips across hers once, twice, three times. On the fourth pass, her hands found his shirt and tugged.

It was all the push he needed, and he pressed his lips to hers on a groan. They were warm and full, soft and eager, firm with just the right amount of give. His lips should be a prototype, she thought for the briefest of seconds, until his tongue teased the seam of her mouth and she opened to him. Rational, organized thought was no longer a possibility once Dave began kissing her in earnest.

Because the man wasn't content to just kiss her. It wasn't a simple meeting of lips and tangling of tongues. His mouth plundered and took, worshipped and claimed, while his tongue teased hers with velvety strokes and licks. He swallowed the little moans she made when he nipped at her lips. Pushed his fingers into her hair to tilt her head back and take the kiss unimaginably deeper. He wound a few locks around his fingers and tightened his hold, the sting at her scalp as much a surprise as the fact she liked it.

This kiss made her question if she'd ever been truly kissed before. Maybe it was the naughty nature of being with a man she hardly knew. The illicit thrill of her first real one-night stand. Whatever it was, she wanted more of it. He kissed her until she was breathless, boneless, even. Except for her fingers that clutched at his shirt, desperate to keep him close. To keep his mouth on hers. He obliged and banded one arm around her waist, while his other hand went to the waistband of her jeans, nimbly working the button free and zipper down in seconds.

Even in her kiss addled mind, this seemed in reverse to V. In her experience, limited and boring as it was, things normally started from the top. Shirt, bra, *then* jeans. Her heart strummed out a staccato rhythm as Dave spread the fly of her jeans open, gently pushing the waistband farther down her hips.

Dave lifted his head to break the kiss on a ragged pant. "One of the first things I noticed about you, Doc," he said, backing her to the side of the bed, "were your legs. The curve of your calves and that glimpse of your thighs made my mouth water." His voice was like gravel poured through a sieve, rough and jagged, and the sound of it rippled through her in luscious waves.

The backs of V's knees bumped the edge of the mattress. Dave's hands floated up to her shoulders and then to either side of her jaw. Tilting her face up, he dipped his lips to hers in a delicate brush. A far cry from the kisses he'd just given her. So light, V wasn't sure if it counted as a kiss. Sliding one hand around her waist, he lifted her onto the bed.

He stared down at her, eyes cataloging all of her, then he bent to take off her heels. After carefully placing them at the foot of the bed, he returned to stand in front of her.

"So," he picked up where he'd left off, "as much as I love the way you look in these jeans—and believe me, I *really, really* love how you look in these jeans—I want to see those legs of yours, Doc. I want to kiss my way up them. I want to taste the softness of the skin at the tops of your thighs. I want to feel the press of them against my hips when you wrap them around me."

Holy crap! Holy crap! Holy crap! How in the world was she supposed to respond to that? *Was* she supposed to respond to that? She had no clue, since *no one* had ever dirty-talked her like that. Although, it was hard to imagine any of her exes having the . . . whatever it was Dave had that let him say those things. Things she wanted to hear more of. *A lot* more of.

Dave's hands came to her thighs, one broad palm on each of her legs and that possessive grasp drove out all thoughts of anyone but him. His gentle squeeze made her squirm and bite her lower lip.

"I've told you what I want, Doc." His thumbs rubbed the seams of her jeans, inches from the spot his words had just brought blazing to life with an achingly white-hot need.

"What I need to know," Dave continued that maddening caress, so close—*soooo close*—and yet so far. "Is whether you're willing to give it to me." Brown eyes clashed into her blue ones when he looked at her.

"Are you, Doc? Are you willing to give me what I want and let me strip these jeans down those gorgeous legs of yours? Let me feel that supple skin beneath my fingers? Kiss my way from your ankle to your—"

"Yes," V said, blushing as much at her eager response as the word she believed he was about to say. A word she absolutely *did not* say, or think, or use to refer to any part of her body. This might be about going outside her comfort zone, but there were limits, for heaven's sake. And that *word* was one of them.

Dave folded his bottom lip beneath his teeth in a sharp sucking sound. "That blush, Doc." He rubbed roughly at his jaw and shook his head. "Goddamn, that blush. Makes me need to know whether you blush like that everywhere."

V's cheeks felt so hot, she was pretty sure they were magenta by now. If he kept talking like this, she might actually burst into flames of . . . she couldn't even say embarrassment. Because while she was feeling a whole lot of feelings, embarrassment wasn't one of them. Not in the face of the wolfish look Dave was giving her, like he was seconds away from devouring her. A not altogether unpleasant possibility.

"I think," he said as his hands moved down her legs, "that blush is the perfect way to measure"—his palms slid over her knees—"just where we are within your comfort zone."

"My . . . comfort zone?" V breathed as his hands reached her ankles.

Dave tucked his fingers under the hem of her jeans and nodded. "That lovely flush on your skin lets me know you like it when I tell you what I want. You might not be used to it, but you definitely like it. Don't you, Doc?"

V nodded and Dave smiled as he pulled gently on the denim. "Thought so."

V lifted her hips to let her jeans slip over the curve of her bottom and begin the journey down her legs. Each inch of the slow retreat of the pants seemed to pull more and more sensation out of her until she was certain the drag of the denim against her skin was an aphrodisiac in itself. Or maybe it was less the act itself and more of the man behind it. The way his eyes raked over each newly exposed part of her, the hard set of his jaw and the growl of appreciation he let out when the waistband of her jeans trailed over her pink painted toenails.

Tossing her jeans to the side, he pulled his shirt over his head, losing a few buttons in the process, and pitched it to land with her jeans. When her eyes went wide at the sight of his naked torso, he said simply, "I need to feel you on my skin." And then settled himself between her knees, hands coming to her inner thighs.

The movement was so sudden it gave her little time to mourn the fact she hadn't been able to appreciate the glory of a shirtless Dave. The quick glimpse she got before he lowered himself to the bed confirmed he was lean and muscular, toned with no additional bulk. Defined shoulders tapered to strong biceps and forearms, which were currently draped across her thighs.

Dave traced a finger over the impression left on V's inner thigh from the seam of her jeans. She fought the desire to shift, to close her legs, or twist away from his perusal. His fingers moved back and forth over the tiny stripe, as though he were trying to erase it from her skin.

"The price of fashion," she murmured.

He looked up at her and again, she battled the need to cover herself. Being splayed out in his bed like this, wearing nothing but panties from the waist down with him settled shirtless between her knees, ignited all sorts of warring feelings within V.

The immediate, ingrained response was that ladies simply didn't find themselves in that position and she needed to recover her modesty and remember who she was. The demure debutante on her shoulder *tsked* in loud disapproval and wiggled a white gloved finger in shame. That response was safe and familiar and was one V listened to without question in the past.

But tonight wasn't about modesty or being the perfectly chaste Southern lady. It was her stepping outside of that role she'd been trained to play her entire life and experiencing a little bit of life on the other side. This was her dipping a toe into Rae's end of the dating pool. The fun end, where people did cannonballs without thinking about the splash, or dove off the high dive without glancing below. Prim and proper had no place in this end of the pool, as the devil in a killer red bikini informed her from her other shoulder.

Without dropping his gaze from hers, Dave pressed his lips to her thigh and gave the skin there the tiniest little suck. Not enough to leave a mark, but just enough to make the debutante pass out from shock and the devil rub her hands together in glee. The pull of his lips against her flesh sent a shockwave straight up the line of her thigh to her core and she couldn't hold in a gasp.

It made Dave smile against her leg and place an open-mouthed kiss no more than an inch higher than the last one. The devil was in full control now, because V's knees bent and fell open, her heels coming to rest at the small of Dave's back. Unsure of what to do with her hands, she fisted them in the comforter. It was either that or shove them into Dave's hair and drag him up the length of her body. But, devil or no devil, she was still herself at the heart of things and wasn't ready for that just yet.

She felt his smile widen as he moved infinitesimally higher to place another kiss just above the last. His tongue joined the party then, slipping between his lips to dance lightly over her thigh. V's body went molten, and the fabric of the comforter squeaked in her clenched fists. Her hips gave a little buck, and he laughed darkly.

"I was about to ask if you were doing okay up there, Doc." His voice was a rough scrape and he chuckled. "But I think I just got my answer."

"Uh-huh," V managed to squeeze out on a sigh as Dave's mouth continued its slow, oh so slow, path up her inner thigh. A trail blazed with kisses, licks, nips, and itty-bitty sucks of her skin. Each one of them sent a different, but no less powerful, charge of lust through V. As though sparking filaments linked his lips to the pool of liquid heat sitting low in her belly.

Dave's mouth reached the crease where her leg became her hip and he nipped at the tendons there. V closed her eyes on a soft moan.

"Initially," he said as he brought his hands to rest on either side of her hips, thumbs hitching under the strappy sides of her panties, "I thought there wasn't anything sexier than that white dress you wore the night we met." His thumbs moved back and forth beneath the satin covered elastic in slow, deliberate movements. "The way it seemed like it had been poured over every curve of your body." Dave smiled up at her. "So fucking sexy." He drew out the words into more groan than sentence.

His eyes dropped from her face to the front of her panties, thumbs still toying with the straps. Dave shook his head. "That dress . . . well, I don't know what it was, but it was enough to keep my focus from straying to what could be *under* it. But now . . ." He brushed a thumb over the front of her panties, touching nothing more than the lowest part of her abdomen, but V still arched into it.

He continued, gaze still on the gauzy lace of her underwear, "I think if I'd known there was even a possibility that you were wearing something like this under that dress, I would've spontaneously combusted on the spot." Brown eyes raked up to hers. "And I definitely wouldn't have made it all the way through dinner tonight without a closer look."

Why was the thought of that so hot?

"I think that may have caused a bit of a stir at such a nice restaurant," V said.

Dave laughed. "You're probably right."

"And I liked the cheesecake there, so it'd be a shame if we couldn't go back," she said, then instantly tried to backtrack. "Not that we would, of course. I wouldn't expect that to happen again this weekend or anything. I mean, I know it was an expensive place and . . ." Her sentence tapered off and *now* her blush *was* from embarrassment.

Dave was unfazed by her babbling. He kissed her stomach just above the top of her panties and then rested his chin on the same spot, gazing up the line of her body. "I'll take you wherever you want, Doc. But first . . ." He toyed with the hem of her tank top. "I'd really like to find out if what's under here"—he gave the shirt a sharp tug—"is as interesting as what I found under those jeans."

Chapter 7

Dave's fingers cramped with the need to touch all of V. To pull her top over her head, snatch her bra away to bare what *had* to be perfect breasts and finally, *finally* strip away the swath of lace covering her sex and dive headlong into her. From where his chin rested just above her panties, he could feel the heat of her. All that separated him from luxuriating in that luscious, wet heat was the smallest piece of fabric held together by delicate straps that felt as though they would snap with the slightest pressure. It was a feeling he could relate to. One he'd had since laying eyes on this woman.

But he needed to make sure she was right there with him. Her pleasure was first and foremost in his mind, even as his cock pulsed against the fly of his pants.

"What do you think, Doc?" Dave ran a finger underneath the bottom of her top. "Think I could take a look under here?"

V's answer was to sit up. The shift in her posture made Dave lift his head from where it rested against her belly. He watched as she hooked her fingers in the hem of her shirt and pulled it, inch by inch, up and over her head. Blood roared in his ears at the sight of her breasts—perfection, just like he knew they would be—encased in lace similar to that of her panties. Only the lace that made up her bra was completely sheer. Which made it that much easier to see the taut, pink buds of her nipples straining forward against the delicate fabric.

Dave drew in a sharp, quick breath at the vision of her. Delectable curves and smooth skin wrapped in cream-colored lace. "Jesus Christ, Doc," he said, reaching out a hand to cup one breast. The soft weight of it in his palm made him groan in anticipation. When he dragged a thumb over her nipple, V's entire body shuddered, and he heard her sudden inhale. She bowed her back, pressing her breast further into his hand.

Dave pressed his fingers into the supple flesh and V's eyes drifted closed as her head dropped back. The teasing feel of her through her bra wasn't nearly enough, and his other hand moved around to her back. Searching fingers found their target and seconds later her bra was undone, the straps hanging loosely at her shoulders. Dave relinquished his hold to divest her of it completely.

The sight of her in nothing but her panties made his pulse skyrocket and his cock harden to painful extremes. She was beautiful, porcelain perfection and he hesitated to touch her even as it was the one thing he wanted most. Her skin was achingly smooth and delicately translucent in places, revealing the blue network of vessels giving life to the stunning creature before him.

"Dave," V said, and his eyes shot to her face. She looked at him through hooded eyes, lips slightly parted and cheeks that sexily innocent shade of pink. Settling back onto her elbows, she dragged the heel of one foot up the back of his thigh. "I . . ." She licked her lips and closed her eyes, her blush deepening.

"What is it, Doc?"

The blue that greeted his gaze when she opened her eyes again was like the hottest element of a flame, searing its brand on the deepest part of him. "I want you to . . ."

"Tell me what you need, Doc," Dave encouraged, moving to hold himself above her.

Her blush wasn't limited to her cheeks, but spread over her throat and down to her chest. She squeezed her eyes shut tighter. "Isn't it obvious what I need?"

"Look at me, sweetheart," Dave coaxed, holding her jaw in one hand. "Open your eyes and look at me."

She did as he asked, those blue eyes still aflame with desire.

"Whatever you want, I'll give you. Whatever you need, I'll provide it. All you have to do is ask, Doc."

V pulled her lip between her teeth but didn't close her eyes or look away. Keeping her gaze on him, she said, "I want . . . I want you to . . ."

He waited with bated breath for her next words, because in that moment he would've flown to the moon and back if she'd asked.

"I want you to touch me," she said. Her small fingers took his wrist and tugged upward until his hand covered her breast, her nipple pressing against the center of his palm. She let out a little whimper, and it broke any restraint that was left in his body.

Dave surged forward, draping himself over her, and lowered his mouth to take hers in a bruising kiss. His hand still held her breast, and he kneaded it as he licked into her mouth, swallowing her encouraging moans. Taking her nipple between his middle and index fingers, he pulled and rolled the eager flesh until it was plumped and deep pink.

V moaned into his mouth, and he shifted to give her other breast the same wicked treatment. She arched into his touch, fingers clutching at his shoulders and heels digging into the backs of his thighs. Breaking their kiss, he worked his way down her throat with licks and sucks. Reaching her breasts, he sucked one pebbled nipple between his teeth, trapping it there and torturing it with repetitive laps of his tongue.

V's fingers speared into his hair and her back bowed, pressing her breast tight against his lips. Dave hummed in approval, and she shuddered in response. Moving to her other breast, his fingers clamped around the tormented bud, still slippery with his saliva. He rubbed and pulled at it, even as he used his mouth to do the same on her other breast.

V began to pant and writhe against him, her fingers twined in his hair. She kept him close even as she whined that it was too much. Finally, he released her nipple with a wet pop and nuzzled the skin between her breasts. Kissing his way down her body, he swirled his tongue into her belly button and earned a breathy laugh as she toyed with his hair.

The laugh turned to a gasp when he started to draw her panties down her legs. She stiffened against him, her hands coming to his wrists, and Dave stopped, hands frozen at her hips. "Talk to me, Doc," he said, looking up at her. Her eyes were closed, and tension radiated from her body.

He unwound his fingers from the sides of her underwear and flattened his hands against her stomach. "Doc, tell me what's going on."

When she said nothing, he asked, "Is it time for medical dramas and mint chocolate chip? Because I can make that happen. Just say the word."

That got him a smile and her to look at him. "I don't think we're quite to that point. This is just a bit . . . overwhelming."

"Overwhelming good, or overwhelming bad?"

"There's nothing bad about this," V reassured him. "Except for maybe my reaction."

Dave stroked the skin of her stomach. "There's nothing wrong with your reaction, Doc. I'd much rather you tell me you're overwhelmed than forge ahead like nothing's wrong. There's no enjoyment in that. For *either* of us."

She stared down at him before exhaling loudly and letting her body flop back against the bed and covering her face with her hands. Dave slid backward until his feet were solidly on the floor. Toeing off his shoes, which he'd somehow forgotten about until that moment, he rejoined V on the bed. Lying next to her, he crooked an arm beneath his head and used his other hand to pull hers away from her face.

"Well, this is humiliating," V said without looking at him.

"No, it's not," Dave said, bringing her knuckles to his lips.

"Easy for you to say over there with your washboard abs, magic fingers, and weirdly prehensile tongue."

"I'm not sure if that last one is a compliment, but I appreciate the other two."

V laughed. "I had this grand plan of stepping out of my comfort zone. Listening to Rae's advice for once and seeing what happens. Turns out I'm incapable of leaving my comfort zone. Like at all."

"Why would you want to go outside your comfort zone when it comes to sex?" Dave asked, truly perplexed by the concept. "How could you even *have sex* if it meant doing something you weren't comfortable with?"

"I don't mean sex *per se*, I mean sex with you."

"Okay, that one there, I'm *certain* wasn't a compliment," Dave said, releasing V's hand and pushing to an elbow.

"No, no, no!" V's hand shot to his chest to keep him in place. "That didn't come out right. At all. What I mean is this whole thing. This . . . this . . . casual fling thing. That's not something I do. Like at all. Ever. But then I saw you, and Rae said you had BDE and so I just thought, 'What the hell?' you know? Like why not give the whole sexy bartender thing a whirl and see what happens. Only now, after we've had this great night, which should obviously end with amazing sex, I freeze up like some sort of virgin on prom night and ruin everything. And as if that wasn't bad enough, I manage to insult you on top of everything else."

She sat up, covered her chest, and looked around. "I should probably go, right? Yeah, I should call an Uber and go." Her nod was decisive. "Yep, that's what I'm going to do. Find my clothes, call an Ub—"

Dave put a hand around her bicep. "Doc."

V looked at him, arms still crossed over her breasts. "Yeah?"

"Take a breath."

"What?"

"Take a breath. A real breath. In through the nose and out through the mouth."

When she did as she was told, Dave nodded. "Very good. Now, if you *want* to leave, of course you can. But"—he put a hand on her thigh—"I'd much rather you stay."

"You would? Why?"

At her fully mystified frown, Dave laughed. "Because I enjoy your company. At least, that is, when you're acknowledging my BDE and not semi-insulting me."

V groaned and Dave laughed again, lifting her into his lap and putting an arm around her. "Again, if you want to leave, I'll take you back to the hotel myself. But I hope you'll stay."

In truth, he hadn't been insulted at all. He wasn't an idiot. Even without her saying anything, he'd known this was well outside the norm for her. She was, it seemed to him at least, a woman who'd crafted a carefully constructed life for herself, missing one key element. An element she was adorably embarrassed to admit she wanted. V wasn't a prude or frigid. She'd just never had someone tap into the sexier side of her personality, which, based on the way she'd responded to him, was at once a crying shame and something he was exceptionally happy about. Because it meant he could be the one to provide that missing piece for her. To give her that walk on the wild side she wanted. And maybe, if he played his cards right, show her it didn't have to come with an end date. Because the more time he spent with her, the less appealing it was that after Sunday his time would be up.

V wondered if Dave would notice if she just stayed curled against his chest for the rest of her life. It was so comfortable here. So warm and snuggly. Not to mention the way it smelled. She didn't know how to put into words how to describe it but was certain some romance author would say something like a pine forest after a spring rain, or snowcapped cedars next to a mountain stream. Whatever it was, it made her temporarily forget her pathetic meltdown of a few moments ago.

Everything had been going so well too. That was perhaps the understatement of the century. Dave was . . . woo boy, Dave was *really* good in bed. Scary good. Channing Tatum on the dance floor good. And they hadn't even gotten down to the nitty-gritty of it all before she flipped out. She'd stopped him when the reality of what she was about to do overloaded her brain. When he made the final move to strip off her panties, it hit her that she was going through with this. This wasn't the foreplay at the club, or the extremely enjoyable kissing and other things. This was no-strings attached sex with a man she hardly knew. And that fact slammed her brain into nuclear shutdown mode, and she'd stopped him. Even though every part of her, right down to the last follicle of hair on her head, wanted him to keep going.

And instead of berating her, calling her a tease, or any other asshole move he could've made, he'd praised her for telling him the truth. He hadn't sent her packing, or lost interest once she'd freaked out. He'd gathered her close and asked her to stay. He was holding her against him like she was something worth protecting. Something to be handled with care. Something to be cherished.

She put a hand on his chest, feeling the steady, reassuring thud of his heart under her palm.

His lips grazed the top of her head. "Ready for ice cream, or did you want me to take you back to the hotel?"

His giving over control of the situation to her and her alone emboldened her and gave her more confidence in the choice she'd made to come home with him in the first place. This was something *she* wanted. He was something she wanted, and she had the right to want it. There was nothing wrong with her choice. V took another deep breath, feeling a steely sort of resolve set in. She wanted this. She *deserved* this. Deserved to feel the way she did when this man touched her.

"What if I said neither?" She placed an open-mouth kiss to his shoulder.

Dave's arm stiffened at her back. "Doc, we don't have t—"

"I know that," she said, continuing to kiss her way across the broad expanse of his chest.

His breath shuddered out in a long exhale as her lips traced a path up his neck and along the underside of his jaw. She turned in his arms, her legs unfurling from his lap to straddle him. Her arms came to his shoulders, and she looked into his eyes, dark with concern beneath his furrowed brow. When she bent her knees and drew closer to him, his eyes widened, and his jaw bulged with the clench of his teeth.

"I don't want you to think th—" He tried to say, but V interrupted him.

"I don't want to think about anything either. I don't want to get in my head about things and miss out on spending tonight with you. I want to listen to the rest of my body for a change. I want to obey my skin when it strains for your touch. I want to allow my lips to sample yours until I'm drunk from your kiss. I want to feel your hands on every part of me. I want yo—"

Dave's mouth covering hers kept her from finishing her thought. His hands pressed into her shoulders, molding her breasts to his chest. In one swift move, he stood with her in his arms and turned to lay her back on the bed. Worry lurked behind the lust burning in his eyes. His hands dropped to the waistband of his pants, and he paused.

"You're sure about this, Doc?"

Knowing he'd need her to say it aloud, she responded, "I am." To prove her point, she slid her fingers into the waistband of her panties and shimmied them down her legs until they dropped to the floor, and she was bared to him. She didn't cover herself, didn't shy away from his gaze, just let him look his fill.

He scrubbed a hand down his jaw and closed his eyes briefly. When they opened, V thought it was entirely possible he could set her on fire with the heat reflected there.

"You are," he said as he unbuckled his belt, "without a doubt"—he undid his fly—"the most beautiful woman"—he let his pants hang open to reveal the waistband of his boxer briefs—"I've ever seen in my entire life." His pants hit the floor and V sucked in a breath at the sight of the bulge behind the gray fabric of his briefs. In a blink, those hit the floor with his pants and the strong, hard length of him hung rigidly in front of her.

Wrapping one hand around the base of it, Dave gave it two rough strokes before he levered himself over her. "You see what you do to me, Doc?"

She felt the ridge of his erection press demandingly against her thigh and she smiled. "I feel it too."

Dave laughed, the sound rich and full of promise. "Maybe I need to see whether I have the same effect on you?"

Supporting himself on one long arm, he nudged her legs farther apart and ran a finger along the slick seam of her sex. V gasped and tilted her hips to chase his touch, eliciting a deep groan from Dave. "Fuck, Doc. Is that for me? Did I get you so wet and soft?"

This filthy side of such a sweet man made his touch that much more erotic. The way he spoke to her woke up aspects of her she hadn't known were even there. But now that she did, V didn't think those darker desires would go back to being dormant. More than that, she didn't want them to. Giving in to this newly awakened yearning, V drew her legs farther apart and bucked against his fingers with a nod.

The growl that rattled from his chest was male, possessive, and hot as hell. He lowered himself to kiss her, pressing the entire length of his body to her and molding her into the mattress. V hummed in the back of her throat and dragged a hand up his back to hold him close.

With noticeable effort, he pulled himself away. "Condom," he rasped out and groped in the drawer of his nightstand. Pulling out a sleeve, he tore one off and tossed the rest onto the bed.

V eyed the plethora of prophylactics. "Is it wrong to say that seems ambitious?"

Dave grinned down at her as he tore the condom open and rolled it down his shaft. "I enjoy a challenge, Doc. And I'll make sure you do too."

He gripped himself in one hand and teased along her sex, bumping her clit with the head of his cock. V's body jerked in pleasurable surprise. Dave pressed his other hand at her belly, and continued the short, blunt strokes of that compact bundle of nerves.

"Oh." V tried to move, but Dave kept her there, doling out her pleasure in portions only he controlled. Frissons of energy sparked out from her center and flooded through the rest of her with each pass he made. Her hand came to his forearm, and she bore down on it as she tried her damnedest to move at the pace that would get her what she needed.

"Not so fast, Doc," Dave chided from his position above her. "You'll get there, but don't be in such a rush. Give yourself over to the ride and enjoy it. I'll take care of you, don't you worry."

It was V's turn to growl, hers in frustration as he continued to tease her to the brink of insanity. Each brush, each stroke, each tap of her clit brought her closer and closer to release, but never quite there.

"So eager," he said, his voice becoming more raw and more roughened as his eyes were locked on her sex. "I could look at you all fucking night." He met her gaze with a smile so wicked it was a sin in and of itself. "I guess you do turn pink everywhere, Doc. At least"—he quickened the maddening strokes at her clit—"you do when I'm around."

Her body clenched at nothing as he increased the pace yet again and she felt the building, tightening swirl deep in her belly. Arching into him, she dug her nails into his forearm, and he relented his hold, letting her pulse her hips against him. Pleasure spiraled out from where he touched her until the delicious pressure was all she could feel. It engulfed her until she shattered with a strangled cry.

"That's it, Doc," Dave said, working her clit with his cock. "That's it, beautiful, let it all go. Give it all to me. I can't fucking wait to be inside you. To feel you all around me."

Wave after wave of splintering sensations ricocheted through her and he coaxed her through all of them until she was a twitching heap beneath him. Her eyes drifted closed, and she heard Dave laugh.

"Don't quit on me now, Doc."

She felt the pressure of him at her core and her eyes fluttered open. "I wouldn't dream of it." Hooking one leg over his hip, she angled herself against the head of his erection, earning a muttered curse and a squeeze to her thigh.

Dave began the slow press inside, eyes locked on the place where their bodies joined. V felt her inner walls stretch and roll around the shape of him, at once beckoning him inside and resisting the intrusion. The juxtaposition reignited the pleasurable ripples within her, and she lifted her hips encouragingly.

"Doc." He rasped her name, tightening his grip on her hips. The single word was as much a curse as it was a prayer as he closed his eyes and pushed all the way inside her. The fullness of him stole her breath on a gasp and she clamped her legs around his waist.

Dark eyes opened, and he asked, "Everything good?"

He held himself still, visible tension running through every muscle with the effort not to move, not to give in to the primal urge to take more of her. She saw the restraint in every tendon of his forearms, the bulge of his biceps and the taut lines of his stomach. V had the impression that he would've kept himself like that all night if she asked. His entire body was primed, waiting for her response.

Hers answered with a roll of her hips that made his eyes widen and nostrils flare. His fingers dug into her hips in a grip that was harshly possessive. "Words, Doc," Dave gritted out through clenched teeth. "I need words."

V reached up and put a hand to his chest, feeling both the rapid pace of his heart and the coiled strength there. "I'll be better once you start moving," she said, punctuating her demand with another buck of her hips.

"Thank God." Dave released her hips to come to his elbows above her. The dusting of hair on his chest teased her sensitive nipples. Reaching back, he braced one elbow under her knee and hiked her leg higher against his hip, opening her wide and letting him press impossibly deeper.

V's whole body reacted to the unexpectedly rich sensation of having him fully seated within her. If she'd felt full and stretched before, now she was . . . she couldn't even make words form in her mind to describe it. And when Dave began to move on a deliciously rhythmic slide, her brain went on permanent hiatus. No longer needed for actual thought, because all that remained to do was feel. The weight of him, the warmth of his breath at her neck, the corded muscles of his shoulders beneath her fingertips, the sound of someone's wanton moans . . . no, not someone's . . . *hers.* Guttural, throaty noises that V hadn't known she was capable of making. Noises this man pulled from her with each thrust of his hips.

"Christ, Doc," Dave's rough whisper floated past her ear. "I could listen to you purr like that all night long." His laugh was gruff as his arm slid from beneath her knee, letting her leg fall loosely to the bed. His hand found her breast, fingers pinching her nipple in a rhythm matching the one set by his hips.

"Dave." V gasped, pulling her shoulders back to press her breast more fully into his hand.

He trapped her nipple between his middle and ring finger, stroking the tip of it with his thumb. The blunt edge of his thumbnail scraped the eager tip and sent starbursts of sensation rioting from her breast to her core. Her hips jerked, and he groaned at her ear, increasing the pace of his strokes. Another pinch of her nipple threatened to send her circling the stratosphere. But for the heady weight of Dave's body on hers, V surely would've levitated right off the bed.

"I can feel you, Doc," he said in a rough moan. "I can feel you holding me so tight, strangling my cock while you chase that release. I'm here for you, baby. I'll get you there. Is that what you want? Want me to give you what you need?"

"Yes," V groaned as she thrashed underneath him, hips working in a wild frenzy as the tendrils of another orgasm gathered low within her.

Dave relinquished his hold on her nipple with one final pinch, the sharp prick of exquisite pain followed by release flooded through her on a wave of pleasure and fueled her climax. When his fingers came to her clit in feathery strokes, V was gone—hurtling over into orgasm.

She had no control over the sporadic jerks of her hips as Dave worked her clit and drove himself in and out of her spasming sex. Her hands shoved against the headboard to keep herself locked beneath him at the delicately precise angle she needed to prolong her release. Because she wasn't ready to come down, wasn't ready for the liquid heat thrumming through her to cease, wasn't ready to relinquish the pure physical perfection that was sex with this man.

"I need to join you, sweetheart, but I don't want to stop," Dave's words were a labored groan, emphasized by the slam of his hips into hers. It was a wildly desperate thrust, showing his fraying control, his own need for release.

Looking up at him, V reveled in the power of that moment. Her ability to take this man to the brink warring against his determination to last until she released him. It was intoxicating to skate that razor's edge with him, but she needed him to fall. To topple with her into blissful oblivion.

"I need you with me," she said as she arced up into his thrust. "I need you with me all the way."

V felt him let go, felt the release of his body when he gave in to the sensations that had to be shooting through his as they were in hers. Dave lost his rhythm, his long smooth thrusts replaced with pulsating snaps of his hips against hers. Pressing her body into his, she used those short thrusts to tease her clit, and she was lost to pleasure once again. His fingers dug into her flesh and he threw his head back on a shuddering groan, joining her in the freefall.

Chapter 8

Aligned against Dave's long, lean body, V sighed contentedly. His answering chuckle rumbled beneath her while his hand trailed down the slope of her side to the dip of her waist, coming to rest against the rise of her hip.

"Need anything?" he asked into her hair before pressing a kiss to the crown of her head.

"No, I'm pretty comfortable right here," she replied, letting her hand explore the lines and planes of his torso.

The truth of that statement surprised her, because this situation was not one in which she was normally comfortable. Her fingers slid lower on his abdomen, and it dawned on her she was more than just comfortable. She was relaxed and happy, sated in a way she hadn't experienced. V's entire body was loose and limber, thoroughly and exquisitely used in ways she'd never experienced. She was positively luxuriating in the afterglow of something she hadn't thought she was capable of doing, much less enjoying. And yet, here she was, cuddled up to a guy she'd known less than forty-eight hours with whom she'd only spent a handful of said hours—a good portion of which had been spent delightfully naked.

Dave continued his lazy stroke of her hip. "I'm glad to hear that, Doc. Because if you told me I had to get up and take you back to the hotel . . ." He laughed again. "I honestly don't know that I'm capable of physical movement right now."

V joined his laughter, tickling along his ribs. "So, you want me to stay only because you don't have the strength to get rid of me?"

"I want you to stay, Doc, because I like having you here. In my place. In my bed." His hand tightened at her hip. "Next to me."

Something fluttered in her chest and then moved south to lodge deep in V's belly where it turned warm and molten. She hid her smile against his chest.

Dave's hand resumed its slow glide over her skin. "I know this situation is, uh, not how you normally spend your Friday evenings. Which means I'll do whatever you need to stay comfortable. Even at the risk of my own personal health."

That liquid feeling spread through V at his words, and she snuggled closer to him. "Thank you," she said. Those two words didn't contain near enough appreciation for his acknowledgment of her needs, but they were all she had at her disposal.

"I do have a question, though," Dave said.

"Please don't ask me about a suspicious mole."

She felt him shift to glance down at her. "I'm sorry, what did you say?"

Peeking up at him, she grinned. "You'd be surprised how many times I've been asked about moles."

"On dates?"

"On dates, at parties, in elevators. People hear doctor and suddenly they're pulling up sleeves or tugging down socks so I can 'take a quick look.'"

Dave shook his head in disbelief. "That's . . . I don't even know what to say that is."

"So, your question is not about a mole, then?"

"No." He laughed. "No moles."

"Okay, ask away."

"I've been wondering how someone like you who likes her rules and guidelines, someone who made a point to require a specific amount of advance notice to go on a date . . ."

"Mm-hmm," V said, curious to see where this was going.

"Well, how did someone like you end up with two friends who appear to be a little more go with the flow kind of women?"

V laughed. "Don't let Kez fool you. She's just going through a little bit of upheaval right now. On a normal day, she's much more levelheaded."

"I'll take your word for it. But that doesn't explain Rae."

V laughed. "There *is* no explaining Rae, I'm afraid. At least no explanation she's ever shared with Kez or me. I know there must be some-thing—or someone—from her past that honed her into the man-eating wonder she is today, but she's not big on sharing."

"Well, the three of you seem like a tight-knit, if a little unhinged at times, group."

"Yeah," V agreed, smiling. "Would you believe it was a backpack that brought us together? At least, Kez and me. Rae came post-backpack."

"A . . . backpack?"

V nodded. "A My Little Pony backpack to be specific."

"I need to hear more," Dave said.

"As you know, Kez and I met in school."

"This would be in the great metropolis of Sawgrass, North Carolina, right?"

V laughed. "The one and only. Our teacher alphabetized every-thing—including her students. Which put Kesler Walsh and Vivian Walters right next to each other. Which let me see that she had a spar-kly pink backpack that featured Firefly."

"I'm afraid to even ask."

V pushed up on an elbow and cut him a menacing glare. "Firefly is only the coolest of the My Little Ponies."

"You seem very invested in that belief for a woman not born in the 1980s."

"Fight me," V said, and Dave laughed. "Anyway"—she resumed her place at his side—"I'd never seen My Little Pony, so I didn't know what it was. I just knew her bookbag was pink, sparkly, and awesome. Turned out Kez's mom found it in a thrift store for like three dollars or something, along with all these old VHS tapes of the show. Once I complimented her on Firefly, she invited me over to watch and we've been best friends ever since. Much to the disappointment of my mother."

Why had she said that last part? V mentally kicked herself. Mothers were not a topic to bring up to someone you'd only just met. *Crap, crap, crap.*

Seemingly unbothered by the mention of her mother, Dave asked, "Why is that?"

"That's a road we don't need to go down," V said.

"We can travel any path you're comfortable with, Doc," Dave said. "Whether it's your mom, your favorite My Little Pony, or anything else you feel like talking about."

"Is that some bartender trick or something? Use that soothing tone of yours to get people to open up to you about their deep, dark secrets."

"Never considered My Little Pony as dark, but then, I'm not the expert you apparently are. And no, it's not a trick. I'm interested. In you. And however much of yourself you want to share with me."

He made it sound so tempting. To let down her guard and share things about herself with him. Anything she wanted without worrying about how he'd see her afterward, or whether he'd judge her for what she'd said. But that wasn't what this was supposed to be about. This was casual, not deep. A temporary timeout from real life focused on physical release, not in-depth conversation. Time to steer it back in that direction.

She stretched her fingers out wide over his abs, moving her hand up to his chest. "I think after tonight, there's not an inch of me that hasn't been shared with you."

"And I enjoyed all of them, I assure you." He caught her hand and held it. "But don't do that, Doc."

"Do what?" she asked, not looking at him.

Still holding her hand, he used her own knuckles to tip her face up to meet his gaze. Even in the hazy darkness, she could see his earnest brown eyes staring back at her. "Don't make this just about sex. There's a chance for something more here, and I think you feel that too."

"Dave, I . . ." V sank her teeth into her bottom lip and looked away. "Like I said, I'm only here until Sunday, so we can't . . ."

Bumping her chin with his knuckle, he brought her gaze gently back to his. "I'm not pushing, Doc, just talking."

V didn't pull away from him, even as she said, "But we've already talked about this. You know I'm not . . . that this wasn't supposed to last beyond this weekend. Just a bit of fun. For both of us."

"And it can be," Dave said, still relaxed and casual as though they were discussing whether there were a chance of rain instead of something that set V's heart racing. "If we get to Sunday and that's all you want, where you want things to end, then that's what we'll do. All I want, all I'm asking you to do is keep an open mind about the possibility of something more."

Broad fingers closed tightly over hers and V felt the smallest of tugs. One so light she easily could've refused it. But she didn't. Instead, she gave in to the pull of his touch and let him gather her closer to his side. She refused to consider how nicely she fit against him, or how much she liked it when he said, "There's my girl." There was plenty of time to do the thinking he'd asked for later. V pushed away all thoughts other than the feel of his skin against hers and the stroke of his fingers at her hip. She focused on enjoying the now and forestalled any thought of the future.

Dave woke to a pillow that smelled like flowers and an empty bed. His hand stretched across the mattress but came up empty. He sat up and rubbed his eyes, clicking on his bedside lamp. He scanned the room for V. But she wasn't there. Had she left? Slipped silently out of the apartment without even a goodbye?

He should've kept his mouth shut about seeing where things go. Should've just enjoyed the night with her, made plans for the next day and shut up after that. There had been no need to delve into what could happen once she left, since she was still fucking here. He'd botched things so badly she'd snuck out in the middle of the night so she didn't have to face another onslaught of what-ifs from him. The idea of it was that repulsive to her. *Shit!*

His chest constricted at the thought, and he swung his legs over the side of the bed, where the tender arch of his foot connected with the sharp heel of one of V's shoes.

"Fuck," he swore under his breath and rubbed his foot. He'd never been so glad to be impaled in his life. Unless she'd fled shoeless into the night, which he highly doubted, she was still here somewhere. The bathroom door was open, and the interior was dark.

He'd just reached for his boxers when the door to his bedroom swung open to reveal V standing there in nothing but his T-shirt holding a glass of water. Relief cascaded through him. She hadn't left. Once he'd processed that, he took in the sight of her, all sleep-tousled and drowsy. Desire overwhelmed relief and shot straight to his dick. He bit back a groan.

She paused in the doorway, taking in the sight of him standing next to the bed—naked and holding his underwear. "Uh, what's going on?"

"I thought . . ." Dave gestured generically with his boxers, then dropped his hand back to his side. "Never mind. Where'd you go?"

A stupid question, given she was holding a glass of water. Obviously, she'd gone to the kitchen to get a drink. But she indulged him and answered.

"I was thirsty and didn't want to wake you, so I helped myself. I hope that's okay."

"Sure. Absolutely. Find everything okay?"

V gave him an odd look but nodded and put her glass on the nightstand. Pulling the covers back, she slipped beneath them, still wearing his shirt. A fact he enjoyed. A lot. "So, are you going somewhere, or . . .?"

Dave realized he was still standing there buck naked and staring at her. *Way to convince her to give this a go, dumbass,* he thought as he dropped his boxers and rejoined V under the sheets. She flipped to her side to face him, one hand shoved under her pillow. Dave mirrored her posture right down to the arm under the pillow.

Her brows furrowed, then released, as though she were working through how to phrase something. She opened her mouth, then closed it only to repeat the process and press her face into the pillow with a frustrated *ugh!* noise.

"What's up, Doc?"

V pulled her face far enough from the pillow to roll one eye. He couldn't see her grin, but heard it when she asked, "Been holding on to that one a while, have we?"

He lifted his shoulder. "Let's see, we met approximately forty-eight hours ago, give or take thirty minutes. You've got to carry the one and divide by two"—he drew his brows together in faux concentration—"which means the answer is roughly forty-seven hours and twenty-three minutes."

V laughed and pressed her face back into the pillow. Dave tugged on her shoulder to get her to look at him. "Seriously, though, what's got you looking like you're trying to solve some complex equation?"

She peeked out from her pillow shield and sighed, flopping over onto her back. Swatting her hair from her eyes, she said, "Funny you should mention equations. You know how the tour you provided of your place was somewhat . . . abbreviated?"

Dave laughed. "I was focused on one particular area at the time."

V nodded, her eyes on the ceiling. "Well, when I went to the kitchen, I noticed the frames you had on the living room wall. And, as one does when they notice something like that, I . . ."

"Snooped?"

V cut him a look. "It's hardly snooping if the items in question are hanging on the wall. I'm pretty sure those qualify as items in plain view, for which you have zero expectation of privacy once you invited me into your home."

"I beg your pardon," Dave said, holding up a hand in surrender. "I guess I need to bone up on my *Law & Order* reruns."

"*Anyway*," V said, rolling to her side again. She tucked a hand under her pillow, and it was his turn to brush her bangs off her forehead. "Once these framed things caught my eye," she continued, "I went over to take a closer look."

"As one does," Dave said, now seeing where this was going and interested to hear what she had to say.

"And I happened to notice that one such framed item was none other than a diploma with your name on it."

"Given that I live here alone, it would be weird if it were someone else's."

V smiled and tucked the pillow farther beneath her head. "No question there, so I was glad to see it was in your name and we didn't have some sort of identity theft situation or worse going on."

"No, I can confirm I am the David Robert Richardson named in the diploma and that I did, in fact, earn that diploma myself."

"Okay, so now, we're getting to the heart of what has me confused," V said, propping herself up on an elbow.

"Glad to know it wasn't the identity theft thing. I know we haven't known each other long, but I'd hate to think you'd already painted me as the new Tinder Swindler."

She laughed and poked him in the chest. "You know what I'm about to ask."

Dave gave her the same unbothered shrug from earlier. "Maybe, but there's no way to be certain, so why don't you go ahead and ask whatever it is you want to know."

"You have a college degree."

"We've established that, yes."

"A college degree in computational and applied mathematics."

"Hence the reason I could calculate how long I'd been holding on to that whole 'what's up, Doc' schtick."

V frowned at his attempt at humor, and he regretted his superficial response. She obviously had an agenda and he'd be wise to give it the respect it—and she—deserved. "I'm sorry," he said. "Please, what else would you like to know about my degree?"

"Your degree from a school most alumni feel the need to work into every single conversation from NCAA bracket picks to their thoughts on the debt ceiling. And yet"—her eyes narrowed—"we've had one date, several conversations, and a few delightful text exchanges, and somehow the topic never came up."

"My infusing our text threads with discussions of my alma mater would have made them a lot less 'delightful.' And don't think we aren't circling back to the NCAA bracket thing. I'm very intrigued."

She ignored that. "Maybe it would have, but still, I would've thought you'd have mentioned it."

"You never said where you went to med school, so why would I bring up where I got a bachelor's degree?"

V's lips dipped, and she nodded to concede the point. "Okay, I'll give you that. But, when I said I was a doctor, it was necessarily implied that I went to med school."

"And my being a bartender doesn't scream 'I have a degree in computational and applied mathematics'?"

She had the grace to blush at his question, but he knew that was the gist of what she meant. He knew, because it wasn't the first time he'd heard it, or the first time someone wondered why with this almighty degree of his, he chose to sling drinks for a living.

"In its simplest, most distilled form . . ."

"Ha! A distillery pun while talking about bartending. Very nice, Doc."

"Well, I figured I owe you one after the 'What's up, Doc' debacle you tried." They exchanged a grin, and she reached for his hand. Lacing their fingers together, she said, "I'm sorry if it's rude, or any other number of ill-mannered descriptors, and it's definitely none of my business, so you don't have to answer, but I can't help but ask."

"You haven't really asked me anything yet."

V considered that and then laughed. "I guess not. All right then, why, with the doors I know that degree opened for you, are you tending bar instead of . . . I don't know, applying or computating mathematics somewhere?"

Dave looked down at their joined hands. Just like he had at the bar the night they met, he noticed their utilitarian elegance. The pink polish painted on nails he now knew were kept short because of her job. He brushed his thumb over the scar on her knuckle.

"I went to college because that's what you're supposed to do after high school. Mathematics always came naturally to me, so picking a major was easy. I chose the college impressively stamped on my diploma in letters larger than strictly necessary, because I was smart enough to get in and lucky enough to get a scholarship. My parents love me, but there *are* limits to that feeling and mortgaging their house to pay for my education was one of them. I went, I studied, I graduated, and then . . ."

"And then . . ." V encouraged once Dave's voice trailed off.

He mulled over the best way to divulge the reason for his meandering career path to someone whom it was clear always had a more specific life plan. Dave figured that was a good place to start, so he said, "It's obvious you love your job, Doc. And I'm guessing a big reason why is because it's what you always wanted to do. A pinpoint in a journey you've had mapped out since . . ." He closed one eye and studied her. "I'm going to go with eighth grade."

The rose tint on her cheeks told him he was close, if not right on the money. Her sigh made her bangs feather upward, then settle back.

With a small grin, she confirmed it. "When I was thirteen, our English teacher assigned us an essay about what we wanted to be when we grew up. We had to figure out what degrees were required, how long you had to go to school for it, reach out to schools that offered the required major. Stuff like that. Other kids in the class complained, either because they didn't have a clue what to write about, or because they couldn't write 'astronaut' or 'bass player' and be done with it."

Dave grinned. "I'm guessing it wasn't a hardship for Little Miss Handbook."

She laughed. "Easiest paper she assigned all year."

He pointed at her smile. "That, that right there is what I never had. That early flame of passion about a career that helped blaze the trail of the rest of my life. Like I said, I went to college, because that's what you did. Once college was over, there was no obvious next step for me. At least, not one I wanted to take. I didn't know what I wanted to do, so I did what a lot of confused college grads did."

"Which is?" V pressed.

Dave shifted uncomfortably. This was a topic he didn't like discussing, because it focused on a time in his life he'd rather not think about. But he also wasn't going to lie. "The only thing I knew with any degree of certainty was I needed an income, so salary was the main thing I looked at when deciding where to interview."

"I'm guessing that didn't work out so great," V said in a soft voice.

Dave snorted. "No, it turned out that a great paycheck doesn't make up for a toxic work environment answering to a passive-aggressive asshat. I was just out of school with no real work experience other than a part-time bartending gig, so I didn't recognize it for what it was at first. The way my supervisor always seemed to assign last-minute intricate tasks on Thursday after four o'clock, or send me some scathing email on the second or third day of my vacation. I'd spend the rest of the week keyed up and anxious, only for him to be perfectly fine upon my return to the office. After a while, I found out our department had the highest turnover ratio of any in the company." His lips thinned at the memory. "That knowledge leaked out when someone in HR sent a mass email summarizing the exit interviews of all the people who'd quit because of my boss. It opened my eyes to what was happening, but upper management did nothing because he made them a shit-ton of money. So, they canned the HR person and kept the asshole all for the sake of the bottom line. I wasted too many miserable years there before I quit and moved back to Rochester."

He glanced over at V, but her face gave no indication of what she was thinking. She just gazed back at him with those bright blue eyes and waited for him to keep talking. So he did.

"My parents wanted me to look for something else in my field, but I just . . . couldn't. I didn't want to run the risk of it being the same shit just with a different asshole, you know? I'd bartended in college, so it was easy enough to pick that back up again until I knew what I wanted to do next."

"And that's how you ended up at Tonic?" V asked and he nodded.

"Yeah, that was"—he considered the timeline—"two years ago now."

"And you . . . like it?" Dave could hear the skepticism in her voice. It was easy to pick up since he'd heard varying levels of it from most of his family since he'd moved back.

"It's been good for the most part." He slid closer to settle his free hand on her thigh under the covers. "Meeting you is an excellent example of how good my job can be."

V laughed as his fingers found the hem of the T-shirt and slipped beneath it, curving around the swell of her bare hip. She let him pull her closer, even as she said, "So I'm just an example, huh? The latest in a litany of ladies mesmerized by your skills behind the bar."

His hand drifted to her waist. "Doc, there's only one of us doing the mesmerizing tonight and it isn't me." He swallowed a groan at the feel of her, all lush and warm against him.

Snaking his other arm under her pillow, he inched closer to her, his hand moving from her waist to cup her breast. He could feel her nipple react to his touch, beading tightly just above the tip of his thumb.

"Don't sell yourself short," she whispered on a shaky exhale as he caressed the curve of her breast. He nuzzled her hair, inhaling the light floral scent that seemed to hover around her in a tantalizing cloud. Not overwhelming, or cloying. Just enticingly feminine. He wanted to bottle it and keep it available whenever he needed a hit of it.

"Also"—her hand curved around his bicep—"don't think I'm oblivious to this blatant attempt to change the subject. And"—her breath hiccuped as he dusted a fingertip over her nipple—"as a mental health professional"—she looped one leg over his hip—"I shouldn't encourage your use of avoidance mechanisms."

"Mm-hmm," he replied, continuing the slow drag of his thumb at her nipple.

V's leg tightened its grip against his hip, and he groaned as their bodies aligned.

"But in this case," she said, "I'm inclined to make an exception."

Chapter 9

September 23rd

"Only you could find a way to trip over a hot bartender's dick and land in a relationship with some dude who loves math," Rae said as they were on their way back to the hotel Saturday morning.

"Would you *please* . . ." V shot a glance at the driver in a silent plea for Rae to show some decorum. "Ugh, I'm not in a relationship with him. I just," she snuck another glance at the Uber driver and continued in a whisper, "happened to have mind-blowing sex with him last night."

"Sex so good it made him want to wife you up." Rae's grin dissolved into laughter. "I have to admit that I did *not* see this coming when I told you to hook up with him. Like not at all."

V shushed her with another glance at their driver. "Will you keep your voice down?"

Rae looked at her like she was nuts. "This is a Corolla, Doc, not a stretch limo. I'm pretty sure if a mouse farted back here the driver would hear it loud and clear." She looked at the driver in the rearview. "Am I right?"

The woman smiled. "Painfully, so. You do *not* want to know some of the things I've heard since taking this job."

"I beg to differ," Rae said, leaning forward with interest.

V elbowed her. "Can we get back on topic, please?"

Rae pouted at being denied Uber After Dark stories, but she refocused on V. "What do you want me to say, V? You've got an easy out here. Just tell the guy thanks for the D, but I'm not interested in anything further. What's he going to do? Kidnap you and keep you here?" She shook her head. "All you have to do is say no. Match his honesty with some of your own."

Green eyes twinkled at V. "That is . . . assuming you *want* to say no and have no interest in seeing Dave after this weekend."

"What would that even look like?" V deflected. "He and I are too different, not to mention we don't live in the same state."

"Not an answer to the question. Do you want to see if there is anything there with this guy? If you do, then it can look however you want. Maybe it's a month-long torrid affair full of sexting and dick pics. Maybe it fizzles out before you get on the plane. Or maybe it's something unexpected. Something you didn't even know you wanted. It can be whatever you want it to be. You just have to decide you want it to be something in the first place. The specifics can be worked out later."

She pulled her sunglasses from her purse and slid them on. "He said there was no pressure, right? Just wanted you to think about it? So, think about it. Try it on and see if it fits. If it doesn't, get on the plane and don't look back. Problem solved."

"He's a person, Rae, not a pair of shoes or an outfit."

Rae sighed. "Look, I'm the absolute last person who would encourage you to let a one-night stand linger around for any portion of the following day much less anything beyond that. But that's not you, babe! You're a relationship kind of girl, which means if there weren't something more than pure physical attraction, you wouldn't have gone to bed with the guy. A true loss for female kind everywhere, but the truth, nonetheless. If you didn't feel something beyond the objective recognition of Dave as a hot man, last night wouldn't have happened. You know that you're just in denial."

"But he's not my type," V complained.

"Let's face facts here. Your type sucks. It's really that simple. The harder question is if they're even *your* type."

"What's that supposed to mean?" V asked, her tone sharp.

Rae lowered her sunglasses, shooting V a look that was as sympathetic as it was frustrated. "Listen, Doc. I love you, but you've got to face facts. You date these guys—guys you claim are great candidates—but who never amount to anything other than a punchline." She arched an imperious brow. "Need I mention the Weasel?"

V cringed. Wesley Augustus Witzel III, a.k.a. Wesley Weasel as christened by Kez and Rae, was the guy her mother set her up with two summers ago. He was as entertaining as dishwater and about half as deep. He'd also kissed with all the passion of a dying trout. If that trout had suffered from chapped lips and a case of halitosis.

"For the record, I never slept with the Weasel."

"Thank God," Rae said. "He might've siphoned out part of your life force during the act."

She grinned when V laughed, but then grew serious. "Don't you think, Doc, that if the sum of your required relationship criteria continually equals him or someone similar, it's time to shuffle the deck and re-evaluate some things? Think about what's important to you, not your mom or her idea of what's perfect, but the qualities that really matter to your own happiness. What you actually want in a man, as opposed to what you think you should want. That will provide a much better foundation for your own happiness than some pre-ordained blueprint I wonder whether you even believe in."

Outwardly, V didn't flinch, but her insides flopped in response to Rae's observation. Truthfully, her insides had been on a roller coaster ride since she'd met Dave. At first, she'd thought it was just that dopamine hit you experienced from something new and fun. But after last night, she had to admit, even if just to herself, it was more than that. It was also more than anything she'd felt for the guys who checked off a lot more boxes on the boyfriend list than Dave did. Which had her questioning the items on that checklist in equal measure with her unexpected interest in Dave's proposal of letting this . . . thing between them last longer than the weekend.

September 24th

"Hello?" V answered without taking her eyes off the airline website on her computer screen.

"Well, at least I know now you're not dead in a ditch somewhere."

V blanched and looked belatedly at the caller ID to see her mother's contact information confirming that it was indeed her. "Mother," she said. "Hi."

"'Hi'? I've left two messages with no return phone call and all I get is 'hi'?"

V closed her eyes and let out a muted sigh. "Sorry," she said. "It's been a hectic few days."

"I see," her mother said, her tone transmitting loud and clear that she absolutely did not. Failing to call after two voice mails was a capital offense in the etiquette-driven world of Caroline Abernathy Cunningham Walters.

"Sorry," V said again. "I should've called you back sooner."

Her mother's first message came on Saturday afternoon while she and Dave had been at the Strong National Museum of Play. They'd toured exhibits ranging from Madame Alexander dolls to the eGame Revolution exhibit where she'd bested him at Giant Tetris—twice. The thrill of victory couldn't compete with the Butterfly Garden exhibit, though, due in no small part to the epic romance factor of being kissed by a cute boy next to a waterfall in a room full of butterflies. The whole day had been relaxed and full of uncomplicated fun. Something V hadn't known she'd needed until Dave had given it to her.

The second message had come in as they were headed to dinner at the Owl House Saturday night and V meant to call her back early Sunday morning, but had been too focused on moving her flight. And now she was paying the price for it.

Her mother made a noise that could've been agreement or derision before saying, "I'm calling to see if you're free for dinner next Saturday."

Dinner, V knew, would be at the Sawgrass Country Club, or "the Club," as her mother called it. For as long as she could remember, her parents had standing dinner reservations there every Saturday night. Sawgrass was roughly an hour north of where V lived in Charlotte, which was close enough to allow her mother to brush aside any alleged inconvenience involved in V coming for dinner.

"I'm not sure," V hedged. "Is there a special occasion?" Her mother's invitation put V's Spidey senses on high alert, since these dinners were Caroline's preferred way of introducing V to men she thought were suitable son-in-law candidates. Sometimes she gave V fair warning, but there had been times V had arrived to discover an extra place setting that turned out to be for so-in-so's nephew or such and such's grandson, and so on and so forth.

"I need a special occasion to have dinner with my only daughter? The one offspring of mine who remained within the state and is close enough to come home for dinner?" Caroline made it seem as though she had a legion of children, when it was only V and her brother Avery. Their mother had never forgiven Avery for moving to Atlanta, which was too far away for unannounced drop-in visits or last-minute invitations to dinner at the Club.

V took a deep breath. "No, you don't. Just wondering if there was something special going on." *Like a date by ambush.*

"Well." Caroline drew the word out and V knew something was up. Nervous prickles ran down her spine. "There is a new doctor at Sawgrass Memorial that I want you to meet. He's a cardiothoracic surgeon that transferred here from Atlanta. Marcus Copperfield. He also happens to be very handsome." The last information was delivered in a sing-song tone.

And here we go. "Is that so?"

Her mother was good and warmed up now. "Yes. He's thirty-eight, single, and from a good family. Four sisters, if you can believe it. His father runs Copperfield Transit, a shipping company, and his mother is very involved in League activities in Atlanta. A man like Marcus won't be on the market long, Vivian."

League was the Junior League, and all of this information was Caroline's roundabout way of explaining to V that Dr. Copperfield wasn't just a successful surgeon, his family was loaded *and* had the right kind of social connections. All of which boiled down to him being Caroline's dream son-in-law and V needed to act fast before someone else snapped him up.

Rae's words from yesterday drifted through V's mind. *Think about what's important to you.* Was any of what her mother just listed important to her? Had it ever been, or had she gone with the flow because it was easier than pushing back? Had she ever really thought about what she wanted in a guy, or had she been satisfied with plugging in her mother's requirements instead? Partly because she'd focused more on school, her residency, and then work, but in no small part because it gave her some common ground with her mother.

It was no great secret that Caroline wanted a daughter who would float through cotillion like she did, who'd make homecoming court in high school, win prom queen then go to college and come back with an engagement ring from a medical student who happened to be the first son of a fine family. What she got, despite all her efforts, was someone more interested in beakers and petri dishes than cosmetics and varsity quarterbacks.

Her mother was not one to admit defeat, though, and so even after V graduated with a medical degree for her wall instead of a ring for her left hand, her mother continued to devote herself to "getting V settled," a.k.a. married to a guy from the right family, with the right job who could hobnob with her parents at the Club. Marcus Copperfield was the latest in a long line of candidates her mother pitched at every opportunity.

Normally, V wouldn't have pushed back. But now . . . now V questioned whether anything her mother mentioned did more than sketch out a two-dimensional man. A smiling, successful image to plug into a family Christmas card instead of a person to make a life with. Up to now, she'd tried things Caroline's way with zero success in any aspect other than entertaining nicknames and funny anecdotes her friends loved to recite. With startling clarity, V knew she didn't want to continue settling for the 2-D version, because it was woefully short of satisfying. She wanted more. She *deserved* more.

"I'm sure that's true, Mother. But the thing is . . ."

She stopped mid-sentence, unsure of how to continue or what to say. She wasn't ready to mention Dave, because the spotlight of her newfound clarity only extended so far. It didn't illuminate a clear path forward with Dave, so it was better not to mention him. It would raise questions she couldn't answer.

"Yes?" Caroline said when V didn't finish her thought. "What is 'the thing,' Vivian?"

V could picture her mother in the sitting room Caroline used as an office from which to run her social empire. She might not have a job other than ruling over the Club, but she handled it like a true corporate scion. More correspondence and directives were issued from that lavender-walled room than from the desk of any Fortune 500 CEO.

V cleared her throat, searching for the best way to head her mother off without divulging Dave's existence. In the end, she took the coward's way out. "I'm pretty sure I've got to cover an on-call shift on Saturday."

Caroline was no fool, though. "Pretty sure," she said.

"Um, yeah," V brazened on. "I won't know for certain until I get back to the office on Wednesday."

Her mother's sigh was dramatically put-upon. "I need to let the Club know a number by Wednesday or I doubt we can get a table."

V suppressed a snort at that line of bull. No one, unless they had an innate desire to no longer work there, would deny Caroline a table at the country club.

"Then I'll make sure and get you an answer as quickly as I can," V promised.

"Well, all right," Caroline said. "Let us know when you get back in town, okay?"

"Of course," V said. "Love you."

"Love you, too, sweetheart."

V's phone was still in her hand when it chimed with a text from Caroline of a link to Marcus Copperfield's MD page at the hospital, complete with a thumbnail photo of the man in question.

Caroline: *Isn't he handsome? And so accomplished too.*

If nothing else, she had to admire her mother's persistence.

Chapter 10

September 26th

Early Tuesday morning, the sheet slid down to reveal another few inches of V's bare back, which meant Dave did the only rational thing. He traced his lips up the line of her spine, making her hum and stretch. She rolled over, unfortunately tugging the sheet higher in the process, and blinked sleepily up at him.

"Good morning, Doc," Dave said and handed her a steaming mug.

Rubbing the sleep from her eyes, V sat up against his headboard and accepted the coffee with a grateful smile. Settling into the pillows at her back, she took a sip. Then frowned and glanced into the cup.

"Is there Stevia in here?" she asked.

Dave nodded, twirling a lock of her hair between his fingers. "I noticed you used it the other morning, so I grabbed some."

"You don't use it?"

Dave shook his head, rubbing his thumb over the soft blond strands wrapped around his finger. "Nah, I'm a processed sugar guy myself."

"So, you got this . . . for me?"

The hesitant confusion in her tone brought his eyes to hers. "Well, yeah, Doc. Is there a reason I shouldn't have?"

The quick shake of her head pulled her hair free from between his fingers. "No, no. It's just . . . well . . ." V's hand fluttered through the air and then dropped back to the comforter. "I mean, I leave this afternoon, so it just seems like a waste for you to get something like that when you don't use it. That's all."

Dave grinned at her to mask his nerves. "It's not like that stuff has a short shelf life. It'll be here next time you're here."

Blond brows shot up above wide blue eyes. "Next time I'm here." V said the words as though she were processing each one of them individually. Like the thought of coming back hadn't occurred to her. Like they hadn't spent Friday, Saturday, Sunday, and last night together. Like she was going to fly home today and they wouldn't see each other again.

Ignoring the anxious uptick in his pulse, Dave nodded. "Yeah, I mean, I know it won't be in the next few weeks or anything, but I'm *hoping* you'll be back in October at the latest."

"October?" Owlish eyes blinked at him, which did nothing to soothe the tightness in his chest at the thought of her leaving. How could she be so surprised by his wanting to see her again?

He swallowed and kept going, glad he'd taken the time to frame his argument in favor of their giving this thing between them a real chance. "The month that follows this one? Tends to have an overabundance of pumpkins, lattes, and flannels? I think you're familiar with it."

Dave thought, or at least hoped, his bluster did a decent job of hiding the gymnastics his internal organs were doing as he waited for her to respond. Since their first night together, he purposely hadn't broached their continuing to see each other, even though he'd given it a lot of thought. He was counting on the time they'd spent together laying the necessary groundwork for his final pitch. It was a good sign she'd already bumped her flight twice. The deadline V placed on things between them had come and gone two days ago without any discernible regret on her part.

But this was the big test. Because there would be no further delaying her departure and, if she chose to, she could board her flight later that day and never see him again. She could walk out of his apartment and his life without a backward glance. The thought of it made his stomach clench and shoulders bunch, but he forced himself to relax. There would be no pressuring V into this. She had to want it, or there would be nothing after today.

She put her coffee on the nightstand next to her and tucked the sheet higher against her chest. "I know when and what October is. My confusion lies more in my presence in Rochester during that particular month." To her credit, she didn't look away from him when she said this. She looked right at him while she destroyed him.

"We agreed this wasn't going to be anything other than the weekend."

Dave kept his voice calm and light, despite the thundering of his heart. He'd never agreed to that, just acknowledged it was a possibility. "In case you missed it, Doc, the weekend's been over for more than twenty-four hours and you're still here."

V's lips pushed into a reluctant smile. "That is true." She shifted higher in the bed, folding her legs beneath the covers and leaning forward. "What exactly are you asking, Dave? Because as great as this extended weekend has been, I can't wrap my head around how this works long-term."

Dave took her hand in his, his thumb landing on the now familiar scar on her knuckle. "I don't have it all figured out by any means, I only know I don't want today to be the last time I see you."

"I guessed that when you mentioned my being here next month," V said, a half smile curving her lips. "But how can we . . . how can whatever this is between us . . ." She blew out a breath and Dave held fast to her admitting there *was* something between them.

"What I'm trying to say," V continued, her fingers curving around the edge of his hand, "is that I've had the perfect vacation romance with you. Literally perfect. As in wouldn't change any of it. But this has been a semi-break from reality. We've been in this little bubble of hormones, pheromones, and banter with no outside intrusions. And I don't know if it can survive the sharp prick of reality that is my everyday life."

"Maybe it won't," Dave acknowledged, even as it almost choked him. "Because you're right, this definitely hasn't been my average week either. But isn't that reason enough to see if we can't . . ."

V's smile was sad then. "Can't what? What are we really talking about here? Long-distance? With what sort of endgame?"

"Why are you so focused on the endgame?" Dave said, unable to completely mask his irritation. "Why are you so determined to only see the shelf life of things instead of what we could have together?"

V laughed. "You said it yourself, Dave. I'm the girl with a handbook. The one who takes comfort in rules and plans and structure. So, I'm asking if you want this thing between us to extend beyond today, what's our plan to make that happen?"

The scrutiny in her blue eyes was intense as she waited for him to give her an answer. An answer he'd started outlining in his head as soon as she'd pushed her flight that first time. Because he knew he couldn't wing it with her. He had to give her reasons, good reasons, if he wanted to convince her to give them a chance. Ironically, preparing for this conversation with her felt a lot like when he'd had to show his work during exams. He couldn't just give her the answer of their being together, he had to walk her through the steps of how they got there.

"Well, like I said, I don't have this all figured out quite yet. But we can start small and go from there."

Her brows dipped along with the corner of her mouth. "What does that mean?"

"It means we see how each of us feel about things once we're each immersed back into our own lives. If it's too much to try to continue seeing each other, then we'll know it won't work."

"Your grand plan is to just see what happens once I get back to North Carolina?" V laughed and shook her head. "That sounds more like flying by the seat of your pants than a real plan."

Dave swallowed back the words that were on the tip of his tongue. That he already knew he'd do whatever he needed to make things work between them. That she was worth whatever sacrifice he had to make. But blurting that out wouldn't advance the ball. He had to stick to the plan if he wanted V to see what he already knew—that the two of them had something special. Something that deserved to be cultivated and cared for until it reached its full potential.

"Look, Doc," he said. "Let's break things down to their lowest common denominators, okay? I like you. A lot. Based on all the empirical evidence I've gathered the feeling appears mutual. Can we at least agree on that?"

V chewed her lip but nodded. "Yeah, we can agree on that point."

"Okay, common ground, that's good. I think we can also agree that the sex is great. Acrobatically phenomenal to be more accurate."

He watched the blush creep out from beneath the sheet to spread over her chest, up her neck, and tint her cheeks as V nodded again. "Yeah," she said, voice soft. "That's a decent description of it."

"Excellent, we've now got two strong pillars to support a decision to continue seeing each other. What if I said that after spending the last few days getting to know you, I wanted to know more? To learn all there is to know about you—from your shoe size to your feelings on the elimination of daylight savings time."

Laughing, V said, "Do you know anyone in favor of the time changing?"

"I don't want to presume," Dave said with a grin. "But I am serious when I say I want to get to know you. Not just in the bubble you described, but in your real life. I want to know all sides of you. And I want you to get to know me too. So that I can be more than just some guy you met once on vacation. I want to be more to you than that, Doc. But first, you have to let me."

"I . . ." V closed her eyes and leaned against the headboard. When she opened them, she gave Dave a frustrated grimace. "I want to argue with you. To say we're jumping into this without giving it enough thought or planning. But when you say things like that . . ."

"When I say true things out loud?"

She grinned at him. "When you say things that make my insides go all melty and swoony, it makes it a lot more difficult to think of the reasons this won't work."

"Does it help you think of ones it will?"

Her laugh was rich and warm. The sound of it coasted over him like velvet. "It doesn't help me think at all. Except to wonder if I couldn't get away with one more day here with you."

"Why settle for one more day, Doc, when my offer is for so many more than that?"

"Ugh!" Her eyes looked to the ceiling, and she threw up her hands, dropping them quickly to prevent the sheet from gaping off her chest. The glare she leveled on him was tinged with suspicious humor. "For someone who claims I'm the one who with a handbook, this was a well-plotted question and answer session, Mr. Richardson. It makes me question whether you're just as much of a planner as I am, only more closeted."

Dave leaned in to kiss the tip of her nose. "Maybe you've rubbed off on me, Doc. Does this mean we're up to a three pillared foundation?"

V looped her arms around his neck, letting the sheet drop away from her body. "It means that thanks to this morning's little charm offensive, it wouldn't matter to me if the foundation of this decision were made of quicksand. I'm in simply because you are."

V handed her suitcase to the driver of the rental car bus. Stepping on after her luggage, she nabbed a seat and set her purse on her lap. When she shifted, the hard edge of something pressed into her thigh. With a frown, she glanced down and saw the corner of a package sticking out of the back compartment of her purse.

"What the . . ."

She pulled out a small square wrapped in brown paper with a crude sketch of either a very odd dog or a horse with an extremely short neck. "Doc" was written in strong, block letters in the top right-hand corner of the box.

Her heart did a little shimmy, and she brushed a thumb over the letters. Then glanced quickly around to make sure no one had seen her do it. Satisfied neither the exhausted mom with twin toddlers, nor the group of elderly men dozing to her left had any interest in what she was doing, V flipped the box over and worked a finger beneath the taped seam of the wrapping. Pulling it off, she tucked the scrap into her purse and opened the lid of the box.

On a thin strip of cotton bedding, in all her pink and blue glory, nestled a tiny Firefly complete with two blue glittery lightning bolts on her little pink rump. V pressed her knuckles against her smile as she lifted the toy from the box. A crisply folded note sat in the center of the cotton. V placed Firefly carefully on the seat next to her and picked up the note.

DOC,

I THINK THIS IS THE PONY YOU MENTIONED. SORRY IF SHE'S NOT AND FOR MY PICASSO-LIKE RENDITION OF HER ON THE WRAPPING PAPER. I KNOW I DIDN'T DO HER JUSTICE. ALSO, WHO KNEW OF THE RABBIT HOLES YOU CAN GO DOWN RESEARCHING MY LITTLE PONY? THERE ARE SOME . . . INTERESTING PEOPLE ON THE INTERNET. I PROMISE SHE DIDN'T COME FROM ANY OF THEM, THOUGH. ANYWAY, MISS YOU ALREADY.
DAVE

V picked up Firefly and ran her thumb over the blue mane and tail of the diminutive pink horse, smiling from ear to ear. It was like holding a piece of her childhood. How in the world had he found this? Tucking the pony back in her box, V dug out her phone.

V: *I can't say I've ever had someone risk their internet search history for me in quite this way before.*
Dave: *If I end up on a government watch list or To Catch a Predator, I'm blaming you.*

V: **lol* Like anyone would believe your story.*
Dave: *Good point. Hold please while I wipe my hard drive.*
V: *Seriously, though, thank you. This is one of the sweetest things anyone has ever done for me. How did you even remember her name?*
Dave: *I pay attention, Doc.*
V: *I'll remember that.*
Dave: *I hope so. Fly safe and let me know when you get home, okay?*

There was a twinge and then a pull in V's chest, as though heart-strings were a real body part and his words had strummed right over them.

V: *Sure thing.*

Pumpkins and Possibilities

Chapter 11

October 12th

Dave: *Good morning, Doc.*

V: *Hey. *sushi emoji**

V: *Crap, ignore the random sushi.*

Dave: *What is, "Words I never thought would be texted to me"?*

V: *LOL, sorry. My phone has started to drop in random things at will. Last week I texted my brother a line of starfishes.*

V: *Also, I miss Alex Trebek.*

Dave: *One of the greatest Canadians of our time. Anyway, just wanted to say good morning and that I hope you have a great day.*

V: *Thanks, that's very sweet! *beaver emoji**

V: *Oh God, no!*

Dave: *Doc, I'll accept any beavers you want to send my way.*

V: *GIF of girl covering her face*

"Well, look who's back from the Great White North!"

V laughed. "I've been back for almost a month, Avery. And that's Canada, not upstate New York."

Her brother's handsome face frowned back at her from the screen of her tablet. "There's a difference?"

"Um, pretty sure the Canadians would say an awful lot."

"True, but then what they don't know won't hurt me." A car horn blared from somewhere off to his right and Avery muttered something unintelligible but assuredly rude. "Anyway, I'm headed to the gym, but wanted to see your face when I tell you that I heard through the family grapevine you've been begging off dinner with some hot doctor and absolutely breaking our mother's heart."

The last was delivered in such a perfect impression of their mother's voice, V couldn't help but laugh. "I see you've talked to Mom."

"Talked?" Avery cocked his head to the side in consideration. "I wouldn't say 'talked' as that implies an exchange of words. I did, however, listen to her bemoan your decision not to join them for dinner at the Club upon your return. As well as her absolute heartbreak over your continued refusal to meet this doctor of all our dreams."

"Your husband would be saddened to hear that," V teased.

"Neil knows my heart only belongs to him, but even he's not above a naughty doctor dream every now and again. You know how he feels about McDreamy v. McSteamy." He adjusted his earbuds and said, "But don't try and change the subject, dollface. I want to hear about whatever it is that has you dodging Dr. Dreamboat like the plague."

"It's hardly anything that dramatic," V hedged. "I told Mom that I ended up covering another doctor's on-call rounds the Saturday I got back, which meant I would've missed dinner even if Dr. Dreamboat hadn't been coming."

"Mm-hmm." Avery's lips twisted. "Sure, okay. What about last Saturday, then? What's your excuse for it? And don't think I don't know what 'covering' means, V. You weren't on call and volunteered to take someone else's. Which means you deliberately dodged dinner."

V laughed. "Nothing gets by you, does it? You should start a true crime podcast, Super Sleuth."

"In all my spare time." Avery snorted. "As in, I'm five minutes from the gym and you need to give me the details starting now. What's got you bucking our mother's version of Mystery Date?"

"He's not a what, brother dear, he's a who and his name is Dave," V said, unable to hold back a smile. A fact her brother immediately pounced on.

"I knew it!" He pumped a triumphant fist in the air. "*Dave*, is it? Tell me, do you write his name in little hearts on the corners of your medical charts?"

V stuck her tongue out at him. "All our charts are digital, thank you very much, so there is no doodling in the margins."

"That smile says you're doodling his name somewhere in a heart. There's no hiding that from me. Tell me about this Dave. Who is he, who are his people, what does he do and"—he leaned into the phone for a lascivious eyebrow wiggle—"how well does he do it?"

"You are a disgusting pig hidden beneath a perfect haircut and Lululemon joggers," V replied with a shake of her head.

He shifted the phone to his other hand and leaned forward, presumably to open the door to what she assumed was his gym. "Girl, please, my prurient personality is my biggest selling point." He grinned again and shot her a devious wink. "And I notice the part of the question you immediately focused on was the sexy portion, so I think we've got a bit of the kettle calling the pot a pervert here."

Ambient street sounds disappeared and were replaced with the pump of upbeat music and muted conversation. "But I guess I can make my own assessment of this Dave in person later this month," Avery said, nodding at someone V couldn't see.

"Oh? And how will you do that? Planning a trip to Rochester?"

Avery smirked at her. "Not ever, ever, *ever*. But our annual Halloween party is next weekend and now I know you're bringing a plus one."

V's eyes went round. "Avery, if I do bring Dave, you are *not* allowed to do any sort of weird big brother stuff to him."

Her brother's mouth dropped open in offended shock as he pressed a hand to his chest. "Vivian Walters, I cannot believe you'd even suggest such a thing."

"*Avery*," V warned, pointing a finger at the screen. "I haven't forgotten senior prom."

Avery's lips twitched. "And I'm guessing neither has that insidious cretin Phillip Kelly. But you forget he was the one bragging about his grand plan to divest you of your virtue that night."

"He was a harmless seventeen-year-old idiot," V said with a giggle. "You know every other boy had the same plan on prom night. It didn't mean it would happen, nor did it mean you had to dye him purple."

Avery's top lip lifted in a chic sneer. "It faded after a day or so."

"But didn't go away for a full month. He looked like a corpse in all his graduation pictures."

Avery's grin was all pride and zero regret. "Served him right."

"My point," V said, trying to remain serious, "is that *if* Dave comes with me, you cannot do an—"

Avery interrupted her. "Sorry, sis, heading into the locker room and they don't take kindly to FaceTime in there. So, I have to run. Love you, bye!"

The screen went black, and V tossed her tablet onto the sofa next to her with a laugh. She should've known her mother would bend her brother's ear to the point of breaking after V had declined all opportunities to dine with Dr. Copperfield with little in the way of an excuse. Sooner rather than later, V would have to tell her mother not only wouldn't she be meeting Dr. Copperfield, but that she didn't want to. And tell her why.

Namely, that in the past two weeks with Dave, she'd been happier than she could ever remember. Just the thought of him brought a smile to her face, as Avery had just seen. Which meant she had zero interest in meeting someone else. A fact that she needed to make clear to her mother before Caroline dropped Dr. Copperfield off on her doorstep with a note that said "For Vivian" pinned to his chest.

V's doorbell rang, and she experienced a moment of panic before shaking off her paranoia. Caroline was determined, but she wasn't deranged enough to deposit a man at her daughter's door without warning. It was, however, seven on a Wednesday evening, so she wasn't sure who she'd find at the door. Her phone rang as she got off the couch. Glancing at it, she saw it was Dave.

"Hey," she said. "Someone rang the bell, so hang on for just a second."

"Sure, no problem" came Dave's easy reply.

Through the fish-eyed lens of the peephole she saw a guy in his early twenties standing on her stoop holding a white bag with a food delivery logo emblazoned on it. V hadn't ordered dinner, so this poor guy was at the wrong address.

"Looks like someone's lost," she said to Dave. "Hang on another quick second while I see what's going on."

"Right here with you, Doc." She shouldn't have gotten as warm and fuzzy on the inside as she did to that simple response, but damned if she didn't.

Opening the door to the hapless delivery guy, V said, "Hey, I hate to tell you, but I didn't order anything."

He frowned and checked the receipt stapled to the outside of the bag, then stepped back to check her address. Still frowning, he asked, "Vivian?"

Startled, V blinked at him. "Yes, that's me."

"And this is 4098 Honeysuckle Lane, right?"

"Well." V paused. "Yes, but I didn't . . ."

"Take the bag, Doc," Dave said in her ear.

"What?" she asked.

"Take the bag from him."

"But I didn't order any—"

"I ordered you dinner," Dave said. "Now take the bag before I have to double his tip or risk a bad rating."

Still confused, V took the bag from the now slightly annoyed driver. "Sorry," she said with an apologetic smile. "I didn't think I'd ordered dinner."

"Right," the guy said, drawing out the word as he backed down the steps.

"Thank you," she called as he retreated quickly to his car.

Shutting the door, she asked, "What is going on?" In response, her phone bleated in her ear to signal Dave was switching the call to FaceTime. With a quick glance in the mirror by the door, she smoothed her brows and bared her teeth to check for . . . well, anything. Satisfied there was no roughage in her gumline, she clicked Accept.

When Dave came into view, he was seated at the small table in what she recognized as the breakfast nook of his apartment. He'd positioned the phone behind the place setting in front of him. In the corner of the screen, a beer sat to the left of his fork, and she could hear soft jazz playing in the background.

More confused than she had been when the doorbell rang, she asked again, "What is going on?"

"Since I'm working all weekend, we're having date night tonight," Dave said, unfurling a napkin and dropping it in his lap.

A fizzy sensation started in V's chest and buzzed outward when she looked into the bag and saw the logo of her favorite restaurant. One Dave had never been to. She looked back at the phone and into the brilliance of his grin, which made a smile tease at the corners of her mouth too. "How did you . . ."

He reached for his beer and winked at her. "You mentioned that place had the best chicken piccata, so I figured it was a safe bet for dinner."

She had zero recollection of that conversation, but it was just another example of how he didn't just hear things she told him. He *listened*. Whether it was big or small, if it came to her, Dave paid attention. The fizzing in her chest continued, like a row of champagne bottles preparing to pop.

Tucking her hair behind one ear, she glanced down at the loose pants and long-sleeved T-shirt she'd changed into after work. "I'm not exactly dressed for date night."

"You look gorgeous, Doc. Now get a plate, a glass of wine and let's eat before your dinner gets cold."

Surprising V, Dave had learned in the past two weeks, was incredibly difficult. Now that she was no longer in vacation mode, her schedule was crammed from what seemed like the moment her feet hit the floor to the second she set her alarm to do it all again the following day. He'd expected her work to take up huge chunks of her time. She was, after all, a doctor.

What he hadn't expected were the additional demands on her time. Like the article she was writing for a medical journal, or the speaking engagements she had throughout the remainder of the year. Add in the fact she worked out at some godforsaken hour at least three to four times a week, took the occasional cooking class and was on rotation to volunteer at the local women's shelter and Dave wondered how she even found time to sleep.

It wasn't that he had no outside interests. He did, although not as many since he'd moved back to Rochester. He'd found a weekly basketball game, but his schedule made it more difficult than he'd imagined. The shift to working nights hadn't been that easy, and his body had taken time to make the adjustment. Leaving work at three or four in the morning sometimes left him wired and ready to play a quick game of three-on-three with guys starting their day as his ended. But lately were more times than not when he was dead on his feet, having come in early to deal with any manner of bullshit resulting from Ryker steering the ship. So, his attendance at those games had suffered, along with several other aspects of his life outside work. He'd missed his nephew's baseball games, ducked out early from poker night with his dad, and canceled more than one fishing trip with his brother-in-law because of some last-minute shit at the bar. Dave could almost relate to V's on-call shifts, except hers were scheduled and his were the result of poor planning by an idiot.

Thankfully, no crisis had arisen tonight, although he'd already planned to ignore it if it did. They'd hired Ryker—not him—to manage Tonic, and it was about time the guy started doing just that. Because he was spending tonight, remotely at least, with his girl. Dave knew V was used to taking care of and doing for others. It was practically in her job description, but he could also see it in her relationship with her friends. Her needs often took a back seat to those she put ahead of herself. He'd decided that at least one night out of six that week, she'd be the one to be taken care of. It was a risk to order food without telling her first, but luck was on his side as she'd had to stay late that afternoon to finish charting.

On the screen of his phone, she was staring back at him, her expression still a little confused—like she couldn't fathom this was really happening—but enthusiasm slowly crept in to push out the last bit of uncertainty. A sunny smile banished it completely.

"This was so sweet of you," she said, and he watched kitchen cabinets appear in the frame behind her as she walked. His view shifted to the side, and he heard her set the food on the counter and saw the corner of a cabinet door as she opened it to pull out a plate. The rustle and clink of silverware followed.

"Don't forget the wine," Dave said, sipping his beer.

"Please," she said with a side-eyed glance. "Rae would unfriend me if that were even a possibility."

Dave laughed. "She's something else."

"That she is," V agreed. Once the table was set, she returned to the kitchen.

"Forget something?" Dave asked.

She smiled and held up a little tripod.

"Did I just discover you're a closet influencer?" he teased. "You've certainly got all the gadgets."

She gave him a mock glare while positioning the phone in the tripod behind her plate. "I told you, I have that to use when I'm cooking and on the phone."

"Earbuds work just as well for that."

"Not when your best friends are bigger fans of FaceTime than most college freshmen," she said with a laugh. "And anyway"—V swept a hand in front of her—"it's certainly working out for you tonight."

"True enough, Doc," he agreed and sliced into his own dinner of roasted chicken and fingerling potatoes. "Tell me about your day."

While she regaled him with HIPAA compliant stories from her day, Dave enjoyed the simple ritual of having dinner with his girl after work. They might've been separated by more miles than he cared to count, but there was still a tender intimacy between them. Neither of them had earth-shattering news, or huge developments or anything even slightly remarkable to discuss, but just having that moment together to unwind and share a meal was special.

"Oh," V said, then held up a hand to finish chewing, "I forgot to mention I talked to Avery today."

"How are things in Atlanta?"

She smiled. "I'm sure they're fine, but he was more focused on hearing all about you."

"About me, huh?" Warmth filled his chest and spread like smoke over an old-fashioned, at the notion she'd mentioned him to her family.

V nodded, popping in another bite. "Mm-hmm. Mainly because my mother . . ." She froze mid-chew for a second, as though she hadn't meant to say the last part.

Dave lifted a brow. "Because your mother what?"

"Well, the thing is . . ." V sipped her wine and looked away from the phone, pulling her lower lip between her teeth. The buoyant feeling in his chest started to deflate with each second she hesitated. The flush he normally loved seeing peeked out from the neckline of her shirt and began the familiar path to her cheeks.

V took another drink of wine. "My mother has certain expectations that I consistently seem to fall short of meeting."

Of all the things she could've said, that was the one he'd expected the least. "How is that possible?"

V smiled ruefully. "Trust me when I say it is. The latest example is my graduating summa cum laude from med school instead of M-R-S."

Her laugh was sad, and Dave's heart constricted. "Are you saying she's *disappointed* you're a doctor?" The thought was unfathomable to him. His parents would've been ecstatic if he'd gotten into medical school and invited his entire town to his graduation once he finished.

"No," V said, a decisive shake of her head. "Not disappointed that I'm a doctor. Just that no marriage license accompanied my medical license. She likes to be able to tell people I'm a pediatrician."

Dave's brow furrowed. Not at her mother's outdated viewpoint, which he didn't need to point out was ass-backward. He was more concerned with the mischaracterization of V's career. V worked with troubled kids. Kids who needed someone to help them work through their problems and figure out how to untangle their knotted synapses, so they fired more easily. Her work let kids live a more normal life. At least, that's how he understood what she'd told him about her work.

"But you're not a pediatrician." When she flicked a glance at him, he hurried to add, "I mean, you are, obviously, but it's more than that. What you do, it's . . ." He fumbled to find the words to express what he wanted to say. "You give people hope for their kids and you give the kids opportunities they wouldn't have without your help. You give them someone in their corner. Someone who goes out of their way to understand what they're going through when no one else does. You're there for them in a way a lot of other people aren't."

Her smile was a brilliant flash of white teeth and flushed cheeks. "Thanks," she said.

"For what?" he asked.

"For understanding the difference."

"It's not hard to see it," he said. "All you have to do is look."

"It's safe to say that is a side of life my mother would prefer *not* to look at," V said. "My work in child psych doesn't make for good cocktail chitchat or dinner conversation. It's not fit for polite conversation, so she adapts the narrative."

"And tells people you're a pediatrician with no further details."

V nodded and sighed. "Yep, allows them to ooh and aah over her accomplished daughter, without getting into any sort of uncomfortable specifics. I'm not even sure if she does it on purpose, or if dodging anything other than polite conversation is just a part of her DNA."

A surge of irritation pulsed from somewhere deep within Dave as he thought about the absurd idea that anything about V's job was something to be embarrassed by.

"You do know that's total bullshit, right?" He had to work to keep an edge out of his voice.

V's smile wobbled a bit, but it was still there when she said, "Yeah, I do." She rubbed briefly at her temple, then dropped her hand to her lap. "But it goes perfectly with her continued attempts to marry me off to someone suitable. Appearance *is* everything, after all." Blue eyes rose to meet his. "Which is why I'm going to tell her I met someone."

Realization dawned hard, fast and unpleasant, dropping like a lead weight in his gut. "Because she has someone else in mind for you."

"Bingo," V said with a little laugh, seeming not to notice the tightness in his voice. "He's a doctor that just transferred to the hospital in Sawgrass."

The meal that had been so enjoyable began to curdle in Dave's stomach. He asked, "And how did that go?"

V's brows dipped. "What do you mean?"

Dave swallowed and did his best to keep his tone even. "When you met the doctor. How did that go?"

"When I met the . . ." Her forehead wrinkled and her eyes narrowed. "What are you talking about?"

Now it was Dave's turn to be confused. "You just said you met this doctor your mo—"

Her face cleared with a laugh as her quick headshake cut him off. "No, no! My mom *wants* to introduce us. I've never met the man."

Relief whooshed in with Dave's next breath. "You haven't?"

She laughed again. "No, you dummy. I haven't met him because I've already met you." A blush stole across her cheeks with lightning speed, and she bit her lip. Looking at him from beneath her lashes, she said shyly, "I mean, I know we haven't said this is . . . well, that we are . . . or that we're not . . . but I thought . . . that is in my mind it's . . ."

Dave jumped in before she could start yet another attempt. "Doc, are you asking me to go steady?"

She covered her face with a groan. "Oh, God, that sounds so fifth grade *and* 1950s all at the same time."

Dave laughed. "Don't you want to hear my answer?"

V peeked at him through her fingers, which only made him laugh harder even as he tried not to. Because laughable or not, she seemed to think there was a possibility he was interested in other women. Women other than the dynamically exquisite one hiding behind her pink manicure on the screen of his phone. And that was something he could not have.

"Doc," he said, his tone serious and all laughter gone. "I'm not interested in seeing anyone but you. And, if I'm honest about it, the idea of you meeting Dr. Dork makes me want to break something. Of his. That cannot be replaced. Like his grandfather's priceless monocle."

V's hand fell from her face, and she laughed. "I don't think his grandfather is the guy from the Monopoly game, but then, I've never met him, so if he is, it sounds like the monocle is safe for now." Her smile turned hopeful and the sight of it made Dave's heart leap into his throat. "So, that means . . ." The words drifted off as she raised her brows at him, the movement completing the rest of the question.

He hated that he couldn't touch her, couldn't wrap his arms around her and cover her mouth with his in a kiss that confirmed she was the only woman he wanted. But he couldn't. Because he was in his apartment, and she was in her townhouse and wishing those miles away did nothing but make his heart ache.

"It means, Doc, that you are without a doubt, one hundred percent mine and I'm yours. Which leaves zero room in this for Dr. Dork, as much as that may disappoint your mother."

Chapter 12

October 14th

V: *Hey, so . . . now that we're going steady, want to be my date to my brother's annual Halloween party? To be clear, he's already insisted that you come, so this is less of an invitation and more of a command performance.*

Dave: *Question. Are costumes involved and does yours have the word "sexy" in it?* *devil emoji*

V: *Well, the norm at his party is that if you're a couple, you have a couple's costume. Which means if I'm a sexy witch, then so are you.* *bat emoji* *witch emoji* *seahorse emoji*

Dave: *I'm guessing the seahorse was extraneous, but then going as two sexy seahorses should give us an edge on the competition.*

V: *I HAVE to get a new phone. How could a seahorse be sexy?*

Dave: *If you're wearing the costume, Doc, it's sexy. Trust me, I'm an expert on these matters.*

V: *Does this mean you're in?*

Dave: *Send me the date so I can check with work, but as long as it's not on actual Halloween, I should be able to swing it. Does this mean we're going as sexy seahorses?*

V: *I've got a little something different in mind. The party's next weekend (10/21). I know it's last minute, so if you can't make it work, I totally get it.*

Dave: *And miss you dressed as a sexy seahorse? No way, Doc. I'll have to fly into Atlanta Saturday morning. But I could stay through Monday night.*

V: *I'll take you for as long as I can get you.*

Dave: *When you put it that way, Doc . . .*

"What exactly are we looking for?" Kez asked. Her question was punctuated by the repeated *snick* of hangers sliding down the long rolling rack of dresses.

V peered around the rack she was perusing. "Anything that looks old Hollywood, like 1930s or early 1940s. With a skirt that twirls."

Kez looked over her shoulder at V, lips working against a smile. "I'm sorry, did you say a skirt that 'twirls'?"

"I did," V said unabashedly. "It needs to twirl if I spin around and sort of float out there."

"Mm-hmm," Kez said, returning to the rack she'd been rummaging through. "Twirls and floats," she muttered with a chuckle.

"Something funny over there?" V called from her own rack of vintage dresses.

"Nothing at all," Kez replied. "I'm just happy you've found a guy who makes you feel like floating."

"You're one to talk," V said with a laugh. "You've been walking on air since we got back from New York. I didn't know your face was capable of holding a smile that long. I thought that was beaten out of you in law school."

Kez sighed. "So did I until now." Selecting a dress, she turned to face V. "What about this one?"

The dress was pale gold satin with thin beaded straps. The beading continued down each side of the low, yet tasteful, V-shaped neckline to cross in the center and curve around the back. The skirt was gossamer layers of material that fluttered when Kez shimmied the hanger. Except for where the straps crossed, the dress was backless to the waist.

Kez held it up to V. "Eat your heart out, Greta Garbo. There's a new starlet in town."

V laughed. "If it's my size, I think it's perfect."

"Already checked, and it is," Kez assured her. "You'll have to wear some hella heels with it though, since we can't get it altered." She fingered one of the delicate straps. "But you have those Valentinos that would be perfect and are essentially stilts, so you should be fine."

"I think you're right," V mused, touching the neckline of the dress. "I don't think I'd need a necklace or anything with this beading."

Kez nodded in agreement, then glanced at her watch with a frown. "We've got to meet Rae for dinner in like twenty minutes. Go make sure that dress is everything you want it to be, and I'll let her know we're almost done."

"Are you sure you didn't want to look for your costume here?"

Kez waggled a finger at V. "Ah, ah, ah," she said. "You know I've never disclosed my costume prior to the party in all the years we've been going. Don't think bringing me to a costume shop the Saturday before the big event is going to get you the inside scoop."

"Does Jackson know how serious you are about this costume contest?"

Kez snorted. "Does he know? You should've seen the way his eyes lit up when I told him about it. If anything, he's worse than I am. He wanted to know why I hadn't said something about it earlier." She grinned. "The tiny detail that we met less than a month ago seemed not to matter. So, yeah, it's safe to say he's as invested as I am. What about Dave? Is he keen on being the Fred to your Ginger? Which I think is freaking adorable, in case I haven't mentioned it."

V nodded. "I think he was just glad I came up with something that didn't require him to wear a mask. Does Jackson feel that way too?"

"Ha! Nice try, Doc." Kez pointed to the dressing rooms. "Now hurry. You know Rae cannot be trusted alone during happy hour."

October 17th

This is Vivian Walters, I'm sorry I missed you, but please leave your name, number, and a detailed message, so I can get back to you as soon as I can. Thank you.

"Vivian, this is your mother. I know you're going to see Avery this weekend at his annual Halloween extravaganza. Please remind him that the deadline for the team registration for this year's Snowflake Scurry 5k is in two weeks and he and Neil are my secret weapons I plan to use to defeat Margaret Ann and her ungodly annoying nieces Tawny and Tammy. Why someone would name their children after a color and a televangelist, I'll never understand, but to each their own I suppose. And *don't* think I can't tell when you're avoiding me, Vivian. It's as plain as the unfortunate nose on that Tawny's face. You've been dodging me, and I *know* it has something to do with this new boy you're seeing. That you told me about *in a text* of all things. With some sort of bizarre miniature swordfish at the end. Texting is wholly insufficient, young lady, so we are having lunch at the Club upon your return, and you are going to tell me whatever it is that you don't want to tell me. End of story. Give Avery and Neil my love when you see them. Kisses, darling."

This is Caroline Walters. I'm so sorry to have missed your call. If you'll leave your name, number, and what you need, I'll be happy to give you a ring back just as soon as I'm able. Thanks so much.

"Hello, Mother. I hate I missed your call earlier, but I was with a patient. I will remind Avery about the 5k, but keep in mind you weren't a big fan of the team name they picked last year. Fair warning, I'm sure he intends to be equally salacious this year. And I'm not avoiding you, I promise. I've just been busy with work and over at the shelter. Lunch next week sounds great. Let me know when. Love you."

October 19th

You've reached the office of Dr. Vivian Walters. If you've reached this recording during business hours, I'm either with a patient or in conference. If this is an emergency, dial 9-1-1. If not, you may either leave a message here, or dial "0" and ask to speak with my nurse, Rhetta Taylor. Thank you.

"Vivian, it's your mother. Again. I'm beginning to consider dialing 9-1-1 if I don't hear from you. *theatrical sigh* But then I know how busy you are. I just wanted to catch you before you left for Atlanta tomorrow, so we could firm up lunch plans. And tell your brother that the name St. Nick's Sacks is not acceptable and that if he doesn't want a pound of coal in his stocking this year, he'll change it immediately before anyone else sees it. I thought Janice Danderbrook was going to have a coronary until I convinced her it was clearly a typo. Slap your brother for me. Kisses, darling."

This is Duvall Walters, and you've reached my cell. I hate I missed your call, but it's only because I'm doing something more important, like skeet shooting. Hah! All jokes aside, leave me your name and number and I'll call you back once I'm off the clays course.

"Hi, Daddy, it's your favorite daughter. You really should consider changing that message before Mother hears it and does it for you. I was hoping she would be with you, since I couldn't get her on her cell or the house phone. Anyway, let her know I'm *not* ducking her calls. Evidenced by my *returning them and leaving voice mails.* Things are just really busy right now, since I'll be out of town through Monday. But if she wants to set up lunch at the Club on Wednesday after I'm back, I'll move things around to make it work. Love you, bye."

This is Vivian Walters, I'm sorry I missed you, but please leave your name, number, and a detailed message, so I can get back to you as soon as I can. Thank you.

"Hey baby girl, it's your dear old dad. Sorry I missed you, I actually *was* shooting clays when you called. And as for your mother, why do you think I have that message other than to get her good and riled up? *Heh Heh* I'll pass your message along, although I think she's spending the day with her tennis ladies over at Margaret Ann's. You know, I think your mother's taken a real shine to that Tammy and Tawny, which is nice seeing as how one of them bears an uncanny resemblance to Margaret Ann's mother and will need all the help she can get. Anyway, I'll let her know Wednesday works for you. Love you, baby. Hug your brother for me when you see him and give Neil my best."

October 20th

V's phone buzzed with an incoming call from her mother. She was about to answer when the flight attendant appeared next to her. "I'm sorry, ma'am, but I'll need you to put your phone in airplane mode for takeoff."

"Right," V said, thankful and regretful all at the same time. She declined her mother's call, obeyed the attendant's instructions, and dropped her phone back into her purse.

"Saved by the proverbial bell," Kez said from the middle seat next to her.

"Is it really being saved when it only delays the inevitable?" V asked with a wry twist to her lips.

"She still hounding you for details about Dave?" Kez asked, and V nodded.

"Yes, she's moved on from being distraught that I 'lost my chance' with the doctor she wanted me to meet to becoming fixated on discovering more about Dave. Thankfully, I've been too busy with work and all sorts of other things to get up to Sawgrass to see her."

"Caroline still living in fear of the big city?" Rae chimed in from her seat across the aisle.

V laughed. Caroline viewed Charlotte as the modern-day version of Sodom and Gomorrah only more dangerous and with worse traffic. No matter that V's townhouse was in one of the safest neighborhoods in the city, Caroline still viewed it with cautious suspicion and rarely made an appearance.

"That remains the status quo, unfortunately."

"So, what have you told her about Dave?" Kez asked.

V flicked a cautious glance at Jackson's slumbering form in the window seat next to Kez. Kez rolled her eyes. "Don't worry about him.

The man has the uncanny ability to sleep through takeoff and not wake up until we land. I didn't believe it either until I experienced it on our flight up to see Nana. It's like the plane is his own personal Ambien subscription."

"Are you sure?" V asked.

"I'll prove it," Kez said. "Listen, Doc," she said in a louder voice. "What are the chances we'll see some celebrities at Avery's party? I think if I got a few drinks in Jackson, I could convince him to have a threesome with Ryan Reynolds."

The three of them glanced over at Jackson. Zero response. Not a muscle twitch or flicker of an eyelash. Just pure, peaceful slumber.

"Is he drooling?" Rae asked and wrinkled her nose.

"Not yet," Kez said. "But stay tuned for that possibility if we're ever on a longer flight." Gold eyes flipped to V. "Now that we've confirmed my boyfriend is in a coma, this isn't the longest flight, so lay it out for us. What does Caroline know about Dave?"

"Just that I met him in Rochester and that's still where he lives. And that he's not a doctor. Nothing much beyond that."

"So, what are you going to tell her?" Rae asked.

V sighed. "I'm thinking as little as possible." She twisted the ends of her hair. "Y'all know the way she's always been so focused on me having this perfect life, with the right man from the right family to provide her with the also perfect grandchildren to show off at the Club and occasional Sunday at Sawgrass Presbyterian. It comes from a good, if uniquely old school, place, but it's still a lot of pressure."

"Pressure you didn't use to mind." Kez pointed out. "In fact, there were times I thought you honestly appreciated her quest to find you the perfect guy, because it was one less thing for you to worry about."

"You're not wrong," V said, giving voice to something she'd been thinking about since September. "It was easier to show up on command. But more than that, it gave us something in common at a time when there wasn't much else, you know? Her pursuit of the perfect guy for me left me free to concentrate on my own goals with minimal conflict. All I had to do was accept her version of perfect and we were all good. But now . . ."

"Now there's Dave," Kez said.

"Now there's Dave," V agreed.

"I'm just playing devil's advocate here, okay?" Rae said. "Isn't Dave close to meeting Caroline's criteria of perfect?" Seeing V about to question, Rae held up a hand. "Just go with me on this, okay? I mean we can all agree he's a good-looking man, seemingly genetically blessed with features that are more symmetrical than the average face. So, the cute future grandkids shouldn't be a problem. We don't know much about his family yet, other than the bare minimum that he assumedly has one and didn't burst fully formed from a cocoon like some hot alien butterfly."

"Your mind is truly a strange place," Kez said. "But I'm with you so far, so what does that say about me?"

Rae ignored her. "And maybe most importantly, he's got that fancy degree in some kind of math that would allow him to calculate the exact circumference of the earth in his head. She'd swoon over his alma mater."

"She would," V agreed. "*If* he were using it in a way other than measuring how much vodka to add to a Moscow mule."

Kez's head angled back, and her brows lifted. "Is that a Caroline comment, or is that a Vivian comment? Because I have to be honest, that sounded a wee bit like it was your concern too."

V hadn't meant to say that. Hadn't intended to vocalize the niggling worry that had tickled her brain since that first night in Dave's apartment.

But she had, and now it was too late to backtrack. She shot another cautious glance at Jackson before continuing.

"Does it bother me that my new boyfriend is allowing his applied mathematics degree to gather dust on his apartment wall while he slings drinks to coeds every weekend? Why on earth would that matter to me?"

Kez laughed. "Not all of us were born holding a stethoscope, Doc."

V shook her head. "You don't have a leg to stand on and you know it. You've been a lawyer since we were eight and Tanner Simpson tried to argue girls couldn't play kickball. You Title Nine'd him before you even knew there *was* a Title IX."

"So, Dave is taking some time to figure out his next move," Rae said. "What's wrong with that?"

V peered again at Jackson and found him still a resident of dreamland. "Nothing," she said. With a guilty sigh, she let her head drop back against the headrest. "Don't get me wrong. I admire him for taking himself out of a shitty situation. For valuing his mental health over a paycheck. That I understand. But I can't wrap my head around why he's wasting his talent—and his brainpower—working at Tonic. That Ryker guy seems like a complete dick, from what little Dave has told me. Not just a dick, but someone who has no business being the boss at all. And yet, Dave's making no move to change. That's the part I don't get. If you have options, real options, at something better . . . why stay?"

She could tell things at Tonic weren't great, even though Dave usually danced around the topic of work or steered the conversation in other directions when she mentioned it. His avoidance didn't keep her from hearing the strain in his voice, or seeing how tired he was when they FaceTimed. He put up a good front, but V could still see it in the circles under his eyes and the way his mouth tightened when she asked how work had been. He was unhappy there, and it didn't take a genius to pick up on it.

She tugged at the ends of her hair. "But, then again, we've been together just shy of a month, so it's not my place to question his life choices. Even though I'm dying to, because the man has potential to be so much more than he's letting himself right now. A fact my mother will certainly key in on with lightning speed. And I don't want to deal with all of her questions and doubts when I'm trying to keep a handle on my own and not let them overshadow how *happy* I am with Dave."

"So don't let her," Kez said.

"I'm sorry," V looked at her wide-eyed. "I was under the impression you'd met my mother."

Kez laughed. "Oh, I've met Caroline and been subjected to her side-eye. It's not like I'm her favorite person on the planet." She squeezed V's hand. "But you didn't let that stop you from being my best friend. Because you saw something in me that you liked, despite me being a tad uncouth for Caroline's tastes."

"What are you saying?" V asked.

"I'm saying, Doc, that I'm living, breathing proof of your commitment to people you care about even in the face of your mother's disapproval. You decided I was worth it. Now you just have to decide whether Dave is too."

Chapter 13

October 20th

"What do you mean there's only four kegs?" Dave asked the delivery driver. He pointed to the purchase order in his hand. "We ordered eight kegs, not four. It says so right here."

The delivery driver pulled an invoice off his clipboard. "I don't know what to tell you, man. My paperwork has four kegs listed and there's four on the truck. I can bring more if you need them, but not until tomorrow. I have other deliveries today."

"Can I see that?" Dave asked, feeling a tension headache brewing behind his right eye. The driver handed him the slip and Dave scanned it quickly, confirming there were only four kegs listed. Nodding at the guy's tablet, he asked, "Any way you can look up the original purchase order?"

"Sure," he replied. "But it's going to say the same thing."

"Humor me," Dave said and rubbed his right temple.

The guy tapped away on the tablet, swiped up a few times, and turned it to face Dave. "Here you go."

Dave took it and frowned. On the screen of the tablet was a scan of the purchase order where he could clearly see the "8" he'd typed into it crossed out and replaced with a scrawled "4" and the initials "RJK" next to it in bold black ink. *Fucking Ryker.*

With a sigh, he handed the tablet back to the driver. "Thanks, man. Looks like there was a mix-up on our end. Sorry for the hassle."

"No worries," he replied. "I'll get the four kegs unloaded. If you want the other four, just shoot over a new PO to the warehouse and they'll get you squared away."

Dave nodded. "Yeah, thanks."

He needed to talk to Ryker. Now. Pushing through the back door of the bar, he called to one of the barbacks working on garnish prep. "Hey, Nicco, can you handle getting the kegs in the cooler? I need to talk to the boss." He almost choked on the word, but did manage to say it.

"Sure thing," the kid replied and hustled out the back door.

Dave rapped on the frame of Ryker's office door before walking in. The man himself was seated at his desk, paging through some sort of catalog. Dave dropped the purchase order he'd located on the desk. Ryker looked at it, then Dave. "What's this?"

"You tell me," Dave said, struggling to keep his temper in check. "Because I thought it was the purchase order we submitted to the distributor for kegs of IPA. You know, as a part of the special 'Craft Draft Night' we have going on tonight? Only instead of eight kegs, we got four because someone changed the PO."

"What's your point?" Ryker asked, turning back to his catalog that Dave could now see was for high-priced boats.

"My *point*," Dave said, his voice tight, "is that we've been advertising this Craft Draft Night for the past two weeks and people are going to show up expecting to drink draft craft beers. Only now, because *someone* changed the PO, we don't have enough kegs to last the night. Hell, we might not even last the first few hours."

Ryker's eyes slid over to Dave's, flat and hard. "Whaddya mean? Eight kegs are way too many for one night. Not to mention how much those fucking things cost. Four is plenty."

Dave's temple throbbed and his eye felt like it could pop from the socket from the pressure building behind it. He shoved down the urge to leap over the desk and throttle Ryker. "Craft beer kegs are smaller than standard kegs. Smaller by more than half. Which means, we had to order twice as many as we normally do to make sure we had enough." *Which you'd know if you paid attention to one single fucking thing around this place.*

Ryker's bushy brows dipped as he considered Dave's point. He pulled at his fleshy lower lip, stretching it into a grotesquely bulbous pout. Releasing it, he looked at Dave. "Fix it." His eyes returned to the catalog.

"Fix it?" Dave repeated the demand as a question.

Those flat eyes looked back at him over the glossy picture of a boat cutting through the ocean. "Yeah, that's what I pay you for, so go fix it."

Ryker's dad, not Ryker, paid Dave but pointing that out wouldn't solve the current problem this idiot had created. Dave released a careful breath. "The distributor can't get us another delivery until tomorrow morning."

Ryker didn't even lift his eyes when he said, "Then I guess you better figure something out and quick, since we'll be open for business in a few hours." He turned a page. "Get the door on your way out."

Dave seethed at the dismissal and had to restrain himself from slamming the door behind him. Pissing Ryker off wouldn't do any good. When he'd been installed as—whatever the fuck his title was since he didn't do anything but create more work for other people—midway through the year, Dave had seen it as the dump job it was. As in, Ryker had been dumped here since he'd fucked up everywhere else and his dad figured he'd do as little damage as possible here. Due in large part to Dave's presence. Which didn't make stomaching the callous ineptitude any easier. But bitching about it wasn't going to solve anything, so he needed to get down to it.

After six phone calls and a mad dash to a local brewery, Dave had enough craft beer to get through the night. He also had a pounding headache and the overwhelming desire to punch Ryker in the face.

Fuckups like the one today were becoming commonplace and left the rest of them scrambling to come up with solutions. Dave would've hung Ryker out to dry, but the only ones that would've suffered were the rest of the staff who'd have to deal with pissed off customers denied their promised craft beer on draft. Rather than force them to deal with the consequences of Ryker's idiocy, Dave called in favors and righted the ship once again.

The thing that got him through the mad scramble was knowing that in less than twenty-four hours, he'd see V. Not just see her, but hold her, touch her, kiss her, and *be* with her. Inhale that floral scent he'd forever associate with her. Hear her laugh and hold her hand.

His phone buzzed in his back pocket while he set the last keg under the tap and cleared the final set of lines. Dave used the hem of his shirt to swipe at the sweat on his forehead, which earned him a wolf whistle from Shay. He shot her a quick middle finger and pulled out his phone.

V: *Hey handsome, thinking of you.*

The accompanying picture put his heart into overdrive and had him seriously considering walking the fuck out right then. V stood in front of a stained glass window, dressed in a sleek red dress with her normal skyscraper heels. Her blond hair fanned out over her shoulders in a waterfall of curls, and her smile hit him as hard as ever.

Dave: *You look amazing, as usual. I can't wait to see you tomorrow. Don't let Rae and Kez get you in any trouble tonight.* *wink emoji*

V: *I don't know, babe, you seemed like a pretty big fan of their kind of trouble.* *wink emoji* *baby bottle emoji* *baby bottle emoji* *baby bottle emoji*

V: *IGNORE THAT! No babies or baby bottles!!!!*

He laughed and shook his head. The woman needed a new phone.

Dave: *It takes more than being bombarded by bottles to scare me off, Doc.*

V: *Good to know.* *kiss emoji* *raccoon face emoji*

Dave: *Random wildlife won't work either. See you tomorrow.*

October 21st

V: *I'm at the airport, so just text when you land.*

Dave: *Did you park in hourly like I told you to?*

V: *No, I'm in the cell phone lot. I take it you've landed?* *spoon emoji*

V: *Ignore the spoon!* *another spoon emoji*

Dave: *Doc, I told you that cell phone lot is sketchy as hell, and you*

should park in hourly. Tell me Jackson and Kez are with you.
V: *No, those two weirdos are already at work on their costumes, and you know how secretive they've been about it. But it's fine. I just had a very interesting conversation with a man who appeared at my window.*
Dave: *WHAT???????*
V: *I'm kidding, I'm kidding.*
Dave: *You'll pay for that one, Doc.*
V: *I can't text and drive, see you soon! *kiss emoji**
V: *That emoji was on purpose, just FYI.*

V had gone in search of the ladies' room as soon as they arrived, which left Dave alone in the vestibule of the trendy Atlanta house her brother had rented for the Halloween party. He was pocketing the claim check for their coats when a voice behind him said, "You *must* be the boyfriend."

After thanking the coat check hostess, he turned around. A tall, slender man with lime green hair that somehow managed to look stylish stood grinning at him and holding a drink. The grin was emphasized by the Joker makeup he wore and yet, he was still good-looking. There was no way the suit he wore was a costume, despite its deep shade of burgundy. It was too well-tailored. The leopard pocket square was a departure from the Joker's typical look, but an interesting touch. There was something familiar about the guy, but Dave couldn't place him.

"Excuse me?"

One side of the man's lips hiked up impossibly higher. "I said, 'You must be the boyfriend.' As in, the boyfriend V's kept hidden away up in New York." He gave Dave an unabashed once-over. "I do get it though," he said. "If I had you, I wouldn't want to share, either."

Dave's cheeks heated, and he shifted nervously, which only made the man laugh. "Calm down," he said. "I'm not going to conk you on the head and drag you back to my fabulously decorated gay lair." He angled his head with a thoughtful frown, as if considering his statement. "Although, I *do* see the appeal in having one." Holding out his free hand, he said, "I'm Avery Walters, V's older, but equally attractive, brother."

Dave took Avery's hand, relief washing over him at Avery's welcome. "Right! Sorry, I should've known it was you from the pictures V showed me."

Avery gestured to his face. "Well, I'm a bit incognito tonight." He regarded Dave's tux. "I have to say, I applaud the two of you treating this as a prom, though. Very cool choice."

"Oh, no," Dave said. "That's not wha—"

"Don't let Avery fool you," V said, reappearing next to him. "He knows good and well we're Fred and Ginger. He's just being an ass."

She gave Avery a playful shove. "Stop torturing my date."

"What?" Avery said, the picture of innocence. "I'm merely doing my big brother duty by engaging in a little light hazing. Nothing untoward."

"Right," V said, smiling at her brother. "Where's your better half?"

"Last I saw the Riddler, he was getting skincare tips from Wednesday Addams."

"Do I hear my name being taken in vain?" Another tall, good-looking guy joined their group. A guy who, judging by his green spandex bodysuit, was *very* secure in himself. He wore a silver mask behind which brown eyes looked askance at Avery.

"Never," Avery said, giving him a reassuring pat on the shoulder. "I was just filling the prom king and queen here in o—"

"Fred and Ginger!" V emphasized her displeasure with a sharp poke to Avery's ribs.

"Ouch! Your freakishly tiny fingers still hurt when you ram them into my flesh, baby sister."

"Anyway," the newcomer interrupted the squabbling siblings and held out a hand to Dave. "I'm Neil, Avery's husband."

"Dave Richardson."

"Nice to meet you," Neil said, giving Dave's hand a firm shake. "You'll have to forgive these two. When they go without seeing each other for a while, they have to get all the sibling rivalry out immediately or their heads could explode."

Dave laughed. "Noted."

Neil gestured toward what Dave assumed was the living room of the house, a corner of which was visible from where they all stood. "No reason to stand out here all night, when there's a perfectly good party going on inside. Let's get you two some drinks, shall we?"

"Lead the way," Dave said.

He and V followed Neil and Avery through a large living room. The furniture had been moved out in favor of small cocktail tables and a bar along one wall. Every surface they passed was draped with fake spider-webs and topped with jack-o'-lanterns grinning wickedly. Witches, goblins, and ghouls were positioned in various corners and would cackle or moan in response to movement. Cauldrons of varying sizes foamed with fog.

"I can see why you rent a place for this," Dave said.

"Could you imagine if it were at our house?" Avery said with a stylish shudder of shoulders. "The cleanup of that would give me worse nightmares than any scary movie. This is much better. All we have to do is show up and have a good time."

"And schedule a cleaning service for the morning after," Neil added.

"Sounds like you guys are practically professionals," Dave said.

Avery looped an arm around Neil's waist. "What do you think, feel like walking away from managing all those portfolios and starting a party planning business?"

Neil shook his head with a laugh. "Like you could possibly leave academia and let your baby sister be the only doctor in the family."

"Oh, I'd still be a doctor," Avery insisted. "The PhD isn't going anywhere."

"You'd make our customers call you 'Doctor?'" Neil asked.

"Of course I would," Avery said. "I'd be the party doctor, there to diagnose all their planning woes." He moved to tap a finger to his chin, but stopped when he remembered his Joker makeup. "That does have a nice ring to it."

"God help me," Neil said.

"I don't even think he can help you with this one." V jerked a thumb in the direction of her brother, who in turn stuck his tongue out at her. "Just remember, you're the one who chose to marry him, despite all my best efforts to get you to save yourself the hassle."

"Why did we invite you again?" Avery asked.

"Same reason you invited us. To show all your fuddy duddy friends how to have a good time."

Dave turned and barked out a laugh. Kez, or at least someone he *thought* was Kez, stood behind them dressed as Axl from Guns 'N Roses, right down to the leather pants and motorcycle boots. A fake cigarette dangled from her lips and aviator sunglasses hid her eyes, but that hair— even stick straight and parted down the middle—was a dead giveaway.

Jackson stood next to her as Slash, recognizable only by his beard. The black curly wig and top hat made him even taller than normal. A guitar hung from a shoulder strap, and he gave them his best rock 'n roll scowl behind his own pair of aviators.

"Oh. My. God," Avery said. "*This* is to die for." He glanced around them. "But weren't you coming wi—"

"Looking for me darling?" A black gloved finger tipped with a . . . claw(?) tapped Avery on the shoulder. Green eyes glittered from behind a mask and red lips parted in a wicked smile.

"Meow," Rae said and wiggled her leather encased hips, which made the bullwhip resting there bounce suggestively. Dave had no idea how she'd managed to wiggle her way into that Catwoman costume but had to give credit where credit was due. It was impressive.

"I'm sorry," V said, giving her friend a long once-over. "But how in the world do you plan to pee tonight?"

"We make certain sacrifices for fashion," Rae said. "Love the prom dress, by the way."

"Right?" Avery chimed in as V glared at both of them.

"Who needs a drink?" Dave asked before the fur could fly.

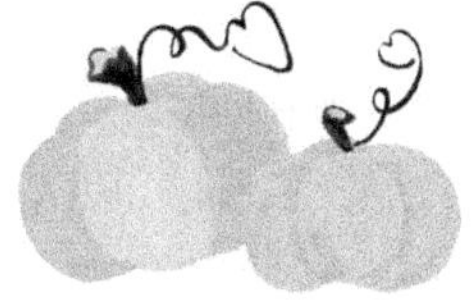

Chapter 14

V watched Dave inhale his third crab puff and look hungrily around for anything more substantial. He snared a canapé from a passing tray and popped it into his mouth. After swallowing the delicate morsel, he asked, "Is there going to be actual *food*, or are we going to have to hit a drive-thru later?"

V laughed. "Unfortunately, I think you just sampled the largest item on the menu. Avery's parties tend to rely heavily on bite-size tidbits and the perfect cocktail." Dave's crestfallen face made V laugh again. "Don't worry, though," she said, taking his hand and leading him toward the side of the room. "I think I've figured out where the caterers are keeping some extras."

"Tell me you're serious," Dave said, his eyes widening with interest. She loved the way they lightened when he was excited. Like a whirl of caramel blending into milk chocolate.

"Absolutely," she replied, tugging him along to the far wall. She ducked between two bubbling cauldrons and pressed her hand against a square in the paneled wall. A soft click sounded, and a hidden door slid open just an inch. At her touch, it swung open on silent hinges. Upon their entrance, undercabinet lights came on to provide guidance in the darkness.

"Jackpot," V murmured, grateful she'd guessed correctly.

When Dave shut the door behind him, the sounds of the party outside muted to dull murmurs. "What is this?" he asked, taking in the small space.

"A butler's pantry," V responded, crossing to the glass front fridge against one wall. Pulling it open, she surveyed its contents, eyes alighting on a charcuterie tray brimming with meats, cheeses, nuts, and spreads. Next to it was a fruit tray, equally well laden with choices.

"I knew it," she whispered, taking the large trays out of the fridge and setting them on the expansive countertop next to it. From the adjoining wine fridge, she took a bottle of champagne. "Can you grab a couple glasses from the rack over there?"

Following her direction, Dave pulled down two champagne flutes from the far wall and set them next to the bottle. "Want to tell me what the hell a butler's pantry is?"

Clearing her throat, V's voice took on an extra-cultured tone, each syllable pronounced with crisp perfection. "A butler's pantry, also known as a scullery, is an intermediary station between the kitchen and the dining or entertaining areas of a home. A true must for those who enjoy lavish parties and need additional food storage or staging space."

"How do you know things like that?" Dave asked on a laugh.

V shrugged. "My parents have one. Something my mother insisted upon in the last remodel. So, I've learned to spot them in other houses."

"I see."

Dave opened the champagne with practiced ease, the cork releasing with a pop made louder in the small, darkened space. At the sound, their eyes met in the furtive glance of teenagers pilfering their parents' liquor cabinet. It made V giggle, which in turn made a broad grin spread over Dave's face.

Accepting the glass of champagne, she said, "This all feels a little forbidden, doesn't it?"

Dark eyes flickered dangerously as he finished the beer he'd brought with him. The clink of the bottle hitting the granite counter sent a shiver down V's spine. His hand spanned her hip and gentle pressure there drew her toward him.

"Why, Doctor Walters," Dave said, his voice low and lush, "are you regretting slipping away from the party with me? Scared of what could happen behind closed doors?" His hands slid up to her waist, the heat of his palms seeping through the bodice of her dress.

Her tongue wet her suddenly dry lips, and he tracked the movement, brown eyes going molten. "Should I be, Mr. Richardson?" she asked, her voice a feathery whisper. "Do you have plans to debauch me in the scullery?"

Dave leaned down and brushed his lips along her jawline. "When you put it like that," he said, nipping at her earlobe, "how could I do anything else?" He pressed a kiss just behind her ear, making all the little hairs at the nape of her neck stand on end. When he sucked gently on the sensitive skin, her nipples hardened into eager points, as if begging to be next.

"Well," she whispered, gripping his biceps, "I *am* the one who led you in here."

His laugh stirred the air at her ear in a warm huff. "Are you saying, Doctor Walters," his voice was a low rumble as he kissed his way down her neck and under her jaw, "the lady herself has indecent intentions?"

His mouth teasing down her throat, kissing and caressing, made it hard to focus, but V gave it her best shot. "I think," she said, letting her fingers steal into his hair, made dark gold by the shadowy space, "that if you were to try, I would be helpless to resist you."

She felt him smile at the base of her throat. "Helpless to resist?" He nipped at her collarbone and her knees wobbled. "Or eager for me to continue?"

God, this man! "Desperate for you not to stop," she said, trying to draw him up for a kiss. She wanted his mouth on hers, the press of it, the sheer heat of it. Her body burned for more of him.

But Dave held back, kissing her chin, then lifting his head. His eyes were so dark she could barely see his pupils. "Doc," he said, his fingers curling into her sides, "if I kiss you the way you want right now—the way you need—then everyone out there will know exactly what we were doing in here."

In that moment, absolutely zero part of V cared about anything outside their private space. She cupped his face in her hands. "What if I said I didn't care?"

He turned his head to kiss her palm, then said, "I'd know that wasn't true, because I pay attention to what matters to you, Doc. You blushed when I kissed you at the airport earlier. Privacy is important to you. Which means what happens behind this door needs to stay behind this door."

His words burrowed their way inside her chest, latching on to a portion of her heart. At this rate, there wouldn't be a spot on it that didn't bear his stamp. He noticed. He noticed so much about her. Things she wasn't conscious of doing or saying. He noticed all of it. More than that, he valued the things he noticed. Filed them away and kept them to use to make her feel treasured and respected.

But all that realization did was make her want to kiss him that much more.

V pouted. "Then what if we just stay in here until Christmas? There's enough food in here for us to make it to New Year's, if we conserved."

Dave's smile was wicked. "Pretty sure that cleaning crew your brother mentioned might notice our presence. But I don't think I'll need until Christmas to give you what you want, V."

"But you just said . . ."

Dave's lips moved up her wrist, and he kissed his way along her forearm to the crook of her elbow, the drag of his tongue making her shiver. "What I *said* was that I couldn't kiss you. I never said there would be no debauching."

"What do you—Oh!" V let out a surprised gasp when Dave lifted her up and sat her on the opposite counter. He stood between her spread knees, his hands resting against her thighs. The heat of them was a burning caress through the gauzy skirt.

"I can't remember if I've told you how beautiful you look tonight," Dave said, his fingers skimming over her thighs to the curve of her hips. "This dress," he said, using his grip on her hips to pull her to the edge of the counter. "This fucking *dress*, baby." He licked his lips and shook his head, hands moving up her back to the thin straps at her shoulders. His fingers danced down her back to land between her shoulder blades. Heat pooled in her belly as she felt his fingers find the tiny clasp between the straps and easily undo it.

"You look like a goddess in this," he said. Reflexively, V put her hands to the top of the bodice to hold it in place as he pulled the straps down her shoulders.

Dave leaned in and kissed her shoulder, his fingers still looped through the straps of her dress. He played with the beading, then tugged gently. "Don't hide from me, baby. Let me see you." His lips moved over her shoulder and along her collarbone, his slight stubble buffing over her skin in a luxurious scrape. The feel of his mouth, kissing and suckling its way to her neck, then upward made her hands drop from her dress. The fabric fell away from her breasts in a silky slide.

His breath was hot at her ear when he purred, "Good girl." The two words shot sparks through her and made her knees widen. Her heels hooked around the backs of his thighs, pulling him closer. She felt as much as she heard him chuckle at her response.

Dave's hands came to her sides, then moved just under the curves of her bare breasts. Lifting his head from her neck, he angled backward to let her arms slide completely free of the dress. His eyes roamed over her, and she arched her spine, aching for his touch to slide higher. He teased the pads of his thumb over one nipple, then the other in alternating tortuous swipes that drove her higher without providing any real relief. She whimpered, the sound equal parts pleasure and discontent, making Dave chuckle.

His eyes went hooded as he watched himself touch her. V shifted, putting her hands behind her and pushing her breasts further into his touch. The movement brought his eyes to hers, their dark depths glowing with lust. "You're so beautiful," he said, his hands coming up to fully cup her breasts in a possessive clasp, drawing the tips of his fingers down to her nipples. The first sharp pinch was stingingly perfect, making V's breathing go ragged and her legs clutch more tightly around his.

"Yes," she hissed, eager for him to continue.

Her eyes fell shut as he toyed with her nipples, teasing them with tugs, tweaks, and rhythmic pinches. Each time his fingers touched her, fiery sensation spiraled through her, transmitting directly to her core. The brush of his fingertips on the very tip of her breast made her ache with need and clench his wrists, dragging him closer.

"Please," she whispered, nails digging into his skin.

"Please, what, Doc?" Dave asked, dipping his head to place a kiss on the center of her chest. "What do you need?"

V squirmed. "You know what I need. You always do."

His smile was hot on her skin, and he turned his head, licking the undercurve of one breast, sucking lightly at the fullness there. "I do, but you know I love it when you tell me. Nothing sexier than when you ask me for what you want. What you need. What you *crave*." He shifted slightly, his tongue darting out in a wicked flutter, barely touching her nipple, but it was so sensitive by then that V moaned.

"That." She gasped, putting a hand to his cheek, and nudging him fully to one breast. "I need more of that."

"More of what, V?" Dave teased her with another flit of his tongue, and she thought her eyes might cross. So close to what she needed, but not quite enough. And he knew it, dammit. He knew it, but wanted her to say it.

Lust fought against chastity, although it was apparent that battle was over since she was currently topless on a counter in the pantry. Dave's breath coasted over her nipple and that sealed it. "I want your mouth on me," she said. "I need your lips, your tongue, and your teeth. I need you to—oh!"

V's head fell back when Dave's lips finally latched around her nipple, pulling the tender bud between his teeth in a nipping suck. The wet, torrid sound of it thrilled her and her hands came to the back of his head, holding him there as his tongue undulated and stroked her, while his fingers mimicked his movements on her other breast.

She knew in the recesses of her mind she needed to be quiet. That she couldn't let anyone hear them. But she couldn't stop the tumble of sighs and moans from escaping as Dave continued lavishing her with exquisite torment. Each swipe of his tongue or tingling graze of his teeth was at once too much and not enough. The tantalizing roll of his fingers blended with the heat of his mouth and overwhelmed all other thoughts she could have. Her one singular focus was on how good it felt when he touched her. But still . . . she needed more.

As though reading her thoughts, Dave lifted his head. "I need to know how far this is going to go, Doc." He nuzzled one breast. "Believe me, I could spend all night on your gorgeous tits if that's what you want." His fingers brushed her ankle, then dipped under her skirt and slid along her calf and over her knee to spread out over her thigh and come to a stop. A trail of heat blazed up her leg in the wake of his hand. "But I think you want more." His hand squeezed the slope of her thigh, thumb stroking the sensitive skin of her inner thigh and eliciting a sharp gasp from V. "Do you?" he asked, giving her breast a teasing bite.

Emboldened by the way he looked at her, V raked her fingers through his hair and asked, "Do you?"

His laugh dusted over her breast, and she shuddered. "Baby, I think by now you know I want to bury my face between your legs and not take a breath until you're limp, boneless and begging me to stop."

V struggled to breathe as her clit pulsed in response to his words. *Challenge accepted!* she seemed to be saying in some sort of bodily morse code.

Dave's other hand came to her skirt, bunching it up above her knees, then sliding beneath it to rest on her other thigh. His thumbs made tandem strokes just below the edge of her panties, and all she wanted to do was inch downward until he could feel how much she wanted him.

As if reading her mind, he asked, "Are you wet for me, Doc?" His whisper was a deep rasp that she was sure she could feel on her skin.

Knowing what her words would do to him, how they'd light that dangerous flame in his dark eyes, she widened her legs. "Why don't you check for yourself?"

"With pleasure," he growled and slid one finger into her panties. He groaned. "Goddamn, baby, you're fucking soaked." When he teased along her seam, V hummed with pleasure. "Is this all for me, Doc?"

She nodded as he continued to tease her, skimming around where she wanted his touch.

"Say it, Doc." The command was more of a growl than a sentence. "Tell me," he ordered harshly.

"It's for you. It's all for you."

Her answer let the beast off its chain. Dave's hands went to the band of her G-string and tore it down her legs, barely giving her enough time to lift her hips so it would come off in one piece. Using the breadth of his shoulders he pushed her legs farther apart at the same time he drew her to the very edge of the counter where the granite bit into the flesh of her backside. Falling to his knees, he draped first one, then the other of her legs over his shoulders and shoved the skirt of her dress up to bare her to him completely.

Cupping her ass in his hands, he placed his thumbs on either side of her most intimate space and drew her open. Using the flat of his tongue, he licked all the way up in one smooth stroke. V collapsed onto her elbows, her head dropping back against the wall on a soft moan.

His breath tickled her oversensitive flesh as he whispered, "Mine," then slipped two fingers inside her as his lips locked onto her clit. V's hips bucked against the counter and Dave used his other hand to still her thrashing movements. His fingers curled and stroked within while his tongue flicked in hard, short thrusts against the tiny bundle of nerves.

"Oh, God." V moaned, trying to keep quiet, but powerless against the jagged sensations rioting through her and powered solely by the talented fingers and tongue working her into a complete and utter frenzy. Every lick, every curl of his fingers, each delicious pull of his mouth drove her higher and higher. Her legs stiffened around his shoulders as his free hand moved to her ass, pulling her tighter to him and pushing his fingers deeper inside her. She clenched around them, and he groaned against her, the vibration of the noise an electric shock against her tightening arousal.

"I know you're close, baby," Dave said, punctuating his claim with a fluttering lick that made V gasp and nod. "I can feel it," he said, thrusting his fingers in and out in quick succession. "Fuck, V, you're so close. Give it to me, please, baby."

He lowered his mouth back to her and sucked her clit back between his lips, flickering the trapped bud with his tongue, all while continuing the relentlessly glorious pumping of his fingers. V's whole body tightened down and her eyes squeezed shut, waves of color and pleasure washing over her as she neared the peak of orgasm. The whirls of Dave's tongue spun her closer and closer. She flexed her hips, riding the swirls and strokes faster and faster. Her nails scratched against the countertop as she fought for purchase, trying to stay anchored into the feeling.

Dave's other hand released her ass to move to her breast, fingers clamping onto her nipple in a tight pinch that was the final push. "Yes!" she cried, her fingers coming to fist tightly in his hair as she rocked against his mouth, straining and working the last edges of her release until she crumpled backward with legs shaking and chest heaving. She couldn't get enough air in her lungs, but lacked the strength to care.

Dave dropped kisses along her thigh, then gently slipped her legs from his shoulders and stood grinning down at her.

"What are you smiling at?"

Reaching up, he grabbed a napkin from the shelf above them and wiped his face. The smile remained when he lowered the linen. "At how fucking gorgeous you look right now," he said, tracing a line between her breasts.

Laughing, V sat up. "Somehow, I doubt that. After what we just did, I'm sure I look a mess."

Dave shook his head. "You've never been more beautiful," he said, letting his thumb brush over her nipple. As it peaked at his touch, he adjusted himself with a pained grunt.

V reached for his belt buckle, the flat of her palm brushing the outline of his cock. Dave sucked in a harsh breath as she stroked him, but he grabbed her hand before she could get to his zipper. "What's wrong?" she asked, confused by his intervention.

"We've been gone too long as it is, Doc," he said, lifting her hand to his lips and kissing her knuckles. "We need to get your dress back together and get out there before someone misses us."

"But you're . . ." Her words drifted off as she looked at his crotch.

"Trust me," he said, smoothing her skirt back down and lifting her bodice back into place. "I know exactly what's going on with me and, if you keep looking at me like that, I won't be able to leave this room for another fifteen minutes."

V smirked and reached for him again. "Fine with me," she said.

"V," he cautioned, catching her hand and trapping it between them. His eyes flashed a warning. Leaning in close, he said, "Do you really think there's a single part of me that doesn't want to bend you over this counter and fuck you senseless right now? To feel that hot little vise of yours clench around me while I make you come again?" V forced a swallow past her tight throat and unclenched her hands to wipe her now damp palms on her skirt.

Dave closed his eyes and blew out a pained sigh. "But, like I said, we can't make that happen right now." His eyes opened, and he dipped a hand inside her loosened bodice, flicking one nipple with his finger and making her thighs clench. "But trust me, it *will* happen."

Chapter 15

Dave let V slip back into the living room in front of him, then pulled the hidden door closed. Just as it snicked into place, he heard a familiar throaty laugh from his right. His shoulders hitched guiltily before he could stop them.

"Find what you needed in there?" Rae asked when he turned to look at her.

He didn't have a chance to answer before Kez chimed in with a sly grin at V. "Looks like *someone* got what they needed."

V blushed and Dave wanted to tuck her under his arm, but didn't have the chance before Avery added, "She's not wrong, baby sister. You're positively languid." He angled his glass toward the pantry access. "Either the caterer stocked some interesting additional herbs in there, or you've been sullied in the scullery."

"This is like a sexy game of Clue," Kez said.

"Dr. Walters and her dashing beau in the pantry," Rae added with a chuckle.

"We know the room, we know the culprits and"—Avery gave Dave a once-over—"the *weapon* in question." His eyebrows waggled impressively when he continued, "That just leaves the . . ."

"That's enough," Dave said, cutting off any further lines of inquisition. He put a protective arm around V's shoulders and she gave him a grateful look. "Doc and I were just grabbing this." He held up an unopened bottle of champagne, its yellow label catching the light. Rae's eyes lit up and Dave shook his head, holding it out of her reach. "Misbehave and you can't have any."

Rae looked down at her costume, then back at Dave. "How am I supposed to do anything but misbehave in this getup?"

"Who's misbehaving?" Jackson joined their group and dropped an arm around Kez. She pushed onto her toes to give him a kiss. Seeing Slash and Axl in a loving embrace was more than a little strange for Dave.

Avery wasn't as bothered. He cocked his head, brow furrowing. "You two are giving me real Slash and Axl fanfic vibes. I didn't know that was something I was into, but you're convincing me it could be."

Not wanting to consider that any longer than he had to, Dave said, "Why don't we scare up some glasses and pop this?"

"Sounds like a plan to me," Rae said and headed to the bar. Kez and Avery followed, letting V and Dave bring up the rear.

"Nice touch with the champagne," V said, hooking her arm through his. "I didn't even see you grab it."

He grinned down at her, enjoying having her hand on his arm. "I thought we might need some cover on why we were coming out of a closet."

V's cheeks went pink, and she pulled her bottom lip between her teeth. "No doubt," she said, casting a knowing glance up at him. "But no matter what they said, I don't think any of them suspect . . ." That lovely pink dusted her cheeks, and she looked away with a giggle.

The sound of it coupled with her demure reaction made him want to toss her over his shoulder and head back into the pantry. Dave leaned down so his lips were close to her ear. "Suspect what, Doc? That you had your legs locked around my shoulders while you rode my face?"

He felt her shiver against him and luxuriated in her quick intake of breath. "Yes," she said with a shuddering exhale. "That."

God, he loved talking dirty to her. The way it made her voice go breathy and her eyes sizzle, with goose bumps spreading over her skin. As though the words themselves were slipping over her in a filthy caress. *Fuck*, it was hot. Made more so by the knowledge *he* was the only one who could talk to her like that. His dick, which was still trying valiantly to fight its way out of his pants, twitched with anticipation. How long did they have to stay at this thing, anyway? Was an hour long enough before bundling V back to their hotel room to peel her out of that fucking wet dream of a dress?

"Drink up!" Avery cried, breaking into Dave's thoughts, and handing him a champagne flute.

They toasted, and Dave resigned himself to the fate of spending the next several hours lusting after his girlfriend with no hope of a reprieve. She drifted over to her friends, and he shifted his stance in a failed attempt to relieve the ache in his groin, regretting his earlier refusal of a quickie. *Later*, he told himself as he sipped champagne and watched V laugh at something Rae said.

With a loving squeeze of her leather clad ass, Jackson stepped away from Kez and came to stand by Dave. "Glad you could make it down, man."

"Me too," Dave responded and clinked his glass to Jackson's. He sipped at the bubbles, but they weren't really his thing. A little too delicate to start with a helluva punch to wake up to the following morning.

Jackson took a similarly muted sip, frowned, and inclined his head to the bar across the room. "Feel like trading this in for something a little less . . . exuberant?"

Dave laughed. "Lead the way."

Rae stepped in front of them with a squeak of leather, green eyes flashing teasingly behind her mask. "I know the look of two Neanderthals who are about to swap expensive champagne for some sort of draft beverage." She wiggled her fingers. "Hand them over, gentlemen."

Dave looked at the still full glass of champagne in her other hand. "How are you going to juggle these?"

"Don't question a professional," Rae said, free hand extended with fingers waggling. "Just hand over the good stuff and no one gets hurt."

"You're a truly terrifying woman, even without the costume," Jackson said, passing over his still full flute of champagne.

"I'll accept that as the compliment you intended," Rae said, snagging Jackson's glass between her index and middle fingers. She waggled her ring finger and pinky at Dave. "Don't be shy, big guy, just slide it right in there."

Hesitantly, Dave did as he was told and notched his glass in the open space between her fingers. Miraculously, not a drop spilled, and the glasses didn't even shimmy. Rae grinned and dipped a little curtsy. "Be on your way, then. Your cheap swill awaits."

"I heard that," Avery called from his spot next to V. "Regan Murphy, you of all people know the last thing I'd do on the cheap is booze."

Dave and Jackson left them to their bickering and headed to the bar.

"So, how are things, man?" Jackson asked while they waited for their beers. "Haven't heard much from you lately."

Dave shrugged, tucking a few dollars into the tip jar. "Things are good. Sorry we didn't connect while you were upstate last week, but work has been . . . intense."

As only an old friend could, Jackson read between the lines to pick up what Dave wasn't saying. "Ryker being a dick?"

Dave smirked. "You ask as though there is some possibility he wouldn't be."

Beers in hand, they meandered back toward their group. After a pull of his beer, Jackson said, "I'm sorry, man, but I don't understand what the fuck you're doing keeping that job."

Dave blew out a breath and sipped his own beer without responding.

"Seriously," Jackson continued, "You've bailed before when that job down in Boston went bad. And leaving that had to be harder than what you've got going on at Tonic. I mean, shit, they fucked you when they brought in Ryker. It's not like you owe them anything."

Dave tugged at his collar. A tux had seemed like a good choice initially, but now the collar was too tight, and he wanted to loosen a few buttons. Without realizing it, Jackson hit on the reason Dave was hesitant to make the leap. Because he'd done it before without a plan and landed right back in the soup. Maybe not initially, but with the introduction of Ryker, his position was as bad, if not maybe a little worse than it had been at his old job. At least there he'd been getting paid more. Now . . . shit now he didn't know what do to. Only that he needed to do something. And that feeling, that hollow, hopeless feeling, was growing with each thankless shift he worked. Before long, it was going to swallow him whole. Either that or he'd choke on the futility of his current position.

From beside Kez, V looked over at him and smiled. The sight of it loosened the band around his lungs and he could breathe again. Dave was done with this conversation. He didn't want to let his job or his concerns for his future ruin his night with her. This weekend was about them spending as much time as possible together. At least half of which he hoped was spent naked, alone and wrapped around each other. Problems at Tonic could wait. They certainly weren't going anywhere in his absence and would probably only multiply. Which was all the more reason to stop wasting time thinking about that and get his ass over to his girl.

He touched the neck of his bottle to Jackson's and said, "Yeah, I know, man. And I appreciate the concern, I do, so don't take this the wrong way, but . . ." Dave glanced back at V and then flashed Jackson a quick grin.

Jackson nodded before Dave even finished his thought. "Point made. Let's not keep the ladies waiting."

October 24th

Dave: *On the plane, Doc. Miss you already.*

V: *Miss you too. *teapot emoji*

V: *Crap, sorry about that. I'm putting "get new phone" on my to-do list for the week.*

Dave: *Honestly, I'm sort of used to the emoji bombs *bomb emoji* by this point and I'll miss them when you upgrade.*

Dave: *This weekend was just what I needed. Seeing you was what I needed.*

V: *I feel the same way, babe. Let's not make a habit of going this long without seeing each other, okay?*

Dave: *The image of you in that dress is burned into my brain, Doc, so it's safe to say I'll being seeing you every time I close my eyes.*

V: *I'm glad you liked it.*

Dave: *I especially liked the way it looked hiked up around your hips when I pushed you up against the wall of the hotel room.*

V: *I . . . have no response to that.*

Dave: *Yeah, you were sort of without words then, too, Doc.*

October 25th

"Sorry I'm late, Mother," V said, dusting a kiss to her mother's cheek before sliding into the chair across from her.

"It's fine," Caroline said, dropping a lemon slice into her water glass. "It gave me a chance to catch up with Margaret Ann for a moment. She may join us for coffee after lunch."

V bit her tongue to keep from reminding her mother that she had patients that afternoon. She'd fight that battle when she was forced to. No sense in putting her mother in a snit before lunch was served. She settled for a noncommittal "Mm-hmm" as she glanced over the menu.

Gray eyes flicked over V's shoulder and Caroline's face instantly softened, her smile a welcoming flash of radiant white teeth. "Marcus," she said with a little wave. "I thought that was you."

Marcus? Who in the world was Mar—

V gave a half turn to see to whom her mother was speaking, and her internal question screeched to a halt. Over six feet of handsome male stood behind her in what was without question a custom suit, with its charcoal fabric draped perfectly over broad shoulders while the lines of his crisp white dress shirt emphasized his lean physique.

"Caroline," said the fashionable Adonis who was, apparently, named Marcus. His smile revealed a dimple in his left cheek and a slightly crooked tooth at the corner of his mouth. "It's nice to see you again."

Dark blue eyes focused in on V. "I'm sorry, where are my manners?" He extended his hand. "Dr. Marcus Copperfield." Realization slammed into V like a freight train as she shook his hand. *This* was the doctor her mother wanted her to meet last month.

Caroline jumped in. "Marcus, this is my daughter, Vivian. She's a doctor too. A pediatrician down in Charlotte."

"Nice to meet you, Dr. Copperfield," V said, as warm, smooth skin enveloped her palm in a firm, but not overbearing handshake.

"Marcus, please," he said.

Caroline glanced around him. "Oh, there's Margaret Ann. I need to catch her before she leaves. Excuse me, won't you?" She was off like a shot, seeming to have forgotten she'd only just seen Margaret Ann.

Marcus watched Caroline rabbit away for a second, then rubbed at the back of his neck and sent V a rueful grin. "I've got four sisters."

V blinked in confusion at the somewhat random fact about his family. "Congratulations?"

Marcus laughed and shook his head. "I've suffered through enough rom-coms to know forced proximity when I see it. I also saw Margaret Ann when she pulled into the lot a few minutes ago, so I know she isn't about to leave."

V returned his smile. "My mother is a bit of a force of nature when she gets her mind set on something. In this case, I'm sorry to say the 'something' appears to be my meeting you."

He gave her a good-natured shrug and shook his head. "No need to apologize to me. I'm a thirty-eight-year-old unmarried surgeon. My mom's been trying to marry me off since my first year of residency."

V laughed. "Well, you have my deepest sympathies if she's anywhere close to as single-minded as Caroline."

Marcus tapped his chin and gazed thoughtfully at the ceiling, then his eyes came back to hers, alight with humor, but nothing more. "Caroline makes my mother look like a complete amateur. I wish you the best of luck."

"I appreciate it."

He took her hand in his, giving it a gentle squeeze before walking away. "A pleasure, Vivian."

Her mother reappeared at the table once Marcus had taken his leave. "Isn't he divine?"

V crossed her arms. "Really, Mother? Please tell me you didn't orchestrate this entire lunch for me to have some random meet cute with Dr. Copperfield."

Caroline fluffed her napkin across her lap with an irritated snap. "How could I know he would be here? And it wasn't a 'meet cute' I just wanted you to see the man, for heaven's sake. Is that so bad?"

"I thought you wanted to have lunch to hear more about Dave. You know, the man that I'm seeing. The man I dropped off at the airport yesterday after spending the weekend with him in Atlanta."

Her mother looked at her, the arch in her brow rising just enough to signal danger. "So tell me about him. This wonderful man you've been seeing for an entire month about whom I know nothing other than his name."

V sipped her water, wishing for something stronger. "Well, he's . . ." She paused and considered the best way to translate Dave's best qualities into something her mother would appreciate. "He's very . . .

sweet." V wanted to pull the word back as soon as she said it, because it sold Dave woefully short.

"Sweet?" Caroline repeated. "I see."

The waiter came to take their lunch orders and once he'd left, V said, "Dave is ver—"

"His LinkedIn page doesn't show a current job listing," Caroline interrupted. "Which is surprising, given he graduated with honors from such a prestigious school. What made him leave his last job?"

V was flabbergasted. "His . . . LinkedIn page?" she asked weakly.

V's face must have been something to behold, because Caroline laughed. "Don't look so shocked, Vivian. Your mother can google, you know. And, considering the sparse details you were willing to provide, what choice did I have?"

"You . . . googled him?" *So much for Caroline knowing nothing but Dave's name.*

"You didn't?"

V sat back in her chair. "I . . . no, I didn't."

Caroline shook her head. "Well, that's just as well, since I'm not interested in what the internet says. I want to hear more from you about this boy. Starting with why you're interested in a man who seemingly left a good job to do . . . nothing in the past few years."

"He's not doing 'nothing,'" V defended Dave. "He's working."

"Oh?" Caroline asked. "Doing what?"

V swallowed. "He's . . . tending bar at a local place in Rochester."

"Tending. Bar." Caroline enunciated the words as though they were each a separate sentence. "In Rochester." She might as well have said building pipe bombs in a basement, given the look on her face.

"Yes," V said. "But only until he . . . figures out his next step." At least, that's what V hoped was the case. Dave wasn't forthcoming on his future plans, but he also didn't seem wedded to the idea of working at Tonic forever. And she couldn't picture him being happy with that long-term.

"Shouldn't he already have that figured out?" Caroline asked skeptically. "And is he going to 'figure out' something here or there?"

"I . . . I'm not sure about the here or there part, Mother," V said. "We've only been seeing each other for a month, so it's a little early for that."

"It's never too early to tell someone your expectations," Caroline said. "You need to make it clear to this young man what you want. Not just for your own life, but for the person you're considering sharing it with. The sooner you do, the easier it is to determine whether they're going to live up to the standard you've set."

"I . . ." V stopped talking. How could she tell Caroline she no longer saw the standards she'd used in the past as her own? That finally, after years of accepting Caroline's standards, she was ready to set some of her own. Ones she believed would matter in the long run. "I think Dave has the potential to meet whatever standard there is," V said.

Caroline blinked. "That's high praise. Especially for someone who seems to be floundering at the same time you're flourishing."

V pushed down the hot flash of anger at her mother's description only to be slapped with a generous dose of guilt, since it was nothing more than a sharper phrasing of the concerns she'd voiced to Kez and Rae a few days ago. Could she really criticize her mother when she'd had a version of the same thought herself?

"All I'm saying," Caroline went on in the face of V's silence, "is that I don't want to see you waste your time, or lose out on anything *or anyone*"—her emphasis on the last word left no question that Marcus Copperfield was the "one" she was talking about—"because you've gotten tangled up with someone who isn't on your same trajectory. Dead weight like that will only hold you back, Vivian."

"Dave is not 'dead weight,'" V said, fighting to keep any edge from creeping into her tone. Caroline wouldn't look too kindly on their having any sort of disagreement in the dining room of the Club. After all, what would people say?

"Maybe not," Caroline conceded. "But you need someone who's going to be more than cargo you're responsible for carrying, darling. You need someone who can chart their own course alongside yours. And, if I'm honest, it sounds like this young man has veered so far off course at this point, that I wonder if he can find his way back."

Chapter 16

October 31st

Dave: *Happy Halloween, Doc. *jack-o'-lantern emoji**

V: *Right back at you. *witch emoji* *pumpkin emoji* *pig nose emoji**

V: *Crap, ignore the last one.*

Dave: *Whew, I wasn't sure if that were some sort of disguised diss. I see you're making real progress on your to-do list.*

V: *I'll get around to it eventually, I promise. And, if I were going to "diss" you, I wouldn't disguise it, lol!*

Dave: *Are you making fun of my hip lingo, Doc?*

V: **smh emoji* This one is absolutely on purpose.*

Dave: *Send me a picture of your costume tonight.*

V: *I will, but I already told you, we're going "basic witch" tonight since I'm just handing out candy in the driveway.*

Dave: *You are anything but a basic witch, Doc.*

"How much candy did you buy?" Rae called from inside V's pantry.

"Do not judge my candy buying habits," V snapped from her place at the stove.

Rae emerged from the pantry holding up two huge variety bags of candy. "More like candy hoarding habits. I thought you gave some out at your office today."

"That's why there's only two bags left," V said, tasting the chili bubbling on the stove. "Come here and tell me if this is too spicy."

Rae took a dainty taste from the extended wooden spoon. She licked her lips. "That's good, Doc." After a few more smacks of her lips she asked, "What's that I'm tasting in there?"

"They wouldn't be secret ingredients if I told you what they were." V rinsed the spoon and put it in the dishwasher. Turning the heat down to simmer, she covered the chili and faced Rae. "You remembered the rules about costumes, right?"

Rae rolled her eyes. "Don't worry, Catwoman is safely back at my place." She wiggled her eyebrows. "I've gotten *a lot* more use from that costume than I originally planned."

V held up a hand. "No, nope, not doing that. Not talking about that. Not even thinking about that."

Rae shrugged. "Suit yourself. But I'm telling you, it was a good investment."

"What was a good investment?" Kez entered the kitchen carrying two shopping bags, her purse, and a garment bag. She slung all of it onto the island and sank onto a stool.

"Trust me when I say you don't want to know," V said. "What's all this?"

Kez dug into one of the grocery bags and pulled out bags of peanut butter cups and Milky Ways. "I wasn't sure of your candy situation, so I brought the extra we had at the office."

"You passed out candy at your law office for Halloween?" Rae asked with a skeptical brow. "That many kids seeking emancipation these days? Ready to strike out on their own with a new company fueled by nothing but their own determination and peanut butter cups?"

"Har har," Kez said, dropping the candy back into the bag. "The office complex had a trunk or treat, and we participated."

"What's in the other bag?" V asked.

"That's the Tupperware I borrowed the night you made lasagna," Kez said, leaving her seat to come to the stove and inspect the chili.

V smacked her hand away from the pot lid. "That's hot." She handed her a potholder. "Use this. And I made that lasagna like three months ago."

Kez inhaled the steam rising from the chili. "That smells amazing. And I didn't know there were due dates for Tupperware returns."

"Only if you aren't a total barbarian," Rae said, the top half of her body hidden behind the open fridge door. She emerged with two beers, a hard seltzer, and a bag of shredded cheese.

Kez took one of the beers and passed the seltzer to V. "Grab the sour cream, too, please," she said to Rae. "And you bring yours back so quickly because you're desperate for a refill."

"What can I say?" Rae asked, depositing the sour cream and cheese on the counter. "If you don't want me to hang around, then don't feed me."

"Isn't that what they say about stray cats?" Kez asked.

Rae lifted a shoulder in a careless shrug. "I've been called worse." She grinned. "And V can call me whatever she wants, so long as she continues to call me for dinner."

V pulled down bowls from a cabinet and grabbed three spoons, setting it all on the counter by the stove. "You've got nothing to worry about there, my friend. You're welcome at my table any time."

"Same," Rae said. "I'll make reservations for us any time, any place."

"All right, you two," Kez said, grabbing a bowl. "That's enough of this love fest. I'm freaking starving. It was all I could do not to inhale that bag of Milky Ways on the way over."

"We look like a low budget version of *Macbeth*," Rae said, straightening her witch's hat.

Kez warmed her hands over the Solo Stove they'd set out in V's driveway, careful her black crepe skirt stayed far from the flames. "Speak for yourself," she said. "This skirt is vintage Prada."

"That's going to smell like a campfire after tonight," V said, settling back in her lawn chair and adjusting the rope belt at her waist. "Why would you wear Prada to trick-or-treat?"

"Because the skirt that came with this ensemble was ugly as hell and looked like a black mushroom cloud."

"You're insane, you do know that, right?" V said.

"Hey, now, Doc," Jackson said as he strolled up the driveway. "Take it easy on my girl, okay?"

"You look like an extra from the *Pirates of the Caribbean*," Rae said, passing him a beer from the cooler at her feet.

He took it and leaned down to kiss Kez on the cheek, his pirate's bandana trailing over the leather vest stretched across his broad shoulders. "Sorry I missed dinner," he said. "I got caught up waiting on materials for a last-minute project."

Kez grinned. "No problem. I hope everything arrived okay."

Jackson nodded, sipping his beer. "Yep, just a bit delayed, but none the worse for wear." After a bit of maneuvering with his sword, he sat in the chair next to Kez. "What have I missed?"

"Other than a parade of mini ghosts, goblins, and ghouls?" V asked with a laugh. "Not a whole lot."

"Don't forget tiny Cher," Rae reminded her.

"Or the Three Little Pigs!" Kez said.

V's phone buzzed in her pocket, and she fished it out.

Dave: *Where's my pic, Doc?*

"Crap!" V said, standing to snap a quick selfie.

"What's going on?" Rae asked.

"Nothing. Dave just asked for a picture of me in my costume an—"

She was interrupted by V and Kez emitting a simultaneous and childish, "Ooo!"

"Grow up, you two," V laughed and held her phone high enough to get her entire costume in the picture. Along with Rae waving in the background.

V: *Sorry! Rae and Kez distracted me with Tupperware due dates and candy bags.*

Dave: *Not even going to ask what that means, but I love the costume.*

V: *Thanks! I wish you could see it in person. *fish emoji**

V: *Dammit!*

Dave: *I'm really going to miss these emoji bombs.*

V: *I didn't think I'd hear from you tonight. Figured you'd be super busy at the bar.*

Dave: *I'll always make time for you, Doc. Want to see my costume?*

V: *Absolutely.*

V waited until the bubbles at the bottom of her screen were replaced by a picture. When they were, she tapped the screen to make the photo bigger. Dave smiled back at her, but he wasn't wearing a costume. And was that . . . using two fingers, she zoomed in on the background. The extremely *familiar* background of the tulip magnolia in the yard across the street from her townhouse.

"What the . . ."

"Happy Halloween, Doc."

V jumped at the sound of Dave's voice and bobbled her phone, almost losing it to the Solo Stove.

And then he was next to her. Putting an arm around her to steer her away from the flames. "Whoa, easy there. No need to tumble into your cauldron on my account."

She blinked up at him, then down at the phone, then back to his face. She pointed at the picture on her screen. "But you're supposed to be there."

Dave laughed. "I am there."

"But you're here," V said.

"Turns out tonight there"—he pointed to her phone—"and here are one and the same. Spooooky!"

"You're here," she said again, a smile spreading over her face. "You're right here!"

"I sure am," he said, laughing as she launched herself into his arms.

"Surprise!" chorused Rae and Kez while Jackson wore a piratical grin.

V pulled back from Dave. "Wait, you two knew about this?"

"Of course we did," Rae said with a laugh. "What other 'last-minute project' did you think Jackson was talking about? He missed dinner to get Dave at the airport."

"I can't believe you're here!" V said, choking up a little at the gesture.

Dave dropped a kiss to her wobbly smile. "Right where I want to be."

"Can I ask you something?"

The tentative note in V's voice paused Dave's hand in drying a glass. They were alone in the kitchen after sending Rae home with the leftover chili and Kez with Jackson and the rest of the Milky Ways.

"Always." He gave the glass one final swipe with the dish towel and placed it in the cabinet. Folding the towel into a neat rectangle, he draped it over the lip of the sink and leaned a hip there. "Fire away."

Even with the invitation he'd provided, V hesitated, chewing her lower lip and straightening an already aligned stack of mail on the island. Her pointer finger tapped at a corner of the bottom envelope. *Tap. Tap. Tap.*

"Doc?" Dave prompted, uneasy with her silence. It never boded well when someone wanted to ask you something and then took their time in doing it. The question turned out awkward at best and debilitating at worst.

V looked at him, indecision clear in her eyes. "I'm trying to figure out the best way to ask you something."

Dave arched a brow. "Isn't the best way usually just opening your mouth and letting the words tumble out?"

Her lips twitched. "You'd think so, but in this instance, I'm having trouble doing that." She met his gaze. "I think because you've been less than forthcoming when I've tried before."

He stiffened with surprise and not an insignificant amount of trepidation at her accusation. "Okay, now I really need you to just rip the Band-Aid off and ask what you need to ask, Doc."

V went back to fidgeting with the mail. "I'm not trying to start a fight or anything."

Dave reined in his defensive response. "How about this," he said, careful to pull any strain out of his tone. "Put it out there and we'll pick up the pieces of my fragile ego afterward." He'd been aiming for teasing, but it came off more petulant than humorous and V winced.

"I didn't mean . . ."

He shifted against the sink, simultaneously eager for her to ask whatever it was she wanted and dreading the moment she would. "I know, Doc. But the suspense is probably worse for both of us than what you want to ask, so let's hear it."

"It's just . . ." V sighed and shook her head, looking out the window behind him into her darkened back patio. She pulled her lip between her teeth once more before saying, "I know I don't have the whole backstory or anything, but based on what you've told me . . ." Her eyes moved from the window to his, an apology plain in their blue depths. "Sorry, but it just seems like things at Tonic aren't going that great for you these days. And your boss, Ryker? I don't think he gets how much you do there, or if he does, then he doesn't seem to care. So, I guess I don't understand why you're still there. Or, even more than that, aren't anxious to make a change or find something that suits you. You're capable of so much more, so why not at least see what else is out there?"

Dave chafed at her description of his life, at the way she made it seem as though he were stuck in some purgatory. Or not even stuck, *content* to sit there with no plan of escape. He didn't like her seeing him that way, or thinking of him as someone not in control over his own life. Even though that *was* how he felt, and it was that precise feeling that made sleep elusive some nights. But how could he put those feelings into words to someone like V who'd known what she wanted to do her entire life? Not just known, but *achieved* it. All he'd done was go with the flow and fail miserably his first time out of the gate.

"It's not as simple as you make it sound," he said.

"How can you say that if you don't at least try?" V countered, her hands moving to her hips. "I'm not saying that it will be easy for you to get back into your field, but isn't it at least worth a shot?"

He barely held in the derisive snort but had to look away. Because the truth was, he had tried. He'd *been* trying since the day he'd gotten back from Atlanta. His updated résumé had been submitted through every portal he could find for jobs utilizing his degree. And not just in New York, but here in North Carolina too. Because, yeah, it was early—*very* early in their relationship—but Dave knew he wanted to be where V was, which meant it made more sense to apply to places here than back home. So, yeah, he'd tried. He'd tried and, as of the latest rejection email he'd received while waiting to board the plane to Charlotte earlier that day—made zero progress. Turned out that taking two years off to bartend hadn't made him one of the top candidates for any of the positions he'd sought.

And again, how was he supposed to tell V any of that? The woman was born to succeed. And she'd already judged him for the mistakes he'd made up to that point. That was obvious by her bringing up his failure to live up to his early potential, so he couldn't add fuel to the fire with his latest fuckups. He didn't want to see pity in those deep blue eyes of hers or watch the corners of her mouth turn down in a disappointed frown. He didn't want her to change her mind about him. To regret any of what they had or see taking a chance on what they still could have as a mistake. He'd find a way out of this and be the man she wanted him to be. He just needed a little more time.

Pushing away from the sink, Dave crossed to the island where V stood. Dropping onto a counter stool, he pulled her to stand between his legs. He guided her hands to the back of his neck and settled his own at the small of her back. "Of course it is, Doc." His thumbs brushed the slope of her waist and he nuzzled into her neck. "But do you really want to spend the rest of tonight talking about my job? Because, I have to be honest"—his hands slipped down to cup her ass, pleased to discover the fabric of her skirt was *very* thin—"seeing you in this costume provides me with other ideas on how we should occupy the remainder of our evening."

Lifting his face from her neck, Dave watched V weigh how to respond and saw the moment she decided not to push him, her blue eyes softening and her lips pushing into a smile. Relief flooded through him. This reprieve might not last long, but he'd enjoy it while it did.

She looked down at her costume, then back at him with an arched eyebrow. "Seeing me in a pile of black rags belted with twine gives you ideas?"

"You in a burlap sack would give me ideas, Doc. Namely ideas about how to get you out of said burlap sack."

"Sounds like all of your ideas revolve around the same basic premise." V toyed with the hair at the nape of his neck.

"I'm a simple man with even simpler needs," Dave replied, enjoying the feel of having her so close.

V brushed a stray lock of hair from his forehead. "I like simple."

"Do you?"

She dusted a kiss to his cheek, and he felt her answering, "Mm-hmm" against his skin. Her lips slid to his ear, and she whispered, "Like the simple fact you missed me enough to surprise me on Halloween when I know it was anything but simple for you to get tonight off." She nipped his earlobe, which made his hands tighten their grip on her ass like some sort of perverse Babinski reflex.

V's palms came to Dave's jawline when she pulled back. She looked at him, eyes a darker blue than normal. "I like your kind of simple, Dave. I like it a lot, because it makes me think we can overcome any complication."

He hoped like hell she was right.

A Relationship with All the Trimmings

Chapter 17

November 2nd

"How's the phone sex?"

V choked on her calamari, coughing and spluttering while Kez thumped her on the back. After a restorative swallow of wine, she rasped, "What?"

Rae's martini paused on the way to her lips, and she regarded V over the rim of it. "The phone sex. With Dave. I know it's not the best substitute for the real deal, but . . . I don't know," she waggled her eyebrows, "Dave seems like a guy who'd give great phone sex."

"He seems like . . . what?" V repeated.

Rae's shoulder rose and fell in a carelessly fluid motion. "He's got that good boy look, but with that bad boy smile. Clean cut, but dirty in all the best ways. A guy like that *has* to be good at phone sex." Green eyes glittered as Rae leaned in closer. "Or are you having more than just phone sex, Doc, you saucy little minx? Are you having FaceTime sex?"

"Am I doing . . . what?" V hazarded a look at the tables surrounding theirs, but thankfully the other diners seemed focused on their own conversations rather than the bizarre turn this one had taken.

"C'mon, Doc," Rae said. "How else do you deal with the distance other than getting down and dirty digitally?" She laughed. "I guess that could have dual and equally appropriate meanings in this scenario."

"I am not having this conversation," V said, taking a prim sip of her wine.

"I hate to break it to you," Kez said, spearing a cherry tomato, "but this is a conversation everyone is having these days. There was an article in *Women's Health* about the best sexual positions for FaceTime."

V blinked at her, startled by the casual way her childhood best friend was discussing sex on camera. Like it was an item on her grocery list, or a new hairstyle she was considering.

Rae put her elbows on the table, drink forgotten and fully invested in the conversation instead of idly lobbing word grenades like "phone sex" into it. "Am I to take your . . . we'll go with 'stunned' reaction to mean that you and Dave are *not* engaging in any sort of cyber sexy time?"

V looked imploringly at Kez. "Can you make her stop?"

Kez laughed. "No one can make Rae stop anything until she's ready to give up the ship. And, I have to say . . . I'm with her on this one. I know how hard it is—" She pointed at Rae. "Don't." Rae stuck out her tongue.

"I know how *difficult* it is," Kez went on, "to sustain a relationship over long distance and one of the toughest parts is the lack of opportunities for intimacy. But . . . there are ways to help with that."

"Are you saying you and Jackson have . . ."

Kez shook her head. "No, but I'm not opposed to it. Especially since it's something I was willing to do with Miller."

"You and Miller . . ." V couldn't even finish the thought.

"He was there, and I was here. So, yeah, we did."

V sat back in her chair, absorbing the conversation. She wasn't an idiot, nor was she some sheltered virgin. Obviously, she'd heard of phone sex and sexting and knew of camgirls and other lines of sex work. Sexting was a topic that came up more frequently than she cared to consider in her work. Too many of her patients had to deal with the fallout from an ill-advised picture taken and texted in the heat of the moment.

"What if Miller took a screenshot or something?" V asked.

Kez gave a little shudder. "I'd like to think he's not enough of a creep to have kept something like that, if he took one, that is. But if he did, that's his issue, not mine. And he wouldn't circulate it if he had it. Things between us might have imploded in stunning fashion, but he's not a complete dickhead."

"I'm not advocating anything you're not down with, Doc," Rae said. "You and Dave haven't known each other that long, so I get it if you're not there yet, or if you never get there. But, in his defense, he doesn't strike me as a guy who'd take a secret screenshot." Her smile turned evil. "And if I'm wrong and he did, I would crush him like the insect he turned out to be." Her eyes went to Kez. "Same goes for Miller."

Kez patted Rae's hand. "You say the sweetest things."

To V she said, "Rae's right, V. FaceTime sex is awkward enough the first time when it's something you *want* to do. If it makes you start to sweat in the wrong sort of way, then it goes from awkward to awful and no one should experience that. All we're doing is reminding you it's an available option."

Rae nodded. "Like a sexual flare gun to be used during an orgasm emergency."

"I was thinking more along the lines of a way to combat the distance part of a long-distance relationship, but yeah, sure," Kez said with a laugh.

November 3rd

"Get home safe, Shay," Dave called.

"You too, Boss Man," she replied as she slid behind the wheel of her car. "I plan to sleep for about four thousand years."

"Seeing as how you're on shift with me tomorrow at four, I don't think that's possible."

"Seeing as how that's less than twelve hours from now, it's a pretty dick thing to bring up after the night we just had."

Dave grinned as she shut her door and offered him a one-fingered salute. He waved back and watched her drive away before getting into his own car. Once inside, he cranked the engine and let his head fall back against the headrest. The clock on the dash read 4:45 a.m. He'd been at work since six the evening before. Ryker, in his infinite wisdom, had the brilliant idea of combining 1-2-3 night with their normal Thursday ladies' night. The mixture of $1 draft beer, $2 house liquor drinks and $3 call liquor drinks with no cover charge for their female customers had the entire staff running ragged all damn night. And added an hour to their normal cleanup.

He made a mental note to check inventory tomorrow, because he was certain of two things. One, they'd hit their backroom supply hard and two, Ryker would be too busy reveling in the receipts from tonight to worry about ordering more booze tomorrow. Dave scrubbed a hand over his face, trying to wake up enough to make it home in one piece.

He had enough time to get home, shower, sleep for a few hours and then get up for the phone interview he had with a biotech company at eleven that morning. The company was in Minnesota, but the position was remote. It was the first interview he'd been granted, and he was nervous as hell. Two years was a long time to be out of the game, and it had been even longer since he'd had an interview in his field. Telling himself it was at a minimum good practice for the next one did little to curb his anxiety.

Pulling out of the lot, he let loose a jaw-cracking yawn. At this point, he was sure he could've slept standing up. All he wanted was to grab a shower and fall into bed for as long as he could manage. The only benefit to the hour was that other than a city bus and a few cars, no one else was on the road and his drive home was mercifully short.

Shower. Bed. Shower. Bed. Shower. Bed. The two words were on repeat in his head like a scratched record as he climbed the stairs to his apartment. Tossing his keys onto the table by the door, he toed out of his shoes and headed to make the first of the words happen.

Hot water cascaded over exhausted muscles as he scrubbed the night from his skin. Standing under the steaming spray, he leaned heavily on the tile and enjoyed the pummeling of the water. Rolling his shoulders, he angled his neck from side to side, getting all of the kinks out.

He was toweling off when his phone signaled an incoming FaceTime call. Wrapping the towel at his waist, Dave grabbed his phone from the counter, a smile already on his face.

"Morning, Doc," he said, rubbing at his still wet hair with his free hand.

"Hey there," she responded. Fresh-faced and smiling with her hair in a ponytail, she looked like sunshine. *Jesus Christ, did he need some sleep.*

"How was last night? As bad as you thought it would be?"

The now familiar warmth in his chest lit once more with the knowledge V remembered his prediction the night would be a shitshow. Not just that she remembered, but that she cared enough to ask. Nodding, he answered, "If anything, it was worse. I just got home maybe twenty or thirty minutes ago. I'm getting ready to crash hard."

He almost told her about the interview, but held back. There was still a chance he could fuck it up, or they'd go in a "different direction," words he'd heard too many times to count at this point. No, it was better to keep things under wraps until he had something more concrete to share with her.

His sleep-deprived brain finally registered the black spandex sports bra she wore, and it took less than a millisecond for that information to transmit to his dick. *Fuck,* but she looked good. He'd woken up with her not even three days ago, but it felt like weeks since he'd touched her.

"Headed to work out?" he asked.

"Yeah, since I had an early session this morning, I thought I'd try and catch you before you went to bed. Sorry we couldn't talk last night."

She'd been at dinner with Kez and Rae when he'd left for work, so they'd only texted. "It's okay, Doc. I don't mind this kind of wake-up call."

V laughed and her eyes tracked over his exposed torso. When she licked her lips, he almost groaned. "Neither do I," she said, eyes lingering on his bare chest. He flexed his pecs, and she blushed.

"Anyway," she said, running a hand over her ponytail. "I know you're wiped out and I don't have much time either, but I'd like to . . . ask you about something."

"I'm all yours," Dave said, ignoring the tightness in his chest and hoping she wasn't circling back on the job topic he'd managed to dodge over Halloween. He wasn't going to lie to her, but he wanted to have something solid to tell her before saying anything.

"Well, I was talking to the girls last night and . . ." Her cheeks pinked up, and she looked away from the phone. She wasn't nervous in the same way she'd been in her kitchen before asking him about Tonic. She was . . . nervously embarrassed about something. *Interesting.*

"Uh-huh," Dave said, leaving the bathroom for his bedroom and dropping onto the edge of his bed.

"So, the thing is, after I talked to them . . . I also read this article and it made me start to think about certain things. Things that are important."

"Okay." Dave was thoroughly confused as to where this was going. He leaned back against the headboard, eyes on V's troubled blue ones staring out from his phone screen.

"How do you feel about phone sex?" V blurted and Dave damn near dropped the phone. It fumbled through his fingers, and he scrambled to right it.

Once he was looking at V's face again, he asked, "How do I feel about what?"

The pink tint was now a deeper, darker hue and she closed her eyes. He watched her throat tighten as she swallowed. Opening her eyes, she asked, "How do you feel about phone sex? Do you think that's something we should be doing?"

There was no longer a twitch under his towel. No slight tingle of sensation, or ripple of need. His dick went hard as stone in response to that question. It was his turn for a giant swallow.

Clearing his throat, he said, "Well, Doc, I think if it's an avenue you want to travel down, you can count me in for the ride." Then her words before the phone sex question came back to him. "Wait, did you say you read an article?"

The color in her cheeks wasn't going anywhere then. She laughed, a strangled little sound, and nodded. "Kez mentioned it, so, I figured I should at least look it up."

God, did he enjoy this woman. Only his girl would do research on phone sex. She needed her data to make a good plan of attack.

"And did you?"

Another nod. "I did. It wasn't about . . . phone sex, though. It was about"—she cleared her throat and dropped her eyes to the side when she said—"FaceTime sex."

If he'd thought his dick was hard before, he was wrong. Because when those words passed from V's lips, his cock positively throbbed in response. There weren't words in the English language that could describe it, except for possibly "battering ram" or "painfully erect." Those two seemed the closest to explaining the vigorously solid situation tenting the terry cloth draped around his hips.

"And, uh . . ." Dave searched for words, which was difficult not just from lack of sleep but from the entire ten units of blood in his body all now pumping directly to his crotch. "What did you think of the article?"

"It made some good points," V said, and her clinical answer pushed Dave's lips into a grin.

"Yeah?" he asked. "Like what?"

"That if you acknowledge it's going to be awkward and you're nervous about it, it helps."

Dave didn't like to hear that V would be nervous about this. "Are you? Nervous, that is?"

"Well . . . yeah," she said, her admission as honest as ever. "I mean, to do . . . *that* on FaceTime is going to be super weird."

"If that's how you feel, then don't even worry about it."

"How do *you* feel about it, though? Is that something you'd want? With me?"

The raw vulnerability in her voice hit Dave squarely in the chest and made it hard for him to speak. He knew he had to, because he had to make sure she knew without a doubt that he wanted her in whatever medium she was willing to give herself to him. Whether it was in person, on the phone, or in paint by numbers, he was *absolutely* interested in the experience.

"Doc," he said, his voice rough. "I want it." The thought of watching V's hands glide over her body and pleasure herself almost overheated his brain, so he had to press pause on that while he finished speaking. "If this is a question of what I want, then the answer is a very enthusiastic yes. But only if it's something you're into as well."

V's answering smile was shy and sexy as fuck. "I think . . . I think with you it could be."

A swift thrum of pride spread through him with her words, followed quickly by an avalanche of lust. Sweet fucking Jesus, was this actually going to happen?

"Yeah?" he asked, needing confirmation he wasn't dreaming.

She nodded and his dick responded with *Now? Is this happening now?*

Luckily, his brain won out, and he said, "Okay then. Well, I'm on shift tonight and tomorrow, so . . . Sunday?"

"Sunday," she repeated, her smile less shy and more excited now. "It's a date."

"Sounds perfect, Doc."

"Yeah," she said with a giggle. "Get some sleep, okay?"

"Sure thing," he said. He'd get right on that. After another, much colder shower.

November 5th

The pop of the cork leaving the neck of the bottle seemed too loud to V's ears, the sound of it bouncing against her eardrums. The first *glug, glug* of liquid splashing into the bowl of her wineglass also seemed at a higher volume than usual. The same was true of the brightness of the light over her island and the hard edge of the countertop at her hip. Everything felt *more*, as though what she and Dave were about to do pushed all her senses up to an eleven out of ten.

Sipping the wine, she let the crisp tartness of it coat her tongue before swallowing. The oven clock read 5:13 p.m. Outside her back patio door, dusk gathered into night. Dave was calling her, or rather FaceTiming her, at six. Because that was the hour she'd picked for their . . . appointment? No, that was too clinical a word. Rendezvous? No, that was too French film noir. Session? No, God, that made it sound like therapy. Which she was going to need if she didn't stop obsessing.

It wasn't like she hadn't slept with the man before. She had. Many, many times in multiple and creative ways all of which she'd enjoyed. So, there was no reason for her to be nervous. Except . . . this wasn't sex with Dave. This was . . . something else. Something she knew wasn't wrong, or taboo, or any of the other words that would've been used to describe it during her conservative upbringing, if anyone had dared speak of it.

She wasn't on Rae's level of sexual self-expression by any stretch of the imagination, but V knew that there was nothing untoward or deviant about self-love. It was a healthy expression of sexuality and a satisfaction of sexual desire she had every right to act on. And *had* in the days since she'd seen Dave. *Oh boy had she . . .*

V took another sip of wine and pressed cool fingers to her heated cheeks. No, the act itself wasn't in question. It was the performance of that act *in front of someone else!* that was . . . well, she wasn't sure what it was other than something she'd never before considered. And then she'd read the article Kez mentioned and . . . here she was planning an . . . interlude? That one had promise.

Because she hadn't stopped with the single article. As with anything else, more data was needed for an informed decision. And there was data galore—thank you internet. Data that told her she might be the last woman on the planet who had never had some sort of cybersex. Which was mind blowing to her, because she didn't live under a rock, nor was she a total prude. She was careful and definitely the most conservative of her friends, but good grief, based on the rabbit holes she tumbled down, she was practically nun-adjacent when it came to this subject.

The articles she read contained advice on everything from "know your angles" (well, duh) to "don't give too many instructions" (minimal risk of that) and finally "make it a surprise" (questionable at best, dubious consent at worst). Which meant with—she checked the clock again— forty minutes to spare before going through with this, she had enough random facts, thoughts, suggestions, ideas, and any other manner of things crowded into her overwhelmed brain. Hence the wine. She needed to relax, or she was either going to call this whole thing off, or make it more riddled with awkwardness than she already thought it would be. And, truth be told, V did not want to call it off. Because while the articles had crammed her brain almost to capacity, one thing that stood out was the repetitive promise that the act of sex over the screen would bring back a sense of closeness and togetherness that was missing in a long-distance relationship.

Of course, a lot of these people were in much longer-term relationships, but V could still relate to that feeling. It had only been a few days since she'd touched Dave, sexually or otherwise, and she already missed it. She missed the feel of his hand on her back, or the way her shoulder notched perfectly under his arm. She missed the sound of his heartbeat when she curled close to him and laid her head on his chest. His very broad, very firm, very *male* chest. *Down girl, still . . . thirty-seven minutes to go.*

Their schedules being in such opposition didn't help things, either. They'd made adjustments to accommodate each other as best they could, but nothing would change the fact he worked every night other than Mondays and Sundays. And that his work usually started before hers finished, so they couldn't really talk at the end of the day. Saturdays were better, but he'd usually go in around four or earlier those days, so again nothing at the end of the day. He'd answer her good night texts, sure. And those answers always made her smile. But . . . she wanted to hear his voice. To have the rumbly, rough texture of it tumble into her ear as she lay in bed.

All of these things resembled the experiences of so many women outlined in the articles she'd read. Each of whom swore these sensual on-screen moments with their partners brought back at least a part of what they missed the most. And that was the kicker for V. The single piece of data that pushed the scales in favor of stepping even further outside her comfort zone to bring a little piece of Dave back with her.

Dave smoothed down his comforter for the hundredth time in the last fifteen minutes. He'd also rearranged his pillows at least six times, changed the bulbs in both of his bedside lamps (just in case) and done a set of fifty push-ups both before and after his shower. During the shower, he'd debated what he was supposed to have on when he called V. Was he supposed to be fully clothed, shirtless, in just his underwear? The only thing he could fully discount was calling her completely naked. That, he was certain, was a nonstarter. Namely, because he would feel weird as fuck to call someone while naked. Maybe other people would be cool with it, but he wasn't on that level.

Of course, thoughts of what he was supposed to have on transitioned seamlessly to thoughts of what V would have on. Which required the shower to immediately be turned to cold. And now, he was debating whether he should have just done a quick preventative jerk in the shower instead. Because cold shower notwithstanding, he'd been hard for at least an hour and was now worried that five minutes into this he'd be a two-stroke loser.

He sat on the edge of his bed and took a deep inhale. V was nervous enough. There was no room for him to be a neurotic idiot. She needed him to be calm and composed about this. And he should be able to do that, since it wasn't his first trip down the cybersex highway. He knew the drill, so to speak, so there was no reason for him to be this worked up over it.

Except there was one very beautiful, blond reason. Because regardless of whether he'd done this before or not, he hadn't done this with V. And that made it different. She made it different. Not just different, but important. For her to suggest this with cheeks ablaze and uncertainty in those big blue eyes of hers, it was something she needed. Something he needed to give her. Something he needed to make sure she wanted and would enjoy. So, he had to get ahold of himself, calm the fuck down and focus on making sure this was good for her.

V positioned the little tripod by her bed, a smile hovering on her lips as she remembered Dave's tease from their dinner together. This had certainly *not* been in her mind when she bought the thing, but it was always good to find a dual purpose for something. Dutifully, she checked the angle to make sure everything looked good. Following the advice of her helpful internet guides, she positioned her phone to show mainly her face, with a hint of cleavage. Going full-fledged lady parts view on her first try was so not in the cards. After all, it was known as "FaceTime" not "VaginaVision," so she figured this was a good start.

She'd also taken the time to consider the lighting. Again, the internet often got a bad rap, but when you were semi-panicking over your first attempt at virtually seducing your boyfriend, by gosh it was there for you. V doubted she would've focused on lighting at all, other than keeping things semi-dim. Now, however, she knew to keep the overheads off and use bedside lamps to provide a warmer, more intimate light. Shadows and silhouettes played as important a part in this as light did, according to her sources. And, after doing a quick test run, she had to agree.

The one thing she hadn't needed help with was attire. That had been taken care of thanks to last weekend's shopping excursion with the girls. She'd planned to wear the royal blue lace teddy in person, but decided to give it a try tonight. Its cut wasn't complicated, just two lace panels that formed a halter-style neckline. A thin satin band bisected the filmy lace at her waist, where it became more fitted over her hips. Loops of satin threaded between her legs to keep the teddy in place. Loops that were necessary because the lingerie was missing one piece she normally viewed as vital to any outfit—a crotch.

Upon discovering this fundamental flaw in the outfit, she'd tried to put it back on the rack. Rae's hand on her wrist stopped her.

"What are you doing?" she asked.

"What does it look like I'm doing?" V replied. "Putting this back."

"Why, though? It's sexy as hell, and that color is perfect for you."

"Because," V glanced around the shop. "It's crotchless." The last part was whispered, and she was suddenly desperate to put the lacy garment back where it belonged.

"Doc," Rae said, squeezing her wrist. "Trust me when I say you need that teddy in your life. Even more than that, *Dave* needs it in his life."

"How can he need something he doesn't even know about?"

"He doesn't know he needs it yet, but once he sees it, he won't be able to remember life before seeing it. His life will exist in two stages: pre-teddy and post-teddy, with post-teddy being his absolute favorite part."

V vacillated. The blue was gorgeous, and the lace was so soft and supple.

Sensing her indecision, Rae moved in for the kill. "Look at it this way. If you get it, no one says you have to use it, but it's there if you need to deploy it."

"It's lingerie, Rae, not a parachute."

Admiring the blue against her skin in the full-length mirror, V had to admit she was glad Rae talked her into getting it. It flattered her curves and, while risqué, it still had an elegance that she loved. And, she had to admit, the crotchless aspect would save her from having to wriggle out of anything on camera. She was reasonably sure all the careful angles and lighting in the world wouldn't make the prospect of peeling herself out of this ensemble any less daunting.

Dave glanced at his phone. Should he do another set of push-ups? Fifteen minutes left. Maybe sit-ups instead? He'd managed to stay out of his own head about all of this for maybe ten minutes. But now he was pacing back and forth and questioning his decision to have lube on the ready. Normally, if he felt the need to fly solo, that happened in the shower, so there was no real need to contemplate the question. But tonight . . . dick friction of the unpleasant variety was a real possibility. One he was willing to endure in order not to spook V with either the presence of the lube or the snap of the cap as they were midway through their virtual evening. He didn't want to take her out of the moment, but the reality was that if things went as far as he hoped they did, there was no way he could keep his hand from wrapping around his dick. Something that would be *much* more enjoyable with the aforementioned lube.

How do you feel about it, though? Is that something you'd want? With me?

V asked him that, because she wanted to know what he wanted.

"She wants you to enjoy this, too," he said to the empty room. "And she's a lady, not to mention a medical professional, so the concept of lubrication isn't going to be a surprise to her. Hell, she probably has her own."

Those words hovered in the air, lodged in his brain, and shot straight down to his cock. The concept of V wet, willing, and thinking of him thickened his blood to the point he felt the pulse of it in his entire body. He grabbed his phone and fired off a text without even thinking about it.

Chapter 18

V's phone chimed from the tripod. She capped her last-minute lipstick and hurried to clear the text. Dave would be calling in roughly five minutes, so she needed whoever this was to kindly disappear for the next however long. Only when she checked the screen, the text was from Dave.

Dave: *Doc, I've been thinking about this, about you, about all of it all fucking day. I need to see you. Now.*

The bold printed words sent a shiver of anticipation down her spine and tugged her lips into a smugly satisfied grin. An unexpected sense of power thrummed in her veins, and she allowed herself to bask in it for a minute before aligning her body with the pillows she'd arranged (one more shoutout to her new internet girl gang) and hit the video call button on her phone.

Dave's face appeared after less than a full ring with an apologetic half smile. "Hey, Doc," he said. "Sorry for jumping the gun, but I . . . holy shit, what are you wearing?" His mocha brown eyes went molten, and he looked as though he wanted to climb through the screen to get to her.

V laughed, the sound throaty and deeper than normal. His reaction boosted the confidence from his earlier text. She ran a finger under the edge of the blue lace as she checked her reflection in the tiny corner image. In this position, he could see from her face down to just below her breasts, which meant the press of her cleavage against the lace cups of the teddy was wholly within his eyeline.

"This old thing?" she teased. "Just something I had lying around for the right occasion."

Dave's Adam's apple bobbed with his rough swallow, followed by an animalistic growly noise. "I'm honored," he said, his voice hitting a lower octave as well. "Let me see the rest of it, Doc."

Expecting this, V'd planned the perfect pose to grant his request and maintain her composure. Shifting a bit, she bent the knee of her top leg and canted her hips before panning the camera down her body. The position let him see all of her without really seeing *all* of her.

"Goddamn, Doc." He breathed, and she let the camera pan back up to her face. "I had this whole plan to talk ground rules and limits and, fuck, I don't even know what else because now that I've seen you, I have no thoughts other than how good you look in blue lace and the overwhelming desire to get down there and take it off with my teeth."

Even without those heady words, her effect on him was so palpable she could feel it through the screen. His eyes were hooded, and his nostrils flared. The line of his jaw was taut, and she could see the tense lines of muscle along the inside of his forearm, like he was holding himself back from reaching through the cables connecting them to pull her back with him.

"I take it you approve then?"

"Approve is not the first word that comes to mind," he said with a dark chuckle. "It's more along the lines of worship, revere, or idolize." She watched him rub a hand over his jaw and then tuck it behind his head to just stare at her. "Why haven't we done this before now?"

V laughed and adjusted her hand beneath her head, careful to avoid exposing too much and getting them ahead of schedule. Although, given the look on Dave's face, he wouldn't mind. "You mentioned something about ground rules."

Dave blinked and blew out a breath. "Yes, that's right. Ground rules." His face grew serious, and he brought the phone closer to his face, brown eyes earnest as he said, "I want you to know we can take tonight as far as you want to go, Doc. If you're uncomfortable with anything at any point, all you have to do is tell me and that's the end of it."

He was as skilled with sweet words as he was with dirty ones and his focus on making her feel safe and comfortable was as sexy as the way he'd devoured her with his eyeballs when he'd answered the phone.

"Thanks," she said, pressing a fingertip to the phone. "The same goes for you, you know."

Dave's laugh was a quick burst of sound through the speaker of her phone. "Doc, you could ask me to wear nothing but a lampshade and smile while singing *Oklahoma!* and as long as you wore that when you asked, I'd do it."

"Good to know," she said with a giggle, grateful he was being himself with her. It made things so much more relaxed that while he'd acknowledged this was new to her, he wasn't making a huge deal out of it. Instead, he was helping ease her into the flow of the evening with his normal blend of humor, confidence, and a healthy dose of straightforward attraction.

"Okay," he said, taking another deep breath. "Now that we've established I have no limits on this call, let's talk a bit about yours."

V swallowed, nerves finally kicking in. "Mine?" The word came out in a squeak.

Dave nodded. "I know what you like when we're together, Doc. At least, most of it, I think. Although"—he gave her a naughty eyebrow waggle—"I'm always eager to learn more."

"I'll keep that in mind."

"See that you do," he said. "But as for what goes down when I'm not there to offer my heartfelt assistance with anything you could possibly desire, you're going to have to fill me in."

V's cheeks started to get warm. "I don't . . ." She closed her eyes. "Can't we skip to the sexy part?"

"Look at it this way, Doc. We're making a plan to get to the sexy part. Because, and I want you to really hear this when I tell you, I have one goal tonight and that is to make sure you are not only comfortable with what we do, but that you enjoy it *almost* as much as you would if I were there."

V opened one eye and looked at him. "Almost as much?"

Dave snorted. "Something is very, very wrong if I give better orgasms virtually than in person. So, yeah, *almost* as much." His eyes went dark. "And Doc?"

"Yeah?"

"For the record, there's no amount of lube that could make my hand feel even close to the heaven that is sliding into the hot, wet heat of you, so for me it's always going to be 'almost' at best without you here."

"Oh-kay." V drew the word out on a sigh and barely restrained herself from fanning her face. "I'll remember that."

"See that you do." The heat stayed in his eyes, but softened slightly. He still wanted her, that was obvious. But there was something else in addition to the lust in his deep brown eyes. Something tender and gentle that tugged at her insides.

"I think it's safe for me to assume, given our plans for the evening, that you trust me."

V blinked at him, then glanced down the length of her body with a raised brow. "Yeah, I think that's a safe bet."

Dave huffed out a laugh. "Okay, good. In that case, I'm going to ask you to let me take the lead tonight. Just to get us started. You seem a bit self-conscious, and I have a few ideas about how to alleviate that. But if you're not cool with that, we c—"

"No, that's fine," V agreed eagerly. Because while Dave's easygoing manner and light teasing coupled with the way he looked at her helped start things off . . . now that they were getting down to it, she could feel her nerves rising and tangling together in a knotted mess. She needed him to take over before she freaked out.

Dave smiled at her, and she felt the familiar tingly sensation float through her in response. "Okay, Doc. In that case . . ." His grin turned bashful, and he dipped his chin to peek up at her. "Do you . . . have everything you need?"

"Everything I . . . need?"

He nodded. "For instance . . ." He turned his phone toward his nightstand and the bottle of water-based lubricant sitting on the corner of it. Dave's face came back on-screen, and she thought his cheeks were a tad pink, which was deliciously adorable. He continued, "I've got what I need with me, so I want to make sure the same is true for you."

V's vibrator that she'd chosen with the help of several well-researched blog posts was in the same drawer of her bedside table it always occupied, together with the bottle of lube that came with it. Dave was right, she needed to go ahead and get it out rather than fumble for it in the middle of . . . well, everything.

She must've glanced toward the drawer, because Dave said, "Get what you need, Doc."

Her face went hot as she opened the drawer and pulled out the vibe and the lube, carefully keeping both out of frame. "Okay," she said, shutting the drawer. "I'm good."

That was a lie. She was not, in fact, good. She was more nervous than a long-tailed cat in a room full of rocking chairs, but she wasn't going to let that keep her from experiencing this with Dave. If she could get over this initial reluctance, she knew things would be fine. Better than fine, if FaceTime Dave were anywhere close to In-Person Dave when it came to knowing what she wanted, and her body needed.

He'd asked her to let him take the lead, so all she had to do was give herself over to that. To trust him with the mechanics of this and allow him to guide her through it. She could because she did trust him. As evidenced by doing this in the first place.

"Okay, Doc," Dave said. "I think we need to level the playing field a bit here." Before she could ask what he meant, he reached behind his head and pulled his shirt off. The white of his T-shirt covered the phone briefly, but then he was back and gloriously shirtless.

"Not as fashionable as what you're working with," he said, "but I'm using what I have available."

The angle at which he held the phone didn't give her the full view she wanted, but since she was already thinking about how it would feel to kiss the hollow of his throat, she could make do.

"When you bite your lip like that, it gives me ideas, Doc," Dave said, his voice rougher now.

V hadn't realized she'd pulled her bottom lip between her teeth. Dave rubbed a thumb across his own lips as she nibbled hers before releasing it. The low, rolling rumble of sound he made spoke directly to her nipples, who sat up and took direct notice.

The way his eyes dipped down and held there told her he'd seen that too. His tongue swept across his lower lip, eyes still focused on where the beaded points of her nipples were now trying their best to pierce the filmy lace.

"Doc . . ."

The gravelly rasp of his voice dragged over her in a coarse caress. Her fingertips dusted the upper swells of her breasts and Dave's eyes greedily tracked the movement. He followed each sweep of her fingers, eyes getting darker with each pass. The arm behind his head bunched and flexed, muscles rolling in his bicep as he watched her.

"Tell me what you feel, Doc." His eyes met hers, hot with lust and hooded with his desire for her. Her fingers stuttered at the intensity of his stare. "I need to know what you feel, how your skin feels under your fingers. What that ripple of goose bumps I can see dancing over your perfect breasts feels like."

"I . . . it . . ." V's fingers slid lower on her breasts, dipping into the valley between them and trailing down until she was loosely cupping one breast in each hand. Her nipples pressed sharply into her palms, eager and aching.

"Shimmy that lace down, Doc. Let me see you." It wasn't a question, but a command. One that slammed straight through V to her already aching core.

Even though the touch at her nipples was her own, she still whimpered at the loss of it as she moved to obey Dave's directions. Rising off her stack of pillows, she undid the clasp at the back of her neck and let the lace fall away from her breasts.

"Sweet Christ, Doc," Dave hissed, shifting higher in the bed. The hand behind his head came forward, fingers almost touching the screen. "You have no idea how badly I want to be there right now." His eyes blinked back to hers and his hand disappeared from view. "Do you know what I'd do to you if I were there right now?"

Brazenly emboldened by the smoldering look he gave her, V drew her hand down the curve of her breast to her nipple, trapping the straining peak between her first and middle finger and giving it a delicate tug. "Something like this?"

"Oh, fuck," Dave groaned, dragging a hand over his face. "*Fuuuck*, V. You're killing me, baby. And we're only getting started."

V hummed in response to both his growled praise and the pinch of her fingers at her nipple. She'd never spent much time teasing herself in this way. Normally, if she were out to get off on her own, she got right to the heart of the matter. Now though, with him watching and encouraging her, she recognized it as foreplay with her hands taking the place of his and following his commands.

"Don't be neglectful, Doc. You've got two hands and two breasts, so put all ten fingers to good use for me," Dave said, and she shivered as she heard the distinct sound of his fly being unzipped.

She couldn't see anything other than his face and a portion of his chest, but his hand had once again disappeared from view. The idea of him watching her and stroking himself made her breath catch in her lungs and she hurried to obey his direction. Releasing the pinch at her nipple and cupping her hands over her breasts, she sighed.

"You know what you like, Doc," Dave said, and she could hear the strain of want in his voice. "Roll those tight little buds between your fingers, tease them into hard, aching diamonds for me. Jesus, fuck, if I were there, I'd use my mouth to take turns licking and sucking on those gorgeous tits of yours, Doc. Would you like that? Would you like my mouth on you, my teeth dragging over those pretty little nipples until they were raw and needy from it?"

V pressed her shoulders back, pushing her breasts farther into his, no *her* touch. Squeezing her thighs together, she moaned her answer. "Yes, yes. I want that."

"You look like a goddamn dream right now, Doc. A fucking dream, do you understand me? I would kill to touch you right now. To taste you, to feel the slickness of you on my tongue. Because I know you're wet right now, Doc. You are, aren't you? I can't see it, but I'm guessing you're twisting those smooth, silky thighs of yours together looking for my touch, aren't you?"

His questions were coarse, lewd, and indecent and shot directly to the liquid heat of her sex, making it throb with desire. Her hips rocked as though goaded into action by his filthy words. V's eyes drifted closed, and she nodded. "Yes."

"Yes, what?" Dave pressed, his voice coming out ragged and rough.

"Yes to . . . all of it."

His laugh was the pure embodiment of wicked and the raunchy sound of it made her ache for him. "Good girl, Doc. I always enjoy your honesty, sweetheart. You deserve to be rewarded for it, don't you?"

She pulled her lip between her teeth and gave her nipples a harsh pinch as she nodded. "Mm-hmm" was all she could manage as a response.

Dave's sharp inhale made her eyes flutter open, and there was no longer any doubt what he was doing while he watched her. She'd seen that harsh set of his jaw before when he'd dragged the hard ridge of his erection across her wet, willing folds. His eyes were so dark now they were almost black and the muscles of his chest that were visible stretched impossibly taut, like a perfectly tuned bowstring.

"Are you ready for your reward, Doc? Because I'm holding on by a fucking thread over here, so I need you to be ready for me."

"I'm ready," she whispered and released her right breast to fumble on the bed next to her until her fingers found her vibrator.

She could've looked down to locate it more easily but hadn't wanted to look away from the glorious display of tethered male desire staring back at her. Within the screen of her phone, Dave was primed and ready and she had no doubt if he were there with her there was a good chance her bedframe wouldn't have survived the experience.

His eyes rolled wildly when the sex toy hummed on. The sound he made was guttural and primal, and she pictured the savage stroke he'd just given himself. It made her own sex pulse with want.

"Sweet fucking Christ, Doc, there's a real chance I'm going to spontaneously combust from that sound alone."

When V clicked her vibrator to life, it didn't matter that Dave couldn't see it. Didn't matter that he was hundreds of miles away. Didn't matter that the only connection he had to her in that moment was the thin electronic rectangle he held in his hand. Because he *felt* it in a deeply visceral way. And the way her eyes hooded, her gaze hazy with anticipation of his next instruction, twisted that feeling, coiling it like a spring within him.

Steady boy, steady, he cautioned himself. No need to overheat before the big finish.

Inhaling a shaky breath through his nose, he said, "I need you flat on your back, Doc. Just like you would be if I were there pressing your beautiful body into the mattress. Feeling the heat of you against my cock, begging me to slide inside."

Her lips pressed into a line, then rolled back into a plump pout as she followed his direction. "Good girl," he said. "Now, keep that hand on your breast for me, sweetheart. And don't forget the way I like to pinch that pert nipple of yours. That perfect amount of pressure between thumb and forefinger that goes directly to your clit and makes you buck against me, greedy and desperate for more."

"Oh my God." V's body shuddered in eager waves as she did what she was told.

"That's my girl," Dave said, sliding his hand up and over the crown of his cock, working the lube over his shaft. Thank God he'd had the forethought to use some before things got going, because he'd either have had to put the phone down (no fucking way) or taken his hand away from his dick (no way in hell).

He watched her profile on his screen. The plush curve of her lips, the delicate line of her jaw, the elegant slope of her neck and the restless movement of her fingers over her nipples. The view ended just south of her breasts. The basest part of him wanted to ask her to adjust the angle, to let him see the rest of her. But he didn't, because the truth was that seeing her face, watching her reactions unfurl across her profile was more intimate and private than anything else.

His hand tightened around his shaft, and he gave himself a brutal downward stroke, unable to contain the groan that ripped from his throat. V turned her face to the phone at the sound of it, blue eyes wide and unfocused as she blinked at him.

"You've got me hard as a fucking rock over here, Doc."

"The only problem with that sentence," she whispered, still teasing her breast with her fingers, "is the part where you're not here."

"I couldn't agree more," he said. "But let's see if we can't get you what you need anyway, Doc. Take your buzzing little friend in your hand and rest it against your clit for me." Her body confirmed she'd done it before he could even ask for the words. He watched the jolt of sensation travel through her in a jerky ripple.

"Good girl," he said, roughly gripping his dick. "Does that feel like my tongue, lapping at your sweet, wet center?"

Her response was a garbled set of sounds.

"What's that, sweetheart?"

Her body arched again, and she said, "It's . . . it's, oh God. It's close, but . . ." V rolled her head to the side and said, "It's still not you."

Pride, lust, and need surged through him and wrenched another groan from somewhere deep in his chest. "Fuck, Doc, when you say stuff like that . . ."

"I thought, *mmm* . . ." She shuddered again and lost her words. With visible effort, she refocused to say, "I thought you wanted me to be honest."

Dave rattled out a quick dry laugh. "I do, sweetheart. So why don't you tell me if you're ready to slide that vibe inside you and pretend I'm there."

"So ready," she whispered, and he watched her body roll in response to the toy's entrance. Her shoulders lifted and her head dropped back on a low groan.

Dave's hand increased its rhythm along his dick at the sight of it, the sound of it, the aching *want* of what was playing out on his phone. He gripped the phone so hard he wondered if the screen might crack.

"Doc," he gritted out. "I need to know if that little toy of yours has something to stimulate your clit, because I'm close . . . so fucking close and I can't come without you."

V nodded.

"All right then, sweetheart, I need you to work that over your clit while that toy is inside you. I know it's not as deep as I can go, but think about all the ways I've touched you, the ways you pull me in and wrap those velvet folds of yours around my dick, holding me in and rippling all around me when you're ready t—"

V's sharp cry interrupted his words, and he watched her body stiffen then quiver and roll as she rode out her orgasm. Dave's hand blurred as he rushed to join her, feeling the tingling tightness at the base of his spine build and build until his own release hurtled free on a shout. Bucking into his hand he came hard as he watched V float back down to earth, knowing if he were there, he could gather those tendrils of pleasure she was feeling then and weave them into another tightly coiled knot of need only to snip the thread holding in her second release to send her free-falling once more into orgasm. A selfish thrill came from the fact that she didn't attempt that without him.

The buzz of the toy went silent, and the only sounds were their commingled but separate heavy breaths. V was the first to speak. "Have you ever considered a career in phone sex?" Her head lolled over to look at him. "Is that even still a thing?"

Dave laughed. "Can't say I'm quite ready to seek employment as a cam boy, but I appreciate the compliment just the same."

Her answering giggle was as lazy as the smile that stretched over her face. He wanted to be there to hold her, to wrap his arms around her and enjoy the soft feeling of her body against his as she came back to herself.

V levered herself back onto her pillows, head resting on her hand as she looked at him. "That was . . ." The breath she exhaled made her long fringe of bangs float up and settle back against her forehead. She batted them from her eyes with an impatient swipe as her blue eyes resumed their regular focus.

Dave nodded. "Yeah, it was."

"I wasn't prepared for . . ." Her hand fluttered through the air, then dropped back to the bed. "*That.*"

Dave tried to keep the preening to a minimum, but it was difficult. "If there's one thing you can trust in, Doc, it's that I'll never leave you anything less than completely satisfied. Even from here, I'll get you there every time."

She blushed and ducked her head and it occurred to him that she'd been so lost in what they were doing, so centered in the moment that V hadn't blushed until now. He liked knowing he could take her outside of her own thoughts and give this to her, even though he wasn't there with her. The idea that enough of him was there to let her give herself over to the experience brought a smile to his lips. It also wedged itself tightly underneath his breastbone where he felt it with each thump of his heart.

Chapter 19

November 8th

*D*ave: *Hey Doc, sorry I missed your call. There was a mix-up with the liquor order and I've been up to my ass in Sour Apple Pucker for the past hour. I've got a break around 8 if you're free.*
V: *There's a joke in there somewhere that Rae would love. Sorry you're in crisis mode. I was trying to catch you while waiting for my to-go order. I'll be around tonight, so just call when you've got a second. Miss you.* *kiss emoji*
Dave: *I'm hoping that was an intentional emoji.*
V: *Maybe.* *wink emoji* *samurai sword emoji*
V: *Dammit.*

November 10th

V: *Hey, sorry, I was with a patient when you called earlier. I'm free now if you have a few minutes.* *clock emoji*

V: *Not intentional, but timely . . . get it?*

An hour later

Dave: *Shit, shit, shit! I fell asleep and didn't hear my phone. I'm so sorry, Doc. Fuck. I'm free until 4, so call when you can, okay? Sorry, babe.* *blowing kiss emoji* *sad face emoji*

Two hours later

V: *Sorry, sorry! I've had two initial intake appointments this morning and both of them ran over. I've got ten minutes to shovel this sandwich into my face before my next appointment. I'll try my best to get to you before 4. Miss you!* *kiss emoji* *dinosaur emoji* *dinosaur emoji*
Dave: *No worries, Doc. Miss you more.*

5:17 p.m.

V: *I'm the worst girlfriend in the world, but in my defense I just finished with my last patient and haven't even started on my charting for them. It has been a day! Wish I could see you, and sorry about the dinosaurs earlier.* *kiss emoji*

8:30 p.m.

Dave: *That's my girlfriend you're talking about, and I don't appreciate you badmouthing her. I'm on break until nine, if you're free.*
V: *Calling now.* *lightning bolt emoji*

November 13th

Dave: *How do you feel about parents?*
V: *Yours, mine, or someone else's?*
Dave: *Probably yours and mine.*
V: *Who are four people with little in common, Alex.*
Dave: *That could be a Daily Double right there. But our shared love of Trebek aside, how would you feel about meeting my parents?*

Dave watched the bubbles dance at the bottom of his screen and then V's picture popped up above her number. It was one he'd taken of her in Atlanta after they'd gotten back to the hotel. Fresh-faced with her blond hair scraped into a messy knot on top of her head, she grinned up at him, wearing one of his favorite hoodies.

"Hey, Doc," he answered, already smiling.

"Hey yourself," she said, her voice a little distant and tinny, signaling she was calling from the car. "And I thought my phone was bad with the bombs it throws into our texts. Random emojis of pool slides have nothing on what you just did."

"Come on now," Dave teased. "What about the solid line of masquerade masks? That was pretty disturbing."

"Nice try, but no. We are not moving away from the fact you just asked me to meet your parents. In a text."

"In my defense, I wanted to make sure the question got out there and as much phone tag as we've played lately, I wasn't taking a chance on calling first." He drummed his fingers on the arm of his couch, suddenly nervous. "But now that it is . . . how about it, Doc? Wanna come make me look good to the family?"

Her answering laugh was bright and warm. "I hardly think you need any help in that department."

He considered the tense conversations he'd had with his dad in the last year and knew she was wrong. His parents supported his decision to leave his first job, but they weren't big fans of his delayed re-entry. His father especially. The longer Dave stayed at Tonic, the harder his dad pushed him to get back into his field. Given that he wanted V to say yes to his invitation, Dave chose to leave that fact out. For now.

"Okay then," he said, "how about you come up and meet them because I want to introduce my girl to my parents. And my pain in the ass siblings."

"Sounds truly delightful,'" V said, and he could hear the smile in her voice. "And when would this momentous occasion take place?"

"Well, as you know, I don't have a weekend off until Thanksgiving."

"Painfully aware," V said. Dave didn't miss the irritation in her tone, nor could he blame her for it. Their schedules had been diametrically opposed to one another since he'd flown back after Halloween. Missed calls had been the norm rather than the exception and they'd survived mainly on texts for the last week. Missing calls with her made a shit week that much worse.

As did the call from the biotech firm letting him know they were going with another candidate. The job wasn't perfect, nor had he been that excited about it after the interview, but the rejection still stung. As did the knowledge that, for now at least, he'd remain stuck at Tonic.

Pushing that thought aside, he said, "I was thinking you could fly up that Wednesday and stay the weekend with me. Meet the family, eat some turkey, watch the Bills. You know, standard Thanksgiving activities."

The line was silent except for the hum of ambient noise, so Dave knew the call hadn't dropped. V just wasn't answering. His palms started to sweat, and he cleared his throat. "Doc, you still there?"

No answer.

"Doc?"

Still nothing. He pushed himself out of the chair, trying not to panic. A quick glance at his phone showed the call was still connected.

"Doc, you're scaring the shit out of me."

"Hey, Dave, Dave! Can you hear me?" V's voice blared out in a volume that could've been heard four counties over.

Dave's pent-up breath whooshed out. "Yeah, I'm here, Doc."

"Sorry, God, I'm so sorry. Somehow I hit the mute button on my steering wheel."

He sank back onto the couch, legs going rubbery and heart thudding in his chest. With a weak laugh, he said, "You had me worried there for a second."

"Sorry!" He could picture her face drawn into an apologetic grimace.

"Don't worry about it. So . . . about Thanksgiving?"

"You didn't hear any of that? Oh gosh, sorry, again!"

"No worries, Doc. What do you say, feel like fighting with my brother and sister over who gets the last slice of pie?"

She laughed. "I don't know about that, but I'd love to join you for Thanksgiving. And meet your family. I *may* not be able to watch the Bills, though. Girl code and all."

"We've got to cure Kez of her unfair viewpoint on my team."

V snorted. "Good luck with that, babe. It doesn't help that Jackson is a Pats fan."

"The traitor," Dave grumbled. Pushing aside thoughts of football rivalries, he said, "Does coming up on Wednesday work for you?"

"Absolutely. I took PTO starting at lunchtime on Tuesday that week, so I'm free as a bird."

"And your family won't mind you missing Thanksgiving?"

She made an unladylike noise and laughed. "I never said that. Caroline will be miffed, but she'll deal with it."

"I don't want to cause problems between you and your mom, Doc," Dave said, even as his heart twisted with the thought she might not come. "If it's going to be an issue we c—"

"Dave," V said, her voice quietly serious. "Stop. All my mother will have to do is tell the caterer to set one less place at the table. She'll give me her trademarked and patented guilt trip about missing it, but she will survive just fine. Avery and Neil will be there to soothe her poor, broken heart with an impeccable wine selection and handcrafted pastry puffs from God knows where."

The corkscrew in his chest stopped tightening. "Okay, if you're sure it's not a problem."

"I'm sure," V said with a laugh. "You're not looking for a way out of inviting me, are you?"

"NO! Not at all," Dave said. "I can't wait for you to meet everyone. They're going to love you."

She laughed again. "No pressure, or anything. You'll have to give me the rundown on everyone, so I'm fully prepared to be the picture-perfect girlfriend."

"You don't need any help with that, Doc."

November 14th

A cold wind sent leaves dancing in a swirl across her driveway as V pulled into her garage after work. It had been a long day, made longer by a traffic snarl on 485. She was ready to unwind with a good glass of red and shovel Chinese food into her face while watching trash television. Juggling her tote bag, water bottle, and takeout bag, she struggled to fit her key into the lock and push open the door to her townhouse. Greeted by the incessant beeping of her alarm, she dropped everything but the food on the table next to the door and typed in her code.

The silence that followed was deafening in the way it permeated the space, emphasizing that no one was there to greet her. She'd left a light on in the kitchen, but otherwise there were no signs of life in the tidy space. Dave's unexpected visit at Halloween seemed like forever ago. A sharp pang of loneliness had her reaching for her phone. He'd be at work already, but she could send a text to let him know she was thinking about him. That she was counting the days until the following Wednesday.

Before she could, her phone rang in her hand. Glancing at it, she grinned and accepted the FaceTime call from Kez.

"Hey, girl," V said, moving into the kitchen and depositing her dinner on the countertop. "What's up?"

Kez's profile came into view, illuminated by light from the screen she was currently staring into. Hazel eyes glanced toward the phone and the visible half of Kez's mouth quirked up into a smile. Her fingers clicked against a keyboard. "Oh, thank God. Your phone is not just an endless voice mail dump. For a minute, I was certain you and I would just trade voice mails for the rest of our lives!" Another sideways glance as she continued typing. "Between this freaking appellate case and—"

"And Jackson keeping you so occupied," V teased.

Kez took it in stride, her smile broadening. "I can't even deny it. The man keeps me . . . busy. Just like I'm sure Dave did while he was here over Halloween."

V blushed as she considered all the ways Dave had occupied her free time the entirely too brief period he'd been in town. Even from the corner of her eye, Kez tracked the way V's cheeks went pink and laughed. "Yeah, I thought so. But anyway, your text from this morning said you had news you needed to discuss. So, let's discuss."

"You could've waited until you left the office to call me. Hang on a second, let me switch this to my tablet." Putting the phone down, V grabbed her tablet from its charger and set it up on the counter. After a few clicks, Kez's face moved to the larger device. "Okay, I'm back."

"As to waiting to call, I couldn't have because Jackson is picking me up to go to some prospective customer's fancy schmancy party. There was no sense in my leaving the office, going all the way home and then turning around to come back downtown." She picked up the phone and let it pan down her body—clothed in a lipstick red jumpsuit. "Hence the reason I'm finishing up an appellate brief while dressed to kill."

"And here I thought cleavage cutouts were all the rage in courtrooms these days."

Kez huffed out a laugh. "Pantsuits are as risqué as it gets, I'm afraid." She finished typing with a flourish. "There, all finished. Now I can focus when you tell me your news."

Bright hazel eyes zeroed in on her as Kez leaned back in her chair and clasped her hands in her lap. "I'm all ears."

V's phone signaled an incoming call, the caller ID making her smile. "Hold that thought, Counselor."

Another click to merge calls added Rae. She was sitting in front of a wall that looked to be made of hand-hewn logs. Her long dark hair was stick straight and fell in an endless sheet over her shoulders.

"Evening, Doc. Didn't expect you'd have our legal counsel on with you. Hey, Kez, I see Jackson finally let you up for air." Rae's voice drawled out as she leaned back into the cushion behind her.

Kez didn't take the bait, asking instead, "Spending Thanksgiving with Paul Bunyan, are we?"

Rae wrinkled her nose. "I'm in Vermont on a client planning retreat, remember?" Rae flipped the screen of her phone to show them the lobby of a rustic lodge.

"That explains the decor, but not the outfit. What are you wearing?" Kez said, once Rae appeared on camera again.

"What, this?" Rae angled her phone to give them a better look at her fitted black turtleneck and matte black leopard leggings tucked into fur-lined boots. "This is my après ski outfit."

Kez arched a brow. "Doesn't après ski imply there was a before part where you skied?"

Rae waved a hand in the air. "You lawyers and your semantics. Some of the people I'm here with went skiing, so technically the 'après' still applies."

Kez laughed. "You never said the retreat was in Vermont. Here I was picturing you trapped in some hotel conference room downtown and instead you're living it up in the land where the men are men, and the sheep are nervous."

Rae's lips twitched into a self-satisfied grin. "I can confirm there are some manly options up here. A little more flannel than my normal taste, but definitely some possibilities." She looked at V. "But that's not the point. Reception up here in the boonies isn't the greatest, so let's cut to the heart of it. The group chat says you have news, Doc."

The three of them had a running group chat, the name of which changed with the seasons, girls' trips and birthdays. Right now, it was Pumpkin Spice and Everything Nice (?). Rae had added the question mark.

V pulled the cork from a bottle of wine.

"Must be some news, Doc," Kez said with a laugh.

Pouring herself a glass, V took it, the tablet, and her food to the bar separating her kitchen and living room. "I think it's safe to say that when your boyfriend invites you home for the Thanksgiving holiday, that's pretty big news."

Kez shot forward in her seat, her chair creaking in protest. "What?"

V nodded. "Granted, it's not happening quite as quickly as it did for you."

Kez laughed. "And thank goodness for that." Kez had unexpectedly met Jackson's grandmother within forty-eight hours of meeting him. "When did all this happen?"

V laughed. "He asked me yesterday, hence my text to you two about having big news."

"Wow," Kez said. "Although I'm not surprised. That man is a complete goner for you, Doc."

"Yeah," Rae said. "It's frankly disgusting how loved up the two of you are right now."

"It's so sweet how happy you are for us," Kez replied. "Really heart-warming stuff, Rae."

Rae stuck out her tongue. "Sue me, Counselor. My two best friends are abandoning me in Sexy Singlelandia to move to the much more boring world of Cozy Coupledom. I have every right to complain." Her smile took the spice out of her words and made it clear she was happy for both Kez and V.

"Anyway," Kez went on. "Give us the details. When are you leaving, who are you meeting and does this mean Dave will get the honor of meeting Queen Caroline and her loyal manservant Duvall any time soon?"

V laughed, but the last part of Kez's question was something V'd been considering for the last twenty-four hours. Was she ready for Dave to meet her family? Her mother had been . . . better than expected during their lunch earlier in the month. It wasn't the complete rejection V'd worried about, so it left her cautiously hopeful about the day Dave would meet her family. A day that seemed to be on the horizon, given he'd asked her to come home with him for Thanksgiving.

"I leave a week from tomorrow," V said. "And, according to Dave, I'm meeting his entire immediate family."

"Which consists of whom?" Kez asked, ever the lawyer.

"His mom and dad, of course, and his brother and sister and their spouses and kids. There may be other family, but he hasn't specified."

"And how do we feel about that?" Rae asked.

"I feel . . . good about it," V said. "Like it's the next natural step. But also like it's sort of soon? I mean, we've known each other barely two months, you know?" She blinked at her two friends. "Is it too soon for me to meet his parents?"

"Don't answer that," Kez said to Rae. To V, she said, "I have no real frame of reference, as you know. I met Nana while astride her grandson, so . . . yeah, there's that. But meeting her sped up my introduction to the rest of the family, so it's hard for me to say what too soon would be."

"I would say this." Rae leaned forward, her green eyes sincere. "First, I like Dave. He seems like good people, so I'm sure his family is too. Second, when a man invites you all the way into his life and doesn't hold anything back, that's when you know you've got a shot at something real with them. Is it early for you to meet his folks?" One shoulder lifted in a slight shrug. "Maybe. But that's not what we should be focusing on. The fact that he *wants* you to meet them is the important thing. He wants you to meet his family because he wants you to be a part of his life. A real participant in every part of it, with holidays and family and all the trimmings. And, all joking aside, if it feels like the next natural step to you as well, then I think you two crazy kids have a real chance of making this work."

V and Kez said nothing, just stared at the screen. "What?" Rae asked.

V was the first one to speak. "That was . . . beautifully unexpected, Rae."

Rae waved off her words. "Yeah, yeah, well, you seemed like you needed me to bring you back to the real point, so I did."

"Mm-hmm," Kez said. "You sure that's all it was, Rae? Because to me it sounded like you wer—"

"Listen, I hate to cut this short," Rae said. "But I need to get changed for dinner with my clients, so congratulations, Doc. Make sure and pack that gray mock neck sweater and those dark wash Paige jeans for your official meet cute with the family. It says casually approachable, yet richly glamorous all at the same time. Talk soon, ladies."

Her screen went black, and V and Kez looked at each other for a second before laughing.

"Think she'll ever come clean about whatever happened to her?" V asked.

"I'm more interested in learning who happened to her and whether he's still alive and limping or if his body will never be found," Kez said. "I wish she'd tell us *something* about it."

"Yeah, me too," V said. "Maybe one day she'll open up about it."

"I'm pretty sure the only way that happens is if her other choice is to completely disappear," Kez said with a shake of her head. "She'd much rather get over whatever happened by getting under someone else. God help the unsuspecting men of Vermont. She'll have at least one of them tied up with his own flannel by the end of the evening, I'm sure."

V stabbed at the remnants of her now lukewarm dinner. "What does it say about me that the thought of that no longer repulses me as it once did?"

Kez laughed, flipping her long red hair back over her shoulder. "It says to *me* that it's been too long since you saw Dave at Halloween."

"Thirteen days and"—V checked her watch—"five hours give or take."

"But who's counting, right?" Kez said, her smile sympathetic. "I've done long-distance, remember? At least you're participating in that particular torture for a guy who's worth it."

"Who's worth what?" A distinctly male voice asked, drawing Kez's eyes from the screen over to her left and, V knew, her office door.

If she hadn't recognized Jackson's voice, V still would've known it was him from the change in Kez's body language. Everything about her softened, from her posture to her smile. Even her voice took on a silkier tone when she greeted him.

"Hey, there, handsome. You clean up nice," Kez said.

Jackson appeared in V's frame of view then, as he leaned down to kiss Kez, bracing himself on the arms of her desk chair. "You're not too shabby, either, Gorgeous." His blue eyes swung to the phone, and he smiled at V. "Hey, Doc." He looked back to Kez. "Am I interrupting?"

Before Kez could answer, V jumped in. "No, you're fine. Kez was just commiserating with me over long-distance love affairs."

"Ah, I see. I can give you two a minute if—"

"No, no," V said. "You two go enjoy your dinner. I'm fine."

"You sure, V?" Kez asked, head tilted questioningly. She looked like an inquisitive Irish Setter.

"Yes, of course!" V assured her. "Go! Eat, drink, be merry!"

Kez hesitated, but agreed. "Okay. I'll call you tomorrow, though. We can discuss the rest of what you need to pack to meet the family and make them fall for you every bit as hard as Dave has."

"I'll hold you to it," V replied. "Y'all have fun!" Her tablet went dark, and silence returned to her townhouse.

Once her plate was scraped, rinsed, and in the dishwasher, V took her wine to the living room and settled into the corner of her sectional with a blanket. With reality stars shaking their salads in the background, V thought about what Rae had said. That she and Dave had a real shot at making this thing between them work.

She wanted Rae to be right, because Dave was well on his way to being someone she couldn't imagine life without. She didn't like the prospect of living without the fizzy feeling she had when she was with him, or when she saw his name pop up on her phone screen. Or the way a glance from him or the slightest graze of his hand on her arm sent tingles dancing through her veins. When he'd asked her to meet his family, that same tingle went racing through her and wrapped itself around her heart.

It helped to soothe her worry over each missed call, or delayed text exchange they'd had lately. With their competing schedules, communication was a precious commodity in their relationship. One that had become scarce in the last week or so. She'd also sensed a growing tension in him. It wasn't directed *at* her, but she could see it in the drawn lines of his face when they talked in the mornings and hear the exhaustion in his voice.

Given that she wasn't an idiot, V knew it had something to do with Tonic. More specifically with Ryker. When Dave told her his penance for flying to see her on Halloween was essentially indentured servitude through Thanksgiving, V wanted to say something. To question once more why he stayed at a job that was obviously making him miserable. To encourage him to look into other options. To use the degree she knew he'd worked hard to obtain. To take a chance on getting back into the job market. The *real* job market and stop hiding from life behind the bar at Tonic. Okay, so that last one was a little harsh and she wouldn't have said it out loud, but in the cozy nook of her couch after a great glass of red, she could admit to herself that at least some small part of her brain—the analytical, goal-oriented portion that had pushed her to continually reach for success her entire life—thought that's what he was doing. She'd said nothing, obviously, because she'd seen his reaction the last time she brought it up.

His eyes had shuttered, no longer that warm, gooey brownie color, but harder and darker like a brick of baking chocolate. The lines of his body, usually so relaxed and loose, stiffened like someone stuck a key in his back and wound it as tight as it would go. His verbal response wasn't much better than his physical one, since it was a dodge, pure and simple. A dodge and misdirection into not wasting time talking about it when there were better, sexier things to do. Only, she didn't view it as a waste of time. It was important.

She again thought about what Rae said earlier. *When a man invites you all the way into his life and doesn't hold anything back.* Had Dave truly done that? There was a sensation in the back of her mind, like an itch she couldn't quite reach, that questioned whether he had. Or if the truth were that he was holding back some part of himself for reasons she couldn't understand.

Maybe there would be time next week for the two of them to sit down and talk—really talk without his dodging around it. After all, they were spending five straight days together. Surely there would be an opening. They could figure this out. They would figure this out.

She picked up her phone.

V: Just thinking about you, babe. Miss you and can't wait for Wednesday.

Chapter 20

November 22nd

Then I had to explain to him *again* that surgery was, without a doubt, his only option."

"I see," V said, tucking her headphones into the outside pocket of her purse. Headphones that had done nothing to dissuade her seatmate from talking to her the entire flight. Neither had her polite, yet still monosyllabic responses to everything he'd said. The man had kept up a steady stream of one-sided conversation since before takeoff. V had never been so glad for a plane to touch down on a tarmac as she was in that moment. Freedom—and Dave—were minutes away, and she couldn't get there fast enough.

"Sometimes I wonder why I do this," he said, giving a rueful shake of his head. It made the tethers securing his sunglasses shift against his lemon-yellow polo shirt. "But if I didn't, then who would?"

Literally anyone else who went to med school and wanted to be an ortho-pedic surgeon, V thought. Out loud, she said, "Who indeed?"

"It's all about the sacrifices we make for our patients." He checked the Rolex on his tanned wrist and reached for his carry-on tucked beneath the seat in front of him, its bold "LV" logo pattern impossible to miss.

"Yes," she said. "I can tell you've sacrificed so much by being in the healthcare field."

Oblivious to the cut, he nodded. "Right? I mean, I'm sure you do the same for all your little guys."

Early on, before she knew this guy was a tool of the highest order, V made the mistake of answering his question about what she did for a living. Her simple answer of "pediatrics" with no further details had been the only opening he needed.

"Mm-hmm," V murmured. *How long does it take to park a freaking plane?*

At long last, she saw the crew open the cabin door and the passengers ahead of them gather their belongings and file off the plane. *Thank God.*

Her seatmate continued chatting away, the buzz of his words falling into the background as she hefted her carry-on and headed down the aisle. He kept pace with her on the jet bridge and as they walked into the airport. She considered ducking into the ladies' room, but didn't feel like juggling her purse and carry-on in the tiny stall. So, she trudged onward with his incessant monologue of his trials and tribulations as an orthopedic surgeon.

Finally, the exit came into view ahead of them and V quickened her pace.

"So, what do you think?"

Belatedly, she realized he'd had paused long enough to receive an answer to something he'd asked her.

V turned to look at him. "I'm sorry, I must have missed your question."

He smiled, big square teeth gleaming in the florescent lighting of the terminal. "I asked if you wanted to meet up for a drink later."

Unsurprisingly, he'd missed, or more likely ignored, her response to what brought her to Rochester.

"Oh, well, that's very kind of you, but I—"

The rest of her words were cut off when strong arms encircled her waist, and she was lifted into the air. Those arms held her aloft for a moment, before pulling her flush against a firm chest. Her hands landed on broad shoulders, and she looked into dark brown eyes that held a hint of mischief.

"Hey, Doc," Dave said and kissed her. Nothing more than a brush of his lips over hers, but she felt it all the way to her toes. He glanced behind her, then shifted his hold, looping one forearm underneath her butt and hitching her tighter against him. The move made her hands slip from his shoulders to rest against his chest.

"Did you need something, man?" Dave asked Dr. Clueless who was standing there staring.

He frowned and shuffled backward in his designer loafers. "No, I . . . no, thank you."

As he hustled away, V felt Dave's chest vibrate with laughter before his soft chuckle. "Making new friends?"

She pulled her lips between her teeth to suppress her own laughter. "Not exactly." Gesturing to the ground, she said, "Wanna put me down now, Tarzan?"

His hand squeezed her thigh. "Not particularly," he said, but did lower her to her feet. Keeping his arm around her shoulders, he took the handle of her suitcase into his free hand.

"Ready to go?"

V nodded. "You didn't have to go quite so caveman, you know?"

Dave grinned down at her as they walked toward the exit. "That was me being nice, Doc. Caveman would've been a whole other level."

V's educated, well-mannered brain knew she shouldn't find that hot. Shouldn't be excited by the prospect of her boyfriend going all gladiator on a random guy in an airport—albeit one who deserved it. Nor should her heart have raced at the blatant way Dave laid claim to her. And yet . . . there was no denying the distinct twinge in her lady parts all of that provoked. While the more evolved spaces in her brain might be offended as hell about it, certain others were completely on board and more than a little interested in experiencing true caveman level.

Pushing those thoughts far, *far* out of her head, she said, "Be that as it may, I had the situation well in hand."

Dave opened her car door for her, then stowed her luggage before getting behind the wheel. He put the key in the ignition but didn't start the car. Instead, he leaned over, cupped her jaw in his hand, and kissed her. This was no brush of lips or chaste peck. It was lush and luxurious. Warm, full lips covered her mouth, his tongue teasing at the seam of her lips until they parted on a sigh. His fingers curled around the nape of her neck and tilted her head back as he deepened the kiss. Teasing and tasting her until she was clutching at his shirtfront and dragging him closer.

On a ragged breath, they broke apart and sagged back into their seats, his hand still at her neck, thumb teasing the pulse at her throat. "I've missed you, Doc."

V managed a shaky inhale and swiped a thumb over the lost cause of her lip gloss. "I can see that." With a hand on his thigh, she added, "I've missed you too."

Dave shifted in his seat and turned the key in the ignition. Backing out of the space, he said, "I don't think there's any situation you can't handle. You're one of the most amazingly capable women I've ever met. The fact that you can drive a stick shift alone is enough to make me weak in the knees."

V laughed, but Dave wasn't finished.

"That doesn't mean, however, there will *ever* be a time when I sit on the sidelines and let you fend off some jackass. Can you? I have no doubt. Will I let there be a time when you have to? Absolutely fucking not. That's a fact you need to wrap that big brain of yours around, Doc. Because it's not going to change."

Again, she shouldn't be turned on. Well, that is, she should be. But only from the soul-searing kiss they'd just shared. Not because he'd just said there were things he wasn't going to "let" her deal with. She was a grown woman. A grown, successful woman who handled her own problems, including pushy, irritating morons who thought they were entitled to her time and attention.

It should've made her mad, furious even that he thought he could draw that sort of line in the sand and say this is how it's going to be, and she had to deal with it. And yet . . . mad did not describe at all what his words made her feel. If anything, his words had somehow formed a sort of telegraph line with her ovaries that were responding "Take me NOW!" in morse code.

"Is that right?"

Dave nodded, his hand moving from the steering wheel to rest on her thigh. "It is, I'm afraid. Normally, I have no problem with you taking the lead on things. As I said, you're scarily proficient in almost every aspect of life. At least that I've experienced with you. This has nothing to do with competence and everything to do with the way I feel about you, Doc. You're precious to me and, like it or not, I'm going to protect you whenever I can."

How was she supposed to argue with that? Why would she even want to? Even the most take charge, woman hear me roar part of her was swooning with little hearts in her eyes and doodling Mrs. Dave Richardson on a notebook margin.

"Well, I guess *maybe* when you put it like that . . ." V put her hand over his and gave it a little pat. "I could learn to get used to it."

Dave laughed and his fingers pressed into her thigh. "What more could I ask for?"

What more, indeed?

When he pulled the car into the supermarket parking lot, V lowered her sunglasses and peered out the window. "Wait a second. What happened to that protective streak you mentioned?"

Confused, Dave hurried to put the car into park and looked at her with concern. "What?"

V gestured to the grocery store they'd pulled in front of. "If you're as interested in protecting my well-being as you claim to be, why in the world are you taking me to a grocery store the Wednesday before Thanksgiving? It's going to be a total bloodbath in there!"

He laughed, surprised by her dramatics. "It won't be that bad."

V snorted and pushed her sunglasses back in place. "I don't know what rock you've been living under for the past few decades, but I can assure you it will be."

"C'mon, Doc. I swear, it'll be quick. We just need to grab some . . ." Dave opened the notes app on his phone and scrolled to the list his mother had given him the night before. "Parsley, thyme, and fennel." He glanced up at V. "You know what fennel is, right?"

"Yes," she said, a smile hinting at the corners of her mouth. "I know what fennel is."

"Awesome. We need to grab that stuff, drop it off at my mom's and the—"

"Whoa, whoa, whoa." V held up a hand and angled herself back against the passenger side door. "What did you just say?"

Perplexed, Dave blinked. "Uh, that we need to get the three things fr—"

"Not that," V interrupted. "The second part."

"Dropping them off at my mom's?"

V nodded so hard Dave feared for the integrity of her spine. "Yeah, that one."

"What about it?"

She crossed her arms and huffed, which made her blond bangs take their usual flight up then sift back down around her eyebrows. Impatiently, she batted at them and waved a hand up and down her torso. "Do you actually think I'm going to meet your mama wearing my plane outfit?"

Plane outfit? This is some sort of trick question, Dave thought. *Danger, danger, danger!* Slowly, he ran his eyes over V's outfit. Black leggings with some sort of pattern on them, black long-sleeve thermal and a puffy vest thing. *Shoes, dumbass. You know the shoes are her favorite.* His eyes dropped to the floorboard. Those knitted black boots that every woman he knew seemed to have a pair of. She looked . . . soft and comfortable. What was he missing?

"Uh . . ." Dave hedged while trying to formulate the correct response to a question he didn't understand.

"That question was rhetorical," V said, and Dave couldn't stop the flood of relief. "The answer is NO I am not going to meet your mother for the first time wearing this!" She plucked at her leggings as if they should be torn off and burned.

"But you look great," Dave said, still certain he'd missed something important.

His feeling was confirmed when V closed her eyes and leaned her head back to blow out a long, slow breath. When she looked back at him, her blue eyes were filled with pity. As though he were the slowest kid in the class who'd just been called to the front to solve for X.

"Sweetheart," she said, her voice low and kind. "I cannot meet your mother until I've, at a minimum, changed my clothes and run a brush through this." She tugged at her long blond hair. "Ideally, I'd have time to shower, redo my makeup *and* hair, debate between the three outfits I brought to wear when I meet her and have a glass of wine to settle my nerves."

"Nerves?" Dave cocked his head in confusion. "What are you nervous about? My mom's going to love you."

V made a strangled half-laugh, half-choking sound. "Your golden retriever attitude is one of the best things about you."

"Golden retriever?" If he'd been confused before, now he was hopelessly lost.

"Never met a stranger, always confidently positive of the warm reception you'll receive. It's very endearing. But in this situation, it's entirely unhelpful. I'm meeting *your mother*. As in the woman who birthed you, raised you, and loves you above and beyond anything else. You are her baby boy, and I am a woman with whom you are, at least in her mind, contemplating having sex with. This is not an even ground sort of dynamic. I need to make the absolute *best* first impression possible."

"And you can't do that wearing your plane outfit?" Dave was amazed at the thoughts that went through women's heads sometimes. Both the topics and the depths.

V shook her head. "No. I can do that wearing one of the three outfits I brought specifically for that purpose."

"I understand," Dave said, even though he absolutely did not. "But . . . circling back to the fennel," he said. "Is that something we can fit into this scenario, or . . ."

"Yes, we can get the parsley, thyme, and fennel. Then we can go by your apartment so I can at least change and brush my hair. What are the herbs for?"

Dave looked blankly at her. "Dinner?"

V bit her lower lip and shook her head. "Yes, but what dish? Does she need them tonight to make something, or will they be used to make something tomorrow?"

"Oh . . . uh, I have no idea."

"Give her a call and check, so I have a timetable to work with."

"Right, okay," Dave said and swiped over to his mother's number.

She answered on the first ring, her voice echoing through the car's speakers. "Have you picked her up yet? Was her flight delayed?"

Dave saw V bite back a laugh. "Hi, Mom," he said. "No, her flight wasn't delayed and yes, I've picked her up."

"Oh, so she's in the car with you?"

"No, I shoved her in the trunk with her luggage."

"David Robert Richardson, I've got two pies in the oven, bread dough rising, and two of your nephews using the dining room for soccer practice. Do not test me right now."

"Hi, Mrs. Richardson," V said, the laugh she'd tried to hold in bubbling free. "I'm safely tucked into the passenger seat, not the trunk."

"Oh!" Dave's mom cried, and he could envision her hand touching her cheek and leaving behind a dusting of flour. "Oh," she said again.

"Hello, dear. It's so nice to meet you. Well, not meet you, but hear your voice. And please, call me Sylvia."

"Nice to hear your voice, too, Sylvia," V said. "We're at the grocery store now an—"

"The grocery store? Whatever for?"

"To get the parsley, thyme, and fennel," Dave said.

"Why would you not have gotten that before going to the airport?" Sylvia asked. "There's no reason for you to drag poor Vivian through the grocery store after she's been on a plane all day. Especially not the Wednesday before Thanksgiving!"

V shot him an "I told you so" look with a smug grin.

"Right, well, that seems to be the general consensus, so that's my bad. *Anyway,* I wanted to see whether you needed this stuff like right now, or if we could bring it later?"

"I only need it for the spare dressing I'm making in the morning, so later is fine."

V mouthed, "Spare dressing?"

Dave shrugged, as clueless as to why one would need spare dressing at Thanksgiving as he was about plane outfits, but not eager to delve into either topic. "Okay, we'll bring it later tonight."

"That's fine, honey," Sylvia said. "Your brother is coming by around seven and your sister should already be here by the time he arrives. Maybe you two could come around then and Vivian could meet everyone."

Dave looked to V, who nodded her assent. "Sure, sounds great, Mom. We'll try to be there a little after seven."

He hung up and glanced at V. "It's a bad sign you and my mom are already somewhat on the same page, isn't it?"

"Only if you plan to remain her favorite," V teased. "Now, let's go grab that fennel."

Forty-five minutes later, Dave slumped against the driver's side headrest while V laughed at him from the passenger seat.

"I did try to warn you."

His head lolled to look at her. "Gloating is one of the few things that doesn't look good on you, Doc."

She grinned unrepentantly. "Gives you a whole new respect for your mom putting together Thanksgiving dinner every year, doesn't it?"

"I'll say." He scrubbed a hand over his face. "I honestly thought those two ladies were going to murder each other over King's Hawaiian rolls."

"What about the woman who ran over that man's foot with her buggy?"

"She never even looked back! Even when he knocked over that entire endcap display of Pepperidge Farm stuffing mix."

"Again," V said, "I tried to warn you."

"No warning can prepare for that," Dave said. "It was like a war zone in there, only fewer rules of engagement."

"Only one rule. Every mom for herself." V laughed.

"I need to buy my mom like twenty years' worth of flowers for enduring that every year."

"Well, the fennel is a nice start," V said.

Dave glanced at the bag on V's lap. "What is it even for?"

"Didn't you hear? The 'spare dressing.'"

It was his turn to laugh. "I swear, my mom's not as weird as that comment made her sound. Nor are we expecting, to my knowledge, random drop-in dinner guests that would require spare dressing."

"I think it's sweet she wants to be prepared for the unexpected hungry masses."

"Your mom doesn't make spare side dishes on the offhand chance she runs out of food?"

V's laugh lost some of its luster. "My mom doesn't make side dishes period. Any and all holiday meals are outsourced. Same goes for birthday cakes, school bake sales, and any other culinary requirements."

The mood in the car dimmed by several watts. V's mom was a sensitive subject, Dave knew that much. They hadn't talked a lot about her, but what V had mentioned made it clear their relationship was complicated at best.

Dave waded in carefully, ready to pull back at the slightest inclination he was pushing too hard. "Well, not everyone finds as much happiness in feeding other people as my mom does."

V's eyes were focused on her lap where she was twisting her fingers together. She sighed and looked back at him. "I'm looking forward to meeting your family. Your mom seems great."

Past holiday meals tumbled haphazardly through Dave's mind, different vignettes of his family doling out teasing insults and heartfelt compliments with equal fervor. This year, he hoped, would be no different. And it wouldn't be. Unless his dad tried to corner him about work. He hadn't told his parents about sending out résumés for much the same reason he hadn't told V. They'd never come right out and said they were disappointed in him, but in the last year his dad's gentle nudges to get him back in the job market had morphed into more determined prodding. It let Dave know his parents were starting to worry.

And, at this point, given the minimum interest garnered by the latest batch of résumés he'd sent out on Monday, so was Dave. He told himself it was because of the holiday weekend. That a lot of folks weren't in the office the week of Thanksgiving and there would be renewed interest in the following weeks. But it was hard to keep an optimistic viewpoint when the last month had been nothing but rejections.

Dave cleared his throat, determined not to let his anxiety and dwindling optimism dampen his week with V. Which meant he needed to get her smile back to its regular wattage. He covered her hands with his, loosening the knot of her fingers. "My mom's a character, as you heard. And I may be her baby boy, but don't worry, she gives me my equal ration of shit too."

"Well, I would hope so," V said, lacing her fingers with his. "Can't have you getting too full of yourself."

"No chance of that around my family, trust me," Dave assured her. He started the car. "Now, let's get you over to my place so you can change out of that outfit and into something suitable to meet my mother."

Chapter 21

The delectable scent of Italian spices teased V's nostrils the moment they stepped through the back door of the Richardsons' house and into the kitchen. Instantly, her mouth began to water. An older woman with short blond hair who V assumed was Dave's mother stirred a steaming pot on the stove. Without turning around, she called to the two boys playing with matchbox cars under the kitchen table.

"River and Ryder, don't you dare leave one of those cars out where it gets stepped on. This is going to be the year no one has to go to the hospital on a holiday."

"Should I be concerned?" V asked Dave out of the corner of her mouth.

He shook his head, hand at the small of her back to lead her across the kitchen. "Nah, none of the incidents have been food related or required more than a few stitches. You'll be fine."

In a slightly louder voice, he said, "Hey, Mom. We're here, and we brought fennel!" He held up the grocery bag like a triumphant warrior returning home with his plunder.

Sylvia looked up from her task, a smile brightening her face and putting crinkles in the corners of her blue eyes. Setting the spoon in its rest on the counter, she wiped her hands on the dish towel at her shoulder. "Dave, sweetheart!" She held out her hands and came toward them. "I'm so glad you're here."

Sylvia hugged Dave and then turned to V. "And you must be Vivian."

"Yes, ma'am," V said and extended her hand. "It's so nice to *oof!*" Sylvia brushed past V's outstretched hand and pulled her close. His mother hugged with the power of a woman twice her size, enveloping V in a rib-cracking embrace that squeezed the breath from her lungs.

"I'm just so, *so* happy you're here!" Sylvia said, giving V one last intense squeeze. "Dave told us so much about you that I feel like I already know you, but to have you here in the flesh . . . I'm just so happy!"

"Calm down, Mom," Dave cautioned, peering into the pot on the stove and reaching for the spoon. "You sound like you didn't think V was real or something."

She popped him with dish towel then batted him away from the pot. "Get your hands out of that."

A pretty blond woman appeared in the opposite doorway, holding a bottle of wine in one hand and a decanter in the other. "Mom, is this the one you wanted to use for tomorrow?" Her voice drifted off when she spotted Dave and V, a grin stretching across her face.

"The prodigal brother returns," she said. "And with a date."

"My not coming by here every day like you do doesn't make me a prodigal," Dave retorted, looping an arm around V's waist.

"I can't help if I'm the favorite child," she fired back, coming farther into the room and setting her bounty down on the kitchen table. She held out a hand. "Unlike my mother, I won't make you lose a rib at first meeting. I'm Erika, Dave's sister."

V laughed and shook her hand. "Nice to meet you. Please, call me V."

"V it is then," she said, as River and Ryder careened into her on both sides. "And these are my feral children, River and Ryder." She touched each boy's head in turn. "Boys, can you say hello to your Uncle Dave and Miss V?"

Shyly, they peeked up at V from halfway behind their mother. V waved at them. "Nice to meet you, boys."

They buried their faces against their mother's thighs, and she shook her head. "Enjoy the shyness while it lasts. Soon they'll want you to help them build a pillow fort or join them to watch some toy video on YouTube."

"Don't fall for that one," said the tall dark headed man who joined them in the kitchen while holding a baby in the crook of his arm. "I did that once and before I knew it I'd watched three uninterrupted hours of a guy rehabbing old tin toys. It's a black hole you do not want to go down." He put out the hand not holding the baby. "I'm Tim, Dave's older, more handsome brother."

V clasped his hand. "Nice to meet you. I'm V." She looked at the baby who was watching her with wide blue eyes and sucking on its fist. "And who is this?"

"This is Harrison," Tim said. "The one currently holding mine and my wife's evenings hostage."

An oven timer dinged, and Sylvia shooed them all out of the way so she could pull out a thing of cornbread. At that point, V's salivary glands kicked into overdrive. It smelled divine in the small kitchen.

The back door opened, and she turned to see an older version of Dave step inside with a small black dog on a leash. His sandy blond hair was going gray at the temples, and he had laugh lines around smiling eyes. He hung his jacket on the hook next to the door and grinned. "Looks like a full house tonight."

When he unclipped the leash from the dog, it pranced over to stand expectantly next to Sylvia. She gazed lovingly down at the dog. "Were you a good girl for Daddy?" One single, sharp bark made the dog's beard quiver and its little nub tail wagged. "But you love Mommy the most, don't you?" Another sharp bark was rewarded with a treat from the jar by the stove.

"This is Bianka, my mother's favorite child," Dave said.

"Nice to meet you, Bianka," V replied, leaning down to let the dog sniff her fingers. V must have passed, because Bianka accepted a pat on the head and then made her way under the table to inspect the matchbox car situation.

"Hi, Dad," Dave said, leaving V's side to give his father a hug.

After a few hearty slaps on the back, he stepped back and looked at V over Dave's shoulder. "This must be the lovely Vivian I've heard so much about."

Dave turned and grinned, motioning for her to join them. She did, taking his father's hand in hers. "Nice to meet you, sir."

Dave's father grinned at him. "Pretty and polite. Nice work, son." To V he said, "Abe Richardson, nice to meet you too."

Releasing her hand, he crossed to kiss his wife, eliciting teasing groans from their three children. "Pipe down, you three," Abe said, drawing his wife against his side. "Or else you can all help me clean out the gutters this weekend."

That was met with another chorus of grumbles that made V laugh.

Abe winked at her. "I'll spare you this time, Vivian, seeing as how it's your first visit. But bear in mind, next time you'll be family."

The idea of becoming a part of this boisterous group appealed to V more than she cared to admit out loud. She liked the thought of being one of them, of being a part of their family teasing, of belonging here because she and Dave belonged to each other. Her heart started to gallop a little at the realization that there was a word for how she felt about Dave. Four insignificant letters came together to form a word powerful enough to change everything. Because once you plucked those letters from your mind and organized them into that word, life was different. At least, it would be if she voiced that word to Dave.

She swallowed nervously at the thought of telling him. Of saying it out loud and watching him hear it. Of what his face would look like when she said it. Whether his eyes would turn that warm honeyed brown and crinkle at the corners because his smile was so big. Of hearing him say it back just before he kissed her.

Dave slung an arm around V, startling her from her thoughts. "I'll tell you like I told Mom," he said to Abe. "Please try not to scare her off within the first fifteen minutes."

V laughed and slipped her arm around Dave's waist. "I don't scare that easily," she assured Abe. "And if it means I get the recipe to whatever is in that pot, I'll clean any gutter you've got."

Abe grinned and nodded. "A woman after my own heart."

He turned back to say something to Sylvia and Dave leaned down to whisper in V's ear. "I told you they'd love you."

And I love you, V thought as he kissed the top of her head. *I just need to find a way to tell you.*

Dave listened to the water running in the bathroom as he unbuttoned his shirt. They'd gotten home not long ago, both exhausted in a good way after an evening with his raucous family. When V suggested making it an early night, he hadn't complained.

His eyes trailed over the various indicators of V scattered around his bedroom. Her suitcase tucked neatly into a corner, her phone charging next to his bed, a pair of heels on the floor by his sneakers. It did something to him to see her things in his space. Unlocked a place in his heart and released feelings he'd known were there, but whose full weight he had yet to experience. Feelings related to having her things in his house on a permanent basis. Or rather *their* things commingled together in *their* house. His hands paused mid-button as he considered that thought and all the implications of it.

The bathroom door opened, and the woman in question appeared in the doorway. She leaned against the jamb, shooting him a sly grin.

"Hi," she said, hands behind her back. She'd changed into a white robe covered in bright flowers. Its hem skimmed her knees and when she crossed one leg over the other, it parted to a point halfway up her thigh. The sight of that smooth, supple skin made his throat go dry.

Which meant his answering "Hey" came out low and gravelly.

When she joined him at the foot of the bed, he got a better look at her robe. And the flowers printed on it.

"Are those . . ."

V dug her toe into the carpet. The movement provided flashing glimpses of her upper thigh that made his fingers twitch with the desire to touch her. She toyed with the tie of her robe and smiled up at him. "Peonies. I have a certain fondness for them that started this past September."

Something warm and soft unfurled in Dave's chest. "So do I," he said, watching a blush start at the neckline of her robe and creep up to turn her cheeks a charming pink. He recognized that blush as the one that stole over her skin whenever her thoughts turned racy.

She cleared her throat. "*Anyway*, I know we said we were turning in early, but I thought maybe you might want to . . ." Her finger wrapped and unwrapped the tie of her robe as she looked at him from beneath the sweep of her lashes. "That is, I thought maybe we could . . ."

He took her chin in his hand and tilted her face upward, compelling her to look directly at him. With a grin, he traced the line of her lower lip with his thumb. "What is it you're asking, Doc?"

She tucked a lock of hair behind one ear and bit her lip. "You *know* what I'm asking."

"Maybe so, but I love hearing you say it," Dave said, already picturing what could be under that robe. He slid his other hand around her waist and pulled her close. "Tell me what you want."

Her hands came to his chest, fingers tracing the ribbed cotton of his undershirt. The featherlight touch teased up to his shoulders, where she followed the lines of his deltoids and over his traps. "I've always loved these little dips right here," she said, "where your deltoids meet your trapezius muscles."

"Oh yeah? Why is that?"

V smiled. "It's silly."

"Since it's my muscle group you're mapping, I'll be the judge of that." He stroked her cheek. "Tell me."

Her palms came to rest just above his collarbone. She spread her fingers wide, curling them over his traps so that her pinky and pointer fingers fit into each of the notches she'd pointed out. "Because it's like they were made just for me."

"A perfect fit," Dave said, his hand curving around her jaw.

"That's my view," V said.

I love you, he thought with bone cracking certainty. The feeling was so sharp, so intense, it seemed to stamp the words onto his brain. He opened his mouth to say them. To tell her he was helplessly and completely in love with her. That he had all these thoughts about the future and their stuff being in the same house and her becoming part of his family.

Before he could say anything, V rose to her tiptoes to nibble along his jawline. "You want me to tell you what I want?" she asked, lips just below his ear, "I want to know what you think about the fact I'm wearing just a robe and nothing else."

That fashion report was breaking news to his dick. "Just a robe, huh?" he asked, one hand winding the tie of the item in question around his finger. "So, if I pull this, I'm going to find nothing between us but air?"

"Try it and see," she said, her blue eyes dark and her smile coy.

Dave knew he needed to share his recent love epiphany with her. To straighten out the jumble of thoughts he had on the subject into sensible, straight lines of communication. But all of that flew from his mind as he rubbed the silky cord between his fingers and considered what was under it. After being with her all day, but unable to take more than just the briefest taste of her, he wanted more. He *needed* more. He needed *her*. They could talk later, he decided.

Dave jerked the end of the sash like he was deploying an emergency parachute. The bow unwound and the panels of V's robe slid open. His eyes traveled down the exposed slip of skin, cataloging the hollow of her throat, the hint of her breasts just beyond the loosened fabric, her nipples beading beneath the thin material, the flat plane of her stomach and finally the thin strip of blond hair at her sex.

The air around him seemed to thin as he drank her in. In the raw silence of the room, V's soft breathing accompanied his own struggle to draw air into his lungs. Dropping to his knees, he pushed his hands beneath her robe, splaying his fingers over her hips and drawing her closer. Dusting his mouth over her stomach, he nuzzled into her, kissing his way along her body.

V's hands came to his hair, and she sighed, pulling him closer. Shifting, he teased the underside of one breast with the bridge of his nose, then followed it with a firm suck that drew the sensitive skin between his teeth and made her fingers tighten against his scalp.

"Oh," V said, arching into his mouth as he drew and released her skin with gently biting sucks. Each graze of his teeth against the trapped flesh made her shudder and tug at his hair. One last short pull of his mouth and he released her, licking over the small, reddened spot with the flat of his tongue.

"Did you . . ." V's voice was breathy soft as she gazed down at him from beneath heavy lids. She swallowed and started again. "Did you just . . ."

"Mark you?" Dave asked, flicking her nipple with his tongue and grinning when she shivered. "Absolutely."

"Why would you . . ." Her question ended on a sharp inhale when Dave drew her nipple into his mouth and held it between his teeth, shifting his jaw back and forth slowly while he worked his tongue against the peak.

V's back bowed, and she gave a low, urgent moan that made him smile against her skin as he continued to suckle at her breast with long, slow pulls and rolling licks. He stroked the curve of her other breast with the tips of his fingers, teasing around her nipple, but not quite touching it.

With one last lick, he released her, enjoying the reddened hue of the tight bud and the darker mark below it. He ran his thumb over it and smiled up at her. "You're no longer wearing just a robe. You're wearing a reminder of me and how much I want you. How much I need you. So much that I want to mark my claim on you. On all of you. All over your beautiful body, so you know there could never be a time, place, or reason that I wouldn't want you." He kissed the center of her chest. "You're mine, Doc. And no one is going to change that. Ever."

V's small fingers traced over his cheekbones and down his jaw, settling beneath it to urge him to meet her lips for a kiss. "I'm yours," she said right before his mouth closed over hers. "Always."

It wasn't a flowery declaration of love from either one of them, but in the moment it was perfect. A perfect expression of how deeply they cared about each other. How strongly they wanted each other and how much they needed each other. Neither had said the actual words, but the sentiments were as clear as if they had shouted them.

Rising to his feet, Dave lifted V into his arms and carried her to the bed, settling her against the pillows. She shimmied the rest of the way out of her robe while he divested himself of the remainder of his clothes. He didn't miss the way her eyes scanned the planes of his body, or the slight upturn of her mouth when her glance moved south of his navel.

With a wicked grin, he launched himself onto the bed, which made her laugh and reach for him. Ranging over her, he lowered himself slowly until his body covered hers completely. Her sigh of contentment matched his as the two of them savored the feel of each other.

"Finally," Dave whispered, kissing along her jawline.

"Mmm," V responded as her hands trailed up his back.

"I've missed you," he said, kissing the corner of her mouth.

She shifted her thigh against the hard length of him. "I can tell."

He laughed and dropped a soft kiss on her mouth. "More than in just the obvious way, Doc." Pulling back, he gazed down at her. Her porcelain skin was flushed a light pink, her lips slightly parted and desire burned so hotly in her blue eyes he thought it might singe his flesh. She was so beautiful, and she was *his*. This woman, this gorgeous woman, had picked him. For a moment, he marveled at that fact he'd managed to make that happen.

V shifted beneath him, bending one knee and drawing her foot up the back of his leg. She touched his cheek and smiled. "I've missed you too. In all the ways you can imagine."

Dave turned his face into her palm. "I've imagined quite a few ways in the past three weeks."

He felt her stomach quiver with her laughter. "Care to share with the rest of the class?"

Lifting to an elbow, he slid his other hand down the length of her body and over the curve of her hip. He cupped her bottom in his hand and gave it a rough squeeze, making her shudder before his hand moved farther south along her thigh. Just behind the back of her knee, he tightened his grip to pull her leg out to the side. Tucking it around his hip to match the other, he moved in a slow thrust and V hummed at the contact.

"I'm always up for a little show and tell," he said, dipping his head to kiss her. His mouth slid over hers and she opened to him, her tongue darting out to tease his. Dave groaned at the back of his throat as she licked into his mouth. He followed when she retreated, and he could taste the mint of her breath on his tongue. His hands slid under her, curling over her shoulder blades as his hips pressed her into the mattress. Her breasts rubbed against his chest, her nipples taut points of desire. When she rolled her hips, the hot, liquid slide of her against his cock was beautiful agony. He swallowed her moans as she moved along the ridge of his erection.

V's hands came between them, reaching for him. Before she took him in her hand, Dave pushed a knee into the mattress and rolled them. She gave a startled gasp at the sudden move that had her astride him, ass resting against his thighs. His dick settled against her folds, hard, hot, and insistent.

"Why the switch?" she asked, the question a throaty whisper.

"Because, Doc," Dave said, stroking a finger against her clit and making her eyes fly wide and her fingers dig into his shoulders. "After weeks of fantasizing about you riding my cock, I'm ready to see the real thing." Her eyes blazed in a flash of blue sparks. "I want to watch you slide down onto me, inch by inch, while I stretch you out and fill you up." V's breath stuttered, and a tremor ran through her, the shiver of her body telegraphing her longing.

Dave pushed up against her sex, nudging at her entrance. The primitive part of him strained to plunge into the heat of her body, to take and claim. But he needed more than the welcoming velvet luxury of her. Dave needed to hear V say she was as lost to desire as he was, to confirm she craved what he longed to give her. So, he asked, "Sound good, baby?"

In response, V rocked forward onto her knees, letting her breasts brush against Dave's chest as her legs widened. Reaching down, she wrapped her fingers around his dick, and he flexed into her hand with a ragged groan. She squeezed and moved her hand in a hard downstroke that had Dave's hips rising to meet her. *Fuck*, did he want her. His hands moved to her ass, curving around each delectable cheek, fingers pressing deeply into her flesh. V gave him a self-satisfied smile and guided the head of his cock to the place it most longed to be. "That sounds"—she drew in a breath as he entered her—"absolutely perfect."

Dave's brain went blank to anything but the feel of her clamping down around him. His vision tunneled to the glide of her down the length of him until he was fully seated inside her. His blood roared in his ears, and it wasn't until her hips touched his that he realized he'd been holding his breath as he watched the joining of their bodies. V gave a shuddering sigh and rested her forearms on his shoulders.

They were so close he could see the wavering line of her pupils as they widened into the deep blue of her eyes before her lashes feathered down and she began to move. The feel of her rolling over him, the undulating swell and release of her most intimate space around him was a delicate torment as he let her set the pace. Her hands moved into his hair, and she drew his mouth to hers.

The kiss was brutal in its intensity as she bucked her hips against him. He answered each rock of her hips with a thrust of his own. Gentle wasn't an option as teeth clashed and tongues tangled into a wild, passionate embrace. Her nails scored his scalp as she pressed closer, angling her pelvis to draw him deeper—to the innermost place inside her. He swallowed down her heated moans and forced back the tingle at the base of his spine that signaled his own release. There was no way he was going over without her.

V broke their kiss, panting and flushed. Leaning back, she placed her hands on his knees and arched her spine. Dave brought his mouth to her breasts, kissing and sucking his way back and forth over the dusky, straining buds of her nipples, teasing and stroking them with his fingers as she hummed with pleasure.

She wrapped a hand around his wrist, and he blinked up at her through heavy-lidded eyes. "Touch me," she said, her voice like raw silk.

"Show me," he said, flicking his tongue over her nipple and loving the way it made her skin prickle and tighten.

V's smile was wanton as she drew his hand down the front of her body to where it joined his. Her hand slid from his wrist, her smaller fingers slipping over his knuckles and down his broader, blunter fingers. With a sure touch, she settled the palm of his hand below her navel, pushing it flat and spreading his fingers so his thumb rested just above the juncture of their bodies.

Dave's mouth went dry as he watched her delicate fingers guide his touch lower still until the pad of his thumb brushed her clit. She rocked into his touch with a little groan. "Touch me," she said again, her hand still resting lightly on his.

He began to circle the tight bundle of nerves, biting back a moan as V began to work her hips in a rhythm to match his touch. "Like this?"

Her head fell back, and her long blond hair dusted the tips of her breasts before falling behind her shoulders. "Just. Like. That," she said, punctuating each word with a roll of her pelvis that made Dave's eyes glaze over. He couldn't stave off his own orgasm much longer. The erotic feel of her was too much.

"I need you to come for me, Doc," he said, increasing both the pressure and the pace of his strokes. "I want to watch you come apart."

"I'm so close," she said. "So close. I just . . . I just need," she dropped her knees wider and pulled his hand a millimeter to the right, curving his thumb slightly upward. That minor adjustment made her body go rigid and her breath rush out on a gasp. "Oh! Oh, yes! Right . . . yes, right there. I just . . . I . . ."

V's inner walls clenched around him in rippling waves as she writhed against him. Her hand fell away from his and she gripped the sheets, her words reduced to syllables as she rode out her climax. Dave stroked and teased and caressed her until she collapsed against him, loose and pliant.

Wrapping an arm around her back, he rolled them once again, nestling her snugly into the pillows. Her hands came to his shoulders, pulling him closer as her knees dropped open, letting him sink deeply into her on a groan.

"Jesus, Doc," he moaned into her ear. "You feel so fucking good." Dragging in and out of her, Dave skimmed a hand up the back of her thigh, hooking his fingers in the bend of her knee to hold her leg out wider. V moaned and arched up as best she could to meet him, hips moving in a greedy circle.

"I can't get enough of you, baby," he said, his thrusts coming faster. "I'm fucking addicted to you. Your taste, your scent, the goddamn electric feel of you. All of it. All of you."

The headboard started to rattle, then thump against the wall. Dave wrapped his other arm under the small of V's back, tilting her hips up. "Yes!" she cried, reaching back to brace herself as he lifted her against him. The slap of skin against skin was salacious and sharp, pushing him even closer. Dave's veins were on fire, sparks of need shooting through his entire body.

The slick grip of V's folds began to pulse around his cock, and he knew she was close even before she said, "Dave, I'm . . . oh, God . . . I . . ."

He released her knee and brought his fingers to her clit. One stroke, two, and then she was gone, and he followed on a broken groan, hips jerking roughly against her as he came. Thoroughly sated and utterly spent, he toppled to his elbows, face buried in her neck. The delicate scent of her perfume mingled with the sharp scent of sex, making his head spin with delirious satisfaction.

V's fingers worked into his hair in light, circular motions. He sighed with pleasure at her touch and felt her laugh beneath him. Pressing a kiss to her collarbone, Dave shifted onto his back and pulled her to rest on his chest. She came willingly, curling into his side. His arm came around her, his hand spanning the curve of her hip.

"You wrecked me," he said, kissing the top of her head.

"Right back at you," V said, dropping a kiss to his chest.

He stroked her hip. "Think my mom will understand if we beg off tomorrow because we're too tired from sex?"

V's head popped up, and she fixed him with a stony stare. "Not a chance, bucko. Your mom's minestrone was to die for. There's no way I'm missing her turkey, or anything else. Fennel included."

"Don't forget the spare dressing," Dave said on a laugh.

"Trust me, I'm already planning to bring my big purse for the spare dressing. Since it's spare, she won't miss it until we're already gone and it's too late."

"Would you be offended if I called you adorable?"

"I definitely should be, but in this instance, I'll let it slide."

What if I told you I loved you? Dave thought. But knew it wasn't the right time. You didn't tell the woman of your dreams you were in love with her when you were naked, sweaty, and discussing Thanksgiving dinner. He'd tell her, that much he was certain of. It was the when and how he needed to work through.

Chapter 22

November 23rd – Thanksgiving Day

The smell of roasting turkey wrapped around V the moment they stepped into Sylvia's kitchen the following morning. Her mouth watered and her stomach growled, despite having eaten breakfast not even an hour ago. She could almost taste the crispy skin and tender, juicy white meat, or the savory richness of the dark meat. She must've made some sort of sound, because Dave laughed.

"Relax, Doc, there's plenty to go around. Despite how it might appear."

How it appeared was complete and utter bedlam. Children of various shapes and sizes careened around adults sipping coffee and mimosas. She recognized Dave's brother and sister and their spouses from the night before. But the five or six other adults milling around the kitchen were a surprise.

"Who are all these people?" V whispered to Dave.

"My Aunt Chloe and Uncle Daniel," Dave pointed to the couple seated at the small breakfast table. "My Uncle Vic and Aunt Carol." The couple talking to Sylvia as she chopped something at the counter. "Carol and Chloe are my mom's sisters and that," he inclined his head at a man loitering around the oven, "is my Uncle Mark, my dad's brother." Loud groans drifted into the kitchen from deeper inside the house. "Sounds like the cousins have already started watching the games."

"Cousins?" V said, trying and failing to keep the hint of panic out of her voice. "When you invited me for Thanksgiving to meet your family, I thought it was just *your family*."

Dave grinned. "This is my family. The whole motley crew of them. And like I said," he said as he tucked her close to his side, "they're going to love you, Doc. All forty-seven of them."

"Mark!" Sylvia leaned around Carol to glare at Dave's uncle. "If you even think about touching that oven handle, you will not like where I decide to put the turkey baster." Wisely, Uncle Mark backed away from the oven with his hands raised in surrender.

Sylvia caught sight of the two of them then and her threatening scowl morphed quickly into a welcoming smile. "There you are! I was wondering when you'd get here."

"It's only ten thirty, Mom," Dave said.

"You say that like it should mean something," Sylvia retorted, but accepted the kiss Dave planted on her cheek.

"Vivian, don't you look gorgeous! Have you met everyone? Oh, what am I saying, of course you haven't!" Before V could blink, Sylvia banged the butt of her chef's knife against the countertop. "Everyone, can I have your attention, please! This"—she gestured proudly at V—"is Dave's girlfriend, *Doctor* Vivian Walters. Let's make her feel at home."

V found herself swept away in a tide of handshakes and introductions, buffeted along by half-started conversations she couldn't finish before the next person came to meet her. It would've been overwhelming, but for the steadfast presence of Dave at her side. His hand rested on her lower back, his thumb keeping up a calming stroke of her spine. After everyone in the kitchen had their obligatory five minutes to speak to her, Dave said, "Okay, everyone. Let's let V have a breath, and possibly a mimosa. She'll be here all day, so there's no need to continue to swarm her."

Erika materialized next to her with the requisite mimosa extended. "My car's parked on the street," she said with a knowing smile. "We can make a clean getaway now, if you want."

Accepting the bubbles with a grateful smile, V said, "No, I think I'm okay, but I'll keep that offer in mind."

Dave's sister nodded. "You'll have to forgive everyone, including my mother, for their excitement over you. They don't mean to make you feel like the newest exotic animal at the zoo, but Dave here hasn't batted *quite* this far out of his league before."

V felt Dave stiffen slightly next to her. She leaned into him, reassuring him with a gentle press of her body. "I don't know that I'd say that."

Erika huffed out a disbelieving laugh. "Then you haven't been paying attention. How this guy landed you is now one of life's great mysteries. Right up there with Stonehenge and the Lost Colony. Not to mention why he's wasting his time working at Tonic. That last one has us all stumped."

V didn't appreciate the putdown, even if it were just sibling banter. Given his body language, Dave didn't either. Sure, she had her own reservations about Dave toiling away at a thankless job, but those reservations weren't the punchline of a joke, or something she'd say to someone she'd only just met. Deciding to wade into the fray, V sipped her mimosa and kept her smile light. "Dave made a choice," she said, "to value his mental health above a paycheck. It takes time to regroup after something like that and only he can say how long is long enough. I'm proud of him for making a decision few people have the guts to go through with. So, if you can't see what I see in Dave, then maybe you're the one who isn't paying attention." Dave's hand at her hip tightened almost imperceptibly in a silent thank you.

Erika's brows shot up and her mouth dropped open, then she threw her head back and laughed. Tapping her glass to V's, she said, "Well, shit, Doc. I think you're going to fit in just fine around here." She punched her brother none too lightly on the shoulder. "Good work, brother dear."

"I would say thank you," Dave said, "but there was that whole thing before the good work part that wasn't a compliment." The change in his voice wasn't big, but V noticed the drop in his tone like someone hitting a dimmer switch and she hated it. She'd have to be very careful how she broached the topic of his moving on from Tonic.

"Focus on the positive," Erika said, oblivious to the shift in her brother's demeanor. "I know the rest of us are. I'm pretty sure Mom's already picking out china patterns for the two of you."

"Don't you have a child or a husband that needs you for something?" Dave asked.

Erika smiled. "Relax, Dave." To V, she said, "I'm only kidding."

V laughed. "Just make sure she keeps it simple. Nothing too flashy, right, babe?" She looked up at Dave and winked.

The tension she'd felt in his posture loosened a fraction as he grinned down at her. "Right, Doc."

"That girl of yours is something special."

Dave glanced away from the ragtag touch football game going on in his parents' backyard to find his father standing next to him.

"Yeah, she is."

They stood in silence for a minute or two before his dad asked the question Dave knew was coming. "How does she feel about what you do?"

What his father was really asking was whether V shared his view that Dave was throwing away a great opportunity by not using his degree.

"She's not a fan of my hours, but we make it work."

Abe made a noise in his throat. "She seems to have quite the future ahead of her."

"Yeah, she does," Dave said.

"Are you planning to be a part of that future?"

Dave's hand clamped down on the railing in front of them. "I'd like to be."

Abe sighed. "I'd like that too. And so would your mother. But I think you know for there to be a future between the two of you, certain things need to change."

Now they were getting down to it. It wouldn't be a visit to his parents without his dad bringing up Tonic. He knew there was no malice in what his dad said. That Abe only wanted what he saw as best for Dave. But knowing that didn't make these conversations any easier. "Yeah, I know," Dave said. He didn't add that he'd been trying to make a change, only to gain zero traction in that regard. No need to serve up a second helping of disappointment to his dad. He'd done enough of that already.

Abe went on with his lecture. "Of course, these things have needed to change for a while now, son. You need to think about your future and how it compares to what Vivian wants for hers. And figure out the best way they can come together." When he looked over at Dave, worry creased his brow. "Or risk them tearing you apart."

That had Dave's heart lurching in his chest. His dad's concerns were no different from the ones Dave himself had. But hearing Abe say the words out loud gave them a physical weight, as though once spoken aloud they had a greater possibility of coming to fruition. And the thought of that made Dave's stomach roil and his lungs freeze. But he couldn't afford a meltdown at Thanksgiving and ruin the day, so he forced himself to push down the rising panic at the thought of losing V. She was here. She was with him. And she'd stood up for him to Erika. That had to count for something. Dave blew out a long breath. "Dad, can we not do this today?"

Ignoring his plea, Abe put an arm around him in a quick, firm half embrace. "I love you, kid. But you need to get your head out of your ass about your job. Your hours are shit, you're making a fraction of what you could be if you used your degree, and don't think I don't know things aren't good with that new boss of yours."

Given that Dave had never, not one single time, griped about Ryker to his dad, that last part came as a shock. "What are y—"

Abe waved a hand. "Don't even try it, Dave. Your shifts used to be regular. You didn't have to duck out on family dinners or miss your nephews' ballgames because of some emergency or other at your job. It gave you a chance to decompress when you needed it, after the whole . . . well, you know."

Yes, Dave thought. *I do know. I'm the one who left because I was miserable.*

"Your mother and I completely understood your reason for leaving. Didn't fault you for it at all, because it was what you needed to do. And, for a little while, Tonic made sense. But now, especially over the past few months, it's been one thing after another with that place that's made your presence around here scarce." He frowned in concern, sadness reflected in his gaze. "And that's with people who are fifteen minutes away from you. I can only imagine the impact it's having on your relationship with V."

"We're making it work, Dad."

"But why should you have to *make* something work? You've got options. *Good* options that you need to think about even more now that you've got someone like Vivian in your life. Don't you think she deserves more than what you're giving her now? Don't you want to be the man she deserves?"

The words stung for their honesty alone. But if you added the seemingly never-ending stream of rejections generated by his attempt to change things . . . it was downright debilitating. For a second, he considered telling his dad about his decision to get back into his field. But that would also mean telling him his efforts to that point had generated exactly squat. And Dave couldn't stomach the look of disappointment he knew would skate across his dad's face before he did his best to hide it.

So, instead, he forced out a laugh and said, "No one is good enough to deserve V, Dad. She's everything anyone should ever want. Not just as a woman, but as a person. And somehow, for some reason she picked me. Even though, according to my entire family, I'm not good enough for her."

Abe sighed and pushed a hand through his hair. "That's not what I'm saying. What I'm trying to say is you're my son and I want the best for you. I'm thrilled you found someone like V. Someone *you* deserve. But I just want to make sure you get everything else you deserve too. And, whether you're willing to admit it or not, you deserve more than what you're getting at Tonic."

Dave opened his mouth, but his father pushed on. "I know you're as tired of having this conversation as I am. But I keep having it with you because I love you. You need to give serious consideration to what you want to do with your life, especially if you want to keep Dr. Walters in it."

He clapped a hand on Dave's shoulder. "Think about how it would be if you didn't have to focus on 'making it work.' If you weren't constantly juggling your schedule against hers and were free to end your days together, spend your Saturdays together." He squeezed Dave's shoulder. "Why make something harder when you have the power to make it that much easier?"

"Am I interrupting anything?"

They both turned at the sound of V's voice to find her a few paces away, with Bianka seated at her heels. It appeared even the dog was in love with her.

Abe smiled at her. "Not at all." He nodded at Bianka. "You seem to have found a friend there."

V laughed and stooped to give Bianka a scratch under the chin. "She's a cutie."

"She's a holy terror," Abe corrected and earned an arch look from the dog as though she knew he'd just insulted her.

"I've been sent to tell you that your skills are needed in the potato mashing department," V said to his father. "I offered to do it, but was informed that was your job."

Abe shook his head with a wry chuckle. "I mentioned a single time sixteen years ago that the potatoes were a little lumpy, and this has been my atonement since."

"Sounds to me like the punishment fits the crime," V said and earned a hearty laugh from Abe.

"You're probably right." He clapped his hands together and headed inside. "I better go face the music."

Once he'd gone, V took his place at the railing while Bianka scampered down into the yard. "The atmosphere was a little heavy out here," V said.

Dave draped his arm over her shoulders, instantly more at ease with her next to him. "It was nothing," he said.

"Didn't seem like nothing." V put an arm around his waist. "You can tell me about it, if you want to." She angled her head back to look at him. "You can talk to me about anything, Dave. I hope you know that."

Her eyes searched his, like she was looking for a particular response in them.

"Of course, I do, Doc," he assured her, which meant he had to tell her about the conversation with his dad. He would've preferred to just stand there at the railing with her in the stark fall sunshine and watch his idiotic younger cousins try to murder each other with touch football. To just enjoy having her next to him. But that wasn't an option.

He glanced out into the yard as he spoke. "My dad was giving me some career advice."

"Oh," V said, nodding encouragingly.

"Essentially," Dave said, "my dad thinks I'm wasting my entire life."

"I'm sure that's not true," V countered.

Dave laughed and kissed the side of her temple. "Well, not my entire life, not now that I somehow managed to land Dr. Vivian Walters as my girlfriend." V went stiff next to him, and he wanted to kick himself for the way that came out.

"I didn't mean it like it sounded, Doc," he said. "I only meant that my dad expressed similar sentiments to Erika's. Only he took it a step further and said I needed to get my shit together or I had no real chance of keeping you in my life."

"What?"

He nodded. "It's a conversation we've had before, but you were a new element in his argument."

"Dave, I'm sorry. I never meant to—"

"Don't worry about it, Doc. It's the same conversation, you just added a new twist to it."

"But if I weren't here . . ."

Dave turned her to face him, putting his hands on her shoulders. "If you weren't here, Doc, a version of that conversation still would've happened. So don't think for a second your being here is anything other than everything I want. As predicted, my family loves you. So much so, they're confirming something I already know—that I need to do everything within my power to keep you. Maybe in ways that are a bit heavy-handed and irritating, but methods aside, it comes from a good place. If they didn't care, they wouldn't say anything. And they do, which is why I don't push back *that* hard when they meddle."

"Huh," V said thoughtfully. "That's a perspective I've never considered before."

Dave laughed. "I can't speak to your experience, Doc, just my own. But most of the time, as annoying, irritating, and infuriating as it can be, when my parents take it upon themselves to meddle, or advise or even criticize, they do it because they want me to have a great life. Because they think I deserve it. So, I do my best to remember that. Even when I want to hold my hands over my ears and hum Green Day songs to make them stop talking."

"Can't say I've tried that one," V said, putting her arms around him and stepping into his chest. Dave's hands came to her cheeks and turned her face up to his.

"We're all glad you're here, Doc."

"Me, too," she said and pushed onto her toes to meet his kiss.

"All right, you two," Sylvia called from the back door. "That's enough of that. Dave, come help your brother get the leaves in place on the dining room table."

"Just like old times." Dave sighed against V's lips, and she laughed softly before turning and asking, "What can I do, Sylvia?"

"You can help Erika set the table, dear."

Hand in hand, they headed back into the semi-controlled chaos that was the Richardson clan Thanksgiving.

Somehow, they managed to wedge all adults around the dining table, with the children tucked around card tables in the living room. The turkey was carved, side dishes were served, gravy was ladled, bread was buttered, and wine poured, until finally everyone had a full plate in front of them. Dave was about to dig in when V stood up from her place at the table, wineglass in hand.

"Sorry to hold up this feast," she said, drawing all eyes to her. "But I wanted to take this opportunity while we're all around the table together to say thank you for welcoming me today. It means a lot to me to be able to share this with you, because"—she looked down at Dave with a smile—"Dave means a lot to me. As is the norm, he came into my life at a time when it was least expected. He found me when I wasn't looking for him and I can't quantify how lucky I am that he did." She cleared her throat and lifted her glass. "Anyway, thank you so much for having me and making me feel like part of the family. Cheers!"

As the "Cheers" chorused around the table, V took her seat and Dave took her hand in his. There was no real way for him to respond to what she'd just done. For letting his family know in her own way that she saw him as enough and herself as the lucky one. It was an affirmation instead of a confrontation and it made his heart ache with so many emotions, not the least of which was pride. The words were out of his mouth and off his tongue before he could even process that he'd said them.

"I love you, Doc."

Her eyes flew wide, and her mouth parted in surprise seconds before a smile graced her lips. She squeezed his fingers. "Thank goodness, because if you didn't that would've made what I just did super awkward."

He laughed and brought her knuckles to his lips. She leaned over and whispered in his ear, "I love you too."

"And I thought I was stuffed last night." V groaned as she levered herself out of the passenger side of Dave's car.

Dave laughed as he rounded the hood of the car and took her hand. "Is this the same woman who planned to steal my mother's spare dressing?" He shook his head and *tsked*. "My, how the mighty have fallen."

"It's your fault," V said, sending him a mock glare.

"My fault? How is your gluttony my fault?"

"Babe, you've got to try these stuffed mushrooms. You'll love these rosemary potatoes. My mom makes the best pumpkin pie," V said, lowering her voice to imitate his. "You, sir, are an unabashed food pusher and I was your hapless victim."

He laughed, and she loved the lightness of its sound. "Ever hear of self-control, Doc?"

She gave him a playful shove into the stair railing. "It's Thanksgiving, dummy. No one exercises self-control at Thanksgiving. Especially not when their boyfriend's mom has the fastest spoon in the east. She was like Quick Draw McGraw with every serving utensil." V patted her stomach. "And I'm the one forced to pay the price."

Dave grinned at her as he unlocked his apartment door. "Sorry you're such a lightweight, sweetheart."

"After that meal," V said, following him into the apartment, "there is nothing light about my weight."

He laughed and swung her into his arms. "I beg to differ," he said.

V laughed. "Put me down before I puke on you."

"God, you're so romantic," he replied, but obeyed and settled her back on her feet. Tossing his keys into the tray on the foyer table, he asked, "Want anything to drink?"

V shook her head and sank down onto the sofa. "No, I'm good. Thanks."

"No going into a food coma," Dave called from the kitchen. He reappeared seconds later with a bottle of water and joined her on the couch, pulling her feet into his lap and easing off her shoes. She groaned at the first press of his thumb against her instep.

"I make no promises as long as you're doing that," V said, closing her eyes and letting her head fall back to the arm of the couch.

Dave laughed and continued his ministrations. V could hear the smile in his voice when he said, "I'm glad you came, Doc."

She opened one eye and grinned at him. "Me too."

"I know my family can be a lot," he said, working his thumb against the ball of her foot. "But you handled them like a pro."

V smiled. "They're pretty great," she said. "But I have to ask you something."

Dave grinned at her. "Is it about what my aunt and uncle were doing in the laundry room?"

V wrinkled her nose. "What? No!" She laughed, but then sobered and looked at him for a long moment. She didn't want to interrupt their happy afternoon, but she also wasn't sure how many more quiet moments they'd have with the two of them alone the rest of the weekend. Sylvia had given her a rundown of an ambitious itinerary, so if V were going to broach the topics she needed to . . . then she better go ahead and do it.

"That conversation with your dad that I walked up on," she began.

Dave was shaking his head before she could even finish the sentence. "It was nothing, Doc. Don't worry about it."

"Please don't do that," V said quietly, and she knew her tone caught his attention by the way his shoulders straightened and his eyes focused on her.

"Don't do what?" he asked, continuing to massage her feet.

V wanted to keep things as conversational as possible, so she stayed where she was. "Don't try and shift me away from something you think is going to be hard to talk about."

"That's not what I'm doing," he argued, and she just looked at him. "I'm not," he protested again.

"Okay," V conceded. "Then what would you call it when every time I ask you about something that makes you uncomfortable, you change the subject? What would you call that?"

"I don't know," Dave said. "Because I don't do that."

"Oh?" V responded, keeping her voice even. This needed to be a conversation, not a confrontation. "Is that why we've had so many in-depth discussions about whether you're happy at Tonic? Or whether there's something else you'd rather be doing?"

Dave's hands stilled. "We talk about work."

V shook her head. "No, Dave, we don't. I try to talk to you about it, but you . . ." She waved a hand in the air. "I don't even know how to describe it. You. . . change the subject and smile your way around it."

She sat up, pulling her feet from his lap and tucking them underneath her. Putting a hand on his shoulder, she said, "I know work isn't going the way you'd like it. And I want you to be able to talk to me about it. I want you to be able to talk to me about anything. Because I love you and I want to be there for you however you need me. You can talk to me, babe. I'm here for you."

Dave stared into the earnest blue depths of V's gorgeous eyes as she implored him to open up to her. To tell her all the things swirling through the back of his mind. All the doubts, second-guesses, and indecisions he had about the direction he'd chosen for his life. She wanted him to unload all of that onto her. To let her help him sort through the shambles he'd made of his career.

Because the honest truth of the matter, the bleak reality of his situation was that he was in his early thirties stuck in a dead-end job he'd kept for too long against the advice of everyone he knew. He could admit that—at least himself. He had no choice, because he lived the reality of it every single day he went to work. The nonstop thankless bullshit he dealt with proved it every hour he was on the clock. Yeah, he could admit it to himself. But was he ready to say it out loud to V? To admit to her he was a complete and utter fucking failure because he'd been either too proud or too stupid to listen when it counted. And was now suffering the consequences of his own stupidity. To drop all of that on her when she'd had her own shit together since forever.

No, he wasn't going to do that, because if he did . . . she'd see what a real fuck up she was dating . . . and she might wise up and leave him. That was the single, purest fear he had in his life. One that pierced through him each time he got turned down by another company. That V would wise up and leave his ass. Because his dad was right, he didn't deserve her. And if he didn't get his shit figured out soon, she'd realize it too.

She didn't need another problem to solve. Some other sad story she could come in and salvage, like she did for so many others. He needed to fix this on his own. To find a way to be the guy she needed by her side. To be someone she could be proud of, not someone she needed to help save.

He brushed her hair off her shoulder, letting his hand come back to curve around her jaw. His thumb stroked her cheekbone, and he smiled at her. "I know that, Doc. And it means the world to me."

She smiled and leaned into his touch. "Okay, so . . . lay it on me. Let's problem solve."

Dave brushed his lips over hers. "I've got it under control, Doc. Trust me. There's nothing for you to worry about, okay?"

V pulled away from his kiss, her brow furrowed. "Dave, don't."

"Don't what?" he said, letting his free hand slip around her waist and lift her onto his lap. He nuzzled her neck, but she pushed at his shoulder.

"I'm serious," she said, and he heard the steel in her voice.

Lifting his head, he looked into her cool blue eyes. Determination reflected back at him, and he sighed. "Doc, I love you. So much it feels . . ." He swallowed and tried again. "It feels like you're a part of me. Like it would be easier to lose a limb than it would be to lose you."

She stroked his cheek. "Who says you're going to lose me? I finally got you to admit you loved me, so I've got no plans to go anywhere any time soon."

Dave smiled. "Glad to hear it. But that's just it, Doc. I feel like my job creeps in on us enough without my devoting any of the time I get with you to it. I don't want to ruin seeing you with discussions of why my job is a pain in my ass, or what Ryker's done lately to make the staff want to walk out. I have to deal with that every day, and the last thing I want is for it to taint my time with you." He touched her cheek in a gentle caress. "I just want to *be* with you, uninterrupted by work, or any other assorted bullshit, for the next few days."

When she didn't reply right away, he dipped his forehead to hers. "Please, Doc. Just do this for me, okay? Let me enjoy having you with me these next few days. We've got plenty of time for the other stuff, so there's no need to ruin the rest of our weekend together with work shit, right?"

Her sigh whispered against his lips. "Okay," she said finally and he thanked God she'd agreed. He knew it was a lull, a brief pause in her desire to talk things out, but he'd take it. He'd take it and keep pushing it until he had the answers he needed to show her she wasn't making a mistake by loving him.

Mistletoe Mishaps

Chapter 23

December 4th

To: drichardson@gmail.com
From: jeanette.mickleson@loseyourcompassbrewing.com
Re: Résumé / Interview Request Malting and Brewing Technologist

Dave,

Thank you for submitting your résumé for our consideration in filling the above referenced position. Given your unique background, we'd like to set up a Zoom interview to determine whether you'd be as good a fit here at Lose Your Compass as it appears on paper. Please let us know your availability in the coming weeks. I know with the holidays scheduling is difficult, so we will try to be as flexible as we can. I look forward to hearing from you.

Jeanette

Jeanette Mickleson

President and Brewmistresss

Lose Your Compass Brewing
1045 East Nowhere Boulevard
Charlotte, NC 28277
(980) 985-2222 - Telephone

Dave blinked at his laptop screen, trying and failing to keep his excitement at a reasonable level. He'd seen the position posted on one of the multiple online job posting sites he now reviewed each morning. After checking to confirm there was indeed a Lose Your Compass Brewing and an East Nowhere Boulevard in Charlotte and this wasn't some elaborate catfishing scheme, he'd submitted his résumé before Thanksgiving.

Rereading the email, Dave made a mental note to use the phrasing "unique background" to describe his work history from then on. He reached for his phone, pulling up V's contact information. But he stopped before pressing the call button. This was just an interview, not a job offer. It wasn't a sure thing, so there was no need to mention it to her yet.

Clearing the screen, he set his phone back down on the table and read the email one more time, fighting back a grin.

December 6th

V: *I'm more than a little mad at you right now.* *red face emoji* *shark emoji*
V: *That last one was oddly appropriate. Maybe they're right about AI taking over the world.*
Dave: *We'll put a pin in the whole AI thing, because I'm more interested in finding out why you're mad at me.*

V: *For ruining one of my favorite Christmas songs.*

Dave: *Um, how did I do that?*

V: *By pointing out that A Christmas to Remember is essentially about two strangers shacking up! Dolly and Kenny's Christmas albums will never be the same!*

Dave: *It's right there in the lyrics, Doc. It's not like I played the song backward or anything. And anyway, does anything capture the magic of Christmas like a casual tryst in Lake Tahoe with someone you just met on the ski slopes?*

V: *You're a terrible person. An actual grinch who ruined Christmas.*

Dave: *Ah, but you're forgetting that he SAVES it in the end.*

V: *There's nothing you can do to redeem yourself here, Richardson. Nothing.*

Dave: *Even if I told you I just marked off the weekend of December 15th to come meet the parents?*

V: *Are you serious?*

Dave: *Depends. Are you still mad?*

Bubbles dancing . . .

V: *You've turned me into a weak woman, Richardson. So weak and desperate to see you I'm willing to overlook you besmirching the national treasure that is Dolly singing with Kenny.*

Dave: *Does that mean your heart just grew three sizes at the thought of seeing me next week?*

V: *You're the green guy in this scenario, not me.*

Dave: *Doc, you should know the size of my heart since you've had it in the palm of your hand for quite some time now.*

December 9th

The white Corinthian columns at the front entrance to the Sawgrass Country Club glittered in the bright winter sunlight when V pulled in. After passing her keys to the valet, she traversed the marble stairs before another young man opened the massive oak door to the elegantly understated lobby. The luxurious Aubusson carpet muted the sound of her footsteps as she walked to the hostess stand in the far left corner.

"Vivian Walters," she told the smiling hostess. "I'm meeting my mo—"

"Of course, Dr. Walters," she responded before V could finish. "Ms. Caroline is already seated. If you'll follow me, please."

Obediently, V trailed along behind her through the maze of tables covered in pristine white linen and dotted with fresh flowers—poinsettias this week, in a nod to the season. Her mother was seated by the window at her usual table and she stood to give V a small embrace and dust kisses to her cheeks.

"Thank you, Darcy," she said to the hostess, who looked like she was contemplating dropping a curtsey before she thought better of it and nodded instead.

V took her seat in the chair across from her mother. "You're looking particularly festive today, Mother."

Caroline glanced down at her red cashmere sweater. A gold reindeer with a ruby nose was pinned jauntily above her left breast. "Thank you," she said. "It's not often you call me for lunch, so I thought I better dress for the occasion."

Ignoring the not-so-veiled dig, V smiled. "Well, I wanted to make sure you and Daddy would be available next weekend to meet Dave while he's in town."

Her mother didn't visibly flinch, but her hand did hover for a split second over her silverware before she adjusted it into a more symmetrical arrangement. "You want us to meet him?"

V swallowed back her trepidation. "I do."

"Things are getting serious between you two?"

"You know they are," V said, smoothing her napkin into her lap and praying for patience. "Why else would I have met his family over Thanksgiving?"

"Are you sure this is the best thing for you?" Caroline asked. V's face must've transmitted something because Caroline shook her head. "I just wonder whether he's . . ." She looked away from V and out at the golf course in the distance. "I want what's best for you, darling. Like I always have."

"Mother," V said, working to keep her voice level. "I appreciate that, and I know you're disappointed with some of the choices I've made in life. And that you've b—"

Caroline's eyes snapped back to V's. "Disappointed? Why in the world would you think I've ever been disappointed in you?"

V blinked at the surprise in her mother's tone. "Well, I . . ." She fumbled for words. "It's just that you, or rather that I . . ." V took a sip of water, trying to organize her thoughts. "I don't think I've ever been the daughter you expected, is all I'm saying. Our interests never really lined up. I hated cotillion and had no interest in pledging a sorority. I preferred science camp to ballet, and . . . well, everything else. It would've been easier for you to have someone who excelled at all that stuff instead of me."

"Instead of . . ." Caroline's eyes went wide, and she touched the diamond pendant at her throat. "Vivian, I . . . I certainly knew we had different views on a great many things, but that doesn't mean I've ever been anything other than proud to have you as my daughter. Why would you think otherwise?"

V recoiled a little at the question and the honest shock on her mother's face. "How could I not? You constantly remind me about my needing to get a move on and find a suitable husband before they're all taken. Like I'm not a whole person without the all-important ring on my finger. That my getting my MD was somehow less important than getting married. That none of my other achievements matter, because I've yet to walk down the aisle with some man you've hand-selected to carry on the family bloodline. And now that I've found someone I'm crazy about, you're here to tell me that he, too, is some sort of disappointment or doesn't check the right box or is one more way I haven't lived up to your standards."

For the first time V could remember, her mother looked completely flummoxed and out of her depth. Her hand remained at her throat, fingers drumming at the delicate chain there. She swallowed, then cleared her throat and took a sip of water.

"Vivian, I . . ." She stopped to collect herself, putting a hand palm up on the table. V stared at it for a minute before covering her mother's hand with hers. Strong fingers wrapped around hers in an unfamiliar maternal squeeze.

Her mother's eyes were soft and sad when she looked at V and said, "I've only ever been proud of you, Vivian. Proud to the point of being honestly mystified at how I produced a daughter who is as smart as she is gorgeous and who in her young life has accomplished things I never even dreamed of."

After another squeeze of V's hand, she continued, "I didn't have your options, sweetheart. Not only because I'm nowhere near as smart as you are, but because my parents didn't see their daughter as an investment equal to their sons. Sons were born to continue the family legacy. Daughters were a mild inconvenience redeemed only by their ability to make a good match. The single option presented was marriage, with no possibility of making a different choice. College wasn't a springboard to better things. It was to catapult you into the higher echelon of the marriage market. To make you a more well-rounded selection for those aspiring lawyers, doctors, and future business magnates."

Gray eyes dampened briefly, then cleared. "Which means when I had a daughter who was whip-smart and so . . ." Caroline's laugh was genuine and heartfelt. "So uniquely gifted in ways I'd never been, it threw me for a loop. I didn't know any approach to motherhood other than the one I'd experienced. Which included cotillion and ballet and any other manner of things I'd been taught that well-bred young ladies needed to learn. And you did all of them without complaint, so I just assumed . . ."

Caroline let the sentence taper off, but then asked, "Why didn't you ever tell me you didn't want to do any of it?"

V's own smile was a tad watery when she said, "How was I supposed to tell you, possibly the most glamorous woman I'd ever seen, that I didn't want to do something? Especially when they were things even as a child I could see meant so much to you. I wanted to make you happy. So, I tried." She laughed then. "Tried and failed miserably at most of it."

"Vivian Walters, you've never failed at anything in your entire life. That's complete nonsense."

V laughed again. "Well, maybe failed is a strong word, but I was nothing compared to you, Mother. You sailed through all of it like an elegant swan, and I struggled along in your wake."

"You were never in my wake, dear, because you've been too busy forging your own way. And I couldn't be prouder of everything you've done. You've shattered any standard anyone could've set for you, sweetheart, and I'm sorry it's taken me this long to make sure you knew that."

Tears prickled behind V's eyes as she basked in the glow of her mother's words. "That means a lot, Mother."

"I love you, Vivian. So much it's a little terrifying at times. I've never seen you as anything other than extraordinary just as you are. You knew what you wanted out of life so early, and what you wanted was something so foreign to anything I'd ever imagined for myself that I struggled to find ways to offer any sort of guidance to you." Her shoulder rose in a fluidly sophisticated shrug. "So, I concentrated on the one area I felt most qualified, which apparently coincided with the area you hated the most."

They exchanged smiles before Caroline continued. "And I know you don't *need* a man. Honestly, I do. But I also know how happy your father and I have been for the last forty-something years, and I want that for you. I want you to have someone who makes you happy the way Duvall makes me happy, infuriating man that he is. You have this life that is so close to perfect, Vivian. And the only thing missing, at least in my view, is someone to share it with."

This conversation filled with long overdue questions, explanations, and affirmations both of them needed would take V a long while to unpack. Which would probably result in her and Caroline needing to delve more deeply into the topics they'd only skimmed today. But there was one part of this emotionally charged lunch that V believed wholeheartedly she could resolve right then. She squeezed her mother's hand. "I think I've found him, Mother. I just need you to give him a chance, okay? Because I'm in love with the guy."

Her mother blinked at her without speaking for a long few seconds, until finally she said, "You're in love with him?"

"Hopelessly and without question," V said.

"Well, then, he must be better in person than he is on paper, because no daughter of mine would fall in love with a man who truly lacks initiative. You'd have been bored within a week."

December 11th

To: drichardson@gmail.com
From: jeanette.mickleson@loseyourcompassbrewing.com
Re: In-person Interview Request Malting and Brewing Technologist

Dave,
We all enjoyed meeting you over Zoom last Thursday and would like to invite you down for an in-person interview the week of December 18th. I understand that is the week before Christmas and, as I said in my prior email, we are flexible given the holiday. However, as we discussed last week, there is an education piece of this that will need to be factored into the start date of the selected applicant. Given that, we'd like to move forward with your interview at your earliest convenience.
Jeanette
Jeanette Mickleson
President and Brewmistresss
Lose Your Compass Brewing
1045 East Nowhere Boulevard
Charlotte, NC 28277
(980) 985-2222—Telephone

To: jeanette.mickleson@loseyourcompassbrewing.com
From: drichardson@gmail.com
Re: In-person Interview Request Malting and Brewing Technologist

Jeanette,

As luck would have it, I will be in Charlotte the weekend of December 15th and won't be flying out until December 19th. If we could set something up for the afternoon of December 18th, that would be ideal. Thanks again for the opportunity.
Dave

To: drichardson@gmail.com
From: jeanette.mickleson@loseyourcompassbrewing.com
Re: In-person Interview Request Malting and Brewing Technologist

Dave,

Thank you for accommodating our need to fit the interview in before the holidays. If it works for you, we can meet at 2:30 on December 18th.
Jeanette
Jeanette Mickleson
President and Brewmistresss
Lose Your Compass Brewing
1045 East Nowhere Boulevard
Charlotte, NC 28277
(980) 985-2222—Telephone

December 13th

Dave: *What would you say if I told you my sister's friend's girlfriend's mom was able to get me a seat on a flight out tomorrow instead of Friday afternoon?*

V: *First, I'd comment on the wholly bizarre structure of that ticket connection. Second, I'd say "Are you serious? Because, if this is a joke, I'm filling out the Amazon return slip for all your Christmas presents right now." Third, if you confirmed this was indeed not a joke, I'd make a bunch of random noises that sounded like an excited dolphin.*

dolphin emoji *dolphin emoji* *dolphin emoji* *life preserver emoji*

V: *I swear I didn't type that last one. We are experiencing the rise of the machines.*

Dave: *At least we'll face AI Armageddon together when I land a day early.*

V: *GIF of happy dolphin*

V: *That also means you can come with me to Kez's cookie party.* *party hat emoji* *cookie emoji* *gingerbread man emoji*

Dave: *I'm almost afraid to ask.*

V: *You'll love it, I promise.* *kiss emoji* *heart emoji* *warthog head emoji*

Dave chuckled and slid his phone into his pocket, only to pull it out and reread the email from Jeanette at LYC. He was still trying to keep his expectations low, but the Zoom call had gone so well it was difficult not to let the "what-ifs" tumble through his mind. This job was the perfect opportunity. Literally *perfect*. He was even excited about the classes on beer brewing he'd have to take before starting. Classes that were offered within a fifteen-minute drive of his apartment. Sure, it was a full semester, but LYC would fund the cost of it and provide him a stipend in the interim. Which would let him cut back his hours at Tonic, if not quit entirely.

LYC was a smaller company—hence the stipend instead of a salary while he took a semester's worth of classes—but had tapped in, so to speak, to a lot of good publicity by participating in a statewide beer festival the prior year. It generated a lot of interest in their product and, as a result, they were looking to grow. In short, if everything went according to their plans, the sky was the limit for them. And him, if he became a part of the company. Try as he might to keep from letting the thought take root, Dave couldn't help but picture what life would be like if he landed this job. Regular(ish) hours doing something interesting with people who seemed genuinely excited about what they were doing. And, best of all, it was in Charlotte. With V.

For what could've been the hundredth time since the initial email from Jeanette, Dave considered calling V to tell her about the job. Part of him was bursting at the seams to share every detail with her. To see the excitement on her face as she absorbed and analyzed every angle of it. To let her start making her plans and checklists for when he moved down.

But another part of him—the scared, self-conscious, and insecure part he'd managed thus far to keep mostly hidden from her—kept him from picking up the phone. Because what if once again he managed to screw things up? Tanked the in-person interview, or found some other way to fuck up and land right back at Tonic. And so, again, he made the decision to wait. To say nothing until Jeanette made him the offer and he had the job. It was better to not get both their hopes up and risk disappointing V.

Chapter 24

December 15th

V blinked up at the dark outline of the ceiling fan in her bedroom. Next to her, Dave's rhythmic breathing let her know she was the only one having trouble sleeping. Carefully, so as not to wake him, she lifted her phone from the bedside table. Three thirty-five in the morning. Suppressing a groan, she rolled back onto her pillow and resumed her staring contest with the fan.

Dave had been different since Thanksgiving. Lighter almost. The tired circles under his eyes were still there, given the hours he worked that wasn't a surprise. But the exhaustion in his gaze had lifted somewhat. The tightness of his features that was usually present when he first came on-screen had abated. His smile was easier and broader, fully reaching his eyes and lighting up his entire face.

Even yesterday, when he'd come to her office after his flight got in, he'd been almost effervescent with happiness. It radiated from his freaking pores. And as much as she wanted to take credit for his elation, she knew it was based on more than seeing her for the first time in three weeks.

Whatever was going on was obviously good, based on his body language alone. But he'd said nothing to her. Zip, zero, nada. Even as she'd given him every opportunity to tell her, he'd made it seem as though there were nothing new. But she knew that wasn't the case. What she didn't know was why he wouldn't tell her about whatever it was. If it was good, why was he holding back? Why not let her into the celebration of whatever had happened? It made no sense, which meant she kept coming back to it, turning it over and over in her brain trying to figure out both what was happening and why he was keeping it a secret.

The conclusion she'd reached earlier in the week was that whatever it was had to be good for him, but bad for *them*. It was the only thing that made sense, because it tracked with the kind of person Dave was. Even if he won the lottery, if he thought it would negatively affect her, he'd do his best to figure out a way to guard her feelings. *You're precious to me*, he'd said. His protective instincts had to be behind his decision to keep her in the dark about whatever was going on with him even as he couldn't completely mask his own happiness.

Which convinced V of one thing—the owner of Tonic had finally told Dave Ryker was on the way out. And if Ryker were on the way out, then Dave would most likely be next in line for that job. So, he'd get a promotion and Tonic would no longer be toxic.

But where did that leave the two of them? If Dave stayed at Tonic, what did that mean long-term? How would that work? And if he were truly happy there, was it right for her to expect him to leave? Unfortunately, the ceiling fan offered no answers to any of those, or the litany of other questions that cascaded through her brain once she'd let down the floodgates of consideration.

V was sure Dave had his own answers to these questions. Answers he wasn't willing to share with her, which didn't bode well for their future. And he was supposed to meet her parents on Saturday. The timing couldn't be any worse. She wanted to scream with frustration but settled for flopping onto her side and pressing her face into the pillow. She had to get some sleep.

Coffee. Someone was making coffee. V blinked open a bleary eye and took another deep inhale. Yes, that was absolutely coffee she smelled. Reaching out a hand, she felt the still warm sheets where Dave had been. The warm, *empty* sheets. He couldn't have been up long. Shifting to her other side, she grabbed her phone—8:30 a.m. V dropped back onto the pillows with an exhausted sigh. She'd finally fallen into a restless sleep a little before six and longed for a few more hours.

Her bedroom door swung open, and the enticing smell of coffee entered first, followed by Dave carrying one of her favorite mugs. It was emblazoned with the words "Sorry for having great tits and correct opinions on everything." A birthday gift from Rae. He grinned when he saw she was awake. Offering the coffee to her, he said, "Good morning."

She took the cup and sniffed the warm aroma of caffeinated heaven. "Thanks," she said and took her first sip. "Mmm."

"Good?" Dave asked, and she nodded.

"I think you make it better than I do by now," she said with a smile.

He brushed a kiss to her temple. "I know how seriously you take your coffee, Doc. I just want to stay on your good side."

"I don't think there's much of anything you could do to get on my bad side," she said, giving him an opening. Eyeing him carefully, she added, "Although, I'm not a huge fan of secrets, good or bad."

V wondered if she imagined the slight stiffening of his shoulders in response, before he grinned at her. "So that means no surprise birthday parties, or last second getaways?"

"Neither of those mesh terribly well with my need for a plan," she admitted. "I much prefer being in the know. Good, bad, or otherwise."

Again, she wasn't sure if she'd *seen* the blip of a shadow in his eyes, or if her subconscious was putting it there. "I'll keep that in mind, Doc," he said easily. Jerking a thumb over his shoulder, he said, "I'm going to head back down and get breakfast started. Come on down when you're ready." He kissed her forehead again and was gone, leaving V alone with the same thoughts that had been spinning through her head all night.

She bit her lip to contain a frustrated groan. It appeared she was going to have to confront Dave head on to get an answer. And she hated that. Loathed was a more apt description, actually. She didn't want to hound him to tell her anything. She wanted him to come to her on his own and share his excitement with her. But he hadn't, and in failing to clue her in, he'd left her with no other option.

Only when was she going to do it? Certainly not today, the day of the Christmas cookie extravaganza Kez's mom hosted every year. There was no way she was going to ruin that by staging some sort of good news intervention with Dave the same day. And tomorrow was out too. Because there was no chance in hell she was adding fuel to the anxiety fire that was Dave meeting her parents. Her nerves wouldn't survive it.

That left Sunday, their last full day together since she'd be working Monday. And what if the conversation didn't go well? How would she carry that forward into work? And what would he do when she went to work on Monday? Sit in her house and stew about it until she got home? Not an ideal scenario when he was flying out the next day. Nor was the possibility he'd just get an earlier flight.

In essence, there was no good time for them to talk about whatever it was Dave wasn't telling her. There were only bad, slightly worse, and completely horrible times to have the discussion. V wanted to bury herself under her duvet and not come out until all of this had been sorted in her absence. That wasn't an option, either, though. They had to talk. It was just a question of when it would happen. And how much it would hurt when they did.

V looks tired, Dave thought as he watched her walk into the kitchen in her robe, the one covered in peonies, twisting her long hair into a ponytail. She'd told him the weeks leading up to Christmas break were some of her busiest, so maybe she was just worn down from work. That he could certainly relate to, given Ryker had been even more of a pain in the ass than usual since Dave's Thanksgiving break. But V was normally energized, not deflated, by her work. And deflated was the perfect way to describe her, as though someone had reduced her to two dimensions instead of three.

Could it be the stress of introducing him to her parents? He hoped not, and V had assured him she wanted them to meet him. That she'd already told her mother how she felt about him, and Caroline was, at least to some extent, looking forward to meeting him.

No, he thought, taking in her jaw-cracking yawn, and the pillow creases on her cheek. It had to be something else. But, for the life of him, he couldn't imagine what.

"Hey, Doc," he said from the stove. "Eggs will be ready shortly and bacon's on that plate there." He angled his chin at the paper towel covered plate next to the stove. "Want a mimosa?"

She perked up a bit at the mention of food, so maybe it was as simple as her working too hard. "I'm good with coffee for now, thanks," V said, grabbing a piece of bacon and crunching into it with an appreciative hum.

Maybe all he needed to do was get her mind off work and into the weekend they had laid out in front of them. Gently turning the eggs, he said, "Tell me more about this thing we're going to this afternoon."

V leaned a hip against the sink, bathed in morning light filtering in through frosted over kitchen windows. A chilly reminder they were less than two weeks from Christmas. "I told you," she said, "It's a cookie party at Kez's mom's house down in Sawgrass. She hosts one every year. We make cookies and have drinks and food and just hang out."

He plated the eggs and handed her one with a kiss to her forehead, resisting the urge to dip a hand beneath the panel of her robe. For now.

"And it's not like a cookie exchange or whatever?" His mother had hosted her share of those while he'd been a kid and they didn't sound like anything V would be that interested in.

She shook her head with a laugh. "No. You'll see when we get there, it's going to be fun, I promise."

They took their seats at the breakfast bar. "I trust you, Doc," Dave said, and V's head swiveled quickly toward him, eyes bright.

"You do?" she asked.

He barked out a laugh, a forkful of eggs halfway to his mouth. "Of course, I do," he said, puzzled by her surprise. He gave her thigh a reassuring squeeze. "You know that."

Her answering smile was tinged with a hopefulness that Dave didn't understand, but preferred to the wan look she'd worn upon entering the kitchen. He pointed to her plate. "Eat up, Doc."

After a few bites, Dave asked, "How long have you been going to this thing?"

V held up a finger as she chewed. Swallowing, she asked, "To the cookie party? Since I was a kid." She shot him an impish grin. "I'm not sure you're truly prepared for what awaits at Kez's parents' house."

One thick brow arched, and he gave her a questioning half smile. "What is there to 'be prepared for'? And if it's not a cookie exchange, then what exactly is it?"

V's face softened as she reminisced. "Well, it started with Kez's grandmother—we all called her Granny—and her sugar cookies. She'd made them for years, but once she had grandkids, she was only too happy to have them 'help' with the Christmas baking. Which was less help than an explosion of flour, sprinkles, and general mayhem when Kez and Hudson got involved."

"I can see that," Dave said with an easy grin.

"Well, as more and more cousins came into the world, the baking extravaganza got a little bigger each year. Then, it expanded to include friends."

"Which is when you joined the fun, I'm guessing."

V grinned and nodded. "I think Kez first invited me in like second grade or something." Her eyes grew wistful. "I loved that house. It was so different from the holidays at my house. My mom was much more in favor of elegant and stuffy Christmas parties, high teas, and other generally child-unfriendly events."

She sighed. "Granny's house was so much more . . . alive and she welcomed me with open arms. Told me to jump right in with the rest of the rambunctious group already elbow deep in dough, flour, and decorations."

As V talked, Dave pictured a warm and inviting house, with well-worn linoleum in the kitchen and pine-paneled walls, complete with the scents of vanilla and sugar.

"The first year was my real favorite, though. I'd been icing a gingerbread man." She mimed holding an icing bag and drawing lines. "I was so careful with my outline of him, but then someone bumped into me, and the icing bag slipped out of my hand. This giant dollop of sugary goo landed on one of Granny's tea towels on the counter. I just knew she was going to kick me out, ban me forever, but I still had to come clean. So, I took it over to show her, already about to cry."

The memory put a smile on V's face that touched a deep place in Dave's heart. "Granny wiped her hands on her apron and took the dainty little towel from me with a smile. I'd expected her to yell or something, but she just patted me on the head and said, 'If that's the worst thing that gets spilled today, I'll count my blessings.'" V giggled. "Then she whispered in my ear, 'Last year, Kez dumped an entire bowl of molasses onto the floor, stepped in it, and left molasses tracks all down the hallway.' She waggled the towel. 'At least *this* I can put in the wash.'"

V shook her head. "She was so great."

"What happened to the gingerbread man?" Dave asked around a bite of bacon.

V laughed. "She looked at the half-finished cookie and said, 'Now, let's go finish dressing that young man. Can't have him scampering out of here without a full suit of clothes!'"

Still laughing, she said, "After a few more years, Granny called in reinforcements to help corral everything *and* everyone. Which is when Kez's mom stepped in. Once Granny passed away, Kez wanted to keep the tradition going, in a bit more of an adult capacity. Cookies are still baked, but mimosas are also served, along with any other manner of adult beverages. Kez and her mom also expanded the invitation list to the point where I'm not even sure who all is coming, but it's always a good time with plenty of food, drink, and enough Christmas sweaters to stock a boutique."

Dave glanced down at his gray thermal shirt. "I hate I left my Rudolph sweater at home."

V laughed and popped the last bite of bacon in her mouth. "I think you'll be fine." She took his now empty plate. "Since you cooked, I'll clean."

Dave rose from his seat to let her pass, and when she moved in front of him, her familiar floral scent hit his nose. It tapped into his ever-present desire to be close to her. To feel the smoothness of her skin, the softness of her touch and the velvet luxury of her mouth on his. Reflexively, he reached out and wrapped her ponytail around his hand.

V stopped short. "What are you do—oh!"

Her words drifted into a pleased sigh when, with a gentle tug, he tilted her head to the side to expose the long, slender column of her neck. Starting at the edge of her robe's collar, he kissed his way up to just behind her ear. "The dishes can wait," he murmured into her ear, and the plates hit the island with a clatter.

V's body melted back into his, her head dropping to his shoulder while a lazy smile teased her lips. He took the cue she offered him and kissed his way along the line of her jaw. Another tug on her ponytail brought her lips to his, and she hummed in pleasure. Turning in his arms, she draped hers around his shoulders and rose to her toes. Her lips parted and his tongue dipped inside in a languorous sampling of her mouth.

When they pulled apart, Dave released his grip on her hair and lifted V to the counter across from the island. Her robe opened with one tug of the sash.

"What is it with you and countertops?" V asked in a husky whisper.

"C'mon, Doc, give me a little more credit than that. You know it's the combination of you and any flat surface that really does it for me." He nuzzled her throat, kissing the rapid thrum of her pulse.

His hand found her breast and palmed it, pleased with the way her nipple drew tight beneath his touch. Pulling it between his two fingers in the way he knew she loved, he kissed her again. This time a slow, teasing exploration of her mouth that left them both breathless.

"We don't have much time," she said when he pulled away, and yet her hands fisted in his T-shirt and drew him back in for another kiss.

His fingers slid between her thighs, and he teased her with his middle finger. Her knees widened, and she gave a little whimper in response. Dave laughed against her mouth. "As wet as you are, Doc, I don't think we need much time."

V fumbled with the drawstring of his pants and kissed her way along his jaw. "Less talking."

"When you put it that way," he mumbled while sliding his hands beneath her ass and shifting them over to where the cabinets met in a corner.

"What are you d—"

He silenced her question with a quick kiss as he opened the door of the bottom cabinet and placed her foot on it while pulling her to the very edge of the granite top. Shoving the waistband of his pants down, he stepped into the center of the V formed by the cabinets and lined himself up with the center of her.

With one swift thrust, he was inside her. Her head dropped back on a groan, and she used her foot on the cabinet door for leverage as she matched the rhythm of his hips. Her nipples dragged over his chest, and he moaned. "Jesus Christ, Doc."

"I'm already almost . . . oh, God." Her nails sank into his shoulders and the cabinet door creaked. He worked her harder, adding a thumb at her clit because he was just as close as she was. Her breath was hot and desperate at his neck, and he dropped his forehead to her shoulder, nipping at the slope of her breast.

The pressure built to an unbearable level until finally he felt the first ripple of her orgasm around him, and he let go, slamming his hips home on a ragged breath, his rhythm now uneven and desperate with his release. "*Fuck, Doc*," he growled as the last of his orgasm subsided and he slowed to long, languid thrusts to tease out every ounce of her pleasure.

Hazily satisfied blue eyes met his. "How did you . . ." She wiggled the door with her foot. "That was genius, if I may be so bold to say."

He laughed and said, "Applied mathematics at its finest. Angle, thrust and force, all calculated to perfection."

Chapter 25

Vivian! Davis! So glad you could make it!" Kez's mom—Sudie Grace, V had told him on the drive over—a diminutive woman with deep auburn hair and kind blue eyes, exclaimed when she flung open the door. Dave couldn't dwell on her calling him "Davis" because he was blinded by the Christmas sweater she wore. It had a succession of . . . cats stringing tinsel and lights. Lights that lit up and were currently blinking at a rate that required a warning for those with seizure disorders.

Kez appeared behind her, shaking her head. "Mama, this is *Dave*, not Davis." She gave Dave an apologetic look. "Don't feel bad, she mixes up me and my sister all the time." Leaning closer, she added in a stage whisper, "I think it was all that time spent 'studying' with her fellow free spirits in grad school." Kez pantomimed bringing a joint to her lips, which earned her a slap on the arm from her mother.

"Kesler, that's quite enough of your smart mouth." She gave Dave a sheepish grin. "Although she is right about the name thing. At some point in the near future, I'm going to start saying 'Hey, you!' and accepting whoever responds." The door opened wider, and she waved a hand, urging V and Dave inside. "Come in, come in. It's freezing out there."

After handing their coats and other winter gear to Kez, Dave hesitated next to V in the entryway. Kez jerked her head toward the interior of the house. "Don't wait on me," she said. "Head on into the maelstrom. Jackson is in there with Hudson and the kiddos, along with God knows who else. I'll be back in a second."

Before either of them could react, Sudie Grace propelled them down the small hallway and into . . . absolute and utter mayhem. Christmas music played in the background, drowned out for the most part by the steady hum of conversation. The kitchen was packed with people ranging in age from infant to elderly, all of them talking, laughing, and generally enjoying themselves. Various types of food lined one counter and there was a bar of sorts set up in the far corner of the living room visible across the open concept space. The real action was at the large island, where kids of varying ages and sizes were doing their best to spread a bag of flour over the entire surface.

Through the resulting white haze, Dave spotted Jackson looming over the children. A redheaded girl of about three kneeled on a bar stool between his arms, tongue poking out as she concentrated on rolling out a mound of cookie dough. She glanced back at Jackson, and he nodded encouragingly, swiping at his forehead and leaving behind a trail of flour. His eyes landed on Dave, and he grinned.

"Hey, man," Jackson called above the din. "Glad you could make it!" Turning, he signaled to someone behind him, and a dark-haired, slightly older version of Kez came up to relieve him. Dave assumed she was Kez's sister Hudson.

Once Jackson was satisfied the little girl was secure, he came over, grin getting wider by the second. "Welcome to the party," he said with a laugh, giving Dave a slap on the back and V a kiss on the cheek.

Dave surveyed the chaos unfolding around them. "I feel like I've walked into . . . I'm not sure what to call it."

Jackson laughed as V said, "I tried to warn you."

"Yeah, it's a lot to take in," Jackson said, dropping an arm around Kez's mom's shoulders, having to stoop and bend at the knees to accomplish it. "Sudie certainly does know how to throw a party."

The older woman flushed and swatted Jackson's abdomen. "Sweet talker." She used her thumb to wipe the flour off Jackson's forehead. To Dave she said, "Vivian has experienced the swirl around here since she was a little girl. It started out as just a thing we did for the kids, you know, getting the family together to bake cookies. Well, then the kids grew up and had their own kids and . . ." She swept an arm in an arc to encompass the mass of people. "This happened."

The atmosphere was so much like his own family holidays— cramped, frenzied, and thoroughly enjoyable—that Dave understood why V fit in so well at Thanksgiving.

Kez appeared next to Jackson and handed him a drink in a glass shaped like . . . a nutcracker? The one she handed V was a wineglass with Rudolph as the stem and the bowl of the glass designed to be his nose.

"Cheers," she said and clinked her reindeer to V's. An evil gleam came into her eye as she looked at Jackson and Dave. "You know what, Mama? I forgot to tell you that Dave here has a fancy degree in math, some sort of applied computational something or other. And we already know Jackson"—she looped an arm around her boyfriend's waist and gazed too lovingly up at him—"can fix just about anything. Which means"—she sipped and the smile that unfurled all the way up her cheeks would make a certain green guy quake in his fake Santa booties—"they're the perfect gentlemen to help you with the last part of the Village."

V coughed into her drink as Dave and Jackson exchanged a look.

"I'm sorry, the 'village'? What is that exactly?" Dave asked, trepidation creeping up his spine.

Sudie Grace's eyes lit up almost as brightly as her sweater. "Oh, it's my Christmas Village. I've been collecting pieces of it since the late eighties." Her smile dimmed a bit. "But this is a party, Kesler, they don't want to spend it working on th—"

Jackson jumped in. "It's no problem. Whatever you need, we can help. Right, Dave?"

"Uh, well, I . . ." Jackson shot him an imploring look and Dave knew what it meant. The guy would've jumped through flaming hoops of death if it put Kez's parents firmly on his side. And, after all, he had Jackson to thank for meeting V in the first place, so . . . "Sure, no problem, Mrs. Walsh. Happy to help."

Kez's mother looped her small arms through each of Dave's and Jackson's. "Oh please," she said, "call me Sudie. And the real issue is Mr. Fezziwig's. I can't get the light to stay in place. And then there's the issue with the train station."

"Train station?" Dave asked and looked back at V while Sudie Grace led them away.

The wicked little nymph just grinned and waved. "Have fun!"

Around a substantial bite of chocolate pie, V asked Kez, "Has Jackson mentioned anything about Dave to you?"

Kez paused in licking a glob of chocolate off her own fork. "About Dave?" She swallowed and shook her head. "No, why?"

V hesitated, scraping her fork across her plate and debating how to answer.

"Doc?" Rae asked from her place on the other side of V. She'd shown up just after V and Dave. Upon her arrival, they'd tucked themselves into an unoccupied corner of the kitchen with three identical slabs of Sudie Grace's legendary chocolate pie.

V huffed out a breath. "He's just seemed . . . so happy lately." She knew how ridiculous it sounded before she even said it.

Kez's brows rose and her lips twitched. "And that's . . . bad?"

"No," V said, then added, "Maybe?" She groaned and dropped her face into her palm. "I sound nuts, don't I?"

"Much more your area of expertise than mine," Rae quipped. "But I have to agree it is a bit odd to be concerned because your boyfriend is too happy." Her forehead wrinkled. "You don't think he's cheating, do you?"

"What?" V's head whipped toward her. "No, I don't think he's cheating. I think he's . . . well, I don't know what to think. But I'm certain whatever is going on has nothing to do with another woman."

"What exactly *is* going on?" Kez asked.

"I don't know," V said with a frown. "He's been different since Thanksgiving. I mean, you know him, he's never someone that's in a funk, or anything. But lately, it's like some sort of weight's been lifted off him." She set her plate on the counter behind her. "I have to believe it has something to do with work."

"You sure it wasn't the swapping of the 'L' word that happened in Rochester that's got him walking on air?" Rae asked. "He seems like the sort that would float around for a while like little cherubs were hanging onto his ears afterward."

V laughed but shook her head. "No, I don't think it's that."

"Have you asked him?" Kez asked.

"You mean have I said to him, 'Hey babe, you seem unusually happy these days. What gives?'" V shook her head again. "No, I haven't. Plus, we've had so much going on, that I haven't had the cha—"

"Bullshit," Kez coughed into her hand. "You of all people should recognize avoidance when you see it. Why haven't you said something to him?"

"Because," V said and paused. Kez and Rae watched her expectantly, twin patient expressions on their faces. "Ugh." She groaned. "Because what if it's something *he's* happy about, but thinks *I* won't be happy about?"

Kez and Rae exchanged a look. "And what would that be?" Rae asked.

"What if . . ." V pushed a hand through her hair. "What if he's gotten some promotion at Tonic? What if they're finally giving Ryker the boot and giving Dave the job he should've had all along?" *And what if that means he's now fully committed to staying in Rochester?* V thought, but didn't voice.

She didn't need to, because her friends followed her train of thought like it was their own.

"Well." Kez spoke first. "He hasn't said anything to Jackson about it that I know of. And I'm pretty sure Jackson would've told me if the news were something like that."

"Sounds like you and Dave have a few things to talk about while he's in town," Rae said. "You know, after he meets your parents and you are both super relaxed because that won't be stressful *at all.*"

V stuck her tongue out at Rae. "Thanks for all the support."

"It's what I'm here for," Rae said, with a deep bow. She squeezed V's elbow. "Seriously, though, you know we're here for you."

"I do," V smiled, putting a hand over Rae's. "And I also know the two of you are right. I've got to talk to Dave before I make myself even more crazy over something that could be nothing." She glanced at the clock on the microwave. "For now, though, should we go rescue the boys from the Village? It's been over an hour."

Kez grinned widely, and V expected a cackle of wicked glee to follow. But she agreed. "You're probably right. I need to confirm Jackson's cookie skills are up to par—rolling, cutting, *and* icing."

"Was he aware he would be participating in the twelve trials of Christmas today?" Rae asked with a laugh. "What's next, catching the partridge in the pear tree?"

"Careful," Kez warned. "Don't let my mom hear you or she'll try and get us a live partridge for next year."

Drinks in hand, they made their way to the formal front parlor of the old farmhouse where Sudie Grace always set up the Village. They crept silently down the hall, careful to avoid the one creaky floorboard next to the curio cabinet. The three of them peeked around the doorframe and found Jackson crouched behind a table holding one end of a measuring tape while Dave scribbled on a legal pad next to him. Sudie Grace watched them fondly while holding the other end of the tape. Dave showed the legal pad to Jackson who frowned thoughtfully before nodding.

"Yeah, I think if we shift the commercial district over by the window, we should have enough linear feet of cord to pull that off."

Dave nodded, brows knit together in concentration. "I still think it's a good idea to elevate the Christmas Carol scene in some way. Make it the focal point."

Jackson scratched his beard. "I don't know. Victoria Station and the opera house are impressive too. Is there some way we can organize it to highlight more than one vignette?"

Dave tapped the end of his pencil against the pad of paper. "Maybe. I'd have to run some more numbers on our available surface area to be sure, though."

Kez looked at V and mouthed, "Surface area?"

V shrugged and put a hand to her mouth to smother a laugh.

"What about spotlights?" Jackson asked.

With a snort, Kez strode into the room. "What's going on, fellas?"

Jackson looked up at her and grinned. "Hey, Gorgeous. We're just reviewing your mom's blueprints and if we tweak some things, we can smooth out traffic flow in the Village."

Kez pulled her lips between her teeth as she picked up a figurine of a carol singer. "Traffic flow, you say?"

Jackson nodded, rising to his feet and carefully retracting the tape measure. "Yeah, the way everything is set up now creates a snarl near Fagin's place. But if we take th—"

"Sweetheart," Kez interrupted. "You do know these figures are wholly sedentary, right? As in, when you place them, they do not move."

Jackson nodded. "Yeah, but with certain adjustments to the layout it won't be as crowded." He surveyed the room filled with ceramic buildings, people, animals, and infrastructure. "What do you think, Dave? It shouldn't take us longer than a day or so to get it a—"

Dave nodded. "Yeah, that should work. Unless we want to explore that spotlight idea a little further."

Kez looked at her mother. "You've created monsters."

Sudie Grace laughed. "I told them we had blueprints, but they insisted on giving things a fresh eye."

"Yeah, well, I'm sure Hudson needs fresh hands in the cookie dough and decoration department, and that trumps the redesign of the Walsh Village. Did they fix the light issue?" Kez asked.

Sudie Grace nodded. "Oh yes, everything is up and running."

Kez clapped her hands together. "All right, gentlemen, your work here is done, and we thank you ever so much for your assistance in getting the Village in tip-top shape."

Jackson looked crestfallen. "But we've made a plan."

Kez patted his chest. "I'm sure you have, and I'm equally sure it's amazing. And will still be amazing next year when you help Mama set everything up *from the beginning* instead of trying to redo everything."

Rae whispered to V, "Guess he passed the first of the Christmas Trials. Next up, flour application followed by dough thickness and cookie cutter placement."

"Don't forget sprinkle spreading and icing design," V whispered back.

"Or cookie consistency and sheet spacing," Rae said, unable to hold in a snort of laughter that made Dave glance their way.

"C'mon, honey," V said to him. "If you're good, maybe Sudie Grace will invite you and Jackson back for another playdate tomorrow."

He shot her a mock glare but put his legal pad and pencil down on a nearby chair. "You realize," Dave said as he crossed the room toward her, "you ladies have interrupted what could be the greatest city revitalization project ever known in Dickensian times."

"Alas, their loss is my gain," she replied and took his hand. "C'mon, Richardson, let's put those math skills of yours to the true test and see how many gingerbread men you can squeeze onto a single cookie sheet."

"Regan Murphy!" Sudie Grace exclaimed, making V glance up from her cookies. The older woman bit back a laugh as she asked, "Did you use red hots to make a pornographic reindeer?"

V swallowed her own snort of laughter as Rae appraised the well-endowed cookie in front of her and sipped her champagne. "I prefer to think of him as anatomically correct."

Kez looked over her shoulder and joined the laughter. "More like genetically blessed." She plucked off the offending cinnamon decorations and popped them in her mouth.

"Hey!" Rae said, affronted at the attack on her masterpiece.

Kez took out another red ball and placed it pointedly on the nose of the reindeer. "You should never be allowed to bake unsupervised," she said.

Dave laughed from his assigned dough station across the counter. "I'm starting to think you could just say Rae should never be unsupervised."

As Rae discreetly shot him the bird, V bumped his hip with hers. "Insults and vulgar gestures. Warms my heart to see you fitting so well into the family."

Dave laughed and nodded at the snowflakes V was decorating. "Looking good there, Doc. You've got such a light touch when you need it."

V bobbled the sprinkles in her hand, dumping a pile of silver sparkles onto the center of a snowflake. Dave smoothed the shimmery shards into the design made by the cookie cutter. "But then"—he shot her a naughty grin—"so do I."

Deftly, he switched her fully decorated batch with the plain batch he'd just cut out. Placing the decorated cookies in the oven assembly line, he grabbed a clean pan and set it to the side. Before going back to his dough, he leaned down to whisper into her ear, "Although by now you're well aware I'm good with my hands and pay attention to the small details."

Holy holly berries, it is hot in here. Her laugh was breathy as she shot him a reproachful look. "Really? Innuendo at a cookie party?"

He gave her an unapologetic shrug. "Can't help it, Doc. With you around, innuendo follows." Dave brushed a streak of flour from her cheek. "I think you've managed to get as much flour on you as you have on the counter."

She stuck her tongue out at him. "I get into my work."

He laughed and rolled out more gingerbread dough. "I can see that from the flour on your face to the sprinkles on your shirt, Doc."

V watched him work for a few minutes, the rolling pin adroitly swiping over the dough, his careful evaluation of whether it was the right thickness before calculating the placement of each gingerbread man. The care he put into it tugged at her heart. He'd thrown himself into cookie day with the same gusto he'd approached renovation of the Village. Not that it was hard to get into the spirit when they were enveloped in the holiday warmth of Sudie Grace's kitchen. But still, he could've participated without being into it. But instead, he'd cut out every shape of cookie from Santa to a certain grouchy green guy and his dog, decorated with everything from icing to sanding sugar and managed to save a batch from burning when Sudie Grace had been distracted by her granddaughter's rendition of Frosty the Snowman.

He'd made a point of asking her about today, found out it was important to her, and then treated it that way. She valued this time, so he did too. The innate romantic simplicity of that stroked over her heart in feathery soft touches. At Thanksgiving, he'd told her she was precious to him, and today had confirmed it. It also made her fall just a little more in love with him.

Dave glanced over at her. His eyes were warm and his skin a little flushed from the heat of the kitchen. He had a touch of flour, or possibly powdered sugar, in his hair and a small streak of what she assumed was chocolate on his right cheek. Grabbing a dish towel, she dabbed at it as she said, "I'm glad you came with me."

He grinned and kissed her wrist as she wiped his face. "Nowhere else I'd rather be, Doc."

"Than up to your elbows in cookie dough, sprinkles, and forced to drink your beer from a Rudolph mug while singing Christmas carols with toddlers?"

He laughed. "As though there is any other way to drink it during December. And I happened to love Edith's rendition of Frosty. She could teach River and Ryder a thing or two, I'm sure."

Next to them, the oven timer went off with a shrill beep. "Dave, honey," Sudie Grace called from her position icing cookies. "Can you grab that for me? I'm up to my elbows in buttercream."

Smiling over at Sudie Grace, he said, "Sure, no problem."

V's hand dropped back to her side as Dave went to rescue the latest batch of sweets. Rae sidled over next to her, cookie in one hand and champagne in the other.

"Careful not to swoon into the sprinkles. A few too many snorts of those, and you'll be high as a kite." She bit an antler off her cookie.

"Thanks for the tip," V said, pulling her eyes from Dave's backside.

Rae laughed. "I'm glad he got to come down this weekend. I hate he's going to miss New Year's Eve."

V frowned and picked up the silver sprinkles once again. "Yeah, me too."

Since this was his one weekend off a month, it meant Dave had to work the next two weekends, including New Year's. He was off Christmas Day, but her mother would have a conniption if she missed Thanksgiving and Christmas and she didn't want to jeopardize the semi-breakthrough they'd had. She could hardly ask him to miss spending the holiday with his family if he'd have to fly home the following day. So, this weekend was it until the following year. As she watched Dave laugh at something Sudie Grace said, V discovered it was entirely possible to start missing someone while they were still in the room with you.

Chapter 26

December 16th

Leaning against the doorjamb of the master bathroom in V's townhouse, Dave watched her smooth on a final coat of lipstick. Her hair hung in wavy curls down her back, and she toyed with the ends of them. He couldn't help but grin at the appraising gaze she cast her reflection, cataloging any perceived imperfection. As if there were any. The deep red dress she wore floated around her thighs and a slender gold link belt cinched her waist. Its delicate emblem of interwoven *C*'s glinted in the light from her vanity. Red-bottomed heels waited for her by the door. He doubted he'd ever get used to this luxuriously glamorous woman being his.

She flicked a glance at him in the mirror and caught his grin. "What?"

Dave shook his head. "Nothing."

V's eyes narrowed. "That grin is something, not nothing."

"Just thinking about how lucky I am, that's all."

That made her smile and turn to face him. "Is that right?"

He nodded and stepped forward, unable to keep from reaching for her. His palms landed on her hips, and he pulled her closer, inhaling the delicately spicy floral scent she wore. "And maybe," he said as he nuzzled her ear, "I'm thinking I can't wait to bring you home after dinner and see the best part of this outfit."

"The best part?" she asked as his lips brushed the skin of her neck. He felt her shiver beneath his touch and grinned.

"Mm-hmm." He hummed against the shell of her ear. "After four months together, Doc, I know that no matter how good things look here"—he touched the bodice of her dress—"it doesn't hold a candle to what's underneath."

Her laugh was a little shaky, and she pushed at his chest without any real force. "We can't be late for dinner," she said. When he lifted his head reluctantly, she gave him a flirty smile. "And isn't the anticipation half the fun?"

His throaty growl made V blush and giggle. "You'll get to unwrap me later, I promise."

Dave's hands slipped to her ass and gave it a possessive squeeze. "I'll hold you to that, Doc."

"I'd expect nothing less." She moved out of his embrace. "But we need to get going. Caroline doesn't tolerate tardiness."

V had told him about last week's lunch with her mother. "It's like we were two people having the same conversation, only in different languages, so we could never understand each other," she'd said, her expression as regretful as it was hopeful.

He knew she was tentatively excited it would be the first step on the road to a closer relationship with her mother. Which made tonight's dinner even more important, because he knew he didn't fit the mold of what her parents expected for her. And yet, she was introducing them anyway.

V slipped past him into the bedroom, and he turned. "Hey, Doc?"

"Hmm?" She glanced over at him as she fastened an earring.

It was on the tip of his tongue to tell her about his interview on Monday. To tell her he felt confident about landing the position. That he'd be in Charlotte by June if everything worked out. Because he wanted her to know he was trying to be the kind of man she deserved. The kind of guy her parents would be glad she had in her life. The kind of man worthy of someone like her, even though he knew the last part was impossible. He'd never be worthy of a woman like her. No one would be. She was everything and then some. But he was going to make damn sure he came as close as humanly possible.

V turned to fully face him when he didn't say anything. "Dave?" Questions swam in her blue eyes.

The words were there, ready to roll out in rapid succession. But then he pictured those same crystalline blue eyes clouding with regret if he didn't get the job. And the words vanished along with his inclination to tell her. He forced a smile and shook his head. "Sorry, I was just going to tell you how gorgeous you look tonight."

V cocked her head slightly, and she watched him for several seconds, waiting for him to say more. When he didn't, she gave him a small smile and said, "Thanks, so do you." Gesturing to the door of her bedroom, she said, "I need to grab my shoes and then we can go."

When she walked out, Dave felt like he'd missed a moment. A pivotal one he couldn't get back. He swallowed down the feeling and followed her from the room.

"Ever been to Charleston, Dave?" Duvall asked once their entrées were cleared, and they waited for coffee and dessert.

"Charleston?" Dave asked. "As in Charleston, South Carolina?"

When Duvall nodded, Dave replied, "No, sir, I haven't."

The way Duvall asked the question signaled more than idle curiosity. Dave sensed a shift in the conversation.

"It's a beautiful city," Caroline said, touching the diamond pendant at her throat. "One of Vivian's favorite places."

Beside him, V nodded, but he saw the suspicion in the slight pinch of her brow. "Yeah, it is. Are you and Daddy planning a trip?"

Caroline tittered with laughter. "Oh heavens, no. Who has time for trips at Christmas? I've got too many irons in the fire as it is these days without the added hassle of holiday travel."

"It can be a beast," Dave agreed, curious as to where this was going.

Duvall jumped back in to steer the conversation back to the course he'd apparently set. "Charleston's come a long way in the last few years, businesswise. Tourism is still king, of course, but there are lots of opportunities in the aerospace field. In fact," Duvall said with a grin, "I have a good friend who works with Riverton Aerodynamics down there."

Dave swallowed his own grin as Duvall's plan became clear. While polite questions had been asked about Dave's college experience and interest in mathematics, nothing had been said about his job. Duvall had been biding his time to make whatever pitch this was going to be.

V tensed beside him, and Dave put a comforting hand on her knee beneath the table. Taking a sip of his beer, he responded, "Riverton? I think some guys I graduated with work in their Portland office."

Duvall nodded, leaning forward with enthusiasm. "They're a big operation, as I understand it. And looking to get bigger. Rumors are swirling about a new office in Charlotte. I'm not sure of the timeframe, but I could find out." His blue eyes, so like V's, looked contemplatively at Dave. "If I had a reason to get more details that is."

"Daddy," V said, her tone as rigid as the set of her shoulders. Dave gave her knee a gentle squeeze of reassurance.

"What?" Duvall said, his hands spread wide. "I'm just saying I could. That's all."

"That's very generous of you, sir," Dave said. He debated whether to say anything more, but before he could, V did.

"Dave isn't interested in corporate work, Daddy," she said, putting her hand over his. "I told you that." Her smile was tight and her eyes serious.

Dave's heart skipped a few beats at her unwavering support of him, even in the face of an opportunity that could bring them within a morning's drive of each other. She was standing up for him, for something she assumed he wanted, because he'd never given her any reason to think otherwise. She didn't know things had changed. She didn't know, because he hadn't told her. No matter how many times she'd asked. *Fuck.*

"Well, maybe that first place wasn't the right fit for him," Duvall said, undeterred. "Riverton could be a totally different experience. And it's a damn sight closer to Charlotte than Rochester."

"Can't argue with that, sir," Dave said, which earned him a sharp glance from V. *Shit.* He needed to tell V about his interview. Needed to tell her about everything he'd been doing the last few months. Needed to let her all the way into the life he wanted to make with her. He'd been a moron to keep her on the outside of all of it. A pathetic coward, too scared of his own failure to tell her the truth.

Oblivious to Dave's inner turmoil, Duvall angled toward him. "From what I hear, the Charleston office is hiring now. They have sign-on bonuses and a money-purchase pension plan. You don't find that too many places these days."

"That's certainly true," Dave said, because he couldn't think of what else to say. He felt V go stiff as a board next to him.

When she spoke, her voice was like steel coated in velvet, soft but unyielding. "I didn't invite Dave to dinner so you could ambush him with a job he doesn't want, Daddy. It's nice of you to mention it, but like I said, Dave tried the corporate world and decided to do something different."

Jesus Christ, Dave thought. He felt like such a dick. Here was V defending his job—a job he no longer wanted—and championing the decision she assumed he'd make. Because he'd been too chickenshit to tell her the truth. He had to say something before things went any farther off the rails.

"Well," Dave said, drawing V's gaze back to him. "Maybe your dad's right. Maybe that just wasn't the right place for me. And it was a long time ago. Maybe somewhere else could be a better fit."

V's eyes rounded when she turned in her seat to face him. She blinked several times before saying, "A . . . better fit?"

Dave nodded. "Yeah, who knows? Maybe it's time for a change."

"Time for a change?" V parroted, looking at him like he'd grown two heads and he felt like an asshole for blindsiding her, but there was nothing he could do about it now.

Duvall picked up on the tension radiating between the two of them and cleared his throat. "Well, like I said"—he glanced at Dave—"think about it and let me know."

"I appreciate that, sir," Dave said, just as the waiter appeared with dessert and coffee.

"I think that went well," Dave said, unknotting his tie and breaking the icy silence that descended between them the moment they'd gotten in the car. V hadn't said two words to him on the drive home and he knew why. She was angry—and deserved to be—because of the way he'd reacted to her dad's offer.

V made a noncommittal noise from inside her closet. He walked over to the doorway and said, "Things seem to be going well between you and your mom too."

She slipped her heels onto the shelf and turned her back to him as she unzipped her dress. "Yeah, she was on her best behavior tonight."

As her dress began to gape, Dave couldn't resist stepping forward. His fingers slid around hers and he helped ease the zipper the rest of the way down. When he stepped forward to kiss the silky junction of her neck, she didn't relax into his touch. Instead, she juked away and stepped out of his embrace. She shimmied the dress the rest of the way off and tossed it into a dry-cleaning bag.

"Doc, I know you're mad. And I get it, okay?"

"Do you?" V asked without looking at him as she knotted her robe.

She moved past him into the bathroom. The hum of her electric toothbrush whirred, and he leaned in the doorway. She wouldn't meet his eyes in the mirror, seemingly transfixed by the faucet fixtures.

"Yeah," he said, coming farther into the room. "I do and I'm sorry. I should've mentioned to you that I . . . that things at Tonic weren't working out, and I was considering . . ." He rubbed a hand at the back of his neck, frustrated with his inability to express himself.

She set the toothbrush on its base and pulled out her dental floss. Dave closed his hand around hers before she could open it. "Doc," he said, voice quiet but firm. "I fucked up, okay? I know that, and I'm sorry."

Her hand dropped to the counter, his still resting atop it. When she looked at him, her eyes reflected her feelings in whirling pools of angry blue. "Is that supposed to make it all better, Dave? An apology? For making me look like I have zero idea what you really want? In front of my parents, no less." She shook her head, irritation in every movement.

V pulled her hand from beneath his, tossing the dental floss onto the counter. Her hands went to her hips. "I'm sitting there getting mad as hell at my dad for even mentioning this Riverton thing. Thinking the whole time that you're suffering in silence next to me, being the good sport because the last thing in the world you want is an office job and then . . ." She laughed mirthlessly and closed her eyes. "Then out of freaking nowhere, you're all, 'gosh, that'd be great if you find out more for me. Thanks so much.' What was that?"

Dave rocked back on his heels. "You know things haven't been that great at Tonic, so I ju—"

V cut him off. "No," she said, her voice like ice. "I don't *know* anything. I can guess. I can surmise. I can speculate. But the one thing I can't do is *know* anything about your job. Because you won't freaking talk about it! I've asked. I've begged. I've pleaded with you to talk to me. To open up to me. To let me in. And I got nothing. Nothing but a consistent brushoff and a 'Don't worry about it,' or 'Let's not waste time talking about work.' And now . . . *now* my dad says one thing over dinner after you've known him less than an hour and suddenly you're considering a career change?"

"It's not exactly sudden," Dave said, and instantly regretted it.

Her brows snapped down and her lips twisted to the side. "It was to me. You know, since this is the first I've heard of it."

She crossed her arms. "You share nothing with me, but lo and behold, my dad says four sentences, if that, and suddenly he's your freaking career counselor. And while I'm standing up for what I have to assume you want for your life, you're asking him to put in a good word." Her glare was a pure blue flame. "Do you know how stupid that made me look? Not even two weeks ago, I'm explaining to my mother how in love we are and how in sync we are and blah, blah, blah. Then tonight, it looks like I don't know the first thing about you."

"Don't say that, Doc," he said, reaching for her. She backed away.

"Why not? It's true. All I've ever done is ask questions that deserve answers. And, until tonight, I thought maybe I had at least some of them. But now . . ." V's hands went to her forehead and flicked outward. "All that's been blown to hell. I just don't understand!"

"Of course, you wouldn't understand," Dave said, his insecurities lashing out in the face of her anger. "How could you when you've known what you wanted to do with your life since the womb? Not all of us are that lucky, okay, Doc? Some of us had to figure some shit out, make a few mistakes along the way before we realized our experiment with something other than the tried-and-true path was a colossal failure."

V glared at him. "How could I know is right, considering you never told me anything! I had to pry little breadcrumbs out of you about your job. About whether you were happy, or what I could do to help you. About anything at all! You say you love me, but if you did . . . if you truly loved me, you'd let me all the way into your life. You wouldn't hold back or shut me out of things."

Dave jolted backward like she'd struck him. He felt her words for the blow they were because they echoed his own thoughts from earlier. Fear gripped his heart in a cold vise. "What are you saying, Doc?"

"I'm saying . . ." her voice cracked, and she swallowed thickly. "I'm saying that when you love someone, you trust them. You trust them with your brightest joy and your deepest, darkest fears. You trust them with your worst days as much as you do your best days. You trust them to be there for you when you need them, even if you're scared to ask for it. You still trust them enough to ask." She blinked back tears, and it gutted him to watch. "When you love someone, you trust them with everything. Without trust, there can be no love." A single tear tracked down her cheek. "And you don't trust me, Dave. If you did, I'd have known more than you being unhappy, or that Ryker was a dick. I'd have known all of it, because you would've trusted me enough to tell me."

She looked at him with red-rimmed eyes. "All I wanted you to do was talk to me, Dave. Tell me you wanted something different. What changed? When did it change? Why did it change?"

She let out a strangled laugh. "You know, until tonight, I thought you'd gotten a promotion at Tonic and didn't want to tell me."

"What?" Dave's shock made him bark out the word. "Why would you think that?"

V lifted one shoulder in a listless shrug. "You've seemed happier lately. Not as tired or frustrated with work. And I wondered why. Like, what would be something that would make you happy but you wouldn't want to tell me? The only thing I could think of was the owners finally realized they should replace Ryker with you. And you thought I wouldn't be happy for you, because of what it could mean for us."

The raw hurt in her eyes nearly sliced him in two.

"Doc," he said, wanting so badly to reach for her. "That's not . . ." He shook his head. "No, Ryker's still at Tonic and will be for the foreseeable future as far as I know."

"Then what . . ." V cleared her throat. "What are you afraid of telling me?"

"I have an interview with a company here in Charlotte. It's a brewery. And it's technically the third interview. The final piece of the interview process, I guess you'd call it. I'd have to go to school for a bit before moving, but—if I get the job—I'd move here to start in June."

The words came out in a tumbled rush, falling over top of each other like rocks in a landslide. And as they spilled out, the relief from finally telling her mixed with fear he'd waited too long. That by keeping it from her, the weeks she'd spent wondering what he was hiding tainted the big reveal. That she thought he'd been shutting her out, when what he'd been trying to do was protect her from the fallout of another misstep on his part. What he'd seen as guarding her feelings, she'd viewed as a lack of trust.

V's mouth dropped into a perfect O and she stared at him without saying anything for a few seconds. Recovering, she spluttered, "Wh-what? You were . . . interviewing?"

Dave nodded. "Assuming I don't fuck up on Monday, then I'm pretty sure they'll make the offer."

Her face was a ravaged mask of disbelief. "Why wouldn't you tell me about that?"

"Because," Dave said, pushing a hand through his hair. "I didn't want to disappoint you if I didn't get the job."

"Disappoint me?" V blinked at him. "Why would I be disappointed in you trying to get a new job?"

"Not for trying," Dave said. "For failing. Again."

V rocked back on her heels, surprise making her eyes go wide. "What are you talking about?"

"The last time I did anything worthwhile was my college graduation, Doc. Since then, it's been a downhill slide." He smiled sadly. "At least until I met you. You are the one thing I've gotten right in a long, long time."

V shook her head, blond curls bouncing. "I don't understand."

"I picked the wrong job out of college and had to leave. Then, instead of getting back out there like I should have, I took the job at Tonic. It was only going to be for a little while, I told myself. Only two years clip by and I'm still there. Still there and now with a worse boss than my first job. Worse boss, worse pay, worse prospects for change. I know the last one is true, because I've been applying for jobs since mid-October and tomorrow is the first time I've gotten something more than a 'thanks for your interest' email, or courtesy interview."

"You've been looking for a new job since . . . October?"

He winced at her wounded expression. "I . . . had to."

"Because of Ryker?"

Dave shook his head, eyes never leaving hers. "No, Doc. Because of you. You're what changed everything, or at least made the light come on in my dim bulb brain and admit things needed to change. I had to stop muddling through life and actually *make* a life. A life with you, which wasn't going to happen if I kept working at Tonic. I started sending out my résumé, sparse though it was."

"Why would you keep that from me?" V asked, and the anguished note in her voice nearly brought him to his knees.

"Because, Doc, the last thing I wanted to do was disappoint you by adding another failure to my list. It's hard enough knowing I've disappointed my parents. I couldn't do that to you too."

V shook her head and looked past him for a few weighted seconds. With a sigh, she met his gaze, a deep sadness in her eyes. "The only thing that disappoints me is the knowledge you didn't trust me enough . . . you didn't trust *us* enough to tell me the truth. You didn't believe enough in what we have together to talk to me about any of this."

"Doc, that's not true," he protested, fear twisting his gut. "I love you. You know that. It's why I couldn't stand the thought of letting you down."

V made a frustrated sound deep in her throat. "You keep saying that. But how could you trying to land a job here possibly be a letdown? What part of that would do anything but thrill me?"

"The part when I didn't get it."

"No!" The vehemence in her voice pushed Dave back a step. "No," she said, more softly. "That's when I'd be there for you. That's when I want you to know you can turn to me for comfort and support. I'd be disappointed *for* you, but not in you. Never in you. And it breaks my heart you don't know that."

Her words pierced his own heart. "Doc, I ju—"

V shook her head. "I don't want any more rationalizations, Dave. I need . . ." She sucked in a breath. "I need some time to think, okay?"

Her eyes closed and Dave wanted to wrap her in his arms and tell her a thousand times how sorry he was. But he didn't. He didn't because he knew she didn't want that. That she wouldn't accept his comfort. Wouldn't accept him.

"Doc, I . . ."

"Don't," she said without opening her eyes. "Just don't, okay? I don't want to hear how sorry you are, or anything else from you right now. I just . . . I just can't."

Dave felt his heart shatter into a thousand jagged pieces that tore his soul to shreds. "Doc, please, don't do this. Don't shut me out."

Her laugh was brittle. "Why not? It's what you've done to me the whole time."

Chapter 27

December 17th

V blinked. Or at least she tried to. The slime stuck to her eyelashes, a combination of dried tears, moisturizer (because skincare mattered even in times of crisis) and the last remnants of her mascara made moving her eyelids more difficult than normal. She rubbed the base of her palms against her eyes and managed to get both open. The smell of coffee wafted in and hit her brain seconds before she remembered her coffee maker didn't have an automatic start. Then she heard a door open. Someone was in her house! Searching her bedroom for anything that could be used as a weapon, her eyes landed on the paperweight Kez gave her last Christmas. Within it, Kez, Rae, and photo V smiled deliriously while toasting luminous glasses of wine.

Snatching it off her nightstand, she crept to her bedroom door. Sound carried up the stairs, including muffled voices and the opening and closing of cabinets. Steeling herself and adjusting her grip on the paperweight, she padded down the stairs. Reaching the landing, she pressed a hand to her chest to calm her pounding heart. Adrenaline had her pulse racing, and she took a deep breath. She would count to three and then round the corner. Belatedly, she remembered her cell phone charging next to her bed and groaned inwardly at her stupidity.

V glanced back up the stairs, wondering if she should chance a trip back up to get it.

"She's not up yet," came a familiar voice from the hall, "I'll just go an—" Kez's words ended in a gasp and then a shrieked, "ShitFuckDammit!"

"What's going on?" Rae called and V heard her scrambling footsteps on the hardwood floors. She skidded to a stop in the foyer where Kez sagged against the wall, a hand clutching at her chest and drawing in deep breaths while V remained poised on the landing in her rumpled pajamas, paperweight weapon in hand.

Rae's eyes swung back and forth as a large grin spread over her face. "I see you found her," she said to a still wheezing Kez. Her eyes went to the paperweight in V's hand, then V's face. "Do you always carry us around with you? Or is this some weird morning thing where you prop it up while you have coffee and pretend we're all together?"

V pressed the knuckle of her free hand into the corner of one bleary eye. "I thought you were . . . intruders."

Rae's lips quirked up into a half grin. "Who made coffee before robbing you? And you were going to what, weight us down until the police arrived?"

"No, I was going t—" V stopped and gave her head a shake. "Never mind, it's not important." She looked between her two friends. "What are you doing here?" She knew how they got in, since they both had keys *and* her alarm code.

"We're here," Kez said, "because I found Dave sleeping on Jackson's couch this morning. Which means you've got some explaining to do, young lady. As in, what the fuck is going on?"

"Let her at least shower first," Rae said. Before V could read too much kindness into the suggestion, she added, "You'll feel better once you wash off those mascara hieroglyphics going on under your eyes right now."

With a resigned groan, V trudged back up the stairs to shower and change. Upon her return, Rae emerged from the powder room. She took in V's tattered jeans and ancient sweatshirt, stopping for a long period at her well-worn Converse. "Is this some sort of protest outfit?"

"I'm dressing how I feel," retorted V.

"No one," Rae said drily, "has ever felt *that* bad about anything."

"Thanks for your support," V said and made a move to go back upstairs.

Rae grabbed her hand. "I see we aren't ready for the humor portion of today. Duly noted. Let's move to the greasy food and all-men-are-pigs segment and see if we can't breathe a little life back into you, okay?"

She plodded dutifully behind Rae into the kitchen where they found Kez dishing up eggs and bacon onto three plates.

The three of them took their seats around V's small breakfast table. "Okay, Doc," Kez said, picking up a piece of bacon. "The floor is yours."

"Men are pigs," V said, with a half-hearted smile.

"Agreed," Rae said. "But I need more than that. What happened?"

After a fortifying swig of coffee, she told them. All of it. Every detail about how Dave hadn't trusted her enough to tell the truth about how unhappy he was with his job. That he'd started to want something different, something more, something she had no clue about because, again, he hadn't told her.

"The bottom line," she said, getting up to refill all their coffees, "is that he doesn't trust me. And if he doesn't trust me, then he doesn't love me. It's as simple as that."

Rae and Kez exchanged a look. "Um . . ." Kez stirred cream into her coffee. "There is very little about this scenario that sounds simple to me. Actually, none of it sounds simple."

"It sounds like less of a trust issue and more of a fear issue," Rae chimed in.

V snorted. "Fear of what?"

"Fear of not being enough for you, Doc. Fear of admitting to the woman who is the epitome of having their shit together . . ." Rae eyed V's outfit. "An exception to every rule, I suppose."

V glared at her, but Rae went on. "As I was saying. If he told you about all these doubts, all these fears, concerns, regrets, or whatever you call them. If he'd told you about any of them, he'd be admitting he wasn't sure what he wanted to do with his life. That he was, in essence, a man with no plan."

V waved her comments away. "That's crazy."

"Is it?" Kez asked. "Because you said his family was pretty hard on him about things. Including what he needed to do and changes he should make to keep you in his life. Is it that farfetched that he'd want to figure a few things out before talking to you?"

"Are you saying he was right not to tell me about the interviews? Or how unhappy he was at work?"

Kez shook her head, and Rae mimicked the gesture. "Not at all. The mature, grown-ass man thing to do would have been talking to you about how he was feeling and getting your input."

"But we also recognize," Rae said, picking up the thread, "how hard it would be, because you've always known what you wanted. Not just wanted it, but *gotten* it. You're at the pinnacle, the tippity tip toppest top of it and he's getting ready to start over at the bottom."

She sipped her coffee and pinned V with a look. "Imagine, just for a second, how it would feel to talk about restarting his career with someone who's never deviated, much less faltered on their entire career path. From high school through med school to now. Would that be a conversation you'd be eager to have? Or would you maybe want to see if you couldn't put something together before broaching the topic?"

"I . . ." Any snappy retort died on V's lips as she considered what Kez and Rae were saying. "Well, damn."

"Ah, she's starting to see the light," Kez said.

V's brain buzzed as she processed through what she'd just heard and thought about something Dave said last night. That she'd have no way to understand anything he was going through, because she'd never wavered from her own course. But still, shouldn't he have trusted her enough to know she'd have been there for him? Maybe he was scared, maybe he was ashamed, maybe he was a lot of things and maybe all that really sucked. But so what? He said he loved her and love, at least to V, went hand in hand with trust. You couldn't have one without the other. He couldn't love her if he didn't trust her.

"He should've talked to me," V said stubbornly.

"He still can," Rae said. "The question now is whether you're will-ing to listen."

V sighed and chewed her lip. Not because she didn't know the answer to that question, but because she did. She'd known it even as she'd been livid with him. She'd known it while crying into her pillow. She knew it because she knew she loved him too much not to. If he were willing to talk, V would listen. And she had a few things she needed to say too.

December 18th 8:37 a.m.

V: *Good luck today.*
Dave: *Thanks, Doc.*
Dave: *I missed you last night. I'm so sorry. I know you don't want to hear it, but I am. I'm so sorry, Doc. I'll make it up to you, I promise.*
V: *Focus on today, Dave.*

December 18th 4:04 p.m.

Dave: *I think it went well. I'll hear from them by Wednesday if not before.*
V: *I'm sure it went great.*
Dave: *I'd love to see you before I fly back, Doc. We've got a lot to talk about.*
V: *I agree. But I'm still thinking about what to say.*
Dave: *I love you, Doc.*

Bubbles, bubbles, bubbles. No response.

December 18th 7:43 p.m.

Dave: *I got an earlier flight out.*
V: *Fly safe, please, and let me know when you land.*

December 18th 10:36 p.m.

This is Vivian Walters, I'm sorry I missed you, but please leave your name, number, and a detailed message, so I can get back to you as soon as I can. Thank you.

"Hey, Doc, it's me. Made it back to Rochester in one piece. I . . . uh . . . fuck, I don't know what to say. Except I love you. And I'm sorry. I'm so fucking sorry, Doc. I'm here when you're ready to talk, or yell, or test out a scalpel . . . whatever you need. I'm here for you. I love you, baby. Sleep tight."

December 19th

Number of times Dave reached for his phone to call V: 8
Number of times V reached for her phone to call Dave: 8
Number of texts typed and deleted from Dave to V: 11
Number of texts typed and deleted from V to Dave: 9
Abject misery level of all parties involved: Hard 10 out of 10

December 20th 10:45 a.m.

To: drichardson@gmail.com
From: jeanette.mickleson@loseyourcompassbrewing.com
Re: Malting and Brewing Technologist—Offer Package

Dave,
After your interview, it should come as no surprise the Malting and Brewing Technologist job is yours. I've attached our written offer and accompanying paperwork. Read through the attachments and let me know if you have any questions. We're delighted to offer you the position and can't wait to have you on board.
Jeanette

Jeanette Mickleson
President and Brewmistresss

Lose Your Compass Brewing
1045 East Nowhere Boulevard
Charlotte, NC 28277
(980) 985-2222—Telephone

December 20th 11:05 a.m.

To: vivian.walters@CMHA.org
From: drichardson@gmail.com
RE: Wanted You To Be The First To Know FW: Malting and Brewing
Technologist—Offer Package

December 20th 11:47 a.m.

To: drichardson@gmail.com
From: vivian.walters@CMHA.org
RE: Wanted You To Be The First To Know FW: Malting and Brewing
Technologist—Offer Package
I never had a doubt in my mind. Congratulations!

V listened to the whoosh of the email heading into cyberspace and wished she could ride its electronic trail all the way to Rochester. Not talking to Dave in the last two days had been harder than almost anything. She'd only known the man since September and had lived the majority of three decades without him, but now that she'd known life with him in it . . . a life without him was a cold prospect she couldn't fathom.

She'd thought a lot about what Rae and Kez said during their breaking and entering breakfast and tried to consider things from Dave's perspective. While she still firmly believed he was an idiot for not telling her his plans, hurt no longer blinded her to the reason why. He'd been protecting himself as much as her by staying silent. What he'd failed to realize was how much easier it would have been for him if he'd told not just her, but his family too. The Richardsons would have circled around him in one big, schmoopy family group hug. But the male ego was a fragile, tender thing and Dave's had taken a beating in the last few years. Which meant he saw things in a darker light than she or his family would. Where they would have been proud of his efforts, he was ashamed of his lack of progress. She was going to have to shake some sense into the big dummy, and that couldn't be done by email, text, or a phone call.

V: *Still got that hookup at American Airlines?*
Rae: *Yeah . . . why?*
V: *I need a ticket to Rochester. Tonight.*

December 20th 11:38 p.m.

Stepping into the rear cooler, Dave relished the chill. After four hours of constant motion, his T-shirt clung to his back. He couldn't tell if his arms were sticky from the beer someone had spilled, his own sweat, or a combination of both. But for his fear of recreating a version of the lamppost scene from *A Christmas Story*, he would've leaned against the freezing wall of the walk-in. Valuing both his shirt and the skin of his back, he settled for a long stretch and a few inhales of frigid air.

While he thought about V. Just like he had since leaving Charlotte two days ago. He'd wondered if he'd hear more from her after her congratulatory email. But his phone remained silent, no matter how many times he'd pulled it out to check for a missed call or text. Jackson had been no help, either.

"Sorry, man," he'd said when Dave called him on the way to work. "I'm with V on this. You should've said something about all this shit. Not just to her, but to all of us. That's what we're here for, dumbass."

"I called for some insight, man," Dave complained.

Jackson grunted into the phone. "Here's some insight. Find the man hiding within the pathetic human being I'm on the phone with and tell V the truth behind your own hesitation. Get your head out of your ass and talk to her. About all of it."

Not exactly *Eye of the Tiger* material, but Dave had to admit Jackson had a point. And he would talk to V. Just as soon as she gave him the chance.

Dave knew he couldn't idle long. Shay was alone behind the bar, and it wouldn't take long for the lines to queue, even longer than they were currently. People were desperate to cram in those last few good times before being stuck with their relatives over the holidays. Sighing, he worked his way back to the rack of kegs on the far wall and found the one he needed. Heaving it onto his shoulder, he left the cool silence of the freezer.

Music, body heat, and the barest scent of cigarette smoke hit him when he pushed open the door behind the bar. Smoking hadn't been allowed in Tonic in years, but the tobacco of days gone by permeated the walls so deeply it always reappeared on crowded nights. The cold weight of the keg dug into his shoulder, and he shifted it to a more comfortable position.

"Hey, Dave!" Shay called.

He couldn't see her, since she was on the other side of the keg. Throwing up his free hand, he yelled, "One sec!" God only knew what fresh catastrophe awaited him. But he couldn't juggle that and the keg. "One thing at a time," he mumbled.

At the line of beer taps, he adjusted his grip and lowered the keg. Shay bounced up next to him. As in, she bounded up like Tigger on springs and jiggled around from foot to foot. From his crouched position, he gave her a curious look. "What's up?"

"We have a . . . customer who needs you," she said.

Dave was not in the mood to deal with whatever was happening. "Can't you handle it?"

"Nope," Shay responded. Her lips were twitching almost as quickly as her feet were tapping.

"What's up with you?" he asked, maneuvering the keg into position and connecting the taps.

"Nothing!" she said. "Nothing. I just really need your help with this . . . customer."

"Fine," he said, dragging himself up to stand. "Where are they?"

"*She* is at the other end of the bar," Shay said. "A knockout blonde. You can't miss her."

Dave glanced down the bar, but another bartender stood in his line of vision. Before he could ask any more questions, Shay skipped away with a cackle.

What the fuck was going on? Dave headed in the direction she'd indicated.

The other bartender moved, and Dave saw a long-haired blonde at the far corner of the bar. He blinked, certain he was seeing things. The hairs on his forearms rose in tandem with the ones at the back of his neck just before she turned to look at him. He skidded to a stop, pinned in place by a pair of beautiful blue eyes. The sudden shift in momentum seemed to throw his heart into his throat. He *had* to be hallucinating—that was the only explanation for it. Grinding the heels of his hands against his eyes, he tried to clear his vision. But when he opened his eyes, she was still there. Every gorgeous angle of her face was right there, like he'd willed her into being in the thousands of times he'd thought of her over the past few days.

Dave's throat constricted around the lump in his throat and his feet started moving again, bringing him to stand right in front of her. His consciousness tunneled down to her and her alone, cutting out the customers waving for his attention, the pounding thump of the bass, the damp heat of the crowded bar. All of it faded into the background, leaving only V.

V watched Dave absorb her presence as something that was happening and not a figment of his imagination. His face had gone totally slack when he'd seen her, and he'd jerked to a stop before coming toward her with slow ungainly strides, like his legs had been frozen and had only begun to thaw. But that lurching pace brought him to within an arm's length of her. So close she could see the sweat beaded at his hairline and the line of condensation left on his shirt from the keg he'd carried out.

"You're here," he said in a voice barely audible over the crowd and the music.

"I'm here," she said.

Dave took a second to let her confirmation sink in before asking, "But I thought . . ." His words trailed off, and he shook himself, as though throwing off whatever he'd been about to say. "What are you doing here?"

"I'm here because I'm in love with you," she said. Given that she had to shout it to be heard above a remix of Britney's greatest hits, the couples on either side of her turned to stare. V blushed but carried on. "I'm here," she repeated, "because I am one hundred percent hopelessly in love with you."

An arm appeared in front of her face. "Can I get an Amstel Light, please?"

Neither Dave nor V had a chance to respond to the interruption, because the girl seated on the stool to V's left slapped at the hand with definitive violence. "What is *wrong* with you?" the girl shouted at the dumbfounded, and possibly injured, man. "Can't you see they're having a fucking moment here? Jesus!"

When the poor guy threw up his hands and backed away, V's unlikely ally patted her on the shoulder and said, "Go ahead, sweetie."

"Um, thanks," V said and turned back to find Dave staring at her with a lopsided smile on his face.

"That doesn't mean I've forgiven you," she said, and the smile fell from his face while their impromptu audience gasped. "But we've seen what happens when one of us chooses to keep the other in the dark and I think we can agree the last thing we want is a repeat of the past few days, right?"

Dave gave her a sheepish look, but he nodded. "Absolutely."

"I don't want you to take the job in Charlotte unless it's something you really want," she said. He started to say something, but she held up her hand.

"No, I need to get this out. I need to get it all out." Bracing herself, she continued, "You said I was the reason you wanted a change. That you were doing all of this because we met." She shook her head. "I want you to take a job because it's what *you* want. I want you to choose to leave Tonic, because it's your choice. Not because it's what you think I want, or because you think I want you to be someone other than who you are. Because I don't. I don't want you to change for me. I love you as you are and for who you are, not some fictional future version of your-self you cram into a job you hate because you think it's what I want."

"Doc," Dave said, reaching out for her.

V pushed on. "It would be easier if you were in Charlotte. It would be easier if you had a job where you didn't work every weekend. It would be easier if your hours matched mine." She paused, tears pricking her eyes and making her voice tremble. "But I don't want easy. I want you. Not you shoehorned into some version of who you think you need to be for me. But you, just as you are. Because, to me, you *are* the perfect guy. Whether you're working here, in Charlotte, or anywhere, doing anything that makes you happy. As long as you're you, you're perfect for me."

"That's beautiful," V's unlikely wing woman stage-whispered and sniffled. "So beautiful."

The next part wouldn't be so beautiful. V straightened her shoulders and pinned Dave with a sharp look. "All of that being said, whatever you decide to do, this isn't going to work unless you talk to me about what you want and why you want it. No more distracting me from questions you don't want to answer. Even if your method of choice is extremely hot sex."

"Oh shiiiiiiit," said her new friend. "Are you sure about that? Because"—she gave Dave an assessing once-over—"that doesn't sound bad to me."

V flushed and watched Dave choke down a laugh. "I'm serious," she said. "If I want to know something, you tell me. Even if the answer is something you think I won't like, or something you're scared to say. No matter what, you tell me. Okay?"

Dave's expression was unreadable, which made V's palms start to sweat. "Is that everything?" he asked.

V nodded. "Yes, that's everything."

"Nothing else you need to say?" he pressed.

Her head moved in a quick negative shake. "No, nothing else."

Dave flattened his hands on the bar and leaned forward. "Well, that's good, because it means I finally get to do this." In one fluid motion, he pushed himself to land in a crouch on top of the bar. V's hand flew to her mouth when he stood, signaling the DJ to cut the music.

The bass beat dropped to silence, and a groan came up from the crowd, which became a curious murmur when they noticed Dave standing on the bar.

Cupping his hands around his mouth, he shouted, "Ladies and gentlemen, if I could have your attention for a few minutes, please. Yeah, right up here, just for a second or two, thank you."

In the silence that followed, V's erratic pulse thrummed in her ears as she waited along with everyone else to hear what Dave had to say.

Probably should've thought this through a little more fulsomely than "Go big or go home," Dave thought as he surveyed the crowd. He blamed his lack of foresight on the fresh shock of seeing V at the end of the bar. But he was up here now with no way out but through, so he needed to get on with it.

"A friend of mine gave me some good advice earlier today. Namely, that I need to get my head out of my ass about a few things,'" Dave said, laughing along with the crowd. "You see, ladies and gentlemen, I fucked up. I mean I *really* fucked up. Instead of trusting what I had with my girl, I let my own insecurities and doubts creep in until I came close to losing the best thing I ever had."

Boos rang out through the crowd, and Dave rolled his hands in encouragement. "Yes, yes, you're right. I deserve that and then some. I was a complete moron. An idiot. A total and utter crumb worthy of your disdain and ridicule." He glanced down at V who was smiling nervously up at him.

"What I didn't deserve, but was lucky enough to receive, was to have this gorgeous creature show up tonight." Dave pointed at V, who blushed to the roots of her hair. The crowd rustled and jostled, trying to catch a glimpse of her.

"Because it turns out, ladies and gentlemen, that in love, as in almost everything else, she's not only a lot smarter, but a lot braver than I am. I'll never be as smart, but I should've been as brave. Should've known that no matter what I told her, she'd be right there in my corner rooting for me, for us. Cheering me on in all the ways that matter, regardless of the outcome. I should've trusted that instead of being a coward who let his fear of failure almost ruin everything. But starting tonight, that's going to change."

He kneeled down and looked straight at V. "Starting tonight, I'm taking the advice I've been so lovingly given by my nearest and dearest and I'm going to get my head out of my ass and do my level best to be a man worthy of her. And, if she'll let me, I'll spend the rest of my life proving it to her."

He held out a hand to V. "What do you say, Doc? Will you let me?"

Tears glistened in her eyes, but she smiled back at him and took his hand. "If I do, does that mean I have to get on the bar?" She glanced down at herself. "Because, I'll be honest, I don't know how that can happen in this dre—Whoa!"

From behind V, the meaty hands of Rodney, Tonic's head bouncer, gripped her waist and hoisted her to sit on his shoulder. "Allow me," he said with a wink at Dave.

Reaching out, Dave lifted V from her perch on Rodney's behemoth shoulder. She stepped daintily onto the bar, gripping his biceps to steady herself. The crowd cheered and clapped, with several catcalls of approval. The DJ started the music again, making the crowd cheer even louder.

"Well," she said with a nervous laugh that was music to Dave's ears. "I guess I'm stuck with you now, since there's no way for me to get down without you."

Dave drew her hands up to his shoulders. "All part of my plan."

V wrinkled her nose. "This seems like more of an ad-lib than a plan."

Lowering his head, Dave said, "This plan's been in motion since the moment you walked into my bar, Doc."

He felt the whisper of her laugh on his lips. "Is that right?"

"Maybe with a few kinks here and there, but the ending? Oh yeah. All part of the plan."

"Standing on a bar surrounded by strangers five days before Christmas? That was your dream ending?"

Dave brushed a stray hair from her face. "Being with you, Doc. Wherever that is. Whenever that is. That's my dream ending," he said and brought his lips to hers.